Barcelona Harbor Murders

A Novel By

Philip Laurien

Barcelona Harbor, New York.

Santa Maria Replica, Barcelona Harbor

Vineyards, Barcelona Harbor

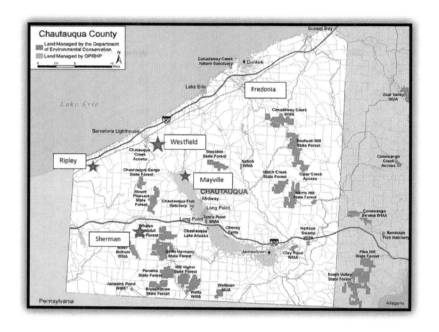

Map Source: New York State Department of Environmental Conservation

Lighthouse at Lakeside Park, Mayville, NY, on Chautauqua Lake

All photos by Philip Laurien

Chapter One

Sunapee, New Hampshire
Sunday, May 14, 2023
Dusk

Heaven sneezed. A crash of thunder shook tall trees and rattled windows. Lightning zig-zagged from a crack in the sky down to an old wooden power pole in a small vale surrounded by dense pine-oak forest. It stabbed the transformer with a fifty-thousand-degree sword, showering sparks and hot oil as it jumped across the wire to the ancient timber barn. Fried pine sap crackled like popcorn as old dry beams burst into flames. The split wooden pole's two halves burned with the stink of melting creosote.

Ten miles away, a fire spotter in his tower saw smoke and called it in. Sirens wailed in the distance as old trucks rolled out of volunteer stations.

First responders Doc and Johnny could see flames above the tall tree line as they drove their 400-gallon Type 6 brush truck past the crooked mailbox that said 'Morrison' in hand-painted letters, down the long gravel driveway, over a creek and past a boulder the size of a house.

"Jeez, Doc, the brush truck ain't gotta chance on this fyah!"

"Pumpah numbah one is on its way, Jawney," replied Doc in his New Hampshire drawl.

"Ayah, but by that time, if Mac's cahs are inside..."

The barn, once built to house cows and store hay, was suddenly ripped by a huge explosion.

"Oh, shit! That's a gas tank for shuah, could be his '57 Stah Chief!"

Orange flames licked the darkening spring sky. The thunderheads threw lightning, but the clouds gave no rain as the barn fire raged on. Its roof sank inward as beams collapsed like molten lava.

Doc sprayed water on the blazing inferno while Johnny laid a hose to a beaver pond 100 feet downhill. When the first pumper truck arrived, it sucked pond water to douse the three-story flames, but it was a losing battle. Johnny soaked the tool shed and construction trailer to save them from drifting sparks.

"Mac's beautiful cahs," said Doc. "Looks like lightnin' hit the pole, Jawn."

"Yah, Doc. What a shame. Mac's whole life was in that bahn."

Meanwhile…10 miles away

Sunapee, New Hampshire
Franken Funeral Home:
The Public Wake for Colonel Abe Solomon (age 100)

The thunderclap also shook the funeral home where Mackenzie 'Mac' Morrison was telling his uncle's life story. 'Big Abe' had enlisted the day after Pearl Harbor. He was an eighteen-year-old giant, too big to stuff into a fighter plane, so the Army Air Corps made him a bomber pilot. With his eagle eyes and natural flying talents, he had outlived the typical two-week life of a B-17 crew. But nothing lasts forever, including luck in war. He was shot down over Belgium on his twentieth bombing mission. It was 1943, and Abe was just twenty years old.

Parachuting out of his dying plane, and separated from his crew, he was pursued by German ground troops, who missed him in the dark Ardennes Forest. Blocked to the west by the enemy, Abe counter-intuitively headed south into France, guided by the stars.

"*Le Résistance*" was a connected underground fighting the Nazis. They helped Abe avoid capture as he walked, rode donkey carts and hitched rides on farm trucks one thousand miles through France and Spain, only to be imprisoned at British-held Gibraltar as a suspected Nazi spy!

Eventually, he returned to England to train new pilots for combat. But that was not the end of his military service. During the Cold War, Abe flew B-52's armed with atomic bombs in 24-hour shifts, ready to strike Russia at a moment's notice.

In 1961 Colonel Abraham Solomon retired from the Air Force to marry French-Canadian Madelaine, ten years his junior. They welcomed their son Jordan a year later, and began a life filled with Abe's 'daily missions.'

He sold travel trailers, logged timber, and built houses. While developing land for a small subdivision, he discovered vast gravel reserves, which he quarried, making a modest fortune.

Abe was sixty when his ten-year-old nephew, Mackenzie 'Mac' Morrison, came to live with them. Raising the rebellious, fiercely independent, and fight-prone young Mac quickly became the toughest 'daily mission' of Big Abe's life.

What Mac remembered most, he told those paying their last respects to this giant of a man, was that his Uncle Abe was good to him.

A policeman appeared at the door, waved to Mac and whispered, "Your barn is on fire!"

Mac jumped in his baby blue '57 Chevy Bel Air and raced home.

When he turned the corner of his long gravel driveway and peered around the huge boulder, his heart sank. The ancient timbered barn was a mountain of blazing rubble.

"Anyone inside?" asked Fire Chief Notting.

"No, Chief. But thanks for trying to save it."

"I'm very sorry, Mac. Lightnin' hit the pole and blew the transformah. Fyah followed the wyah to the bahn. Grass tankah was first, but they didn't have enough watah to knock it down. Once the cahs' gas tanks exploded and those beams caught, we couldn't stop it. But Jawn saved your tool shed and trailer."

Johnny touched Mac's shoulder.

"Mac, we tried, man. Glad you had Abe's cah with you."

Abe had bought the baby blue Chevrolet Bel Air convertible for his 34th birthday in 1957, when he was a hotshot B-52 pilot. He gave it to Mac 32 years later on his 16th birthday. Mac had continuously upgraded it until it was better than new. Driving it to Abe's wake was a way to pay final respects to his mentor.

"Thanks, Johnny."

Mac stripped off his suit coat and popped the Chevy's trunk to get the work clothes he kept in there. He pulled on an old sweatshirt and laced up his tactical boots, the lightweight ones with steel toe and sole plate made for kicking in doors. Then he pitched in to help the firemen. Thoughts of tomorrow and what to do next were already swirling in his head. By dawn, the fire was out, and he had a plan for the rebuild.

It would be different.

*****

Chapter Two

Monday, May 15
6:00 a.m.

News travels fast in a small town. Mac's barn fire was the talk of the table at Eleanor's Café. Mac was there, along with his contractors, friends and Jordan Solomon. Jordan had recently built vacation cottages on a wooded pond that was once Abe's gravel quarry. He rented them to summer tourists and winter skiers.

"Mac," said Jordan, handing him a key, "you can stay in that cottage as long as you need to."

"Thanks, Jordan, I really appreciate that."

"You're gonna rebuild, right, Mac?"

"Yep, but it'll be different. Don't worry, Jordan, I'll be at Abe's burial tomorrow."

Mac turned to Roger Lemonier, his best friend since fifth grade.

"Rog, I need your big backhoe, a loader and three dump trucks as soon as you can get there. Probably gonna need your guys for 2-3 days to clean up the mess."

"You got'em, Mac."

A dark green Triumph TR-6 convertible pulled up to the Café. Mac's longtime insurance agent, Flavius Miller, got out and waved to him. He was wearing his trademark red corduroy vest, white shirt and red leather snap brim cap. Flavius had already visited the fire scene overnight, and begun the claim paperwork.

"Flavius, how's it look?" asked Mac.

"The barn was insured for $500,000, Mac. It's a total loss. The F-350 work truck, '57 Pontiac, tractor and contents should be valued value at $250,000. I'll file today. There won't be any problems, and your payment will be quick."

Mac turned to his friend and attorney, Morgan Hillman.

"Morgan, since I gotta oversee the cleanup and plan for the rebuild, I'd like you to do a few things. I'm giving you power of attorney. Angie

4

can handle my checkbook. Once the insurance money is deposited, pay off the $50,000 mortgage. Next, set up a $200,000 trust for Gabriella with a $25,000 draw per year, unless I override. She turns 25 in nine days and the trust is her birthday present. Last, call Mitch Baker, the surveyor. Tell him to submit the 40-acre final plat."

"You're selling, Mac?"

"Just the front 40 acres. Also, get Jenny Walters to take this listing: *5-acre wooded lots with town road, water and pond frontage. Offers in excess of $100,000 considered.*"

"Mac, as your attorney, I advise you to wait a bit and think this over first."

"Morgan, I've already thought it over. I've been cash-poor and land-rich since the divorce 10 years ago. Abe will be buried tomorrow. Jocko died last year. Gabby has her own life. Now, my timber-framed barn, house, and business that I built and invested in for twenty years are all gone. And I'm gonna be fifty in four days. So, it's time for change. I'm gonna raise cash and make the land self-supporting. But first, I've got debris to clean up, and get my suit cleaned for Abe's burial."

"Mac, I'll take care of your suit," said Morgan. "Anything else?"

"Yes. White dress shirt, XXL, black socks and boxers. Thanks, Morgan."

Next, Mac huddled with his contractors. He wanted a 50' x 100' insulated steel barn to sit on the barn's existing concrete pad, with paved asphalt aprons. It would be flanked by the same-sized steel shed on a gravel pad. The earthwork, both structures and the paving could be built in two months for $205,000, after which Mac could restart his own business building houses.

With his plan committed, it was time to go see what could be salvaged.

*****

As Mac circled the smoldering rubble, he was looking for a miracle: his twelve-string guitar.

He knew where he'd left it, but that corner of the barn was a soggy pile of ashes. However, while scanning the wreckage, he spotted a dirty black shape under a pile of collapsed oak beams.

Grabbing a shovel from the tool shed, he picked away at the debris until he could see it. The big red "J" was unmistakable. When he pulled back the rubble, he unsnapped the hinges and was glad he paid extra for the hard case. His Jonsered™ 920, one of the biggest chainsaws ever made, looked well-used but otherwise OK. He lifted it out, set the choke and yanked the ripcord.

"*Rrring-a-ding-ding!*" The two-stroke engine fired to life! For the first time today, Mac smiled.

"We'll rebuild together, ole buddy" said Mac. He revved its engine and felt the power in his hands.

Putting his Swedish chainsaw with the 36" logging bar to work, he began the huge task of cutting piles of burnt beams that had once been his barn home. He worked like a madman, covering himself in flying sawdust and chainsaw oil. He worked around Roger's big excavator, loader and dump trucks. He worked without eating or slowing. He worked until darkness and exhaustion made him quit.

*****

Chapter Three

The large coffin was positioned under a maple tree, surrounded by headstones dating back to the Revolutionary War. Abe's son Jordan gave the eulogy.

"Abe Solomon was good to all of us. He was my father, my mentor, my confidant, my biggest critic, and my most ardent supporter. While the world has lost a hero, we can rejoice that we knew him for a while and that he enriched our all of our lives. Rest in peace Pop."

As the bugler played taps, the military guard lowered the coffin into the ground next to his beloved Madelaine.

Morgan Hillman approached Mac with his confidential secretary, Angelica Milana Morelli. She was tall, slim and Neapolitan, with dark eyes, hair and olive skin. She was also a CPA and Mac's accountant.

"Mac, there is something I have to give you," said Morgan. His black courtroom suit with white pin stripes discreetly covered his powerful six-foot physique. He pulled out a weathered yellow envelope and handed it to Mac.

"Abe Solomon gave this to Judge Gromley many years ago. Before the Judge died he passed it to me, with instructions to give it to you only after Abe's death."

"What is it, Morgan?"

"I have no idea, Mac, it has a wax seal."

"Huh! Uncle Abe was so generous in life. I cannot imagine what he saved for me in death."

"Well, open it and find out."

"Not now. It'll be Abe's special birthday present in three days."

*****

7

Mac's Barn Site
12:30 p.m.

In just 24 hours, Roger's equipment had done a huge job of debris removal. The concrete pad was clear. The pile of blackened wood was being carted away. The burnt shells of the 1957 Pontiac and the F-350 work truck were sitting on a flatbed.

Mac said "Roger, I'm paying off the $50,000 loan we took out, so our drill rig is free and clear. Since I'm gonna be busy with the rebuild, and your excavation business is booming, let's have Reggie run the well drilling company and keep my share of the income. If he does a good job, maybe someday we'll sell him the whole deal."

"If that's the way you want it Mac, that's generous, but I still want you as my partner."

"Of course, Rog. We've been best friends since 5th grade and that won't change. Let's pull the trailer onto the barn pad and connect it to water and septic lines. As soon as I get power back I'll have an operating office."

"Glad you still have Abe's Chevy, Mac. We'll always have that memory of you and me working on his car for the past 30 years. It's way better than new."

"Those are great memories Rog, but right now I need a work truck. And good used ones are scarce in northern New Hampshire."

"Right! Well, let's finish clearing this site today, and then we'll find you a truck."

*****

Chapter Four

Wednesday, May 17
Jordan's Pond
5:30 a.m.

It was a brisk spring morning, with just enough time for a quick paddle on the pond before heading to Eleanor's Café. Mac pulled on his lightweight terrain pants, tactical boots and hooded sweatshirt before stepping outside into the pine-scented air.

As he approached the old canoe, a rumbling came from beneath it. The closer he got, the louder it got.

'GRRRR!'

When he stopped, the growling stopped. When he took a step, it started. It sounded like a large dog.

The canoe was upside down, like an open-faced sandwich. He slipped the paddle under the bow thwart and lifted it a foot. A large white dog ran into the woods.

Mac scanned the area. There were a dozen cottages on the pond, but it was early season, so nine of them were vacant. The closest three were occupied by retired couples. Since no one was outside, he assumed the dog did not belong to them.

Instead of going for a paddle, or heading for coffee at Eleanor's, Mac started a fire in the outdoor grill. When it was hot, he brought out an iron skillet, bacon and eggs. He smacked a slab of bacon on the skillet and began separating the strips as the fat melted. The smell wafted away. He heard chatter from the three cottages as people brought their coffee outside to see who was cooking.

"Good morning!" Mac shouted. "I'll gladly trade you bacon for coffee!"

"Deal!" shouted an old man in a bathrobe.

Five minutes later, Mac had three unshaven old men at the picnic table with pots of coffee. Their wives were coming out with plates of toast and jam. After introductions, Mac set down a platter of bacon and sat with them.

9

"I saw a white dog under the canoe this morning," he said. "Does it belong to any of you?"

"No," said Mrs. Gerrard. "Oh, look! There he is, by the woods!"

Taking four strips of bacon from the platter, Mac laid them on a plate and slowly walked toward the dog.

'Grrrrrrrrr'.

The dog backed away, but kept his eyes on the bacon.

"It's all right, boy," Mac said calmly, "here you go." He placed the bacon on the ground, turned and snapped a photo over his shoulder as he walked back to the picnic table.

The dog was eating.

He cracked four eggs and dropped them in the pan with four more strips of bacon. They sizzled on the hot skillet. In a minute he slid them on another plate. Mac again set the plate down before the large white dog. He wolfed it down. When he finished eating, the dog walked down to the pond, took a long drink, then came back and stood in front of Mac. He shoved his nose under Mac's arm and flipped it up in the air. Mac gave him a little rub and the dog flipped his arm up again as if to say, 'Pet me some more.'

Mac began gently stroking the dog's ears and scratching his back, which made him close his eyes and purr like a big cat. Mac could feel his ribs sticking out. He smoothed back his fur to look and saw black and blue bruises.

"You're a big baby, aren't you, buddy-boy? You don't have a collar, and you haven't eaten in days. I'm going to make you more eggs. Would you like that?"

'ROWF', the big dog replied.

"OK, can I call you Buddy?"

'ROWF!'

"Well now, what kind of dog are you, Buddy-boy? Look at those crystal blue eyes. You're long and tall like a German Shepherd but broad in the chest with a downy undercoat like an Alaskan Malamute. You just want to be friends, don't you, Buddy?"

The dog raised a giant white paw and placed it in Mac's hand.

"Good boy, Buddy." Mac offered him a bite of toast, and the dog gently took it from his fingers.

"You have a gentle mouth, Buddy."

"Thanks for the coffee, folks," Mac said. "I'll be gone today, but Buddy and I would be glad to join the evening campfire with you."

As his neighbors melted back into their cabins, Mac walked through the cottage door, but Buddy hesitated, looked inside, and sat on the deck.

"You want to stay outside? OK, Buddy, we're going for a car ride!"

*****

North Woods Veterinarian Clinic
7:30 a.m.

Vet-Tech Melanie Taylor waved a wand all around the big white dog.

"No chip, Mel?"

"Nope."

"What breed is he?"

"I'd say Malamute-Shepherd cross by his blocky nose, his downy fur and his blue eyes."

"How old would you say?"

"A year. He's malnourished, or he would be bigger. He's one hundred pounds, but I'll bet if he's properly fed, he'll be one-twenty. His neck is raw from some kind of rough collar, probably a chain. There are signs of abuse from bruises on his back under his fur, Mac. No records in our files for the birth, and we are the only Vet within 20 miles. Unless a breeder is trying to make this strain of dog, I'd say his momma got out and found a new boyfriend."

"Are there any German Shepherd breeders near here, Mel?"

"Closest is Roland Malouin, twenty miles from you Mac. Not a nice guy. Doc filed an abuse complaint against him. He's never been back, and we don't want his business."

"Could this dog have come from his kennel?"

"Well, if this dog was with that breeder, he would have been trained for guard work because he's not a pure bred Shepherd. Come to think of it, Mac, there is a handsome Malamute male that we just neutered, and I think his owner lives near Malouin. Let me check our records."

Mel went away and came back with a file in her hand.

"Mac, this owner lives just a half mile from Malouin's kennel. I go by his house on my way home. He has a gorgeous Alaskan-Malamute wheel-dog on his sled team. Could he have gotten loose and bred Malouin's bitch? Don't know."

11

"But if this is a Malamute-Shepherd cross, it's going to be intelligent, powerful, loyal and protective, but not aggressive. Clearly, this dog didn't like abusive treatment, so he escaped and found you."

"Here's what I suggest, Mac. Let me put him on the internet with a general description, no picture. See if anyone responds. If they do, I'll call you. In the meantime, I suggest you get a chip, collar and a license. We'll give Buddy his starter shots. I can see by the smile on your face that he already makes you happy. Jocko was such a good pal. We all miss him, Mac."

"Let's do it. Buddy, can you pick out a collar?"

'Rowrf!' Buddy reached out his paw and shook Mac's outstretched hand.

Melanie brought out several collars. Buddy sniffed a brown leather one and gently pulled it with his teeth. Mel gave him his shots, and Mac filled out the paperwork as his owner.

"Buddy-boy, we're going to Eleanor's Café!"

'Rowrf!' Buddy stood on his hind legs and twirled.

"Is that your Buddy-dance Budso?" Mac asked.

'Row-rowrf!' Buddy nudged his leg with his nose. *This dog understands me*, Mac thought. *Hunh!*

✻✻✻✻✻

8:30 a.m.

Eleanor's contractor regulars had left, so Mac took a seat by himself at an outdoor table. Buddy lay underneath and rested his chin on Mac's shoes. In just a few hours, it was clear that Mac had claimed Buddy, and Buddy had claimed him.

An older woman with a tangle of gray hair placed a coffee in front of Mac.

"Mistah Mac, I'm so sorry about your fire. But you are OK, yah?"

"I'm fine, thanks, Eleanor."

Eleanor had been in America for 30 years, but she still spoke with a thick German accent. She looked down and saw the tail sticking out from under the table.

"Oh! Du hast einen neuen Hund!"

Buddy's ears perked up. He stood and faced her.

"Mistah Mac, dis dog knows German! Vere did you find him?"

"He found me, at Jordan's pond."

"Vat's his name?"

"Buddy."

"Who gave him dat stupid name?"

"I did."

"HA! Why you don't give him a good German name, like Rolf!"

'ROLF!' barked Buddy.

"I think we'll stick with Buddy, Eleanor."

She scratched Buddy under his chin and walked back into the kitchen. Mac checked the to-do list on his phone. 'Call electric company'. He called. It would be three weeks before he had power. They had the transformer, but a backlog of pole installations was ahead of him.

"Three weeks, Buddy! Well, today we'll go shopping for everything dog! And I need new clothes!"

❋❋❋❋❋

Chapter Five

Thursday, May 18
8:00 a.m.

Mac's cell chirped: *Melanie: Call me.*

"Mel, what's up?"

"We got a hit for Buddy. Bad news, Mac. That breeder Malouin says it's his dog."

"So the dog ran 20 miles to get away from him? How did he identify him?"

"By description."

"Why didn't he have a collar?"

"Said he had a chain wrapped around his neck anchored to a ground stake; must have slipped out of it."

"I'd like to wrap a chain around *his* neck and see how *he* likes it! What else?"

"He just said it's his. He's coming here to get it."

"Mel, you give him my cell, tell him I have the dog."

"He's not a nice guy, Mac. Big guy, too, like you."

"Great. I hope he takes a poke at me."

"Mac, don't go Lone Ranger[1] on him! I know you."

"I can handle it, Mel. Just give him my number."

*****

Mac hung up and dialed Jules Avery, the K-9 Officer for the Concord P.D.

"Jules? It's Mac Morrison. Look, I've got a dog here, a mixed breed Malamute-Shepherd cross. He might have come from Roland Malouin's kennel. Is that where you got your K-9? It is? OK, I need to know the key commands this dog may have been taught for guard work. Yeah, I've got a pencil, go ahead. Yeah. OK, I'll be careful, thanks Jules."

Mac wrapped a towel around his arm to protect it from bites and took Buddy outside to test him. Mel's assessment of Buddy's likely temperament was correct. Buddy was smart and protected on instinct, but he would

14

not attack Mac, his own new master. Mac ran through all the other commands, and Buddy obeyed each one. He tried the one command necessary for safety, and Buddy obeyed it every time. Buddy enjoyed responding to Mac's encouragement with a big whap of his tail against his leg. He was a happy dog.

✵✵✵✵✵

Mac's Cottage, Jordan's Pond
9:00 a.m.

A surly voice on the phone snarled.
"The Vet said you got my dog!"
"Correction," said Mac, "I have 'a' dog."
"Where do you live?"
Mac gave the address and hung up. The trap door in his brain reserved for bullies cracked open.
Half an hour later, a beater Chevy pickup with filthy cages rattled down the gravel road to Jordan's Pond. Mac and Buddy were sitting outside on the deck. At the sound of the old truck, Buddy's head jerked around. He jumped to his feet and spun his head to look plaintively at Mac. His eyes said, 'What's happening? Don't send me back!'
"Don't worry, Buddy, you're mine. He's not getting you again. You stay. Stay, Buddy."
The old truck stopped in front of Mac's cottage. Mac propped up his cell phone on a deck table and hit the video record button. His neighbors were sitting outside in the sun.
"Hey folks, do me a favor and please join me," he called to them.
Three elderly couples trudged over to Mac's deck while a large, unshaven man in dirty clothes unfolded himself from the truck. He was every bit as big as Mac, all of 6'3", and probably outweighed him by 50 pounds. He had an angry look as he stomped up to the cottage.
"Savo! Come!"
'Grrrr!' Buddy stood behind Mac. "Stay, Buddy," Mac said.
"SAVO! COME!!!!"
'GRRRRR! ROWROWROW!'
"He doesn't seem to respond to that name," said Mac.

15

Roland Malouin whipped out a collapsible steel rod and pressed a button. It snapped open the length of a golf club. He raised it overhead and moved towards Buddy.

"WHOA! Put that club away!" Mac said.

Buddy pushed past Mac, leaped off the three-foot-high deck and struck the big man in his chest, knocking him on his back. Then he was on top of him!

'ARARARARARARARARAR!'

"BUDDY!" shouted Mac. "*AUS!*"

Buddy backed away.

The big man leaped up with amazing speed and swung the club at Buddy, but Mac slammed into him first, grabbing his wrist with both strong hands and twisting it up behind his back.

"OW! YOU'RE BREAKIN' MY FUCKIN' ARM!" Malouin shouted.

"DROP THE CLUB, ASSHOLE!" Mac snarled.

Malouin dropped the club, wheeled, and threw an uppercut that would have taken Mac's head off, had it been where he thought it was. But Mac had whirled full circle, whipped his elbow backwards and crushed the big man's temple with a dull thud, like a kid kicking a pumpkin. Malouin collapsed in a pile, rubbing his head.

"Now!" said Mac, "A chip and license says this is my dog Buddy. What proof do you have?"

"My bitch bore him! She got bred by a Malamute that jumped my fence. Figured I could train him for guard work since he's not a police dog, but he's too hard-headed. Wouldn't take guard training, and nobody wants a mongrel Shepherd."

"Maybe he didn't like your abuse, Malouin. So you staked him out with a chain around his neck and starved him, and you brought no proof he's yours."

"You stole my dog!"

"No, this dog ran twenty miles to escape you, and found me. Obviously, he does not want to go with you. And he's NOT going with you!"

Using his body to conceal his hands, the big man snatched the club behind his back, stood up, turned on his heels and swung at Mac's head.

But Mac had anticipated. He ducked, shifted his weight left, then shifted forward and lashed out with his right foot, soccer-style, kicking the side of Roland Malouin's knee with the instep of his steel-soled tactical boot.

"CRACK!" was the sound of Roland Malouin's knee dislocating.

The big man staggered, collapsed to his knees and rolled on his side, dropping the club. Buddy snatched it in his teeth and ran into the woods.

"OW! MY FUCKIN' KNEE! I'LL PRESS CHARGES! I'LL FUCKIN' SUE YOU!"

"Folks," said Mac, "what did you see?"

"He attacked you with a steel rod, Mr. Morrison."

Mac pointed at the cell phone on the table.

"All recorded on here, asshole. Shall we call the police and show them the video? No? Then I suggest we make a deal. I'll buy him, even though you can't prove you own him. How much?"

"$1,000!"

"Hah! Malouin, you're such a piece of shit! No, I'm gonna give you $400, and you sign a release."

Malouin's eyes flicked back and forth. "What release?"

"Mrs. Gerrard?" Mac said.

"Yes, Mr. Morrison?"

"Would you go inside my cabin and get the paper on the table?"

"Of course."

When she reappeared, Mac gave it to Malouin.

"What about my money?" he growled.

Mac slipped four hundred dollars from his wallet and put them on the table. "Now sign, and beat it," he said. Buddy returned without the club.

Malouin signed, stuffed the cash in his filthy jeans, hobbled into his beater Chevy and roared away.

"Well, I love to see a bully get beat!" said Mrs. Gerrard.

"We all do, Mrs. Gerrard," said Mac. "Thank you for being my witnesses. Buddy boy, you are mine, and nobody is ever going to separate us!"

Buddy was visibly smiling with his white tail whapping Mac's leg. He danced around and around him and finally jumped up and gave him a slobbery kiss on the cheek. 'ROWRF!'

***

Mac's Barn site
11:00 a.m.

Roger Lemonier was sitting on his Cat™ D3 bulldozer.

"Hey Rog," said Mac, "I'm surprised to see you here. Just picking up your dozer? The job site's clean. We're all good, man."

"Mac, Jenny Walters said you're selling house lots on the pond. Is that right?"

"Yep, six of them, each one is at least five acres with town water and road frontage."

"I'll buy one, Mac. I want you to build me a new house."

"Be glad to, Rog, just as soon as I get this steel building up."

"Hey, I want to talk to you about that, too. You gonna need all that space, Mac?"

"No. I'm gonna rent four bays, and keep two. The new building will be well insulated with radiant heat, tall overhead doors, offices on the back-side, and a propane backup generator."

"Mac, I need a bigger heated shop and office, plus covered outside storage," said Roger.

"Then let's plan your space, Rog. I can build these bays to suit."

So, the two friends measured and marked the barn pad for interior walls. Then they rough staked the earthwork for the shed and aprons, which Roger's dozer could do in the next week.

Next, they walked the pond lots. While Roger picked the one he wanted, Mac got his chain saw and felled a dozen large oak trees to clear an entry drive. Using his D-3, Roger stacked the logs, which Mac would send to be milled into flooring for his future house. With a dirt driveway cut in, Roger began clearing the underbrush for a view of the pond.

By five p.m., Roger had cleared a spot for a house on his new lot, and decided to rent three barn bays and most of the shed. He would soon be able to walk through the woods from his new contractor's office to his new home. Perfect.

Meanwhile, Buddy-dog was chewing on a stick, swimming with the beavers, and rolling in pine needles, just enjoying his new life without a chain around his neck.

"All right, Buddy-boy," Mac said, "you've been patient. Time for supper, eh?"

'ROWRF!' He thrust his paw at Mac and shook his hand.

Back at their cabin, it was a lovely red sunset over Jordan's pond, as good a day as Mac could remember.

The knock on the cabin door had a familiar cadence: 'Tap-ta-ta-ta-tap!'

Buddy rushed to the door and growled. "Sit, Buddy," said Mac.

"Hey, Angie," Mac said as he opened the door.

"Hello, Cowboy. Morgan is getting ready for trial in the morning, so I brought your birthday present tonight. Got a DVD player in here?"

"Matter of fact, I do. Whatcha got?"

"Impact[3]. It's a 1949 film noir, with one of your favorite actresses, Ella Raines[2]."

"Sweet! Thanks, Angie! And thank Morgan."

"Happy birthday, Mac. You deserve some happiness this year."

"Amen to that, sister! Buddy, make room on the couch!"

✻✻✻✻✻

Chapter Six

It was a glorious dawn for Mac's fiftieth birthday. He was still in good shape from building houses, but he didn't move as fast in the morning, and there were kinks that took twenty minutes to work out. The Gerrards were outside, wrapped in blankets, sipping coffee on their deck.

Mac shouted, "It's my birthday. Please join us at Eleanor's Café, 6 a.m. sharp!"

"Love to!"

✺✺✺✺✺

Eleanor's Café
6:00 a.m.

Eleanor had strung up crepe paper around the umbrella tables. A large cake inscribed with '5-0 Mac!' sat proudly on a round stand. All of her 6:00 a.m. contractor regulars were there, along with Mac's friends. Mac's phone chirped.

"Happy Birthday, Dad! Are you at Eleanor's, as usual?"

"Hey, Gabby! Yes, I am. Where are you?"

"Back in Colorado. It's 4 a.m. here, but I wanted to be first to wish you happy birthday, so I got up early."

"What happened to the ski tour?"

"No snow in the Alps. Anyway, that's not working out so great, so I think I'm done with that. Now I'm working part time at a fancy café. I've got an idea for a business, but it will need some startup capital."

"Well, your birthday is in five days, and I have a surprise that could help you with that. Hey, I'll keep this short. I would have called you sooner, but I don't have a satellite phone and I thought you were still in France."

"That's OK, Dad."

"Our barn burned four days ago, Honey."

"WHAT?"

"Hit by lightning. It's all gone. Nothing left but a concrete pad. I'm planning the rebuild now. The tool shed and the trailer were spared."

"OH NO! But you weren't hurt?"

"No, I was at Abe's wake."

"UNCLE ABE DIED? Oh my God! So where are you living?"

"A tourist cabin on Jordan's pond."

"Did your cars burn?"

"All but our baby blue Chevy. Luckily, I drove it to Abe's wake."

"But without Abe joining you for morning coffee, you're all alone again, Dad."

"No, I've got a new dog named Buddy. He's a one year old white Malamute-Shepherd mix."

"Good, I'm glad for you, Dad."

"Yeah, he came to me at just the right time. Hey, I got a lot of folks waiting to cut this cake, so I'm gonna say I love you, glad you're safe, talk to you soon, OK?"

"OK, Dad, Happy Birthday! Love you!"

"All right, Mac," said Roger, "open Abe's envelope!"

Mac slit the envelope and slid out a battered yellow carbon copy with blue ink.

"It says *'Accident Report: Police Department, Ripley, New York'*. Hey! Ripley was my home town!"

"So, read the report, Mac," said Roger.

Date: May 14, 1983. Time: 8:30 p.m.

Accident Location: U.S. Route 20 and Sherman Road (SR 76), Ripley, NY.

A commercial truck tractor (no trailer), NJ registration, eastbound on U.S. 20 struck a 1970 Red Ford F-100 pickup truck northbound on S.R. Route 76 (Sherman Road). According local auto shop owner Joseph Minetti Jr., he was following the F-100 when it failed to stop for a red light and crossed U.S. 20 in front of the eastbound tractor truck, causing the accident. The pickup truck was struck on the driver's side in the intersection. The impact pushed the pickup 75 feet to the east on

U.S. 20. The F-100 pickup's gas tank ruptured, and the vehicle burned. Damage to the rear of the pickup truck was also noted, but it is undetermined if it was related to this collision. Both the driver and passenger of the pickup truck were killed at the scene. Deceased were Shaun and Claudia Morrison, U.S. Route 20 South, Ripley, NY.

"OH MY GOD, THIS IS MY PARENTS!" Mac yelled. "THIS IS THE ACCIDENT REPORT FROM MY PARENT'S DEATH!"

"Really?" said Roger. "Why would Abe give you that now?"

"Wait," Mac said. "There's another carbon." He unfolded it. "Looks like a State Trooper's report of the same accident. It says '*New York State Police Accident Report, Troop A, Fredonia, New York.*'"

"Read it, Mac."

Mr. and Mrs. Shaun Morrison of U.S. Route 20, South, Ripley, NY, were killed on impact from a truck tractor (no trailer) traveling east on U.S. Route 20 at 8:30 p.m., May 14, 1983. The Morrison's 1970 Ford F-100 pickup truck failed to stop for a traffic signal displaying red while attempting to cross U.S. Route 20 northbound on Sherman Road. The F-100 was struck mid-section on the driver's side by the tractor driven by Juan Martinez of New Jersey. Local farmer Joseph Minetti Jr. was following the Morrison's truck and stated they had run the red light when struck. Mr. Martinez also stated that the Morrison vehicle ran the red light, and he could not stop in time to avoid striking it. Damage to the rear of the Morrison pickup truck appeared to be old damage. This officer determined it was not relevant to this accident.

"Mac," said Angie, "you came here 40 years ago. Weren't you in their truck?"

"No. They went to a farmer's meeting and left me at a neighbor's. I never saw them again."

"Not even at the funeral?"

"They were in closed caskets. Now I know why: they were burned. Uncle Abe and Aunt Maddy drove down from New Hampshire, went to the funeral, packed my stuff, and brought me back here."

"What about your farm?"

"It got sold to pay estate debts and mortgage. I got a little money from it, plus a car insurance settlement. Abe kept it invested. When I got out of the service I used it to buy the 65 acres with the barn."

"You know, Roger," Mac mused aloud, "it's going to be three weeks until I get electric. So, I think me and Buddy will take a road trip to Ripley. These reports meant something to Uncle Abe. Maybe he wanted me to look into it when I was more mature."

"CUT DA CAKE!" Eleanor bellowed.

"OK, OK," Mac said, shaking his head in disbelief at this turn of events. Flavius Miller handed Mac an envelope.

"That's an insurance present, Mac. You got paid."

"That was fast! How much is it, Flavius?"

"Two checks will be wired to your account: $500,000 for structure and $250,000 for contents, including vehicles."

"OK, good, so I've got building capital. Angie, I'm giving you my checkbook. Morgan knows what to do."

"Manny," Mac said to contractor Manny Martinet, "I'm ready to order the steel building and shed. Rural zoning allows contractor's yards, so there will be no problem getting a permit. The existing pad is reinforced concrete with a deep footer so you can set your posts right on it. Angie can give you a $50,000 deposit. Is that enough?"

"That's more than enough."

"Roger, you know what I want. Send Angie the bill for earthwork. All right, my friends," said Mac, "let's eat this beautiful cake!"

*****

11:00 a.m.

Mac stopped for cash and supplies before heading back to his cottage. He packed a bag and put Buddy's gear into the huge Chevy trunk.

After a last look at Jordan's Pond, Mac considered his alternate routes. Instead of taking I-89 and Route 3 into Massachusetts, he headed southwest on rural two-lanes towards Keene, thinking back as he drove.

He'd lost a lot in fifty years: his parents at age ten, their farm, his buddies in Iraq, his lake house and marriage, Jocko-dog, Aunt Maddie and Uncle Abe, and now–everything else he had built in his life.

23

As always, when he looked too hard in life's rear view mirror, it made him sad...and angry.

For ten-year-old Mac Morrison, the sudden move from his parent's New York farm to the cold New Hampshire north woods had made him shut out the world. He was the new kid who talked funny and got picked on. His anger fueled his hard young fists, and he tore into his taunters with a ferociousness that belied his age.

And when he realized he was good at fighting, he began taking on bigger and bigger bullies, until no one in school wanted to challenge him. There were many calls to the Principal's office, with Uncle Abe having to come pick him up. But Abe never punished him for fighting, because young Mac always had a good reason. In fact, Abe was proud of him. He knew he couldn't control him, so he taught him the best he could.

Now, at age fifty, Mac was still stuck in that place, protecting those he cared about and meting out punishment to bad actors when they crossed his path.

He drove through downtown Keene on the widest Main Street in New England, once laid out to allow a full U-turn by a horse-drawn freight wagon. Nowadays it had four driving lanes divided by a center tree-lined median. Wide sidewalks, angle parking and Victorian store fronts with large glass windows completed the Norman Rockwell image of a New England town.

The Chevy was soon tooling its way across the Connecticut River with Buddy sprawled across the front bench seat, his chin on Mac's knee. They would cross southern Vermont on a lazy route through Brattleboro and Bennington before entering New York and picking up I-90 at Rotterdam.

*****

8:00 p.m.

Mac pulled off the Thruway outside of Le Roy, looking for an old-style Mom-and-Pop-owned motor court where he could park in front of his door and walk directly into his room. When he found one, it was half full of old Chevy pickups parked together on one side of a semi-circular driveway with green lawn in the middle. Latin music thumped from a radio on the sidewalk. A cluster of people were charcoal grilling outside the rooms. They turned and looked at the baby blue Bel Air. The smell of tamales and beans wafted over to him.

24

Spring planting season, Mac thought, *must be day labor.*

'Grrrrrr!' Buddy rumbled, with his head hanging out the Chevy's window.

"Sit Buddy, sit." Buddy sat and looked at Mac, who gave him a head rub.

Mac paid cash for an end unit farthest from the other tenants, locked the car and set the after-market alarm. There was an old railroad diner across the road, and it was open. Mac walked across, tied Buddy's leash to the fence rail and went in. He ordered two burgers, coffee and real French fries to go. He and Buddy crossed over the road and took their dinner back to the room.

He watched a Red Sox game on an ancient fat TV, the kind he hadn't seen since he was a kid. Eventually, he turned it off and listened to the hum of the old refrigerator in the corner. The king size bed was clean, the room was quiet, and they dropped off to sleep, with Buddy's long white back pressed against his side.

*****

Chapter Seven

"You can't go back home to your family, back home to your childhood, back home to a young man's dreams, ... back home to places in the country away from all the strife and conflict of the world, back home to the father you have lost and have been looking for, back home to someone who can help you, save you, ease the burden for you, back home to the old forms and systems of things which once seemed everlasting but which are changing all the time–back home to the escapes of Time and Memory."[4]

- Thomas Wolfe

Saturday, May 20
4:30 a.m.

Buddy nudged Mac with his nose until he woke up.
'Grrr!' His growl shook the bed. He leaped off and ran to the door.
"What's up, Bud?"
'GRRRRRRR!'
The ancient clock radio blinked red block numbers. Slipping into his terrain pants and sneakers, Mac pulled back the curtain. Three young men with flashlights surrounded his car.
Mac cracked his door and silently stepped out into the darkness with Buddy at his heels.
"What's up, guys?" he said.
Buddy pushed around Mac to protect him and snarled, 'ROWROWROW!'
The men whirled around with their hands up high.
"STAY, BUDDY!" Mac said. He saw no weapons. "Do you speak English?" he asked.
The middle one spoke.
"We were just looking at your car, Mister. Never saw one like this up close."
"It's a 1957 Chevrolet Bel Air."
"She's so beautiful, Mister. We like the old cars with all the chrome. I would like to own a car just like this one someday."
"I hope you do. What's your name?
"Paco. What's yours?"

"Mac. You're up early, Paco."

"We wanted to see your car before the farmer picks us up. Are you from New Hampshire, Mister Mac? That is a long way for a car this old."

"I upgraded it with a new engine and did a lot more. Be happy to show you when it's daylight."

"The farmer comes before then."

"You guys had breakfast?"

"No. My mother cooks for us when we get home, sometimes after dark."

"That's a long day without breakfast. Tell you what, Paco. You appreciate my classic car, and I like that. How 'bout I buy you guys breakfast?"

Mac handed them a $50 bill and pointed across the road. "The diner is open," he said.

Paco looked stunned. "Really, for us?" he said.

"Car guys stick together. Better get going; the sun will be up and your farmer will be looking for you."

"Mister Mac, *Mucho gracias*! Ramon, Thomas, vamos!"

The three turned and ran for the diner, whooping and hollering.

"Well, Buddy, guess that's it for sleep, eh? Let's get our own breakfast."

He jumped up and smacked Mac in the chest with his giant paws, then twirled a circle around him.

'ROWRF!' Buddy was a happy dog.

*****

6:00 a.m.

New York had been his home once, but that was a long time ago. It did not feel like home anymore.

Mac drove west on Route 5, trickling though the small towns of Batavia, East Pembroke and Akron. He stopped and walked Buddy at a town park above Old Clarence Hollow, just enjoying the pond and the spring morning, and his new dog.

Five miles later, he hit the snarling traffic of Buffalo's suburbs, so he rolled back onto I-90.

In 1989, sixteen-year-old Mac Morrison had driven his Uncle Abe's 1974 Chevy pickup from New Hampshire to summer camp in Dewittville, New York, fifteen miles from his childhood farm. Now, as the mile markers whizzed by, he relived that road trip.

27

Once past Silver Creek, the Thruway was lined by vineyards with perfectly parallel rows of gnarly vines. Mac recalled running down such rows as a kid, popping grapes in his mouth with his terrier Scout barking behind him.

❊❊❊❊❊

11:00 a.m.

Nearing Westfield, Mac's daydreams were interrupted by a 'Whoop! Whoop!'

A State Trooper's lights flashed in his rearview mirror. Mac drifted the Chevy onto the shoulder and glided to a stop. Keeping his hands on the steering wheel, he waited for the Trooper to approach. Buddy was on full alert, spinning and barking.

"Sit, Buddy. Stay."

Buddy sat and growled low in his throat. Mac could see the Trooper running his plate and talking on his radio.

'ROWRF,' Buddy alerted as the Trooper approached Mac's window. He was dressed in gray with a flat brim hat that made him look taller than he already was.

"Sir, would you exit at the Westfield ramp and pull over by the toll booth?" The Trooper turned and walked back to his cruiser, lights still flashing.

"Huh!" said Mac. "Wonder what this is about, eh Buddy?"

So Mac drove his baby blue '57 Chevy to the off-ramp and stopped beside the toll booth apron.

"Sir, may I see your license and registration? The reason I pulled you over was not for speeding, even though I clocked you at 72 in a 65 zone. I would have just given you a warning for that. I pulled you over because your trunk lid is floating up and down."

"Really, Officer?"

Mac got out of the car and walked around back. Sure enough, the trunk latch was stuck jaws-open.

"Huh!" said Mac. "You know, sixty-six year old car, stuff gets stuck."

He lifted the trunk lid, opened a toolbox, and took out a hammer and can of penetrating oil. Giving the latch a spray, he waited a few seconds and then hit it one sharp 'whap!' The steel jaws popped open. He sprayed it again and test-closed it with a reassuring 'click.'

"Thanks, Officer, I appreciate you seeing that. Good eyes."

28

"Well," he said, looking at Mac's driver's license, "it's kind of a slow day, Mr. Morrison. You're coming from New Hampshire, eh? Long drive for a '57 Bel Air."

"You know your cars, Officer...Gregor," he said, looking at his name tag.

"Well, I've got a classic Chevy myself. To be honest, I needed a reason to see your car. It doesn't look like stock ride height."

"Officer Gregor, you just got yourself the nickel tour. Got five minutes?"

"Sure. I'm actually going on lunch break."

Mac popped the hood, and the Officer let out a low whistle.

"Is that a Chevy crate engine?"

"Yep. It's the fuel injected aluminum 383 V-8 with the 4L70-E six-speed automatic. Probably 140 pounds lighter than the old iron 283."

"How many horse?"

"450; I reinforced the frame and added custom exhaust, disc brakes, modern steering and suspension, then repainted it the original Larkspur Blue."

"Did you do all that yourself?" asked the officer.

"Yes, with the help of my best friend," said Mac. "How about you, Officer Gregor? What's in your garage?"

"I've got a 1974 Crimson Red Chevy 4 x 4 with the 454 V-8, new carb, aluminum heads, and intake."

"Huh! My uncle had one like that back in the day. Officer Gregor, could we join you for lunch?"

"Sure. Follow me."

They drove a half mile to Barcelona Harbor, stopped at Todd's Corner Gas n Go, bought subs and cold pop and sat on a wooden picnic table at the pier beneath an old stone lighthouse.

"So, Officer Gregor..."

"Call me Andy."

"OK, call me Mac. Grow up here, Andy?"

"Yep, I've lived all my life in Chautauqua County. Still live in Mayville, over the escarpment. That's the big ridge that runs parallel to the lake. Went with State Police Troop A right out of college. Got twenty six years in; four to go for a full pension."

"That would make you about 48. I turned 50 yesterday, Andy."

"You look younger. Live in New Hampshire all your life?"

"Actually, I grew up just down the road in Ripley."

"No kidding! Are you visiting relatives, Mac?"

"Wish I were. No, my parents were killed in a car accident 40 years ago. I went to New Hampshire to live with my aunt and uncle, and haven't been back in 34 years. The last time I was here was the summer I turned sixteen. I was a counselor at a western riding camp in Dewittville."

"No way!" exclaimed Andy. "You mean the Bar B Ranch with Mr. Barnes and his wife?"

"That's the one. You know it?"

"I was a camper there too, Mac. Wait a minute! You're not 'Mr. Mac' my tent counselor, are you? The cool guy with the '74 square body Chevy truck?"

A little trap door opened in the back of Mac's brain. The name 'Mr. Mac' slid out all fuzzy and wilted.

"Mr. Mac? You know, I think some of the kids did call me 'Mr. Mac'. Wait! Andy Gregor? I think I had you in my tent. You were one of the older kids!"

"That is amazing! Mr. Mac!"

"Andy Gregor! You know, one of the places I wanted to see on this trip was the Bar B. But I Googled it, and could not find it."

"It's gone, Mac. House, chapel and stables are still there, but Mr. B and his wife died years ago. It's Betty Wilson's home and riding stable now."

"How would I find it?"

"Take State Route 394 thru Westfield up and over the escarpment into Mayville. When you come down the hill towards Lake Chautauqua, bear left onto State Route 430. Take that to 633. I think your eyes will remember when you see the old stable barn."

"Terrific. One last thing, Andy; where is a good place for me and Buddy to stay for a few nights?"

Andy pointed to a towering four-story Victorian house with cream yellow wood clapboards, and an elevated front porch that offered a panoramic view of Lake Erie. A shallow balcony projected off the fourth-floor attic under the eaves. In the time of sailing ships it was perhaps the widow's walk for a captain's wife.

"Go see Marybeth. She owns the Captain Murphy B & B. She's a dog lover, with a little cottage out back that would be perfect for you and Buddy. And, she's a fabulous cook."

"Local lady?" asked Mac.

"Yep, and, she was a Bar B camper!"

"No way!" said Mac.

"Yep, popular thing back in the day, sending kids to riding camp. Thank you for lunch, Mac. I'm glad I stopped you. Don't know what your plans are for tomorrow, but it's my day off and my wife is playing golf. Would you like to come over to Mayville around lunch? I'll show you my truck. Maybe we can drive by your family farm. I'd like to see it."

"Let's do it, Andy. Let me get your cell number and give you mine."

✳✳✳✳✳

Chapter Eight

Mac drove five minutes into sleepy downtown Westfield. It looked frozen in 1920 with its stately Victorian homes, leafy tree-lined streets, sidewalks, and a pocket park in front of a Greek Revival Library.

Mac quickly passed out of town and began the drive up and over the thousand-foot-tall escarpment before descending into the tiny village of Mayville.

The quaint three-block downtown was decorated with red, white and blue bunting for the upcoming Memorial Day Parade. He could picture a high school band marching past sidewalks lined with folding lawn chairs and little kids sitting on curbs wearing heart-shaped sunglasses waving tiny flags.

The day was getting warm and Buddy was panting in the un-air conditioned '57 Chevy. Mac dropped the top on the convertible. Buddy got his first taste of open air riding and he liked it.

The expanse of Lake Chautauqua greeted them at the bottom of the hill. Rather than go left for the Bar B, Mac swung the Chevy to the right past the paddle wheeler Chautauqua Belle and into the lake front park. The pace of life was slow, the breeze calm, and the lake waters as crystal clear as he remembered from his youth. There were only a few cars. Some kids were playing tennis, and families were picnicking under large trees.

Buddy swam in circles outside the beach area lapping up cool water and watching Mac on shore. When he was done, he shook off and trotted along as they crossed the narrow rural road to an old wooden ice cream stand painted rainbow colors.

It felt the same as 34 years before. Mac ordered a pistachio cone and a bowl of non-dairy vanilla for Buddy. They sat on a bench under a large oak tree, quietly enjoying a perfect afternoon overlooking the gorgeous Lake Chautauqua.

"Doesn't get much better than this, does it, Buddy?"

'Rowrf!' Buddy replied.

*****

Mac missed the Bar B the first time he drove past. The sign was gone, and the chapel bell tower had been removed for an add-on shed. But the stable was still there, as were the corral and riding ring.

He couldn't help himself. He had to knock on the front door and make an awkward introduction to the owner, Betty Wilson.

"It's OK," she said, "you're another Bar B camper come back to revisit your youth. Feel free to walk around. The mess hall is now our living room. The tent platforms were burned as bonfires, but you can still see the outline of the chapel. It's cluttered inside but you'll find hymnals in the pews and the piano where Mr. B led the songs."

"You sound like a former camper, Mrs. Wilson."

"Six years! It was sad to see it close, but parents don't send kids to camp anymore. Kids play Xbox, or Tik Tok, whatever that is. We just enjoy living here and giving riding lessons. Most of our riders are older folks. There is no substitute for the smell of manure, leather and a sweaty horse. Come back anytime, Mr. Morrison."

"I'd like that, but I live in New Hampshire. This is a trip to see my childhood home."

"Oh, where was your home?"

"Forty years ago, my parents owned the Morrison Vineyard on U.S. 20 by the Ripley exit."

"Yes," she said "I remember it, and I remember when your parents were killed in that terrible crash. After they were gone there was supposed to be a big development of your farm, which was near our store. I was just a teenager, but I remember the hullabaloo with the other grape farmers. They didn't want to see that land paved over."

"When was that, Mrs. Wilson?"

"Goodness, well, a woman never tells her age, but I was a high school senior. I remember because Minetti had just bought that farm, and it's a small town. Everyone knows everyone. I'm almost 60, which means it would have been 1984, I should say."

"That's interesting. So what happened?"

"Now, that I don't remember. There was talk of a big development, but it never happened."

"Well, thanks again for speaking with me, Mrs. Wilson. Maybe I will see you again. I would love to take a trail ride. I haven't been on a horse since my last summer here thirty-four years ago."

"Isn't that something," she said. "I hope you do come back again, Mr. Morrison."

"Well, Buddy, what do you make of that? Remember that library we passed? I think maybe we have time to read old newspapers."

'Rowrf!' Buddy nudged Mac's knee and raced him to the car.

"We have a special stop to make first, Buddy-Boy. Let's go."

*****

12:30 p.m.

The private Morrison cemetery was a small plot of land between summer cottages on the eastern shore of Chautauqua Lake in Dewittville. It was less than two miles from the old Bar B camp. The land had been purchased in the mid-nineteenth century by the first Mackenzie Morrison, after whom Mac was named. His part of the Morrison clan hailed from the Low Country of Scotland. They were looked down upon by their Highland cousins.

In 1847, Mackenzie was a young seaman on a packet ship to America, transporting Irish refugees escaping the Great Potato Famine. Instead of staying aboard for the return trip, he took work riding a barge mule on the Erie Canal. Having traversed New York from the Hudson River to Lockport, he next took a job on a sailing ship hauling lumber on Lake Erie. And that is how he found Barcelona Harbor. He rented a horse to ride up the escarpment for a sweeping view of Lake Erie, but instead was transfixed by the seductive panorama on the other side. He bought the horse, and purchased a half-acre plot on the shores of Chautauqua Lake.

He built a modest home, married, and became a fisherman, supplying the growing community with fresh catch from the clear lake waters. When he died, his children, and his children's children for generations funded the care of the family plot. In the mid twentieth century, the Town accepted the cemetery for permanent maintenance.

It was a peaceful spot, one young Mac had visited many times as a child. He found his parent's simple headstones and cleaned them with rags and chemicals he had brought just for that purpose. Satisfied that they were being well cared for, he put Buddy back in the Chevy and headed over the escarpment to Westfield.

1:15 p.m.

The William A. Banks Memorial Library proudly faced a sliver-shaped park under a canopy of tall trees. Its portico was Greco-Roman, with Doric Columns supporting a stone lintel over tall double doors. The sign said that it was open until 3 p.m. Saturday.

As Mac climbed the stone steps, he looked back at his blue Chevy parked in the shade. Buddy was watching him through open windows.

It was cool inside. The high-ceilinged room was whisper quiet. Two elderly patrons pretended to read magazines, but they were both slumped-over, sleeping.

Mac approached the front desk. A woman with gray streaks in brown hair looked at him over half-glasses. Her name tag read 'Rosemary'. She looked bored.

"Yes?" Her voice was condescending.

"I'd like to look at newspaper archives," said Mac.

"How old?"

"1983."

"Those would be on microfiche," she said. "Do you know how to use a reader?" She twisted her head to hide a sneer.

"Yes."

"What date?"

"May 14, 1983, and the months after."

"I'll pull the 1983 and '84 fiches. You can sit at the reader in the alcove."

"Thank you," said Mac.

"Any particular story?" Rosemary asked. "I can scan quicker if I know what you want."

"I'm looking for a fatal car crash in Ripley."

"Oh?"

"Yes, my parents were killed in that crash."

"Oh," she said, "I see. Well, here are the fiches. Let's see now, here is a story, May 15, front page:"

'LOCAL GRAPE FARMERS SHAUN AND CLAUDIA MORRISON KILLED IN FIERY RIPLEY CRASH.'

35

"Is that the one?" Rosemary asked.

"YES! Yes, thank you," said Mac.

"If I can be of any other help," she added, "I'll be at my desk."

With that, she turned and walked away. She reached down into the pocket of a baggy cardigan that looked like it had been worn every day for ten years. She slipped out a cell phone and ducked into a side room.

"Joe, better come up here," she said, as the door clicked shut behind her.

✱✱✱✱✱

Mac's eyes were riveted to the black and white photos of the crash scene that accompanied the newspaper story. His car-restorer brain subconsciously analyzed what he was seeing.

- Photo #1 was a side view of his parent's 1970 Ford F-100 pickup truck. The driver's door was caved in, and the truck was folded in half, burnt black. The left rear wheel was tucked inward. The sheet metal behind it was wrinkled, indicating the rear axle had been shoved forward.
- Photo #2 showed the back end of their Ford F-100 pickup. The step-and-tow bumper was crushed and lifted up.
- Photo #3 showed a black tow truck with a flat 'pusher' front bumper covered with a scabby rubber mat. It was stopped in the middle of the road next to a Victorian storefront. White block letters said 'Joey's Collision and Repairs' across the truck's hood. There were multiple tire marks on the road in front of the truck.

Mac focused on the photo that showed the back end of his parent's 1970 F-100. At first he was puzzled, then dumbfounded.

Now, the door to that little cubicle in his brain, the door that had been left open for 40 years, the door that would never close, no matter how hard he tried to close it, now that door swung wide open and let his memories flood out with a sharpness that only death can sear into one's subconscious.

May 14, 1983. He was five days shy of 10 years old. His memory reeled back to the red Ford F-100 he was promised when he would turn 16. That was the truck he drove on the back roads of his farm. He vividly recalled that afternoon. He washed and shined that red F-100 before they drove it to a grower's meeting. He knew every inch of that truck. He had never seen it again once his parents drove away. Destroyed in the accident, he was told, towed away and gone.

Now, his eyes stared at the photo of that F-100. Here it was, at the scene of the accident after the fire was extinguished. Its heavy duty step-and-tow bumper, the one he climbed on every day, was smashed in and pushed up!

But, he knew there was no damage to the back of his parent's truck on the afternoon of May 14, 1983. Yet, here it was, a few hours later, crushed!

Wait, he thought, both police reports said they had been struck on the driver's side door by the big tractor truck. So, how did this back end damage happen?

He turned his attention to the news story from May 15, 1983, in the Westfield Press.

Mr. and Mrs. Shaun Morrison of the Morrison Vineyards, U.S. Route 20, Ripley, were killed in a two-vehicle accident at the intersection of U.S. 20 and Sherman Road on May 14 when they failed to stop for a red light and were struck by a heavy tractor truck traveling east on U.S. 20. The impact ignited the gasoline tank in the Morrison's 1970 Ford pickup truck. The resulting fire had to be extinguished before the Ripley Fire Department, assisted by units from Westfield, could remove their bodies. The Morrisons were both declared dead at the scene. The driver of the truck that struck them, Juan Martinez, is employed by ZOL Trucking, Paramus, New Jersey. Local auto body shop owner Joseph Minetti Jr. was following the Morrison vehicle and stated that they ran the red light when struck by the heavy tractor.

Ripley Police and NY State Police from Troop A in Fredonia responded to the scene. The accident investigation continues, but the preliminary police report released today to the Westfield Daily Press concluded it was a case of driver error caused by Mr. Morrison's failure to stop for the red light, misjudging the speed of the oncoming truck, and not allowing enough time to safely cross the intersection.

Mr. and Mrs. Morrison were well known in the Ripley and Westfield area as members of the Growers Co-op. They have operated the Morrison Vineyards for 15 years after taking it over from Mr. Morrison's parents, now deceased. They are survived by a son, Mackenzie, age 10.

Mac stared numbly at the screen. He looked at the following days' stories but there was no new information. However, one year later, a small story in the Westfield Press read, *'N.J. Corporation buying Morrison Vineyard: new development proposed at Ripley Interchange.'*

Six months after that, a second-page story quoted Joseph Minetti Senior saying the Minetti family business had purchased the Morrison farm from a New Jersey Corporation, and were planning to develop an outlet mall in partnership with a developer to be named.

Mac remembered the Minettis. They owned the vineyard next to his. He remembered a cocky twenty-year-old Joey Minetti racing up and down doing burnouts and 'laying rubber.' He always had a hot rod he was souping up. Mac remembered when the Minettis built him an auto repair shop by the fence line close to his father's barn.

Joey Minetti was a genius with cars, and a jerk, Mac remembered that. Joey was making money for the Minetti Enterprise, that's what he told young Mac over the fence. Mac had to ask his mother what an 'enterprise' was. That's what the black and white sign over the gate to the Minetti property said: 'Minetti Enterprises.'

And cruel: Joey Minetti was a cruel son of a bitch. He shot his BB rifle at kids riding bikes just to hear them yelp. If Mac had been a little older, he would have kicked Joey's ass when he shot his Terrier Scout through the fence and then ran away laughing. But he didn't run fast enough to escape the rock that nine-year-old Mac hurled so hard at the back of his head that it knocked him out, and he fell down and chipped his tooth! Joey Minetti did not shoot BBs at Scout after that.

Mac also remembered that Old Man Minetti, as the kids had called Joseph Senior, had approached his father about buying their vineyard, but his Dad refused to sell. His plan was for young Mac to take over in ten years and give the vineyard new life. That's how he reported it to Mac and Claudia over dinner in their country kitchen. And that had been the end of that.

Or, had it?

He copied the stories and photos to a document and then made multiple enlargements. He hit the "Print" button and heard the whir of a copy machine.

Removing the fiche card, he picked up his photocopies and headed for the computers.

First, he called up *Google Earth*™ and looked at the family farm. There was the old house, extended to the rear since his childhood, with several large new warehouse buildings behind it.

Next, he shifted *Google Earth* to the intersection of State Route 76, also known as Sherman Road, and U.S. 20. He looked at it from above, then he went down to *Google Street View*™ and did a 360-degree turn from the center of the intersection. He zoomed in and printed each one.

Using the mouse wheel, he 'drove' *Street View* six hundred feet from the double railroad track north to U.S. 20 the way his father had. He took snapshots as he went and printed them.

He kept replaying the two police reports in his mind.

Using *Street View* again, he 'drove' from the Grange Hall in Sherman north on Route 76 to Ripley, the way his father drove the night they were killed. He remembered driving that road with his Dad as a kid. It had 7 curves. Three had high speed approaches to sweepers. Those were fast and fun, if you slowed in time.

There was a steeper section with four back-to-back curves, like a roller coaster at the county fair. His Dad drove him to summer camp on that road. He remembered how it fell from the top of the escarpment down to the Ripley flats. It was all coming back to him.

Next, he looked up the County Auditor's tax maps and found property records for the family farm. There were several sales transactions. He printed them out.

The web site also had a topography layer. When he overlaid it on the tax map he saw that he had remembered right. It was a 900-foot drop from the top of the escarpment to the Ripley flats. The section with the four sharpest curves dropped one hundred feet as it rounded two curves and then climbed one hundred feet as it rounded two more, just like a roller coaster. The rural road was narrow and heavily wooded.

By now, the throbbing in his temple was a loud warning of a stress headache, or worse. He needed to shut down and chill out. He felt his temple, then felt for the little square box in his pocket. It was there.

He shut down the computer, collected his pages from the printer and walked to the front desk.

"Find what you were looking for?" the librarian asked with a sneer.

"Yes. Twenty prints. What do I owe you?"

"Five dollars."

Mac handed her the money. "Have you lived here all your life?" he asked.

"Yes," she replied, cautiously.

"Do you remember an outlet mall proposed for the Morrison farm near the Ripley Interchange? It would have been 1984."

The woman grimaced as a small tic rapidly winked her left eye.

"No, but my memory isn't so good way back. You know how it is, getting older. Why do you ask?"

"Oh, just curious. Something someone told me today. I also read a story about a proposed development of our farm in the news files. Well, thank you for your help, Ms..."

She paused..."Minetti. You're welcome...Mr. Morrison?"

"Yes, I'm Mackenzie Morrison."

*****

As soon as Mac cleared the front door, Rosemary Minetti rushed to the window and snapped his picture with her cell phone.

Then she went to the printer file history and reprinted the pages he paid for. She went back to the front window and looked out as he loaded his dog into an old blue car. Once again, she slipped her cell phone from the sagging pocket of her old cardigan. She snapped another picture of the Chevy driving down Route 394 towards Barcelona Harbor, then hit her speed dial for 'Joe.'

"Joey, you here?" she asked.

"I sent Gino," he replied, "what's the big deal, Rosie?"

"Not sure. We need a family council tonight."

"Rosie, we're gambling tonight."

"We can go to the casino later. Shouldn't take long, but it could be important. I'll call Gino."

*****

Chapter Nine

Saturday, May 20
3:00 p.m.

T he church bell rang three times. A quiet afternoon was winding down. Few cars moved through the sleepy downtown as Mac walked down the library steps under tall shade trees. As he approached the Chevy, he felt eyes on his back. He walked around the car so he could look back at the library. There was a flash at the window, the curtain shivered and went still.

Someone just took his picture.

He walked Buddy around the small city park. Mostly American cars were parked on the street, but at the far end of the park was the unmistakable shape of a bright red Ferrari.

As he pulled away from his parking space and drove down Route 394 towards Barcelona Harbor, he kept his eye on his rear view mirror. A red Ferrari, way back, was following him.

✳ ✳ ✳ ✳ ✳

3:15 p.m.

The Captain Murphy B & B Inn was a hauntingly impressive Victorian relic. Its architecture was foreboding, but its yellow hue was welcoming. Neat gardens surrounded the front entry. An elegant script sign directed guests to check in at the back door. Mac parked the Chevy to the rear.

Leaving Buddy in the car, he crunched his way across round pea gravel to the porch. When he pulled open the ancient wooden screen door, its rusty spring 'gronked' welcome and then 'whapped' the door shut behind him with a 'bam!'

The large porch had a low shed roof and six square tables draped with white linen tablecloths. A small vase with fresh cut flowers sat in the middle of each.

A delicious aroma wafted out from an open kitchen window to the porch.

41

"Hello! The dogs won't bite," trilled the voice from the window.

It was a smoky, sultry voice that went up and down an octave. It made that one sentence sound like Dusty Springfield's₅ husky '*Son of a Preacher Man*₆.' A guy could fall in love with a voice like that, especially if those delicious aromas were dinner.

Three little dogs ran up and sniffed him. Like poodles, but not poodles, thought Mac. He bent down to let them smell his hand before patting one on the head.

"Marybeth?" Mac said to the face in the window.

"That's me."

She came out of the kitchen wiping her hands on a towel. She had rubber gardening boots on her feet, and was wearing a freshly starched white shirt with a high collar and the sleeves folded back. A beautiful blue scarf was tied around her alabaster throat, which had a touch of early summer tan. A second matching scarf held back her flowing chestnut hair, 1940s Hollywood style. White painter's bib overalls concealed a slim figure.

"Yes? Can I help you?" she said. "Are you looking for a room?"

Her eyes were deep emerald green.

"Uh...wow! Marybeth, did anyone ever say you look like Ella Raines?"

"I'm sorry, Ella...who?" she said.

"Ella Raines, the actress. Hey, I'm sorry, too. I'm Mac Morrison, and I didn't mean to be rude, but I just watched her 1949 film noir, *Impact,* and you look so much like her in that movie, right down to the bib overalls. That's a compliment, by the way."

"I'll take it as one, but I'll check her out on the internet! HAHA! Were you looking for a room?"

"Yes, and I have a dog. Trooper Andy Gregor said your cottage might be available."

"Andy Gregor! Now, don't tell me: he didn't give you a ticket if you promised to stay the night here! HAHAHA! He's always trying to drum up business for me, that scoundrel!"

She laughed so raucously that Mac had to laugh, too.

"You're almost right, actually."

"Well, the cottage is available. Its early season, so I don't have a lot of rooms booked. How many nights do you want?"

"Not sure, let's say two or three, possibly more."

"Breakfast is included, but I can offer lunch and dinner some days if you add the meal plan."

"Sounds good, I'll do it. It's a large dog. Would that be a problem?"

"Is he well behaved, Mr. Morrison?"

"Better than me; call me Mac, please."

She chuckled at that. This was a lady with a sense of humor, he thought.

"OK, Mac. The cottage has a kitchen and its own bath, but it's small, just one room."

"I like small all of a sudden."

"Meaning what, Mac?"

"My house burned last week, so I'm living in a friend's one-room tourist cottage."

"I'm sorry, Mac. Anyone hurt?"

"No, but my house and business were all in that barn."

"What is your business?"

"I'm a builder, and half owner of a well-drilling rig in a small town."

"What town?"

"Sunapee, New Hampshire."

"Hey," Marybeth said brightly, "I ski Mount Sunapee! We have great skiing in Chautauqua County, but our season is shorter, so I go to New Hampshire in spring. Do you ski Mac?"

"Um-hm, pretty much that's what we do in winter, that and sit around our wood stoves telling lies."

"Now you're putting me on. What do you really do in winter Mac?"

"I restore classic cars, like my '57 Chevy out there."

"It has a nice rumble; not too loud, just right. Did you resto-mod it with a new engine, transmission, and suspension?"

"Marybeth! Are you a car nut?"

"Cruise–In Queen three times! That's for the car, not the owner!"

"You'd win for the owner too."

Marybeth blushed.

"What car do you have, Marybeth?"

"1964 Mercury Cyclone with the Hi-Po 289. My Grandad bought it new. It's sitting in the barn out back."

"I've never seen one," said Mac.

"First Cruise-In of summer is tomorrow night, Mac. You bring your Chevy, I'll bring my Merc. It's in the Mayville Lakeside Park by the ice cream stand."

"My dog Buddy and I were there today, Marybeth. Memory took me back to the Bar B Ranch!"

43

"Don't tell me you were a Bar B camper!"

"Yep, six summers. Andy Gregory and I actually remembered each other after all those years!"

"I was a Bar B camper, too! Guess I don't remember you."

"I'm older than you; I turned 50 yesterday," Marybeth.

"Not that much older, Mac, I'll be 44 this June. Some days, I feel 64. It's a lotta work running this place all alone."

"Don't you have help?"

"I have a housekeeper, so I do the cooking. But without a man around the house, I have to do all the maintenance or pay to have it done. This place barely breaks even as it is. Here's a registration card and key, Mac. Your dog can come on the porch. My dogs will check him out."

"Buddy will behave. He listens to me, even though I've had him less than a week."

"Rescue dog?"

"Sort of; I took him away from a bad breeder."

"Say, I need to get back to baking. Do you want to join us for dinner, Mac?"

"Sure. Buddy and I will unload our stuff and take a walk down to the lake. I've got some things to think about. See you at dinner."

"OK, Mac, glad you're staying with us. It'll be nice to have a man to talk to."

Mac thought about that while he and Buddy unloaded their gear and checked into the cottage.

As a builder, he had to check out another builder's work. Walls were extra thick with a heavily insulated door, but it had a cheap lock. Inside, he saw good choices for a rental cottage: birch plywood paneling stained a light maple and finished with satin poly. Two electric hydronic radiators hung on the walls. The cottage would be cozy in winter with no boiler, noise or maintenance.

Mac brushed Buddy's white coat until it glistened. He fed him, and slipped into a clean shirt. They walked side by side across the empty two-lane Route 5 past the old stone lighthouse to the Harbor pier.

Barcelona Harbor's beach lay beneath the shoreline of rural Route 5 with a sharp bank climbing 30 feet up to the road. As he walked, Mac heard water running. He looked up to see a shimmering waterfall shooting out of shale, dribbling down the face of the embankment to the lake. The beach ended with a steep shale wall.

Mac's eyes were scanning as they headed back to the pier, a habit from his two tours in the Middle East.

'Grrrrrrr!' Buddy tapped his leg with his nose and sat. Alert!

"What do you see, Buddy boy?"

Movement caught his eye. A young man with a long mop of dark curly hair was sitting by a replica of the ship Santa Maria, watching them.

"I see him, Buddy. Good boy!"

'Rowrf!' Buddy circled Mac, wagging his tail.

"Let's go see pretty Marybeth Murphy, Buddy!"

Fishermen were returning to the ramp and hauling their boats out on trailers. As Mac and Buddy walked uphill past the stone lighthouse, they heard the unmistakable rasp of an Italian V-12 engine. Mac turned his head in time to see the mop-headed young man driving away in a bright red Ferrari.

*****

6:00 p.m.

"May I join you?"

Marybeth Murphy was holding a steaming bowl of pasta noodles in one hand and a large salad bowl in the other. She had changed into dark blue dress slacks and cordovan loafers to go with her white high collar shirt with a pearl necklace, and a lighter blue ribbon in her flowing chestnut hair.

"Buddy and I would be delighted," said Mac as he quickly rose and pulled out her chair.

She set down the bowls, grabbed a tray of hot toasted rolls
and sat with Mac.

"Smells wonderful, Marybeth. At home I mostly live on microwave meals, so this is a treat."

"It's simple to make, and cheap!

Buddy nudged his arm.

"He's begging for a bite of roll. Will I be banned if I give him one?"

She tossed the salad and shook her head.

"Forgive me, Marybeth. You said the past two years have been tough with no man around the house."

Marybeth stopped tossing salad and looked Mac directly in the eye.

"I'm a widow. My husband passed away two years ago. They said he drowned while fishing. They found his boat and his body floating, still wearing a life vest. I never could accept it. He was a great swimmer."

45

"I'm sorry, Marybeth."

"I've been a long time getting over it, but it still bothers me, Mac. I never had a chance to say goodbye. Isn't that sad?"

"That's very sad, Marybeth. I never got to say goodbye either, to my parents, that is. Then I got some news yesterday that took me back to their deaths here in Ripley forty years ago. Next thing you know, I'm back here. Gonna go see my childhood home."

"Where was it, Mac?"

"The Morrison Vineyards. Gonna drive by the old house tomorrow. I was ten the last time I saw it."

"Why didn't you have a chance to say goodbye, Mac?"

"They were killed in a car crash while I was at a friend's house. Police came and told me my parents were dead. My aunt and uncle came down from New Hampshire for the funeral, then took me back there and raised me. My uncle just died last week. At least I got to say goodbye to him."

"Oh, I'm very sorry, Mac. But at least you have Buddy. I have my three Labradoodles. Their mother died, and they had to be hand-nursed, so my vet asked me to do it. I'm part of a network that rescues dogs, pays for medical care, and gets them to foster homes. These three were so attached I couldn't bear to separate them, so I kept them. They came along just after Jim passed, so they have been my family since."

"What did your husband do?"

"He was an Investigator for the New York Bureau of Criminal Investigation. We were high school sweethearts. When he got promoted, I quit teaching elementary school and converted this big old place into a B & B. That was six years ago, and it's been good because it keeps me busy. But you said the Morrison Vineyard, I can't place it."

"U.S. 20, south of Ripley near the I-90 interchange."

"Oh! Is that the Minetti farm and wine store?"

"Wine store?"

"Yes, they built a wine sampling room out front. You'll see it when you drive past. Speaking of wine, I almost forgot the wine! We can't have pasta without wine!"

She reached around and grabbed a bottle of red wine.

"Hope you like this Mac."

"Is it Minetti's?"

"Gosh, no, I wouldn't buy from them!" she said with a vengeance.

"Why, Marybeth?"

"When Jim died, he was looking into something involving them. He joked their entry sign should read 'Minetti *Criminal* Enterprises.' I believe my husband's death was foul play, Mac, and I believe it was connected to Minettis. But what about you, Mac, what was the news that brought you back here?"

"It was a 40-year-old envelope that contained police reports of the car crash that killed my parents. Those reports told me facts that had been kept from me, so I wanted to revisit my hometown, and perhaps find out more about their deaths. I'll never know why my uncle held that envelope so long, but my guess is something about their accident didn't seem right, yet he didn't know what he could do about it at that time."

"Marybeth, you have to understand that, in 1983, my Uncle Abe was 60 years old. He had retired from the Air Force in 1961 after a distinguished 20-year career that included bombing missions against the Nazis, and his plane being shot down. He had survived the war, worked very hard, and done well. He deserved a peaceful retirement with my aunt, who was ten years his junior."

"For him, with their son grown and away at college, life was finally getting easier. Suddenly, he had the responsibility to start parenthood all over to raise a 10-year-old boy he didn't even know. And I was not an easy kid."

"For me, moving to a dark New Hampshire forest, with no friends, and an old Colonel for an uncle was like being cast adrift in a cold ocean, with no touchstone, and nothing to comfort me but my little dog Scout. I was angry after losing my parents, my home and our farm. I became an uncontrollable hellion, my uncle later recalled, constantly getting into fights and beating the crap out of kids twice my size."

"Anyway, Marybeth, I think Uncle Abe wanted me to have this envelope when I was more mature, to do whatever I thought needed to be done, but after he was gone. Maybe he felt guilty that he had not done more at the time."

"And that's why you're here, Mac?"

"Yes, I wanted to come back, visit their graves, and maybe finally lay the memory of my parents to rest. I didn't suspect anything nefarious. But today, some things happened that made me wonder."

"Like what?"

"I found the old Bar B Camp and knocked on the door. In chatting with the current owner, Mrs. Wilson, she remembered some talk about a big development proposed for my parent's farm after they died. So, I did a little research at the library."

"Property records showed the Probate Court ordered a Sheriff's sale of our farm to clear my parents' debts. It was bought by a New Jersey Corporation, which sold it to the Minettis, who owned the vineyard next to ours. I found a 1984 news article about Minetti's plan to develop my parents' farm into an outlet mall."

"Ironically, the dowdy librarian just happened to be Rosemary Minetti, and the witness to the accident that killed my parents in 1983 was her husband Joey Minetti. When I asked Mrs. Minetti about their family's plans to build an outlet mall, she claimed she had no recollection. I think she was lying."

"But your farm never got developed, Mac. It's still a vineyard today."

"Yeah, I don't get it, Marybeth."

"Mac, Rosemary Minetti plays the part of the frowsy librarian with the baggy sweater and those granny glasses. The Minettis like to gamble. Her casino clothes are designer stuff. Jim said Joey is a heavy loser."

"That's another thing Marybeth: Mrs. Minetti helped me find the story of my parents' death in the archives, but when I questioned her, she was evasive. Then I heard her make a phone call to Joe."

"That would be her husband Joey, Mac."

"And then someone snapped a photo of me when I left the library. I saw the flash from the window. A red Ferrari followed me from the library down here. After that, Buddy spotted a young man with black curly hair watching us at the beach. He drove off in a red Ferrari."

"That's Gino Minetti. Mac, I don't like the feel of this. Those are very unscrupulous people."

"But are they dangerous?"

"I don't really know."

"Well, tomorrow I'm going to take Trooper Andy to the accident scene, and show him the two reports to see if he spots anything hinky."

"So, Mac, forgive me if I change the subject. Are you...alone?"

"I've been divorced ten years, Marybeth."

"Do you get lonely sometimes?"

"I was lonely, when I was married, Marybeth. And I've been alone, but now I have Buddy."

"Well, now it's my turn to apologize for intruding, Mac. Let's not talk anymore about the past. Let's celebrate life with wine, and good food, and interesting conversation."

'Rowrf!'

"Oh, of course, and with you too, Buddy-dog!"

*****

Chapter Ten

Eighty-five-year-old Joseph Minetti waved his hand and the family sat down. The table was long: not as long as a bowling alley, but just as wide, because it had been a bowling alley, and was polished like glass.

Joseph was the patriarch, tall and thin, hardened from years working the vines. He had a trimmed white mane and matching goatee like a skinny Ernest Hemingway. He had led the family from its days as humble grape growers through fifty years of hard times and, finally, good times. He was wise and respected, even though his younger generations ran most of their businesses.

His voice was raspy, but it still had an authoritative bite.

"First, we toast to family, health and business. OK, Rosie, you called this Council, go ahead."

"Thank you, Poppa. Something strange happened today, so it's time for Gino and Gina to know the background history. My darlings, forty years ago there was a car accident in Ripley. Two people died: a man and his wife. They were named Morrison, and they owned this farm next to our old home place. Joey, your father, was driving behind them. He saw them get hit by a big truck. The Morrison vehicle burned, and they died. Joey told the police that Mr. Morrison ran the red light, and got hit by a big truck. The driver of the big truck said the same thing. That was the end of that."

"The Morrisons had a ten year old son. He was not in the car. After the accident, he left here. When the court ordered the sale of Morrison's farm, Poppa bought it. Today, a guy about 50 years old comes into the library, looking up news stories about his parent's death in a car crash 40 years ago. His name is…Morrison."

Joseph Senior put down his wine glass. Rosemary continued.

50

"So, this Mackenzie Morrison was asking a lot of questions about this farm. He had talked to someone who said we planned a development after we bought the land. He wanted to know why it never got developed. I played like I didn't remember, but I don't think he believed me, because he found an article in the paper from 1984 where Poppa was talking about developing an outlet mall."

"When he left the library, I checked the browser history on his computer and reprinted all his pages. He was on the county website checking property sales for this farm. And he printed out newspaper stories, property records and Google Earth views of the accident site where his parents died."

"So, I'm thinking: is this just curiosity with this guy Morrison, or what? I called Joe to come check this guy out and see where he went. Joe sent Gino."

"So, Gino," Joe interjected, "you followed him. Did he leave town?"

"No, he drove to the Harbor and went into the Murphy B & B. He left his car there and took a walk on the beach with a big dog. Looks like a tourist. What's the big deal?"

"OK," said Rosie, "maybe this Morrison guy is just coming home for a look, maybe he's just curious."

Joseph Senior held up his hand. Rosie kept quiet.

"Look," he said, "if this is the Morrison kid, it's natural to come see his old home: natural. So, if this Morrison shows up at the Wine Store, Gina, be nice to him, talk to him. It was his farm before we bought it. Gino, you do the same. If you meet him, if he comes into your business, be nice. This will blow over, and in a few days, he'll go home to...wherever."

"New Hampshire," Gino said. "He drives a baby blue '57 Chevy convertible with white canvas top and New Hampshire plate."

"Ok, good," said Joseph, "we can see him coming. Be nice. All right, that's it, end of discussion. Gina, how were April sales?"

"Best ever, Poppa, over a million dollars. We're developing markets in towns where we've been supplying restaurants. Their patrons are buying directly from us on-line. It's a trend."

"Wonderful, Gina," said Joseph. "You're smart, you keep on top of trends, and you make us money. We're all very proud of you. Thank you for your hard work. OK, Gina, you can go now. I got some business to discuss with the others. Love you, G."

"Love you too, Poppa."

When Gina had gone, Rosemary spoke. "Bad luck he's staying at Murphy's place."

51

Joseph Senior cleared his throat. He spoke in a voice tinged with age, wine and cigarettes.

"Things are going good for us. All the businesses are doing great. We are outta debt. Took us forty years to get here, so we don't want to blow it now! Let's all be careful while this guy's in town. Rosie, you overreacted by calling Joe to watch this guy. Anyway, it's done, can't undo it."

"Gino, there's more to this story, but this is a secret we keep between us three. Gina doesn't know, and we don't want her to ever know, that's why she has her own separate business. But you are in with Joey now, running a very profitable business. But, if you get caught, you could drag Rosie and me down with you. So, I'm gonna tell you this story because, with this Morrison here, you need to know. We are all four involved now. But not Gina, never Gina, got it?"

"Got it, Poppa," said Gino.

"Forty years ago," Joseph continued, "I tried to buy the Morrison farm, but they wouldn't sell. We needed to expand our small vineyard. I offered them more money, but they still wouldn't sell. We had to get other income. Rosie married your father and joined our family. She took a job at the library, and that helped us. Joey was young, but he was a genius with cars. So we built him a garage, and he started a collision shop. He's great, makes cars like new. But there wasn't enough business in this little burg."

"So Rosemary started the wine store, but our sweet wines didn't appeal like California wine, French wine, or Italian wine. It was the 80's, no internet, hard to market outside our area. Rosie tried, but it barely broke even. She stayed at the library, did wines on the side. We were still struggling."

"Then, bad luck. I had a great poker hand in Atlantic City, a chance to make a lot of cash, so I bet the farm, but I lost."

"Next thing, the Jersey casino boys come to see what they own, and they see 'location, location, location' with a toll-free exit off the Thruway. Great spot for a factory outlet mall, they said!"

"But they needed the Morrison farm near the exit to go with ours. So, I talked to Morrison again, offered him more money. He still wouldn't sell! So the Jersey Boys said they'd handle it: play rough and scare him so he'll sell."

"A growers meeting was coming up and Morrison would be there. Jersey Boys planned an accident on his way home, but it didn't go right. When Morrison stopped for the red light, we could have waited and got them later. But Joey, you know your father, he's impulsive. He was driving behind them, so he shoved them into the big speeding truck and, boom! Their gas tank blows up, they die. Roasted like marshmallows!"

"That wasn't the plan; we never intended to kill them. But it's done, can't undo it. It was night time, no witnesses besides the trucker and Joey. Jersey boys paid their trucker to keep his mouth shut. He and Joey both said the farmer ran the red light. Cops said it was Morrison's fault: case closed."

"So this Morrison kid goes bye-bye. Jersey boys buy the Morrison farm at Sheriff's sale and go looking for a developer. But it was early 1984, outlet malls were a new concept, and interest rates were 13%. Banks balked at backing them."

"Then, the state said Mall traffic would require a new interchange and overpass. Cost a gazillion dollars and we still needed planning approval!"

"So then, Jersey Boys said they don't want the land, they just want their money. But they got another idea. They'll sell us our farm back, with the Morrison farm, and hold the mortgage. All we gotta do is 'cooperate' with some of their other businesses. This location, right on the Thruway, in a sleepy little town, with a wine business already operating, was perfect for them."

"Perfect how, Poppa?"

"First, they expanded our wine business to import good Italian wines in big shipping containers. They helped us market the wines to Italian restaurants. We had the license to sell and ship. They got all the vineyard contacts in Italy. And they had restaurant and wholesale contacts on the East coast."

"So now we had container trucks delivering wine to us from New Jersey ports for our store and wholesale distribution, and containers going back through New Jersey ports to Italy. Our Jersey boys got influence in the ports, so no problems. Totally legit businesses, good deal."

"But Jersey had other businesses, some legit, some not so legit, you get my drift. They needed a legit cover for exporting contraband."

"That's why our Minetti wine shipping containers were perfect. They'd pick up our containers full of Italian wines at the docks in Jersey and deliver them on their trucks to us. We'd sell the wine through our retail store and distribute wholesale to restaurants. Then we'd load the containers with vats of our bulk grape juice and crates of our bottled juice, and they would truck it back to Jersey ports. Sometimes, they would reload the container to hide contraband surrounded by our grape juice, packed so it couldn't be seen even if the container were opened. We weren't involved in that part."

"They put the containers on the ship at the Jersey port. They were careful: they matched the weight of the shipment to the weight of just juice to keep things kosher. If any customs inspectors looked in the container, they'd see grape juice, no problem. They shipped to Sardinia, a big Italian island in the Mediterranean Sea."

"Sardinia had easy customs and Jersey Boys got friends there. For high-end cars stolen in New York and Jersey, they made up new Italian titles, and shipped them out to North Africa or the Middle East, no worries. No drugs, they never were involved with drugs. For guns and other contraband, they packed them in Sardinian wine crates for return to the vineyards in Italy. There, they would load our empty containers back up with good Sardinian wines, and send them back to us, to complete the loop."

"It went great for ten years."

"Then, bad luck. A crane used a top lift thing at the dock, and a hook busted. The crane dropped the container, doors busted open, and cars spilled out, but the Bill of Lading said the shipment was grape juice. Customs checked the VIN tags, and the cars came back stolen. Luckily, there was no other contraband in the container, just the cars. Shipper was Minetti Wines, so cops knocked on our door. Joey told them he shipped the cars in our wine container, without our permission, or our knowledge. Because we all had separate businesses, Joey took the hit for the family, and for the Jersey boys. He did some time in prison."

"But by the time he got out, it was the mid-90s, and now there was the internet. Rosie, she was still at the library. She knows about the internet. She says, hey! We can sell our Minetti wines on-line, and import Italian foods, too! Genius! So Joey reopened the collision shop, but now he was also selling salvage parts on the internet."

"Then, late 90s, you kids came along."

"Gina's on-line Sardinian wine sales are now our biggest business."

"Gino, you branched off Joey's salvage business into high-class European cars just when all the athletes started driving Ferraris and Lambos, and wrecking them: perfect timing. And Joey, now he's specializing in repairing high end European cars, since you got parts."

"Three years ago, we had paid off all our mortgages. We were doing great. Then Joey lost big at the casino. Luckily, because we are good customers, they took his marker with high interest. I was too old to remortgage this farm to pay his debt, so Joey called our old friends in Jersey to ask if they could pay it off, and we would return the favor in another way. They came and checked our businesses for collateral, and they saw a wrecked Ferrari that Gino bought cheap from the insurer. So Jersey boys stole another one, same car, and shipped it here in a Minetti wine container. Joey swapped the VIN tags and trackable parts from the legit wreck to the stolen car, got a salvage title, and sold the car to pay off his casino marker and pay back the Jersey Boys. But they wanted to keep doing it, and we owed them."

"So that began your new business. Jersey sends Joey stolen cars in our empty shipping containers to match whatever high end wrecks that Gino buys from insurance companies. Always European cars: Audi, BMW, Mercedes, and high end Italian. Joey swaps the VIN tags, engine and tranny case and even welds chassis sections from the crashed car into the stolen car frame. Gino, you have the titles for the legal wrecked cars so you send the altered stolen cars to New York State BMV inspection. And to make sure they pass, we give an 'appreciation' to an old friend at the BMV."

"Poppa, I know all this."

"No, Gino, wait, you didn't let me finish. Joey shipped a car to California, but something about it, they don't like it. They question the VIN tag; something about the rivets. They don't like the rivets Joey used on the VIN tag. Car got impounded. So Cali BMV calls New York BMV, and they turn it over to BCI."

"I never knew that Poppa," says Gino.

"We didn't want you to know. You were too young, and might say the wrong thing to someone. So, BCI Detective Jim Murphy comes around checking Joey's cars. We got lucky again. Joey was between 'project' cars; he was doing a legit collision repair. Murphy goes away."

"But later, he sneaks in behind a Minetti truck before the gate closes and catches Joey with a hot car. Fortunately, the car had damaged body panels, so Joey tells Murphy, he don't know it's stolen. He was hired to repair the body, that's all. Murphy wants the customer's name. Joey gives Murphy his Jersey contact, and as soon as Murphy leaves, Joey calls the boys in Jersey, figures they could make up an alibi. Jersey's furious!"

"But Poppa," said Gino, "Murphy drowned. Nobody ever came back on us for a bad car, did they?"

"No. We got lucky. Murphy drowned before he got into Joey's business. We had to pay some money to a friend in the Cali BMV, but they fixed the problem with the VIN on that car; all good."

"So Gino, that's why Rosie is worried about Morrison staying at Murphy's B & B. This guy is already curious why his farm didn't get developed, and why we bought it. While he's staying at Murphy's he could talk to her. As far as she knows, her husband drowned. But did she know he was lookin' into Joey? Did he tell her? Maybe she mentions it to Morrison. He could get more suspicious of us. He's asking all these questions, doing research on his parent's death. Why is he really here? Who is he, a detective?"

"So Gino, just be careful what you say around this Morrison guy. We want him to have a nice vacation, go home, never see him again, OK? And Joey, I know you. You avoid this Morrison; you don't even want to cross paths. Got it?"

"OK," Rosemary said, "let's go to the casino."

**

"Rosie, Joey, wait a minute," said Joseph Senior after Gino left the room.

"We got lucky with Murphy drowning. We got lucky again when our friend at BMV took care of the rivet problem. Cost us a little money, but we kept our skirts clean. So, anything you wanna tell me?"

"Tell you what, Poppa?" Joe asked.

"Anything. Maybe, something I don't know?"

"Poppa, we're good," said Joey.

"All good," said Rosemary.

"You're sure, Rosie?"

"We're good, Poppa."

"OK, Rosie, if you say so, I trust you. Joey, you're unlucky at cards, but you got lucky when you married Rosie. She is smart, she takes care of business. OK, we leave in half an hour, go play some cards, eh?"

*****

In Joe and Rosie Minetti's private suite
7:00 p.m.

"I need to call him."

"Joey, Poppa said…"

"I know, I know, Rosie, just to let him know. This is the guy from 40 years ago! He was there! He should know."

"But Poppa said…"

"Rosie, I'm gonna tell him: do nuthin…unless I say so."

*****

56

Chapter Eleven

Mac's Cottage was clean and quiet. Buddy went right to sleep. Mac couldn't sleep. He sat in the dark, wracking his brain. He kept thinking: *What really happened forty years ago?*

He turned on the lamp. Buddy stirred and looked at him. Mac sat up and put his feet on the floor. Buddy sat up and leaned against him, looking over his shoulder as Mac pored over the accident pictures.

Mac's car-restorer brain was churning. He was trying to process what he saw in the photos to somehow fit the story told by the police reports.

And it did not fit.

"What really happened forty years ago?" he said, surprised to hear his own voice in the room. Buddy looked at him, puzzled.

He studied the driver's side picture of his parents' burnt truck. It was folded in half where the big tractor struck it, puncturing the gas tank.

The rear axle was pushed forward out of its shackles. The heavy steel panel was wrinkled *behind* the axle. No side impact would have wrinkled the panel *behind* the wheel like that. And with the wheel tucked inward, the truck would have been *undriveable*. So, that damage was caused by a rear end collision, and had to have happened *during* this accident. It could *not* have been *'old damage'* as Trooper T. Riley determined in 1983.

He again perused the picture taken behind their pickup, showing the heavy-duty rear bumper crushed and lifted up. The Ripley police report noted that rear end damage, so *why did the state trooper dismiss it as old damage?*

The third picture was a south-facing view from U.S. Route 20 looking down Sherman Road. Now that Mac had seen the location on Google Earth, he recognized landmarks in the photo that had not changed in 40 years.

The Victorian storefront stood at the southwest corner of the intersection. In the picture, a tow truck was stopped in the street to its left, facing north towards U.S. 20. Its front push-bumper said 'Joey's Collision and Repair' across the top. That was Joe Minetti's truck.

According to the police reports, Joey Minetti had been following his parents' truck.

The photo was taken after the fire was extinguished, with the tow truck backed away from the corner. Debris and broken glass lay on the pavement in front of it from the initial impact. The tractor and his parents' truck were 75' to the east, out of the picture.

Wide tire marks on U.S. 20 ran crossways in front of the tow truck east-to-west. Were they skid marks? Had a semi-tractor, without a trailer, traveling at the posted 25 mile per hour speed limit, enough momentum to skid seventy-five feet while braking and pushing a 4,000 pound pickup truck sideways?

The fourth photo showed the tractor, a cab-over-engine with no sleeper, backed away from the burnt wreck of his parent's pickup.

Mac did some quick research on his phone. The tractor probably weighed 12-15,000 pounds. Internet data showed such a tractor could stop in 60 feet *if* it had been traveling at 25 mph. Now, he thought of the tractor-pulling events he had seen. When the drag sled begins to dig, the tractor's momentum dramatically slows. So, it seemed to him that a single bobtail tractor traveling at 25 mph hitting a 4,000 pound pickup truck sideways would not take seventy five feet to brake to a stop, *if it was trying to stop.* It also seemed like the tractor would have caromed off at an angle after hitting a moving pickup truck. But in this instance, it shoved it seventy five feet in a straight line.

Something was not right about all this.

No, he thought, *the tractor had to be traveling faster than 25 mph. And it did not try to stop.* It pushed the pickup *through* the intersection with its driving wheels spinning. That would explain the wide tire marks all across the intersection east to west, and the seventy-five feet it pushed their pickup truck.

Now, Mac focused on the third picture with *two sets* of black tire marks *in front* of Minetti's tow truck.

One set was clearly made by a narrower vehicle with skinny tires. The other set was made by a vehicle with two sets of dual rear wheels. The dual wheel marks were *outside* of the skinny tire marks. They had to be made by a *wider track* vehicle.

58

Mac knew that the narrower set of tire marks were _skid_ marks made by a vehicle with brakes _locked up_. His Dad's old F-100 had skinny tires.

The wider marks were made by a powerful truck with four rear driving wheels spinning fast, doing a sustained burnout, _like a dually pushing a narrower vehicle_!

Dad must have locked his brakes and was PUSHED into the path of a speeding tractor truck!

Had to be! How else did his truck get smashed in the ass? Their F-100 had _no rear end damage_ when he washed it just hours before!

And Minetti's tow truck, which was following his parent's truck, had a flat pusher bumper and wide track with four driving wheels. So, Joe Minetti must have shoved his parents' pickup in front of that speeding tractor.

But: why? And why did the cops not see that? But they DID SEE IT, but they dismissed it. WHY? Payoff? Cover-up?

Now, forty years of guilt drowned him.

WHY COULDN'T HE HAVE PROTECTED HIS PARENTS?!

Half a dozen therapists' voices echoed in his brain:

"You are not responsible for your parents' deaths."
"You have to let it go; there is nothing that you can do about it."
"You have an over-active sense of responsibility."
"You can't protect everyone from harm in life, Mackenzie."

He turned out the lamp, and sat in the dark again. His parents' faces haunted him. He envisioned the horror of them burning alive.

His head was pounding! He needed to shut down and chill out.

"Snap!" The sound crackled the air like static electricity jumping from a metal lamp to a finger after sliding stocking feet over a rug in winter. Buddy whipped his head around to find it. He sniffed Mac and touched his cold wet nose to a spot in his temple. It was hot.

Mac felt the hot spot in front of his ear. It was there again, a bulging clot, a big one.

The doctors warned him: "Mr. Morrison, you are predisposed to ischemic stroke. Blood clots in the temple are a warning. Keep the pills handy!"

He reached in his pocket for the little box. He chewed four, to be sure. The gritty orange aspirin dissolved under his tongue.

Now, he wanted soothing music. If no one can sleep, then let there be music.

Picking up his phone, he scrolled the play list and selected 'Nessun Dorma$_7$' (Let No One Sleep), the aria from Puccini's *Turandot*. Luciano Pavarotti's powerful voice was accompanied by the New York Philharmonic Orchestra$_7$.

The melody flowed through the cottage and out the window into the cool night air. He cranked the phone to max volume as the aspirin began to work.

Mac closed his eyes in the darkness, taking deep breaths to relax. Pavarotti's crescendo filled the room.

Dilegua, o note! (Vanish, oh night!)
Tramontate, stelle! Tramontate, stelle! (Fade, you stars!)
All'alba vincero! (At dawn, I will win!)
Vincero! (I will win!)
Vincero! (I will win!)

The orchestra ended with the eight note refrain, and then came a thunderous, rousing ovation.

Suddenly, silence in the little cottage.

The bulging clot melted, the pounding stopped, and relief swept over him.

Like Calaf, the suitor for Princess Turandot, Mac had three riddles to solve at dawn:

- what caused that rear end damage to their truck? That was the key.
- why did the state trooper dismiss that damage?
- why did the police find his father at fault forty years ago?

Mac believed he knew the answer to the first riddle. In the morning, with Trooper Andy's help, maybe he could begin to see the whole picture.

"I'll figure it out Dad," he said to the dark, empty room.

"I'll win, Mom."

Buddy nudged his face with his cold nose as if to ask, 'Are you OK now?'

"I'm good, Buddy. Good boy."

Sleep finally claimed him.

*****

Chapter Twelve

Dawn came strong, searing the Great Lake with a fiery blaze of color and bathing the rows of young grapes with bourbon-colored sunshine.

Mac pulled back the curtains. The world was up and moving. He needed to get in gear.

His forty-year hunt had begun. He now knew why Abe held that envelope so long. An angry young Mac would have gone off half-cocked, lashing out at innocents, while damaging his own life path. As usual, Abe had been right.

Mac was certain he knew how his parents had died, but he needed an expert to confirm his theory, which was *not* what the police reports said.

Buddy was waiting by the door.

'Woof!' He scratched the door and danced a circle.

"Hey, Bud."

Mac slipped on lightweight terrain pants and running shoes, and stepped outside bare-chested. The cool morning air braced him. He breathed in the oxygen, ready to do battle.

"Hey, sleepy-head!" shouted Marybeth. "Come pick strawberries!"

Mac and Buddy trotted over to the garden.

"You like Pavarotti at bedtime, Mac?"

"Oh! Last night? Did I wake you, Marybeth?"

"I sleep with the window open, Mac. So I heard his glorious voice."

"Marybeth, to be honest, I have some ghosts that haunt me. Sometimes I need music."

"…to 'soothe the savage beast'? I get it, and I loved hearing it. It reminded me of Mom. She used to play his records while she baked and I would sing along. Thought maybe I would be a professional singer someday, but then Jim and I settled down, I began teaching school, and now look at my life! Anyway, we have plenty of berries, so you've got 20 minutes 'til Belgian waffles, Mr. Builder. Get a move on!"

"Yes, Ma'am!" Mac hustled back into the cottage and fed Buddy. His cell phone rang: Trooper Andy.

"Good morning Andy! What is your wife's tee time?"

"9:15."

"Perfect. Grab her, and her clubs, and come over to Marybeth's for Belgian waffles. I've got plans."

"Mac, Sandy's best friends with Marybeth. She'll love that."

*****

The kitchen was once again full of wonderful aromas as Mac and Buddy entered the back porch. The windows were down to keep the warmth inside.

"Andy and Sandy Gregor are joining us for breakfast, OK, Marybeth?"

"Great! Coffee urn is on the side table."

A car pulled into the gravel area behind the B & B. Andy and Sandy Gregor stepped onto the porch with a 'gronk' and a 'whap' of the old screen door. Marybeth served giant stacks of Belgian waffles with butter, fresh strawberries and real whipped cream.

"Marybeth," said Sandy, "how do you stay so slim?"

"Hah! Come work with me for a day. I burn more calories than you will golfing!"

"Well, she looks great, doesn't she, guys," said Sandy.

"Fabulous," Mac added with a wink.

"So what are you men up to while we ladies are busy?" Sandy asked.

"Viewing the site where my parents were killed forty years ago," Mac said.

"So, there's doubt in your mind, eh, Mac?" said Andy.

"Yes, there is, Andy. I'd like you to recreate the accident scene, using the two police reports. Then consider the evidence from the newspaper photos, and tell me, as a Trooper, what you make of it."

"This should be interesting: a mystery to start our day."

"Next, we'll drive by my parent's farm, now owned by Minetti Enterprises LLC."

"I think the wine shop doesn't open until after lunch," said Sandy.

"Well, I've got a shooting range," said Andy. "A couple of new lever action rifles were delivered yesterday. We could do some target practice and have lunch at my house, then visit the wine store later."

62

"Sounds like a plan," Mac said. "Marybeth invited me to a Cruise-In tonight. I don't want to miss that."

"And Mac, dinner will be at 5:30 tonight, so don't be late."

"I won't," said Mac. "Hey Andy, you said you had a '74 Chevy square body short bed pickup. Are you coming to Cruise night?"

"Sure. I'm master of ceremonies. We have a DJ and a drawing for prizes. Typical stuff, but I think you'll be surprised at the quality of the cars."

"I'm looking forward to it, Andy. Now, let's eat! Marybeth, sit down and join us!"

"Sandy," said Marybeth, "after breakfast, I'll show you a rose with the sweetest fragrance!"

*****

9:00 a.m.

Mac and Andy stood at the intersection of U.S. Route 20 and Sherman Road. It was a level crossing of two-lane roads at the center of Ripley's tiny rural village, largely unchanged for one hundred years. Narrow sidewalks lined both roads.

"Andy, any changes to this intersection in the past 40 years?"

"A couple of old houses were razed on the southeast corner to create this pocket-park, Mac. Otherwise, there are no changes to the buildings, the roads or the signal."

They noted that the Victorian two-story shop at the southwest corner sat directly on the sidewalk, blocking the view around the corner. North-bound drivers on Sherman Road, like Mac's father in 1983, could not see oncoming traffic to their left until they actually entered the intersection.

Because the other two corners were occupied by a bank and a school, they would have been empty at 8:30 p.m., the time of the accident.

Due to the U.S. Route 20 exit off I-90 four miles to the west, there was a regular passing of eastbound trucks headed to the Co-Op in Westfield.

"OK, Andy, you read both police reports. You saw the pictures with what appeared to be skid marks in front of Joe Minetti's northbound tow truck, and wide tire marks outside those skid marks. You saw additional wide tire marks from the striking tractor running east-west through the intersection."

"Let's set the scene. It was 8:30 in the evening, dusk, with clear skies. My parents were northbound on Sherman Road into sleepy Ripley, where they roll up the sidewalks after dinner. With a school, a bank, and a store all closed for the night, no neighbor had eyes on the street."

"The Ripley police report and the State Trooper's report both charged my father with failure to stop for a red light while crossing *through* the intersection. They determined he was responsible for the accident that killed them when they were struck by an eastbound tractor."

"What is your first observation, Andy?"

"Well, either they ran the red light, and were struck by the tractor truck going east, as both police reports concluded, or they tried to make it through the intersection on a yellow, were late doing so and were struck by the tractor, which, in either case, had the green eastbound."

"OK, Andy," said Mac, "let's break this down."

"Scenario number one: my Dad ran the red light and got hit in the intersection."

"Andy, knowing how carefully my father drove, under normal circumstances, he would *never* run a red light. They were only a couple miles from home. There was no emergency. The signal interval is short. So why would he run a red light when he knew he would have the green light in a minute or less?"

"Furthermore, as you noted, Andy, this storefront on the southwest corner sits directly on the sidewalk. It totally blocks sight distance to the west for a north-bound vehicle on Sherman Road. So, my Dad could not see if there was oncoming traffic on his left until he was actually in the intersection."

"So, why Andy, would he blindly run a red light in front of a speeding truck? That makes no sense."

"I agree," said Andy. "That seems unlikely."

"Scenario number two: they tried to make it through on yellow, and got hit in the intersection."

"If that had been the case, then the eastbound tractor should have been stopped at the red light, and only begun moving when the light turned green. Therefore, he could not have had the momentum, especially running without a trailer, to push their pickup 75 feet east of the intersection, and hit it so hard it exploded the gas tank."

Andy nodded.

"I agree. That does not make sense either."

"Scenario number three: my father was trying to commit suicide with my mother in the car, leaving me to grow up alone in the world."

"No, of course not, Mac."

"OK, Andy, we are left with only one other possible scenario. It's the one that makes physical sense with the facts."

"And that is…"

"Scenario number four: Andy, I draw your attention to the newspaper photos of the accident taken from three angles. Note the damage to the rear of my father's F-100 pickup truck. The heavy duty step and tow bumper is crushed and pushed up. The Ripley police report noted it, but the State Trooper's report dismissed it as old damage."

"But it could NOT have been old damage because the rear axle of my father's pickup is clearly pushed forward, and the tire is tucked into the frame in this photo. That would have made the truck undriveable. And the sheet metal *behind* the axle is wrinkled, clearly indicating it was hit in the ass."

"If the side impact to the driver's door had caused the axle to shift, it would have had wrinkled sheet metal in *front* of the axle. No, Andy, this rear-end damage occurred at the time of this accident."

"Also, Andy, what do you make of these black tire marks in front of Minetti's tow truck in this photo?"

"They look like skid marks from skinny tires braking hard."

"I agree. What about the others?"

"Well, they're a wider double track, and they are outside of the skinny set of marks."

"Like a wide truck with four rear tires spinning its tires hard?"

"Possibly."

"Like a tow truck that was following my Dad, with a pusher blade for a bumper, doing a burnout as his more powerful truck shoved my parents into the path of a speeding tractor truck?"

"Whoa, Mac, now that's a stretch. There is no way to ever prove that."

"But with the evidence we have, it looks like the Morrison pickup truck was *pushed* into the pathway of the speeding tractor truck."

"And Joe Minetti *was* the one driving behind them in a tow truck with a pusher bumper," Andy mused. "He said so in both police reports. Huh!"

"Andy, I remember that day so clearly, even forty years later. I washed my parents' truck that afternoon before they drove to the Grange hall. I wanted it to look good, even though it was old. Just a few hours before this accident, there was *no damage* to the rear of my parents' pickup!"

65

"So," Andy repeated, "under Scenario number four, Joey Minetti pushed your parent's truck into the path of a speeding tractor. And Joe Minetti was the witness to the accident. But Mac, the tractor driver corroborated Minetti's statement that your Dad ran the red light."

"But, Andy, that isn't credible with the facts at the scene as we see it. He could have been paid off."

"OK, let's assume you're right. Was it a spur of the moment decision? Or was it planned? Could the driver of the tractor have been part of the setup, perhaps in two way radio contact?"

"It had to be planned, Andy. Three pieces of evidence prove it."

"First, the rear-end damage to my Dad's truck is the key. It definitely occurred at the time of this accident, *but I am the only one who could know that, other than Joey Minetti*. The Ripley cop noted the damage, but the Trooper dismissed it. There is absolutely no question about it. My parent's pickup was pushed into the tractor. And Minetti had to have pushed it."

"The second piece of evidence is the speed of the tractor. It pushed my Dad's pickup sideways 75 feet past impact. I checked some data online. A normal stopping distance for that tractor traveling 25 miles per hour should be about 60 feet. But it was pushing a 4,000 pound pickup sideways, so it should have been much less than 60 feet. So, we know the tractor was driving much faster than 25 miles per hour."

"Third, because Minetti could not see around that corner, he had to be in contact with the driver of the speeding tractor in order to time the collision. They probably used two-way or CB radios. And remember, Andy, it was a New Jersey truck that killed them, and it was a New Jersey LLC that bought our farm at the Sheriff's sale after their death."

"One more thing, Andy," Mac said, standing on Sherman Road where his father's pickup would have been if he were stopped for a red light. "Nowhere in the police reports is *this* mentioned. My parent's farm is *that way* Andy," he said, turning to his left and pointing west. "My Dad would have been turning *left* at this intersection, *not speeding across it*. And you can't run a red light and accelerate around a blind corner at the same time. The reports assumed he was speeding straight *through* the intersection, but that was not the case. I drove this route with him a hundred times as a kid. He always turned left to go home."

"This was no accident, Andy. This was an *execution*."

"But then the question is why, Mac?"

"Andy, old man Minetti had tried to buy our farm, but my Dad turned him down. After my parents died, and Minetti bought our farm, he announced in the Westfield Press that he was planning a factory outlet mall at the Ripley Thruway interchange, with a developer to be named."

"OK, Mac, let's suppose Minetti wanted to buy your vineyard to develop an outlet mall. Maybe they had some scheme to flip the land to a developer. If your parents wouldn't sell, the motive for murder was money. The giant hole in that theory is the land never got developed, and it is still a vineyard 40 years later."

"It's just a theory, Andy. But it's the only one that aligns with the physical facts of the accident."

"I agree," said Andy, "but you can never prove it."

"You're right. But if that's what they did, I can't let them get away with it."

"Whoa, Mac, what are you saying?"

"I'm gonna win, Andy."

*****

U.S. Route 20, near the Ripley Thruway Exit
10:30 a.m.

The sign read, 'Minetti Wine Shop and Tasting Room: Opens 1 p.m.'

"We're early," said Mac, peering in the window. "Those big steel warehouses weren't there when I lived here."

"Everything behind the front fence is a separate business, Mac," said Andy. "Joseph Sr. is the patriarch. He's about 85 years old. He has labor to run the vineyard. Used to sell their juice through the Co-Op, but now they export it. That's the farm warehouse."

"Daughter Gina's import wine business is the biggest warehouse."

"Joey expanded his collision and restoration shop. That's another building."

"Gino's salvage business specializes in high-end European cars, and that's another warehouse."

"Huh! So, all these enterprises are being run in sleepy little Ripley, New York. Well, Andy, you gonna show me your Chevy?"

"Yep, we'll go to Mayville the back way."

*****

67

They drove Sherman Road out of Ripley, snaking back and forth up the escarpment, turning onto County Road 22, and merging with State Route 430 into the Village of Mayville. A sign proudly said 'Founded 1830'.

Andy lived in a quaint old farmhouse updated with new siding. Broad lawns surrounded it. It was on the leafy rural outskirts of the village, tucked into a hollow with a steep hill behind it. At the top of that hill was downtown Mayville.

"Andy, I don't see any new houses."

"Mac, this area has been losing population for 60 years. Farming is stable, but without new jobs, our kids graduate and move away. Some folks live here and work in Erie or Buffalo's south towns. They stay because it's gorgeous. Local economy relies on agriculture, tourism, and snow."

"Snow?"

"Skiing and plowing. Mac, you were young, maybe you don't remember the lake-effect snow. Snow brings skiers. And many of the Thruway maintenance crews live here. We have some of the biggest plows in the world."

"Let's go see your truck, Andy!"

It was a clone of Abe's '74 Chevy.

"Mac, when you drove that truck to the Bar B, I was 14, and to me, that truck was the coolest thing on the road. I told myself someday I'm gonna have one just like it. Found it in southern Kentucky ten years ago. Rebuilt the engine, and changed the color to match what I remembered. Is it close?"

"It's perfect. So, you're bringing this to the cruise-in tonight, Marybeth is bringing her Merc, and I'm bringing the Chevy. That's a good start."

"Yep; say, while my daughter Janey is making us lunch, do you want to take some target practice?" He handed Mac a rifle.

"This is a Lever Action .22, Mac. It takes a top-mounted scope. This other is a replica of Rooster Cogburn's gun in '*True Grit*'s. Do you hunt Mac?"

"No; I got my fill of guns in two tours in the Middle East."

"Army?"

"Yep. Three years with Desert Storm: combat, mine clearing, building and guarding base camps."

"What about the other tour?"

"Two years with a private security contractor in Afghanistan. I made enough to pay for a nice lake house, which I lost in a divorce. Anyway, that's water under the bridge, Andy. Let's see if I can still shoot."

Mac was rusty, but he was shredding bullseyes by the time Janey called them to lunch.

"Janey, this is Mac Morrison. He was my camp counselor at the Bar B camp 34 years ago. We're driving his childhood haunts."

"We went to Minetti's Wine shop," Mac said, "it's on my parents' former farm."

"Really! I'm friends with Gina," said Janey. "We went to school and played sports together."

"There are several new warehouses," said Mac.

"Those are their different businesses. Everyone in the family has to contribute to the Minetti Enterprise. Their imported wine is the biggest business, thanks to Gina's leadership. She has a staff in the warehouse for wholesale distribution and internet shipments."

"Joseph Senior runs the vineyard and makes their grape juice shipments to Italy."

"Rosie has a small staff to import Italian foods. Everything is shipped to restaurants."

"I met her yesterday," Mac said.

"Bet she was wearing that old gray sweater!"

"She was."

"Gino took over Joe's salvage parts business. He specializes in European high-end car parts. He buys wrecks from all over the country, ships them here, disassembles them and sells parts back to dealers and body shops, all online."

"Then there's Joey's auto collision and restoration shop. He's a genius with cars. OK, these sandwiches are done. Grab a drink from the fridge, and we'll eat out back at the picnic table."

*****

Minetti Wine Shop
1:30 p.m.

The sky was already clouding up for a brief shower when Mac parked. The hum of I-90 was constant. A bell chimed as he opened the front door.

"Hello! I'll be right with you!"

A pretty young woman emerged from a back room. She was tall and slim, with a totally different bone structure and face than Rosemary Minetti.

"Hi. I'm looking for a couple of bottles of wine," said Mac.

"Our Italian wines are excellent, how about a taste test?"

Mac sampled three whites and three reds; he picked out a Vermentino white and Cannonau red.

"My name is Gina. I see your car is from New Hampshire. Are you Mr. Morrison?"

"Yes, how did you know?"

"Rosemary said she met you at the library. She mentioned your car."

"This used to be my family's farm. I remember the house."

"Would you like to come see it?"

"Thank you, Gina, but I want to remember it the way it was. What do I owe you?"

"Eighty-two dollars. If you don't like those, please come back. We'll taste some more, and I'll give you a credit."

"That's very generous, Gina, thank you. Hope to see you again."

"Mac walked back to his car. Buddy greeted him with a poke of his nose and a playful 'ROWRF!'

"Yeah, I know, Buddy; you want to go play on the beach. Let's do it!"

❋❋❋❋❋

Sunday, May 21
2:00 p.m.

Mac drove along the shoreline on rural Route 5 back to Barcelona Harbor. There were peek-a-boo looks at Lake Erie as a spring storm scudded towards shore like a black blimp.

The first sprinkles of rain were soft as they dappled the windshield, but as Mac turned into the B & B, the skies opened, and the rain poured down.

"No walk on the beach, Buddy. We'll run for the porch. Let's go!"

❋❋❋❋❋

"Marybeth?" Mac called, as he and Buddy scooted through the back door. 'Arf arf arf!' The labradoodle gang raced out to surround them.

"In the kitchen!"

70

This afternoon, Marybeth was wearing a red checked cotton shirt with a half collar, three quarter length sleeves and form-fitting jeans that followed the curves of magnificently shaped legs. Her hair was tied in a ponytail as she dusted pizza dough and rolled it out.

"Mac, I need some wood for the pizza oven. Do you mind?"

"You have a wood-fired oven?"

"Yes, it was a bread oven a hundred years ago."

"Where is the wood?"

"In the woodshed, silly, off the back porch. Watch out for the screen door. It's got a wicked strong spring and it'll smack your ass."

Mac gathered firewood in his arms and went back into the large Victorian kitchen.

"Marybeth, would you be offended if we had a sixty-dollar bottle of Minetti Cannonau with our pizza?"

"I guess I can make an exception for a sixty-dollar bottle of wine. Did you meet Gina?"

"I did. Nice girl."

"Very nice. I taught her in fourth grade. She's not like the rest of her family, I can tell you that, maybe because she's adopted."

"Interesting day with Trooper Andy," Mac said.

"Tell me over pizza, OK? Would you go in the barn and uncover my Mercury?"

"Sure, Marybeth."

✲✲✲✲✲

Marybeth's timber-framed barn was eerily familiar. Mac glided the tall wooden doors back on ancient rollers. He could see the shape of a car undercover, a small fishing boat and a lawn tractor. He flicked the switch, and two bare bulbs flickered on in the rafters.

"Not very bright in here, eh, Buddy? Marybeth needs better lighting."

He pulled back the blue cotton cover to reveal a Mercury Comet Cyclone. "Huh!" he exclaimed, "four-speed stick-shift, and bench seat!" With its sleek body lines and NASCAR style roof, the Cyclone looked fast standing still. Not a car he ever saw at New Hampshire cruise-ins. He disconnected the battery tender and turned the key to the accessory position. The

71

dashboard lit up. He turned the key back off, left the barn doors open and ran behind Buddy through the rain to his cottage.

✱✱✱✱✱

5:30 p.m.

The rain let up in time for dinner. Round pea gravel crunched under foot as Mac and Buddy walked to the porch. The dining area was already full, with six couples at six tables. A huge salad bowl and glass tray of iced shrimp sat on a buffet table. Marybeth laid out eight large pizzas.

"Serve yourself, folks."

She motioned for Mac to join her.

"You and I are in the dining room. I want to hear about your day. Buddy has to stay on the porch."

It was a long story told quickly and with little embellishment, but it was enough for Marybeth to frown as she and Mac cleared away the guest tables.

"I don't like it, Mac. It doesn't make sense."

"It wasn't an accident. Certainly looks planned, but I don't know why. This business about future development that never happened just muddies the waters. If my parents refused to sell to Minettis, it might have been the motive to get them out of the way. But that's total speculation."

"Doesn't pass the smell test, does it, Mac?"

"No. Anyway, I've done all the sleuthing I can for one day. Had another great dinner with you, and now we need to get going, eh?"

"Right, Mac."

"Come on, Buddy, we're going cruising."

'Rowrf!' Buddy did his 'Buddy dance' twirling around on his hind legs.

✱✱✱✱✱

72

Chapter Thirteen

Sunday, May 21
6:15 p.m.

Mayville's lakefront was an American panorama. The Chautauqua Belle was docked on shimmering blue water behind the old brick train station, surrounded by classic American cars.

Trooper Andy Gregor stood by the road, directing them to grassy spots reserved with folding lawn chairs. Buddy leaped out of the Chevy and gave Andy a big 'whap' with his tail.

"Your Chevy square body looks proud in this lineup," Mac said.

"Let's see some cars, guys!" Marybeth chirped. "And I want a black raspberry ice cream cone!"

Buddy led them up and down the aisles. He would run ahead to scout, then turn back to see where Mac was. There were already a hundred classic cars, mostly 50s and 60s iron.

As they passed a black 1959 Cadillac Eldorado, Marybeth said, "Love those fins."

"This is Joe Minetti's Caddy," said Andy. "They must be around here somewhere."

Mac snapped into hunt mode, scanning the aisles. Sixty feet down the row was Rosemary Minetti, stylishly dressed like 1959 to match the Eldo. By her side was Joey Minetti, looking directly at him. Rosemary turned to see Mac staring at her. She spoke to Joe, and pulled him away. As they walked off, Joey Minetti looked back at Mac, nodded, and grinned wolfishly. He still had a chip on his front tooth!

Mac nodded back. 'I'm coming for you, Joey,' he said to himself.

Andy broke the silence.

"Mac, I've got someone for you to meet. See the black Crown Victoria with highway bars?"

Mac returned to the moment.

"What? Oh...yeah, I see it."

"Let's go introduce you."

They walked down the aisle and stopped in front of a folding chair. A large man stood up. He was taller than Mac, with a solid build and silver streaks in thick black hair.

"Hello, Andy, how's things?" said the man.

"Good, Tim. Tim, I'd like you to meet Mac Morrison. Mac grew up here as a kid. He was my Bar B tent counselor."

Tim extended his hand, and Mac shook it. It was as large as a bear paw.

"Is this your Crown Vic Police Interceptor, Tim?"

"Yep. She's my old Trooper car, painted it myself."

"Still has the Thruway push bars," said Mac.

"I kept her all original," Tim said. "Love this car. Can I pet your dog?"

Buddy sat down and looked up at Mac, but did not offer his paw.

"Sorry," Mac said. "Sometimes he's like that."

"I had a dog," said Tim. "Shepherd, too. Loved that dog…"

"Tim Riley was the responding Trooper to your parents' accident 40 years ago, Mac."

Mac's head jerked sideways to look at Andy.

Andy continued, "When I read those police reports, I wondered if it could be his father Tom, who was also a Trooper, so I ran the badge number. It was Tim's, so I called him to make sure he'd be here."

Mac said, "So you are Trooper T. Riley? I read your report of the car crash that killed my parents on May 14, 1983, at U.S. 20 and Sherman Road. I've got questions, but let's get Marybeth her ice cream first, OK?"

"OK," said Tim.

They made small talk at the ice cream stand before walking to a picnic table.

"So Tim, do you actually recall anything about that accident? There were two reports," Mac said, "yours and Ripley P.D. They were different."

"Not much. It's been a long time, and my memory isn't so good. I do remember it was a fatal. Once the fire was out, I got called away."

"Called away? Why?"

"Thruway wreck. Tractor trailer jackknifed, a dozen cars piled up. We diverted traffic onto 20, got wreckers and a crane. It was a big mess, took all night to clear it. Hey, Mac, I'd like to see your car."

"Oh, OK, sure, Tim, let's do that."

They walked down the aisle and stopped at the Chevy.

"1957 Chevy Bel Air, Tim. My uncle bought it new. He gave it to me when I turned 16."

"Nice. Original?"

"Restored."

"Nice. Well, thanks for stopping to see my old patrol car. I see some folks, so I gotta go say hi. Maybe I'll see you around Mac. I go fishing almost every day if you'd like to go out for walleye."

"Maybe I would, Tim. I'm staying at Marybeth's B & B."

"I know. See ya!"

Mac watched Tim Riley slouch off, waving left and right at folks.

"Andy, did you tell Tim I was staying at Marybeth's?"

"No."

"Not very talkative, is he Andy? And, he recalled a Thruway wreck better than he remembered my parent's fatal, that seems odd."

"Mac, twenty years ago, Tim's cruiser was hit. He never fully recovered from a head injury. The Troop moved him inside, but he wasn't an inside guy. Eventually, they found a spot for him as station security. He was good at that. But his people skills have really declined. Five years ago, he retired from State Police and took a part time job with BMV."

The sun was getting low behind the hill. A pinkish glow cast across the waters of Lake Chautauqua. Strands of white lights were turned on, and a DJ played Dusty Springfield's '*Wishin' and Hopin'*9. People started dancing. A hand slipped into Mac's and tugged him onto the grass.

"C'mon Mac," said Marybeth, "Dance with me!"

Mac felt the warmth of Marybeth's slim body hugging him. The touch of a woman felt good.

By nine p.m., half the cars had left, but the socializing continued. Folks set up grills. The smell of charcoal mixed with hot dogs and hamburgers.

The rasping shriek of a V-12 engine announced a red Ferrari that slewed across the grass and slid to a stop in front of Andy's Chevy. A mop-headed young man sprang from the low sports car.

"Officer Andy, how's life?"

"Good, Gino. You might want to slow it down, OK?"

"OK. You know me. I like to go, go, go! Sorry I couldn't get here earlier, but I have an order I'm delivering for Dad in the morning. I had to get loaded tonight. Hi, Mrs. Murphy."

"Gino," said Marybeth, "I'd like you to meet Mac Morrison. He's visiting from New Hampshire."

Buddy moved in front of Mac and sat down. 'Alert.' Mac understood.

"Gino, I met your sister this afternoon. The old family farm looks good. You made some changes."

"Yeah, Gina told me she met you. That's a nice car you've got there, Mr. Morrison," Gino said, pointing to the Chevy.

"Thanks, Gino."

And how did you know which car was mine, Gino? Mac thought to himself. *Because you followed me from the library, that's how.*

"Well, I'd invite you to come and see your old farm, but I'm going to be driving this shipment to Conneaut tomorrow. If you're still here after that, I'll be happy to show you around."

"Maybe I will, thanks, Gino."

"Well, Andy, Mr. Morrison, Mrs. Murphy, nice seeing you, but it looks like the party's over except for the dancing, and I don't have a date."

"I'll dance with you, Gino," said Marybeth, "but it's gotta be a fast one. Show me some moves."

Mac and Andy watched while Gino put on a display of amazing dancing. Marybeth kept up the best she could. When the music stopped, she laughed and thanked Gino. He hopped in his Ferrari and took off with a shriek as Marybeth strolled back to Mac and Andy.

She said, "I can't remember the last time I had this much fun, guys, but it's time for me to head for the barn."

"Maybe I'll see you tomorrow, Mac" Andy said.

"Thanks for introducing me to Tim Riley, Andy."

*****

The security light glowed weakly. Mac rolled back the barn door, and Marybeth drove the Merc inside.

"Thank you for a nice evening, Mac."

"Thank *you*, Marybeth."

"What are your plans for tomorrow Mac?"

"Well, for one, I'm going to rehang that gutter that's falling off your porch roof. Then I'm going to the hardware store and buy you some lights for the barn and a new LED spotlight for the courtyard. This is way too dark for your guests, and it's dim in your barn. I don't know how you can work in there."

"You don't have to do that, Mac."

76

"Yes, I do. I need a daily mission, so tomorrow, its handyman repairs to get you caught up. If you want to add to my list, tell me at breakfast."

"OK, and thanks again for a nice evening, Mac."

"Good night, Marybeth. C'mon, Buddy, let's take your last walk."

'Rowrf!' He did the Buddy twist dance and took off for the pier.

The two buddies walked across sleepy Route 5 and watched the after-glow over Lake Erie. It was dark, but a quarter-moon was making its way up, and it would be a clear night.

"OK, Budso, let's go home."

Mac's feet crunched on the pea stone driveway. Before they made it to the cabin door, Buddy cut him off and sat. Alert!

"What's up, Buddy?" Mac whispered.

'Rowrf!' Buddy pointed with his nose flipping up and down, and then ran to the cabin door. He sniffed, walked under the window, then circled around the parking lot, eventually trotting over to the neighbor's yard and sniffing the front door of their rental cottage.

'Rowrf!' He scratched the ground with his paw and pointed at the door.

"Good boy, Buddy. Stay."

Mac returned with a powerful LED flashlight. His cabin door showed no sign of forced entry. The pea gravel had been disturbed, but he could have done that himself. He swung the flashlight in an arc where Buddy had been sniffing. His eye stopped at the cabin next door where Buddy had stopped.

Nothing looked out of place, but as his eye traveled up the door, he noticed something odd. One of the side lights had a bulb with an internal security camera. It was pointed directly at him. And the light was on; the camera was recording.

"Huh! Do we have nosey neighbors, or did we have a nosey visitor, Bud? I don't know. We'll figure it out tomorrow. Race you to the big bed."

As he showered, he made a mental note to buy two more things at the hardware store: a dead bolt lock for the cabin and a security camera.

**

Chapter Fourteen

As Mac pulled back the curtains, moonlight lit the room. Time to move.

Dressing in the dark, he grabbed his wallet and keys and quietly opened the door to let Buddy out. His eyes were still adjusted to the darkness as he scanned for danger. The light bulb camera was off.

Buddy jumped onto the Chevy's bench seat, and the big V-8 quietly burbled the short distance to Todd's Gas n Go. Business was brisk at the bait locker, with fishermen stocking up before launching at the Harbor ramp. Mac gassed up the Chevy and grabbed a coffee and donut.

While making the fifteen minute drive to his old family farm, he reviewed what he knew. The police reports were a cover-up. It wasn't an accident, it was an execution. His parents were murdered. But he could never prove it.

Joe Minetti had to have shoved them into the tractor truck. There was no other way to figure it. The truck driver had to be involved, but he would be 100 years old, if still alive.

His innocent inquiries at the library triggered Rosemary Minetti's paranoid phone call, and the red Ferrari following him. They had to have put up the spy camera, so they must be worried, but why? They had gotten away with murder for 40 years, and the evidence was gone. So, he reasoned, the Minettis must still be doing something illegal, and can't afford to be scrutinized.

Trooper Tim Riley was at the scene of his parents' death. Did he really believe the rear end damage to his parents' truck was old damage, or was he part of the cover-up? Was he being guarded, or was he mentally diminished and could not remember?

Mac sipped his coffee. What was the motive?

It had to be the land.

His father loved the vineyard. Had he been pressured to sell and refused again? But why was their land never developed?

Mac pulled into a vacant lot on U.S. 20, facing Minetti's service drive. There were old trucks parked among the weeds. Mac put the Chevy behind a semi-trailer where he could see under its chassis. He was facing a gated driveway that led to two large steel buildings with signs that read 'European Auto Salvage,' and 'Perfect Collision and Restoration.'

"Gino's gotta be coming out that gate, Buddy."

'Woof'. Buddy nudged him with his nose. Mac gave him a bite of donut.

He shut off the engine, and half-dozed with one eye on the gate.

Buddy growled at 6:00 a.m. The sun was up in the east behind the escarpment, but long shadows still darkened Ripley. A heavy white pickup was coming down the driveway towards him, towing an enclosed trailer. It stopped at the gate.

A man in a baseball cap jumped out, unlocked the gate, pulled the truck through, and then relocked it. As expected, he headed towards I-90. Mac waited until he was well down the road before pulling out behind him. He followed the trailer's lights as it pulled into a truck stop at the Ripley exit.

Mac scratched Buddy's ear, and he purred like a big cat 'hmmmmmmm.'

"You're a goof, Budso! Let's find a hiding spot." It was easy to do behind all the trucks idling while their drivers slept. Five minutes later, Gino walked out of the station with a coffee, filled the tank on the F 350 and headed to I-90.

"Buddy, let's see if Gino was telling the truth."

Mac followed far enough back to see the red trailer with the logo 'Perfect Collision and Restoration' on its back doors. This was Joey's trailer and truck.

Forty-five minutes later, Gino exited I-90 at State Route 7 for Conneaut, Ohio. Mac let him get almost out of sight as they drove a mile-long stretch of divided four-lane rising into the small old downtown. Grid streets that were laid out at a time of horses and wagons now only provided on-street parking to the hundred-year-old brick storefronts. Maybe that was why downtown was pockmarked by vacancies. Time had passed by old Conneaut, but it looked like it was trying to make a comeback.

Gino headed east on U.S. 20, crossed over the Veterans Memorial Bridge and parked in front of an old garage. The sign on the building said 'Kurt's Kustoms'. An overhead door rolled up and a middle aged man in overalls walked outside.

Mac stopped the Chevy behind a cinder block building 300 yards short of Gino's truck. Grabbing his binoculars, he slid out of the car and peered around the corner. Gino shook hands with the man, and unlatched his trailer doors. They rolled out a chassis with an engine mounted. Gino went back into his trailer and came out with a familiar looking hood and front fenders from another 1957 Chevy Bel Air.

Through the open garage door, Mac could see the body of a red '57 Bel Air hardtop lifted up on a four post rack, ready to be lowered. The man handed Gino a check.

OK, thought Mac, its Joey's trailer. So he painted the chassis, the engine, the hood and the fenders, and Gino was delivering them. Nothing suspicious.

Gino did a U-turn and started back towards town. Mac stepped behind the building, waited for the red trailer to pass, and then drove in the opposite direction to the east. A short distance up U.S. 20, he looped behind a '50s style hamburger stand with a famous old brand of barrel root beer and headed back the way Gino had gone.

The red trailer was a quarter mile west, parked by an ancient barn with a dozen 1950s cars on the grass.

Mac drove past until he was out of sight. He backed the Chevy behind an empty store, donned a floppy Bush hat, then leashed Buddy and they walked on the sidewalk. Fifteen minutes passed, but no Gino.

He's got to have made his pick-up by now, Mac thought.

"C'mon, Bud. Let's go!" They jumped back in the Chevy and headed east to the old barn. The truck and trailer were gone.

"We lost him, Bud," he said, driving east and crossing into Pennsylvania. When he saw a sign for I-90 at Route 6N, he said, "Well, Buddy, is that the way he went?"

'ROWRF!' Buddy flipped Mac's arm with his nose.

"OK, that's the way we go." He entered I-90 East and goosed it up to 80 miles per hour. Within two minutes, he saw the red trailer.

"We got him, Bud." Forty minutes later, Gino exited at Ripley. Mac continued on I-90 to Westfield, then back to Barcelona Harbor.

*****

Monday, May 22
8:30 a.m.
Murphy B & B

"Hello!" said Marybeth, as Mac and Buddy walked into the back porch. A few couples were finishing their breakfast.

"You and Buddy had an early morning!"

"Sleuthing," said Mac. "Something smells wonderful! Too late for a plate?"

"Breakfast ends at 8:30, but since you danced with me last night, OK, Mac."

"You better feed me, lady, because I'm going to do some serious work on this old house today."

"Mac, I appreciate the gesture, but really, you don't have to repair my house."

Marybeth put the cast iron frying pan back on the stove and lit the gas flame. Picking up an egg, she reached for the bowl to crack it.

"I want to. It's what I do. And, I need to. If that sounds mysterious, it's because we had a visitor at my cottage last night while we were at cruise-in."

"What?" Marybeth dropped her egg on the floor with a 'splat'!

"I'll clean that up, M. Can I call you M, Marybeth?"

"Funny, Jim used to call me B. Call me anything you want, Mac, just call me," she said with a wink. "Now, what's this about a visitor?"

"Buddy alerted. He scented someone had been at the window. We noticed something. Come outside."

Mac pointed to the house next door. And, there it was.

"See the side light bulb closest to us on their cabin, M? Notice it's different from the other?

"Uh, OK, yes."

"It's a motion-activated security camera that screws into a light socket. See how it's pointed at us?"

"Yes! Why would they spy on me? I've been friends with the Shavelys for six years!"

"Not you, M, me. It's pointed at my cottage. Did they do that, or did we have a visitor last night?"

"Let's go ask them," Marybeth said.

"C'mon, Buddy, let's go say hi."

'ROWRF!' He raced ahead, scouting for Poppa Mac.

*****

Monday, May 22
8:45 a.m.

They walked next door to an impressive Victorian house with a widow's walk on the roof. Marybeth pressed the bell next to a massive front door. A teenage voice shouted 'coming'!

As the door opened, two twin girls stared out at Mac and Marybeth.

"Hi, Marybeth!" They squealed in unison.

"Hi, Linda! Hi, Belinda! This is Mac Morrison; he's staying in my cottage."

"Hi, Mac!" they giggled in unison.

"Girls, we noticed a new security camera on your cabin. It's aimed at my cottage."

"Really? We didn't do that!"

"Can we show you?" said Marybeth.

"Sure!" They bounded down the stairs like kangaroos.

The cabin was in the back yard, facing the rear of the Shavely house, and flanking Marybeth's B & B. There were two outside carriage lights, one on either side of its door.

"Girls, see the odd looking light bulb? It's a security camera," said Marybeth.

"Marybeth, we did not put that up! I'm sorry. I'll take it down right now."

"Actually, girls," said Mac softly while turning away from the camera, "I'd like you to leave it up. Here's $100 for the extra electricity and a good lunch for you two. Is that fair?"

"$100? For us?"

"And your Mom," added Marybeth.

"Sure, that's great!" they said together.

"Please leave the light switch on day and night, OK?" Mac said. "That way, we know the camera is broadcasting. Do you have Wi-Fi for guests, girls?"

"Sure."

"Well, whoever put up the camera is using it."

"Wow! This is weird! Why is someone spying on you, Mac?"

"I don't know, but since they want to see when I come and go, let's let them. Now, promise you won't tell any of your friends about this, OK? Just your Mom and Dad, and they can't tell either."

"Cool! A summer mystery in Barcelona Harbor!"

"Yes," said Marybeth, "why don't you write a story, and submit it for your summer extra credit project."

"OK! Is that all, Marybeth?"

"Yes."

"Can we pet your dog, Mac?"

"Of course you can. Buddy, can you shake?"

'Rowrf!'

Buddy sat and lifted his big paw so each of the girls could shake it.

"He's so cute!" they said. "What's his name?"

"Buddy."

"Oh yeah, you said that!" they giggled. "Well, thanks for checking us out! Call us if you need us!"

"OK, thanks, girls."

"Bye!"

They bounded off like kangaroos, laughing and high fiving each other.

*****

9:00 a.m.

"M," said Mac, "Do you have a security camera?"

"Yes, it's one of those doorbell thingy's."

"Motion-activated?"

"Yes."

"How long can you look back at recorded history?"

"Not sure, never tried."

"Can I see your phone, M?" Mac tapped the app to wake it up. Scrolling back to the previous night's recordings he watched several of her guests arriving.

"Looks like one couple walked down to the lake after dinner. Let's start at 6:30 when we left."

Marybeth sat by Mac. "Your omelet is delayed, mister, because this concerns my home. This is a violation of my space!"

"I see nothing for almost two hours, M. We've got some glare coming off the lake as the sun gets low in the sky. Now, here! At 8:00 p.m. I see a person walking across the street. Because of the glare, I can't make out a face, or even if it's a man or woman. It's just a figure, see M?"

"Yes. Now it's moving onto the Shavely lot, and now he, or she, is...gone!"

They kept watching. Three minutes later, still in the glare, the figure slunk across the lawn and ran across the road to the pier parking lot.

"Well, M," Mac said, "I think that is when the camera was put in. Someone wants to watch me."

"That worries me, Mac. I have a house full of guests; I've got to be concerned for their safety."

"I know, but a light bulb is no threat. And I'm going to use it to my advantage when the time comes. What about my omelet?"

"OK, Mr. Builder, then tell me about your Conneaut trip."

✳✳✳✳✳

Chapter Fifteen

Marybeth said, "So, Mac, you followed Gino to Conneaut. Did you see anything suspicious?"

"Not at all. Obviously, Joe Minetti does some legitimate work in his shop, and Gino was delivering it."

"Which leaves you where, Mac?"

"Leaves me with a free day to work on your house. While you clean up from breakfast, I'm headed for the hardware store. Gonna listen to some good music while I work. Do you have tools?"

"Jim's tools are in the barn workbench."

"I saw a boat in the garage. Jim's fishing boat?"

"Yes. They towed it here after he was found in the lake. It hasn't been touched in 2 years. Why?"

"Just curious."

"Well, go to the hardware! I've got guests!"

✳✳✳✳✳

Country Farm and Hardware had everything Mac needed. He loaded up the giant trunk of the Chevy and scratched Buddy's head as they rolled down Route 394, over the New York State Thruway, past row after row of grapes.

It felt good to have tools in his hands. He made quick work of the gutter. Using a sixteen-foot step ladder, he strung up six new LED shop lights with long pull chains in the barn. They could be lit off the wall switch, or individually.

Mac bored the cabin door for the new deadbolt, and chiseled out a slot in the jamb for the heavy-duty striker plate with the wrap-around steel sleeve. He used three inch screws to seat the striker plate. No one could kick that door open.

He did the same with the new heavy-duty commercial doorknob and latch. It had a wraparound steel panel that folded on three sides of the door, so it couldn't be jimmied. Mac threw the old junk lock in the trash, and moved on to the final job: a new security camera in the back courtyard.

He set his phone on a picnic table so he could clip the screw gun to his pocket. As he was climbing the ladder to mount the camera, Marybeth carried a tray of lemonade and two glasses outside with a 'whap' of the wooden door.

"Break time!"

"Sounds good, M. Let me mount this camera and then I'll come down and join you."

"Don't let it get warm. I'm going to sit here, have a cold glass and watch you work."

Mac's phone rang. "M, could you answer that? Put it on speaker, OK?"

"Hello?" Marybeth said. "Hello?" she repeated.

"Oh, hello, this is Attorney Morgan Hillman's office, calling for Mackenzie Morrison. Who am I speaking with, please?"

"That would be Marybeth Murphy, the owner of the fine B & B where I am staying in Barcelona Harbor, New York, Angie!" bellowed Mac from the top of the ladder.

"You sound a long way away, Mac."

"I'm up on a ladder. What can I do for you Angie?"

"Mac, I have a bill from Roger Lemonier for two 40' x 100' parking pads paved with 12" bank run and 6" crushed gravel. It's also for a 58' x 108' gravel shed pad. All pads are compacted and rolled. He noted the shed pad is ready to be cored for footers."

"OK, good. Pay it, Angie."

"Don't you want to know how much?"

"Is it less than $22,000?"

"Yes."

"Pay it. It's Roger, I trust him. You got my insurance check, right?"

"Yes, both checks cleared and were deposited in your checking account."

"What's my balance, Angie?"

"Your starting balance was approximately $50,000. The insurance checks were $750,000 total. I took $200,000 and put it in the trust account for Gabriella, and paid off the $50,000 mortgage, so your balance now is $550,000."

"Good. Email me the trust. Gabby's birthday is on the 24th. You have her cell number?"

"It's in Morgan's trust file."

"I'd like you to call her late in the day on the 24th and explain how a trust works. Take her first draw request."

"OK, Mac."

"And, Angie, *this is important!*"

"What, Mac?"

"If you do not hear from me before your call to her on the 24th, have Morgan phone Marybeth Murphy at the Captain Murphy B & B in Barcelona Harbor, Westfield, New York."

"Mac, I know you, and I know that tone of voice. What are you into?"

"It's complicated, Angie, I can't talk about it yet. It might be nothing."

"Mac, don't go Lone Ranger[1] on us again."

"Angie, just do those few things, please. Bye!"

"MAC!"

"Hang up, Marybeth."

"Mac, did you want me to hear all of that? You sound like you're expecting trouble."

"Not expecting it, M, planning for it. I was a Boy Scout. Be prepared."

"Was Morgan a Boy Scout?"

"Special Forces, both him and Roger. They are as tough as they come. If things go wrong, he and Roger Lemonier will come like the Hammers of Hell riding black war horses in the night."

"Oh! Mac! You just sent a shiver down my spine!"

"Well, this is my fight. I'll keep you out of it. Let's have some lemonade."

Mac screwed in the camera, aimed it and climbed down the ladder.

"Security system done, lights are up in the barn, lock on my cabin and your gutter is fixed."

"Wow! It's not even noon, and you're done?"

"Hey, I'm Mac the builder, remember? Oh, by the way, is it OK if I get Jim's boat running?"

"Why?"

"Might want to catch a big fish."

"It hasn't run in 2 years, Mac."

"Hey, I restore boats in the winter too."

"Well, go ahead. Mac, Angie had a 'familiar' way of speaking to you."

"She's been my trusted accountant for 15 years. Plus, I helped her during her trial, so we're close friends."

"What trial?"

"For the murder of her sleaze-bag husband."

Marybeth sucked in the air, and her eyes widened like saucers.

"Oh, my God!" she exclaimed.

"Hey! She defended herself!" Mac said. "Jury found her 'not guilty' in 15 minutes."

"Well, how did you 'help' her?"

"I drowned her husband's accomplice until he confessed."

"WAIT! MAC! Now tell me the whole story! And give me the context of why you drowned…almost drowned, this bad guy."

"Marybeth, Angie married a handsome, successful general contractor. Country club set, prominent family. He turned out to be an abusive philanderer, and a two-faced psycho, in my opinion. Course, as a builder, I don't always have the best opinion of general contractors."

"Anyway, one day he beat her up badly. She called me. Her face was a mess. I took pictures for the cops. She said no cops, she didn't want the publicity. So, I told her I would pay him a visit and 'correct' him."

"She said no, don't get involved. She would use the pictures to ensure a quick, uncontested divorce. Except he didn't want a divorce, so he kept on beating his pretty trophy wife."

"She's a CPA, so she began going through his business records and found he was skimming. She told him if he didn't give her an uncontested divorce with a good settlement, she would tell his partners."

"That was a mistake," said Marybeth."

"Yep. So, he was hired to extend a sewer line along a scenic river. He lured her to the site by saying he would take her to a nice restaurant for lunch and discuss a divorce deal."

"*Said the spider to the fly*[10]," Marybeth interjected. "Remember, I taught elementary school."

"She agreed, but in this case it was her '*Spidey-sense*'[11] that was tingling."

"What happened?"

"The site was outside of a small town, hidden from the road. The giant excavator was backfilling a 20-foot deep sewer line using a heavy trench box. It's like a steel sled with walls to prevent a cave-in. Her husband's plan was to walk her along the trench for a view of the lovely river. The backhoe operator would swing around and whack her with a loaded 3-ton bucket, knock her into the trench, and bury her."

"Then they would pretend to dig her out by hand, but it would be too late. Her husband would tell police that she slipped, fell in the hole and hit her head on the trench box. Of course, the backhoe operator was generously rewarded for his part."

"Problem was she wouldn't walk close enough to the trench, so her husband pushed her. She saw the bucket swing, and ducked. It hit her husband and knocked *him* into the hole. He hit *his* head on the trench box, split his skull and killed him."

"The backhoe operator panicked and called the cops. He told them she pushed him in. But she told the cops it was a setup to kill *her*, and the backhoe hit *him* by accident."

"Sounds like a 'he-said-she-said' case, Mac. Why was she charged with murder?"

"She had a million dollar insurance policy on him for accidental death, M. An overzealous prosecutor up for re-election smelled a news bonanza. 'Wife kills socialite husband in murder plot to collect a million dollars.' It would be big press coverage, a slam-dunk case with the backhoe operator's testimony. They charged her with second degree murder, because they couldn't prove premeditation. When they held her without bail, I introduced her to my friend Morgan Hillman, a top criminal lawyer."

"So...?"

"So, I hired the backhoe contractor to do some earthwork around my barn. I live in the deep woods. He came down to look at the job and give me a quote."

"Soon as he stepped out of his truck, I sucker punched him and knocked him cold. Dragged him through shallow water out to the big beaver den in the middle of my pond. When he came to, I shoved his head in their entrance hole, under water, and held him there until bubbles stopped surfacing."

"When I yanked him up to breathe, I told him unless he confessed to the plan to kill her, I would hold him under until the beaver chewed his face off or he drowned."

Marybeth's eyes widened like dinner plates!

"All of a sudden, he was telling me how the 'accident' had been planned."

"I had set up a camera on the beaver lodge and recorded his soggy confession, which I turned over to Morgan, who gave a copy to the state Attorney General, who intervened and suggested the Prosecutor drop her case. She refused, arguing the confession was obtained under duress."

"Wasn't it?"

"Hell yes, it was under duress! It was under water! Hah!"

"So..."

"She got a jury trial. Morgan presented not only the video confession but bank records showing a $50,000 wire transfer from her husband to the excavator's bank account for unspecified 'excavation work' two days before the 'accident'."

"Morgan put the contractor on the stand and asked him what the $50,000 was for, since his office could produce no work records connected to it. He took the fifth."

"Took the fifth?"

"Refused to incriminate himself; it was as good as a confession of guilt."

"Soon as the jury saw the video confession, and the payoff evidence, they went out for fifteen minutes and came back with a 'not guilty' verdict."

"You know, Mac, if everyone would just follow the golden rule, there would be no trouble in the world. No murders, no wars, no violence. Wouldn't that be wonderful?"

"It would be wonderfully naive, Marybeth, because there is a lot of bad in the world. Seems like you have your perfect piece of paradise here inside your Murphy B & B, but what are you going to do when trouble, I mean deadly serious trouble, comes to Barcelona Harbor? You have to fight, M."

"So...that's why Angie said, 'don't go all Lone Ranger.' Are you just friends with her, Mac?"

"Yes, we're just friends, Marybeth. Morgan and Angie became a couple after her trial. She is his woman, for sure. Since my divorce, I haven't dated any woman."

"Once burned, twice wary, Mac?"

"Something like that. Gabriella was only fifteen when I divorced her Mom. She wasn't ready for another woman in my life."

"I really had no right to pry Mac. It's just that..."

"Forget it, M."

"OK, Mr. Builder. How about lunch?"

"Wait, do you have guests for lunch, M?"

"Actually, no, not today, and no one is checking in. My housekeeper will clean, so I have a free afternoon until I start supper around four p.m. Why?"

"How about I buy you a burger and fries at one of the last roadside joints of the 50s? We've got just enough time."

"Great! Where are we going?"

"Conneaut, and don't ask. Hey! Here comes someone up your driveway!"

A Platinum Ford F-350 pickup with dual rear wheels crunched to a stop. Its license plate read '*DedlySrs*'.

The horn double tooted, and a big hand waved out the window.

"Oh, that's Tim Riley," said Marybeth. "Hi, Tim!"

Tim unfolded his large frame, stepped down from the cab, and walked over.

"Nice truck, Tim," Mac said. He recognized it as the truck Gino was driving that morning.

"It's a friend's; he lets me use it to tow."

"What do you tow with it?"

"My wife's horse trailer and a boat."

"Tim," Marybeth injected, "how about some lemonade?"

"No thanks, I can only stay a minute."

"So Tim," Mac said, "did you have any other thoughts about that 1983 wreck?"

"Not really. Sorry, I tried."

"Tim," said Marybeth, "How is Anna?"

"Good! She's in remission. It's a good thing I'm still working part-time, so we have some medical coverage. But her treatments are expensive, and I have a big deductible to pay. Anyway, she's happy, and looks like she's gonna beat it this time. Today she's riding at the D Line, so I dropped her horse off with the trailer, gonna pick her up after I'm done here. Well, I just wanted to stop by, goin' fishing later!"

"Tim, thanks for coming by," said Mac.

The Ford dually backed down the stone driveway, turned and headed for the harbor pier.

*****

"Marybeth, who were the possible players in the plot to kill my parents?"

"Joey Minetti and the New Jersey truck driver."

"Right. Truck driver's probably dead; the police report listed his age as 60 at the time. Who else, M?"

"Well, I'm presuming Joseph Minetti senior had to know, and Rosemary, because there are not many secrets between a husband and wife."

"OK and who else?"

"Not Gino and Gina, they weren't even alive."

"I agree. They had nothing to do with my parents' 'accident'."

"That's it isn't it? I mean, who else besides...the Ripley police officer."

"I checked obituaries. He died 5 years ago, which leaves..."

"Who? Former State Trooper Tim Riley?"

"He was at the scene, and his report downplayed the damage to the back of my parents' pickup."

"But, Mac, Tim has been a friend to my family for thirty years! Well, most of thirty years, until he put up that fence. I grew up in my parents' house next door to him. Tim and Anna didn't have kids. They treated us like we were their kids. You can't suspect Tim Riley!"

"All I'm saying is anyone connected to the original accident forty years ago has to be looked at. And we have to be very careful what we say in front of any of them. I want to keep this close to my vest. If there is a murderer out there, I don't want him to see me coming."

"And you suspect Tim?"

"I suspect him of a cover-up, but I don't suspect anyone other than Joe Minetti of murder, yet. But as I gather information, I need to keep it to myself."

"So, some things in your mind you haven't told me, Mac."

"That's for your own safety, Marybeth. I can keep a poker face, but can you? You live here, you know these people; you might slip. Just a tic of your mouth or a blink of your eyes could tell someone that you know something, even if you don't. I don't want you involved."

"I understand, Mac."

"So, your parents lived next to the Rileys?"

"Yes, they were always good neighbors until Tim put up a fence a few years ago. It encroached on Dad's property. Dad hired a surveyor to set the bounds, but Tim ripped them up and told Dad to get off his land!"

"So, what happened?"

"The police came out and watched the surveyor reset the bounds. The fence was a foot onto Dad's lot 200 feet down the line. The police told Tim he would have to move it, but he refused."

"So Dad went to court and got an order allowing him to remove the fence. He hired a contractor to take it down while Tim was at work, and they piled it in his driveway."

"When Tim came home, he went berserk. He pounded on Dad's door. Dad refused to open it. Tim ripped up Dad's garden. Dad called the police again."

"After that, bad things started happening. Dad's car had flat tires. The bushes along the front border all died. Dad got a restraining order. Tim would yell obscenities whenever they went outside. The stress really affected them. They talked about moving, but they had so many memories in that house, and they really couldn't afford to buy another."

"You are describing a psychotic personality, Marybeth."

"The funny thing is Tim has always been nice to me."

"Well, let's just be careful what we say, and to whom we say it, OK? C'mon Buddy, lets show Marybeth we can have fun!"

"You said classic 50s burger joint?"

"Yep."

"Give me ten minutes; I'll be right out!"

*****

Chapter Sixteen

She came out of her bedroom with ponytail hair, a white sleeveless blouse and flouncy blue poodle skirt. White bobby socks with black and white saddle shoes completed the look.

"Rockabilly, sister!" Mac exclaimed. They jumped in the car, and Buddy sat between them.

"Buddy, sit by the window," Mac said, and pointed. Buddy grumbled, but he moved over, and Marybeth slid next to Mac on the big bench seat. *People with modern cars and bucket seats don't know what they are missing,* Mac mused.

Marybeth laughed, "You two are like an old married couple!"

"And we've only known each other a week," Mac said.

"Now tell me, Mac, is this road trip just pleasure, as in, 'taking your girl to lunch?' Or is this also sleuthing?"

"You are so suspicious, Marybeth."

"Well, you got up at 4:30 and drove to Conneaut. So, you have a reason for going back. Am I right?"

"Almost. It *is* our first date. *That* is the most important part. But I saw this very cool, 1950s Root Beer joint, and it's a beautiful day, so why not take my girl for lunch? We're in my '57 Chevy and you're in your poodle skirt. You'll be the queen of the shake shack!"

"And..."

"Well, just down the street is where Gino made a delivery and a pickup. I thought we might stop and make a couple of inquiries, like any good classic car couple."

"Un-huh, I thought so. What are we looking for?"

"Original '57 Chevrolet full-coverage hub caps. Mine got lost over the years, so I have Pontiac's. Your job will be to bat your eyes and turn any man into a stammering puddle of mush."

"HA, HA! Mac Morrison, you are going to get me in trouble. Nice girl like me shouldn't go out with a dangerous guy like you!"

The forty minute drive was a dream to Mac, with Marybeth's arm looped through his. He steered with his left hand, listening and laughing as she told tales of silly twelve-year-old campers at the Bar B. He exited off I-90 at Route 7 for Conneaut and looped back through the downtown, just as Gino had done. As they passed the old barn with junk GM cars, he pointed it out.

"We'll be stopping there, after lunch."

Next, they drove past the brick garage where Gino delivered the chassis.

"And, here."

"After lunch," said Marybeth.

"Correct. Coming up, the 50s Root Beer juke-joint. Are you hungry?"

"Starving! Looking forward to eating someone else's cooking."

"Well, I guarantee it won't be as good as yours, but it's Rockabilly, baby."

The baby blue Chevy Bel Air cruised into a bustling burger stand with wooden barrel root beer. The horseshoe-shaped open-air counter extended to the sidewalk of U.S. Route 20, with sparkly red stools wrapped around it under a wide roof, just as it had since it opened in the early 1950s. A shady picnic grove beckoned out back.

Cute girls in white outfits ran back and forth from the kitchen. One poured frosted mugs of root beer and handed them off to customers. It was organized chaos.

Shake, Rattle, and Roll[12] was blaring from sixty-year-old counter-top jukebox speakers. Songs cost a quarter, just like 1969.

"Let's grab those last two stools," said Marybeth.

With Buddy trailing on his leash, Mac waved at one of the servers, pointed to the barrel and made a V for two mugs. She nodded.

The root beer was frothy and cold. The taste took Mac back to the Bar B ranch, when Mr. Barnes would bring out wooden cases of cold pop as the campers huddled around the campfire and sang songs. Mac always hoped there would be a root beer. Sometimes there was.

A pony-tailed server said, "We're real busy, but I'll be back in five minutes to take your order."

As the song ended, Marybeth dropped a quarter in the jukebox and pressed F10. Bill Haley and the Comets yelled out *Rock Around The Clock*[13].

One two three o'clock, four o' clock rock!

Ba-dum! (Drum beat)

Marybeth jumped off her stool, swung her poodle skirt and grabbed Mac's hand.

"C'mon, Mac, dance with me!"

Five six seven o' clock, eight o clock Rock!

Ba-dum! (Drum beat)

Nine ten eleven o'clock, twelve o'clock Rock!

We gonna Rock! Around! The clock tonight!

Well, the clock strikes two, three and four,

If the band slows down, we'll yell for more

We're gonna Rock! Around the clock tonight

We're gonna Rock, Rock, Rock, 'til broad daylight

We're gonna Rock, gonna Rock, a-round the clock tonight

Marybeth jitterbugged fast, whirling her poodle skirt. Mac held on, matched her moves, and swung her round and round, lifting her off her feet.

"Whoooooeee!" Marybeth shrieked.

We gonna rock, we gonna rock, we gonna rock around the clock!

Ba-da-da-dump, DUM! (Drum beat)

"Yaaaayyyyy! Woo woo woo!" the counter crowd applauded.

"Whew! I'm whipped," said Mac. "Burger break!"

They ordered two burgers, fries, and a chocolate shake with two straws, just like a first date.

"Oh, Mac, isn't this fun? Look at the old cars! '49 Caddy, '66 Mustang, '63 Stingray split window coupe in white!"

They sipped their chocolate shake, knocking heads.

"Mac, I wish every day could be like today. Sunny, burgers with root beer shakes, and good fun with good company."

"Yeah, that Buddy is good company!" Mac said.

"Knucklehead!" She elbowed him in the ribs.

"Marybeth, this *is* fun, and I'm glad we came. But, if I knew what trouble I would be stirring up, I would never have brought it to your door. I'm sorry about that."

"Don't be, Mac. I feel alive for the first time in 2 years."

"Good!"

The three of them enjoyed their burgers and the beautiful afternoon. Mac and Marybeth leisurely sat and chatted and Buddy howled his approval. When it was time to leave, Mac ordered a shake to go as Marybeth dropped a quarter in the jukebox and punched 'J 12'. Elvis' deep voice crooned over the parking lot.

Wise... men... saaaay...
Only fools... rush... in...

"C'mon, Mac, dance with me!" Marybeth put the shake down and grabbed Mac around the waist. She twirled her poodle skirt and pulled him out into the parking lot to dance.

But I...can't help...falling in love ...with... you[14]

"Hold me tight, Mac," she whispered in his ear. She sang along with Elvis, like a spring bird calling its mate after a long flight home. It was a soulful soprano unleashed after years of idleness.

"Woo-hoooooo," shouted the gallery. "Get a room!"

"HAHAHAHAHA!" Marybeth's laugh was infectious. The whole joint started laughing and clapping.

"OK, Mac, time to go home."

"Yes, my cruise-in Queen, but two stops first."

*****

Chapter Seventeen

Monday, May 22
2:30 p.m.

Kurt's Kustoms was one minute down the road. Mac parked in front of the open garage so Marybeth could step out and swirl her poodle skirt.

It worked.

"Help you?" called a voice from inside the garage. He walked out into the sun, looked longingly at Marybeth, and then at Mac's Chevy. It was the man in the overalls Mac saw paying Gino.

"I'm Kurt," he said.

"I'm Mac, and this is Marybeth."

"Nice Chevy. Looks like you lowered it, but kept the original steel wheels."

"That's why I stopped."

"Want custom wheels, Mac? I can help with that."

"No, Kurt, I'm looking for an original set of '57 Chevy full coverage hubcaps."

Kurt whistled.

"Well, can't help you there. I do customs, not restorations. Hubcap Harry, that's who you want. Quarter mile west, it's the old wooden barn with a bunch of '50s GM cars out front. If anyone would have your hubcaps, it's Harry."

"Thanks, we'll stop there. Looks like you're doing a '57 Bel Air. Resto-mod?"

"Yep, I just got the chassis this morning."

"Nice, I'd like to see it when it's done."

"Maybe you will. I go to Cruise-Ins up and down the Lake."

"I just live…" said Marybeth…

Mac interrupted, "Well thanks very much Kurt. C'mon, Marybeth."

He whisked her into the Chevy. With a honk of the tuned horns, Mac waved at Kurt and backed out.

"Was I about to say too much, Mac?"

"Probably not M, but this guy does business with Gino."

"But you don't think Gino…"

"I don't think yet, M. I'm gathering information. You did OK, just be careful. In small towns, people talk."

"I'll be more careful, Mac. Now let's go meet Hubcap Harry!"

*****

The sign on the faded wooden barn said *'50s GM Parts and Hubcaps'*. There were a dozen cars sitting out front. When Mac pulled into the gravel drive, he could see they were very special cars. Even though they were exposed to the weather, they were up on cinder blocks, not sitting on the ground. There was a blue tarp under every car to keep the weeds down, and keep the damp from rusting the chassis. Grass paths had been carefully mowed around each one.

"Look M: '55 Buick Special, '57 Bonneville, '58 Impala, '56 Cadillac. We are at the right place."

A stooped old man came out of the barn. He blinked in the bright sun and hooded his eyes to see.

"Hello! Can I help you folks? Oh, my wife had a skirt like that! Nice, nice Chevy Bel Air. Can I have a look inside?"

"Sure," said Mac.

He looked inside with rheumy eyes.

"All stock, good, hate it when they junk'em up with stupid steering wheels and purple radios. These were the most beautiful cars ever made."

"I think so. Don't see any Fords or Chryslers in your yard," Mac said.

The old man snorted.

"Them's for others. I'm a GM man, always was. Gotta specialize you know. Lookin' for something?"

"Yes."

"Bet I know," the man said. "Set of '57 Chevy wheel covers. Those are Pontiacs, got the red center with Chief Pontiac. Nice caps, but wrong on that Bel Air."

"You know your cars mister…"

"Harry. Hubcap Harry, they call me."

"I'm Mac, and this is Marybeth."

"Nice to know you, folks. Come inside, and I'll show you why I'm Hubcap Harry. Like a cold soda? I got an old machine in the corner. Ice cold Coke in a glass bottle is still a dime in my barn."

"Thanks, we just had lunch at the root beer stand, Harry."

Buddy walked over, sat in front of the man and held out his paw.

"You want to shake, buddy? OK, I'll shake. Good boy! What's his name?"

"Buddy."

"Buddy, that's his name?"

"Yep, he's my Buddy."

'Rowrf!'

"Can he have a treat? I got a box on my counter over there. Keep them just in case. I love dogs."

"Do you have a dog, Harry?" Marybeth asked.

"Had one, lived to be 15. She died in my arms a year ago." A tear dropped from the old man's eye; he quickly wiped it away.

"You didn't want another, Harry?" she said.

"I'm too old. Can't start over with a dog, probably would outlive me. But I sure miss not having one. Had dogs all my life, but my Roxie was special. She knew my heart. She could read my mind. Never more than ten feet from me, anywhere I went. Loved my Roxie-girl."

Another tear fell, and now he turned away to wipe his eyes.

Marybeth stepped forward and gave him a big hug.

"Harry, I can find you a nice senior dog that needs someone to love her. I'm part of a dog rescue network. There is a senior dog out there that needs you, Harry. Would you like me to do that, find you an old dog to love you, and be your buddy?"

Harry turned and held her hand in both of his.

"I don't have much to live for now," he said. "Since Roxie died, I just putter around and mow the grass. Sell some parts now and then; just biding my time."

"Harry, I think you should get another dog, maybe a senior dog whose owner died. It's waiting at a shelter for a second chance. Harry, you could be that dog's life, and then you wouldn't be lonely."

"Oh, Marybeth, do you think you could find one?"

"I know I could, Harry. Does it matter if it's female or male?"

"No, not really, just a good dog. That would be great, just to have a dog again."

"I'll find you a dog," Marybeth said. "Do you have internet, Harry?"

He snorted again. "Yep, even an old fart like me has internet. He pulled a card from his pocket that read 'Harrys' Hubcaps, Conneaut, OH' with the phone number and email.

"I don't have a website. That's too much work, but I know what I have. If people call me, I usually don't even have to look. Now, Mac, is that your name?"

"Yes", said Mac.

"You might have gotten lucky, Mac. Let's go look."

Inside Harry's old barn, the walls were lined with GM hubcaps from the 40s, 50s and 60s: thousands of them, all in neat rows on nails. They went up ten feet and circled all around the barn.

"Wow, how long have you been collecting hubcaps, Harry?"

"All my life. Before the interstate, U.S. 20 was the main road from Cleveland to Buffalo and those towns were hopping during the big war, lotta traffic. I grew up in this house. Used to ride my bike up to that root beer stand and get a frosted mug for 10 cents. Boy, those were the days, the 50s! Well, the cars used to just whizz by and, you see, we're on a bit of a curve here."

He pointed to the road.

"In spring, we'd get potholes. People would come around that curve, and hit a pothole. Their hub caps would pop off and roll right into my front yard! I'd pick'em up, wipe'em off and hang'em on a nail. Sell 'em back to the same folks who lost them on their next trip!"

He cackled and stomped his cane. "Prob'ly started doing that when I was 6 or 7 years old. I'm 85 now."

"So you've had some of these 70 years?" Mac said.

"Some. I sell some, but some I keep, just because they're beautiful. Now let me see, '57 Chevy. The Chevy caps are on this wall over here. See, I have them sorted, Olds, Chevy, Pontiac, Cadillac, Buick. Aren't they beautiful? The 50s cars were my favorites."

"Mine too," said Mac.

"OK, look up there! Your eyes are better than mine. See up on the top row, way to the left?"

"I see them! You've got a set of original '57 Chevy full coverage hubcaps, Harry! And they look to be in good condition!"

"Course they are. If they have a scratch, I polish them out, like jewelry. There's a ladder over there on the wall, Mac. Can you climb up and get those down?"

"Sure can. Harry, you and Marybeth just made my day!"

"Huh?"

"You have my hubcaps, and Marybeth has my heart. Don't tell her. We just went on our first date to the root beer stand. She stole my heart like a 15 year old."

Marybeth beamed and twirled her poodle skirt.

'Rowrf!' Buddy did the Buddy dance and pushed off Mac's chest.

"OK, Buddy, you helped too. It's been a good day for all of us."

Mac climbed down with the hubcaps. "Harry, these are perfect! What do I owe you?"

"Well, you've got a nice set of Pontiac caps. How about we trade, and maybe you give me $20?"

"Let's pry mine off, and put these on," Mac said. Buddy ahead ran to the Chevy. 'Rowrf!', 'Rowrf!'

"Yeah, I'm excited too Buddy," Mac said, rubbing his head.

Marybeth snaked her arm through Harry's, and they walked out to the Chevy.

"Harry," she said, "who cooks for you?"

"Me," he said, "mostly microwave something quick. Nothin' fancy; eat in front of the TV. I like the old shows. They got streaming now, you know? I can watch old black and white *Perry Mason*[15], those are great. The 50s *Gunsmokes*[16] are my favorites."

Mac on put the new hub caps, and smacked them in with the heel of his hand. He walked back to Harry and handed him the stack of Pontiac hubcaps and two bills folded over.

"We got a great deal, Harry. Thank you so much."

"I got a great deal, too. You folks made my day."

"And I'm going to find you a dog, Harry. I have a Bed and Breakfast in Barcelona Harbor. Do you know it?"

"By the old stone lighthouse?"

"That's the one. You come up and stay the night, my compliments, meet your dog and let me cook for you. Does that sound good?"

"Sounds wonderful, Marybeth." Now, the tears were flowing like rain from Harry's eyes.

"Sorry, I just get sentimental," Harry said.

"God love you Harry!" Marybeth said. "If everyone were as good as you, there would be no troubles in the world."

'Rowrf!' Buddy jumped up and licked Harry's face.

"You big goof, Buddy, you want to be my buddy. Well I'll be your buddy too. Here!" He pulled a treat from his pocket. Buddy gently took it and jumped in the open door to the Chevy.

Marybeth gave Harry a hug. "I'll call you Harry. I'll get you a nice dog."

"That would be wonderful, Marybeth."

Mac shook Harry's hand. "Thanks again, Harry, great to meet you. I'm so happy to finally finish this car. See you again."

Mac started the Chevy with a rumble and waved to Harry, who looked down at the cash in his hand. "Hey, wait!" he yelled. "This is $200!"

"That's the right price, and a great deal at that," Mac said. "Now go to the root beer stand and have lunch on us."

*****

Chapter Eighteen

Monday, May 22
3:15 p.m.

Rain began to pelt the windshield as they hummed north through Pennsylvania. Soon it was a torrent slashing off the windows and peppering the canvas roof.

"Marybeth," said Mac, as the windshield wipers viciously swiped back and forth trying to sluice off the rain, "you sing so beautifully. Did you ever perform?"

"Church choir, school plays, and chapel piano at Mr. B's camp services. I loved that old Chickering upright. It had a great tone and real ivory keys. I bet it's almost a hundred years old, if it still exists."

"Mrs. Wilson said it's still in the old chapel," Mac said.

"Imagine that! I was a music-major in college, Mac, piano and voice. And I sang in a college jazz group, too, loved doing that."

"So why didn't you continue, M?"

"Life got in the way, Mac. Jim went to community college for criminal justice and law enforcement. We married the day after he graduated. I was still in Fredonia's School of Music, so we got an apartment in town. I could walk to campus while he started in the State Police Troop A. Jim was gonna be a Trooper from the day he was born. His life was always gonna be the Troop, and fishing. If he wasn't tracking a perp, he was out on the lake."

"Sounds lonely for you, M. You never had kids?"

"Jim didn't want kids," she said wistfully. "When I graduated college, I couldn't find a music education job here, and here is where Jim had to be. Troop A, it's all he ever wanted. So, I got my elementary education certificate and began teaching fourth graders. I loved that, too, it was sort of a substitute for my own kids. Gina Minetti was one of my favorite students, like my own daughter."

"I didn't see a piano in your house," Mac said.

"It was at my parents' place. I used to go there to play because Jim wasn't musical. My parents would sing and play along with me, Dad on his guitar and Mom on her flute. After they died, it was too painful to sit at my piano without them. I had an estate sale and sold it."

"You need to start singing again, lady. I love your voice."

Marybeth smiled and hugged his arm.

"Such a romantic ending to a storybook afternoon, Mac. I felt like that 15 year old girl that stole your heart."

Mac smiled back. "It was a great afternoon, M, the best in ten years." He began softly whistling in time with the wipers.

"Mac," she exclaimed, "you whistle symphonically! Perfect tone, perfect syncopation, and note-for- note! It's uncanny, and I should know!"

"M, I don't even realize I'm doing it. Don't ask me how, but the music reveals my inner thoughts. I must have a thousand melodies in my head, and my subconscious selects the one to play and tells my brain, kinda like punching the buttons on that old jukebox."

Marybeth suddenly caught the melody and began singing along...

"When you're strange...Faces come out of the rain"[17]

"Very good, Marybeth, the Doors, *People are Strange*[17]."

"So Mac," she said, *'faces come out of the rain'*: is that like the faces you've met, to figure out which ones were involved in your parents' death?"

"Yes. So, Marybeth, do you know Dylan's *All Along the Watchtower*[18]?
She nodded.

"Well, said Mac, "I feel like *'There's just too much confusion; I can't get no relief'*. And furthermore, M, *'two riders are approaching'*, but I can't see their faces, *'and the wind begins to howl.'*

"Do you always speak in musical metaphors Mac?"

"Only with people I like," he grinned. She hugged his arm as they drove on through the rain.

"You know, Mackenzie Morrison, you're kind of an old soul. You drive a 66-year-old car. You say an actress in a seventy-year-old film looks like me. You play forty-year-old Pavarotti at midnight, and you whistle fifty-year-old rock-n-roll tunes."

"M, I'm an old soul because I was raised by my Uncle Abe and Aunt Maddie in the New Hampshire north woods. They were two generations older than me, and their son Jordan was twelve years older than me, so the music in our house was an eclectic collection of records from the 40s through the 70s. Don't forget, this was not a cultural mecca. It was the early 80s. No internet, no cable TV, just rabbit ears on top of our TV set, with maybe four stations playing old movie reruns. We didn't even have good radio, so whatever old stuff they had, I devoured: books, records, art."

"Maddie was sweet and wise. She taught me French, so when we visited her relatives in Quebec, I soaked up their culture like a sponge."

"Abe was the Colonel, the stern task master. He taught me many things. He showed me how to work on cars by rebuilding his Chevy. I learned how to build houses by helping him build his post and beam barn. He was a bird watcher, so he taught me how to be stealthy in the forest. Most importantly, he taught me how to be a man, to protect your friends and family, and to take the fight to the enemy, before they bring it to you."

"So Mac, now you take on others' fights for them, don't you?"

"Sometimes I do, Marybeth, for a sympathetic situation. Not everyone can fight, M. Some don't have the strength. Some don't know how. Some don't have the will. That's the most important quality, the will to fight, and to finish it."

"So you go 'Lone Ranger,' like Angie said, and intercede for others."

"Believe me, M; I don't go looking for trouble. I have plenty in my own life to keep me busy."

"But it seems to find you, doesn't it, Mac?"

"Sometimes...maybe someday you'll understand, Marybeth."

"Well!" she said, changing the subject. "It's almost 4 o'clock. We are going to get back just in time. I was going to grill out, but this rain does not look like it will be over anytime soon."

"I can grill in the barn with the doors open," Mac said.

"That sounds like a plan. After you set up the grill, would you come in and set tables for me?"

"You bet, M. Hey! I noticed stacked sandbags in the barn. Is that a pistol range?"

"Yes. Jim was an avid shooter."

"Do you have his guns?"

"Yes, and since you put up new lighting, we can shoot."

Mac stopped the Bel Air by the B & B's back door and shut off the engine. The rain thudded on the canvas convertible top.

Marybeth said, "Mac, I'm gonna run for the porch. Thank you for a wonderful afternoon. It was a great first date!" She kissed him quickly and patted his cheek. "Now get busy, Mister!"

"Yes, Ma'am! C'mon Buddy!"

Buddy raced into the cottage. Mac fed him first and then he pulled on his rain slicker before heading back out into the weather. He yanked back the barn doors on their squealing rollers and dragged the grill inside out of the downpour. It was one of those big stainless steel jobs with the roll-over top and plate tables on the sides. Mac could just imagine Jim standing at this grill, happily chatting with Marybeth on the back porch while she made summer salads. It made him sad.

So, once again, he began mulling what he knew.

Tim Riley was a bit slow. He could turn from nice to nasty. He can't or won't recall a fatal accident he covered up forty years ago. He's 62, Mac thought, pulling out his cell phone. On a hunch, he looked up 'Westfield High School Yearbook 1979'. He found senior class photos. There were huge Elton John glasses and long hair on boys and girls. Prom pictures showed powder blue tuxedos.

He trotted through the rain, left his slicker on the back porch, and shouted.

"Ready to set tables!" he yelled.

Marybeth stuck her head through the open kitchen window and said, "Let's do red vinyl table cloths. They're in the buffet. Dishes are in the big cupboard, and silverware in the buffet drawer."

"Do you use cloth napkins?" Mac asked.

"Not with steaks! You'll find large paper napkins in the cupboard. Left side of the plate, please."

"Hey! I can set a table, lady!"

"We'll just see, won't we? I'll inspect."

"How are you coming in the kitchen?"

"Good. Dinner is at 6:30 tonight. We'll have time to shoot a few rounds."

"Can I use your computer, Marybeth?"

"Sure, whatcha need, Mac?"

"Password?"

"Now you're getting personal, Mister, but since I kissed you, maybe I can trust you."

Marybeth booted up the computer and looked over Mac's shoulder as he searched.

"Tim Riley is 62," he said, "which should make him class of '79. Let's find the 1979 Westfield High School yearbook."

"Radford, Reminger..."

Riley, Timothy.

"Whoa! Long hair does not look right on this guy," said Mac. "He was a big dude even in high school."

Favorite Line: Seriously?
Sports: Football, rifle club
Awards: SW Regional First Team Left Tackle, 1978, 1977, 1976
Hobbies: Cars, hunting, fishing

"Let's scroll down to the M's."

Minetti, Joseph Jr.

"Woo! Look at the mullet!"

Favorite Line: Deadly Serious
Sports: Rifle club
Awards: 1st place, 1979 WNY Auto Dealers High School Auto Trouble Shooting
Hobbies: Cars, cars, cars, hunting, fishing

Mac said, "*Faces come outta the rain*, Marybeth. Now let's look through the senior event pics. Look at this Rifle Club team photo. This looks like a young Tim Riley towering over a young Joey Minetti with his arm slung around his shoulders. Like best buds."

"Wow," said Marybeth, going back into the kitchen, "makes you wonder..."

"Certainly does. Especially since Trooper Tim couldn't recall my parents' accident, but it was his best bud Joey who witnessed their death. That's not something I would forget. Was Tim Riley covering for his buddy forty years ago by suppressing the rear end damage to my parents' car?"

"Maybe, but you can never prove it, Mac."

"You're right M, but I'm getting warm. OK, enough mystery for tonight."

❖❖❖❖❖

As Marybeth unlocked the gun safe, Mac noticed a fine looking six string guitar leaning against it.

"Your guitar, M?"

"Dad's. I haven't touched it since he died. Probably should put it away. Do you play?"

"Mm-hm. OK, M, let's see these guns."

"Mac, this is a replica of Steve McQueen's gun in *Wanted Dead or Alive*[19]."

"Never seen one in person," Mac said. "Hey, that's a Colt 1911 replica."

"Yes. .45 caliber."

"Uncle Abe had one in WWII; he gave it to me, but it burned in my barn fire."

"And this is a .22 Target Pistol, 11 capacity mag. 2.75" barrel, Mac. Slips into my back pocket, but I prefer holsters. Not for fast draw."

"In a firefight, accuracy beats fast draw every time, M."

"Let's both use the Ruger, Mac."

"OK, M. Slip it into your back pocket and cover it with your shirt. Load it in here and I'll bring the second mag in my pocket, tucked under my slicker. I don't want the spy camera to see us carrying guns."

"Oh, see, now I already forgot about that thing, Mac!"

They went out to the barn, and Marybeth hung up targets.

"My phone will ping when guests enter the front door, so we have a few minutes. Let's both shoot three, compare, and then seven more."

"Ladies, first."

Marybeth got into a one handed shooting stance and ripped off three quick shots, all bullseyes.

"Good shooting, M! Should I toss a silver dollar?"

"OK, hot shot," she retorted, "let's see if the man can beat that."

Mac stood right arm outstretched and steady.

First shot: low, third ring. Second shot: high, second ring. Third shot: bullseye.

"Pretty good for never having shot that gun, Mac."

"You're being kind. Let's see you shred that target, M." And she did. Five more bullseyes and two in the first ring. -

"Very good, M!"

"OK, now see if you learned anything from your first three, Mac."

Mac put three in the second ring, two in the first ring and two bullseyes.

"Not bad Mac, for a man!"

"Ho Ho! Thanks, but the sandbags weren't firing back. Makes a big difference."

"Well, let's hope we don't have anyone firing at us."

"Let's hope, but be prepared, M."

"Hey, it's 6 p.m., Mac. Some folks always come down early."

"I'll wash up. Buddy will stay in the cottage while we eat."

"Mac, thank you again for a wonderful afternoon. Now get outta here and let me change. No poodle skirt for supper!"

*****

Chapter Nineteen

The rain let up and the skies cleared, putting a spring chill in the air. Everyone donned sweaters for dinner. Mac wore a sandy pullover with nubbly wool that could have come off a Greek fishing boat.

"You look warm and comfortable, Mac," said Marybeth as she touched his sleeve.

He got six steak orders, grabbed a huge platter from Marybeth and headed for the barn. Then he opened his cottage and let Buddy out.

"Well, Bud, we're gonna have bones for you." Buddy danced ahead as Mac carried the platter of steaks to the barn. The sizzle of fat on the gas grill filled the air. Buddy drooled on Mac's shoe.

"Here you go, Buds!" He tossed Buddy six bones.

'Rowrf!' Buddy dropped to his belly and began gnawing.

Mac carried the platter back inside, grabbed two more steaks and returned to the barn. Buddy was chomping and smacking his lips.

"Buddy, we're gonna have to wash your face and belly tonight, eh?"

'Rowrf!'

Ten minutes later, Mac was seated with Marybeth at her candlelit dining table.

"No business talk, Mac, just us."

"Agreed."

"It's really nice to have you here, Mac. I didn't realize how lonely I've been. To push it aside I've been working every minute, trying not to think about Jim and my parents. You've taken me away from that, it's good. Thank you."

"I feel the same, M. I closed my heart ten years ago. Only my dog and my daughter had the key to get in."

"I'm glad. Well, let's see how this red wine pairs with our steak!"

After they had eaten, and the candles burned half-way, Marybeth checked on her guests. A few were talking softly, looking out over the pretty back garden, lit by solar low-lights.

"Ready for coffee, M?"

"Mac, let's clear the tables. Then we can have our dessert alone."

*****

Monday, May 22

7:30 p.m.

"So Mac, you've been suspicious of Tim Riley from the start. Why?"

"First, when Andy introduced us at the Cruise-In, Buddy sat and refused to shake his hand. Remember?"

"Uh, did I miss that?" Marybeth said.

"Maybe you did. Anyway, Buddy was telling me '*watch out*!' Even though I've only had this dog a week, he's looking out for me. Some dogs can smell trouble."

"Second, because he was at the scene of my parent's accident 40 years ago. His report contradicted the Ripley P.D. report by determining the rear end damage to my parents' truck was not related to the accident. And, he was evasive when I questioned him about it."

"Also, Tim is a retired New York State Trooper who drives a twenty-year-old cop car and still works part time for the BMV. With Anna's medical bills we know he needs the money. But he goes out on the lake fishing almost daily so he must have a fairly expensive fishing boat. How does he afford that?"

"Well, good point," said Marybeth. "I've been fishing on Tim's boat. It's big and fast."

"How big, M?"

"Let's stroll down to the pier, Mac, I'll show you."

With Buddy tagging along, they walked past the stone lighthouse, down the sloping parking lot and over to the moorings.

"It's this one here," Marybeth said, pointing to a black off-shore sport fisherman. *Deadly Serious* was painted on her stern. "Tim first took us out on it three years ago, Mac. I think he said it was only a year old at that time."

"M, do you remember the words under Joey Minetti's yearbook picture?"

"Mm, no."

"Same as the license plate on his big truck: '*Deadly Serious*.' So, this is Joey Minetti's boat, not Tim's." Mac took out his camera and snapped a picture with the flash. A light went on in the cabin as a voice boomed.

"Who's out there!" Tim Riley's head stuck out of the cabin door.

'Grrr!' Buddy rumbled deep in his belly, and nudged Mac's knee with his nose.

"Buddy, shh!" said Mac. "Hello, Tim."

"Did you take my picture?"

"I took a picture of the harbor, but your boat is in it. Do you mind, Tim?"

"No, I guess not. Want to come aboard?"

Buddy sat: 'Alert!'

"I can see inside from here, Tim." Mac looked in the cabin. There were two beds, head and a galley kitchen."

'Grrrrrrr!' Buddy bared his teeth.

"Is that dog mean?" Tim asked, stepping backward and reaching for a pistol lying on the cabin shelf.

"Only if he doesn't like you," said Mac. Tim pulled his hand away from the gun and gripped the ship's wheel, as if he were just steadying himself.

"I'm sleeping aboard tonight," Tim said, "going fishing early, guys."

"Is Anna going out with you tomorrow?" Marybeth asked.

"No, she's going riding. Well, guess that's the full tour, gotta turn in now, so g'night."

"Good night, Tim. And good luck fishing tomorrow," said Marybeth.

Tim closed the cabin door and clicked the lock as the lights went off.

"Let's take a stroll, M," said Mac.

They meandered around the square pier, then stood and gazed down at the beach. Buddy sat and scouted the area with his eyes.

"How much do you think a four-year-old 34' Pursuit off shore fishing boat with twin 400 engines costs Marybeth?"

"I was wondering the same thing," she said.

"Let me Google that," said Mac. "Let's see, Pursuit Sport fishing boats for sale...here's one, used. 2017 Pursuit, OS 325, 34', twin 400 HP Yamahas. Want to guess?"

"I don't know much about boats, Mac. $200,000?"

"$340,000, in Sandusky, Ohio, so it's a Lake Erie boat."

"So, M, three years ago, it probably cost $400,000. Business must be good at Perfect Collision and Restoration," Mac said. "Marybeth, what does Tim do for the BMV?"

"Some kind of inspection, Mac. He only works when there is an appointment. Let me use your phone, I left mine in the kitchen. I know all the state websites. OK, here it is:

> *'The BMV Inspection station is by appointment only. Vehicles declared a total loss can be returned to operational status if they pass a state inspection and a salvage title is issued.'*

"Aha!" said Mac, "so BMV Officer Tim Riley is inspecting vehicles that were totaled by insurance companies and rebuilt. If they pass that inspection, the BMV issues a new salvage title. Let's follow the money, and connect the dots, M."

"Joey Minetti owns a very expensive boat and the very expensive truck that tows it. Those two combined would have cost him a half million dollars several years ago. That's pretty pricey for your average body shop owner."

"Joey Minetti is also in the collision and vehicle restoration business. Gino Minetti buys totaled high end cars from the insurance companies for their parts. Joey's best bud, Tim Riley is the local BMV inspector for salvage vehicles."

"And, Joey was previously convicted for selling and shipping stolen cars."

"Marybeth, I bet Tim Riley is getting paid by Joe Minetti to pass a salvage title inspection on 'rebuilds' that are actually stolen high-end cars, whose trackable parts were swapped out for legit parts from other wrecks that Gino buys. And Joe lets his buddy Tim use his truck and his boat as a favor."

"All right, M," said Mac, "another piece of the puzzle drops in place. If I'm right, I think this is what Jim was looking into, and it got him killed. You didn't believe he drowned. I agree with you. Now we have to find who killed him, and punish them. I'm sorry to dredge this up, M, but if I'm right, we have to make them pay."

"Mac," said Marybeth, "wait a minute! You came here to look into your parent's deaths. Are you going to look into Jim's death too? Are you now taking on my fight?"

"You're a sympathetic situation, lady. Yes I am, if you will work with me to find Jim's killer."

"Of course I will, Mac! This is what I've wanted to do for two years, but I didn't know how. If we could prove who killed Jim that would give me some closure."

As they looked at the lake in silence, Marybeth slipped her hand into Mac's and held it tight. When the red sun disappeared below the water, they walked back to the B & B. Approaching the spy camera, Mac pulled Marybeth close to face him.

"Is that for me, or the camera, Mac?"

"Both. You invited me for dinner, so I'm calling this our second date. Best girls get a real kiss on the second date." He lifted her up and gently kissed her, and she hugged him tight.

Buddy ran into the barn and emerged with two bones in his mouth.

"Two? You got two bones in your mouth?"

'waRuff!'

"M, I gotta clean up Buddy. Do you have some old towels in the barn?"

"Yes, in the tool locker, Mac. Well, guys, it's been quite a day, but I'm beat. Breakfast prep starts at 6 a.m., so I am going to say good night."

"Night M."

"C'mon, Buddy, let's clean you up."

*****

Monday, May 22
9:00 p.m.

A thin band of clouds turned the sky into purple twilight, but it was bright inside the old barn with the new LED lights. Mac was wide awake. His brain had opened the door to the hunt mode cubicle. Sparks were flying out, and he knew he would not sleep tonight.

Not yet.

He found the towels, soaked one at the hose bib, and washed Buddy's face and belly.

A fine layer of dust covered the Tracker Pro Guide V 175. Its single Mercury Outboard engine hung on the transom. *Plenty of boat for calmer days on Lake Erie, but small for rough water*, Mac thought.

Using a high powered LED flashlight, he inspected it bow to stern, paying special attention to the gunwales. The boat had been swamped, not sunk, towed in and returned to Marybeth as found. Other than a crease of black along the port side gunwale, he saw no damage. He spotted a booster pack by a barn wall outlet and connected it to the battery.

Next, Mac removed the engine cover, grabbed a socket wrench from Jim's tool box, and unscrewed each of the spark plugs. They were a nice tan color, not sooty or corroded. He took a can of WD-40™ and pre-lubed the cylinders with a squirt.

The fuel in the gas tank didn't smell bad, even though it was two years old. A bottle of fuel stabilizer on the tool shelf suggested Jim had used it in Marybeth's Merc and his boat. Mac added some fresh gas from a red plastic can next to the lawn tractor.

Next, he went outside and dumped the plastic rain barrel, rolled it back into the barn and dipped it under the outboard engine's prop shaft. With the barrel standing upright, he got the hose and began filling it until the water intake was well covered.

With the spark plugs still out, he connected the battery and turned the key to engage the starter. The engine turned over, and a little oil sprayed out of each cylinder. He reinserted the plugs, replaced the engine cover and, with the booster set on full, he reached over the gunwale and turned the key. The engine spun over and fired with a brief puff of oily smoke. The propeller roiled the water in the barrel, and the engine ran smoothly: the wonders of modern fuel injection.

He let the engine get up to operating temperature, then he revved the throttle to 3500 rpm, holding it there for 20 seconds before idling down and shutting it off.

So Mac now knew there was nothing mechanically wrong with Jim's boat the day he died. They said it was swamped when they found it, and his body was nearby in the lake.

Mac pulled out his cell phone and Googled the County Sheriff's website. Under the Marine division, he found the tab for accident reports and downloads. Scrolling back two years, he kept looking until he found the report for James Murphy.

He sat on a stool and read the report.

Buddy came and lay at his feet, placing his chin on Mac's toes. He purred.

"Hi, Buddy. Been ignoring you, haven't I?" He reached down and scratched his head. Buddy closed his eyes and purred louder. "You are a funny boy, Budso."

The report said Jim's boat was spotted by men fishing two miles offshore and a mile north of Barcelona Harbor. It was swamped with no operator. Upon searching the area, the men spotted Jim's body in the water with his floatation vest still strapped around his chest.

115

The fishermen assumed he had fallen overboard and drowned. They were able to haul his body onto the swim platform behind their boat and secure it, after which they brought Jim's body, with his boat in tow, back to Barcelona Harbor. The Sheriff's Marine division took possession of the boat and body.

The Sheriff's report noted that Jim had a possible head injury from a crease on his skull. The officer speculated he might have hit his head on a boat cleat when he was pitched overboard.

"Hmm!" said Mac out loud. Buddy lifted his head off his toes. "Did I wake you, Buddy? I wonder. Marybeth said the autopsy determined it was accidental drowning."

A man-sized life vest lay in the boat. It was dirty and had marks like it had been scuffed or dragged. If this was the vest Jim was wearing, then it could have gotten scuffed while being transported on the swim platform.

"Hm," said Mac again. "Bud, let's go walkies."

'Roof!' Buddy jumped up and whapped Mac's leg with his long tail.

Mac grabbed the vest and an old beach towel from the locker. He paused as he stood at the barn door. The spy camera was on and pointing in his direction. He did not want to be seen. With the bright lights in the barn, he scanned the big room and found a rear door.

"C'mon, Bud."

They slunk out into the darkness, moving around to the side of the barn to get behind the Shavely's cabin. Walking quietly, Mac and Buddy stayed on the side of the cabin and walked down the Shavely's driveway behind a privacy fence that ran all the way to the road.

At this time of night, Barcelona Harbor was a ghost town of a few dozen houses, the marina, Todd's Gas n Go and the stop sign at Route 394. Mac and Buddy crossed over the road and dropped onto the lawn below the stone lighthouse. In a minute, they were on the beach.

Mac stripped down to his boxers, strapped the flotation vest around his chest, and waded into the lake. The water was cold, and it chilled him. Buddy watched and started in after him.

"Stay, Buddy." Buddy stood in the water up to his belly and watched.

Mac walked out until the water was over his head. The vest held him up. He bobbed up and down to see what would happen. The vest held him upright. He tried to swim free style or sidestroke, but it kept forcing him back face-up. He could only do breaststroke tipped forward at the shoulders with his head well out of the water.

And he was larger and heavier than Jim.

He paddled awkwardly toward shore until he could touch bottom. Buddy nudged him with his nose, happy to have him back on the beach.

"I was safe, Buddy. You were gonna come and get me, huh?"

'wuf!'

"Shh, Buddy."

Mac toweled off and slipped on his quick-dry terrain pants, dark knit shirt and running shoes. The air was cool against his damp skin, but it felt a lot warmer than the water. Mac and Buddy retraced their steps, and in two minutes they were back inside the blazingly bright barn.

He flicked off the lights and the barn plunged into darkness.

"Let's go, Bud."

Checking the spy camera, he could see it was pointed at the cabin. He walked Buddy to the nearest pee tree before they went inside.

Mac hung his clothes up to dry, stepped into a scalding hot shower and washed away the lake smell of old fish. He used the hair dryer to comb his curly mop before he laid his head down. He was a good tired. A few more pieces of the puzzle were going into place. A big picture was forming in his mind.

He picked up his phone, scrolled down his playlist and slipped between the sheets, pulling a blanket over him. Buddy lifted his head, spun around and settled next to Mac's side, laying his big head on his chest.

Mac was thinking of what Maddie had told him when he had just divorced his wife, and was feeling low. Maddie was dying, and she knew it. She wanted to be alone with him one last time. She had said:

"Mackenzie, in a good marriage, there has to be passion and partnership. You never had both, like Abe and I have. Find a good woman who will sing with you, dance with you, build with you, and take you for who you are. Not a woman who wants you for what you have; that was your wife, and she was a mistake, you know that now. But she did give you a beautiful daughter to always love and cherish. Find one who will sing with you, sweetheart, and be happy after I am gone."

Now Mac was thinking of Marybeth's angelic voice as he tapped the button for one of Aunt Maddie's favorite songs. He could picture Abe and Maddie happily dancing in the living room on a Saturday night while the Platters sang *Twilight Time*[20].

Heavenly shades of night are falling
It's twilight time
Out of the mist, your voice is calling
It's twilight time
When purple colored curtains
Mark the end of the day
I hear you, my dear, at twilight time
Deepening shadows gather splendor
As day is done
Fingers of night will soon surrender
The setting sun
I count the moments, darling
'Til you're here with me
Together at last, at twilight time

❀❀❀❀❀

Chapter Twenty

'Wuf!' Buddy licked Mac's nose and grinned big teeth as his long tail whapped the bed like a machine gun. Happy dog.

"Mornin', Buddy."

The white curtains had a golden glow from the rising sun glancing off the lake. Mac swung his feet to the floor and slipped on his dry pants, reached in his dresser for a clean pullover, slipped on socks and sneakers and gave his hair a quick comb.

"Shhh," he whispered to Buddy.

They crept out the cabin door and quickly moved to flank the spy camera. He rolled back the big barn door and flicked on the lights. They blinded his night eyes, and he blinked to adjust.

Mac went to the tool locker and found a razor blade and brought it over to the boat. There were a dozen mayonnaise jars screwed to the underside of a shelf on the barn wall. Mac unscrewed one of the glass jars, dumped the nails onto the tool bench, and unscrewed the jar's lid from the shelf.

The black crease on the boat's gunwale was not rubber, as he had thought. It was a smoother finish like paint, but maybe not regular paint. Using the razor blade laid flat, he took scrapings from the gunwale's outer stainless steel rail and dropped them into the clear glass jar and capped it.

He put the jar in a shopping bag, carried it outside and placed it in the Chevy trunk. Without turning towards the spy camera, he and Buddy walked quietly toward the back porch.

There was light in the kitchen window. He swung open the wooden screen door with a 'gronk' of the rusty spring and turned the handle to the interior door. It opened.

Holding the door so it didn't bang shut, he let Buddy in and followed. Buddy ran straight for the kitchen, and one second later, Mac could see him through the window, standing with his giant paws on Marybeth's shoulders, licking her laughing face.

"Good morning, Buddy," she said, "where's your Poppa?"

"Right here, Marybeth."

'Arfarfarfarf!'

Three little Labradoodles came running out to greet Mac. He bent down to pet them, and when he looked up, Marybeth gave him a quick kiss on the cheek.

"That was for a very nice day yesterday, Mac. Well, you are an early bird, aren't you?"

"This is normal wake up time for me, M. In New Hampshire, a group of us contractors have 6 a.m. coffee at Eleanor's. She's an older German lady who cooks a mean breakfast. We let each other know what jobs we are working on, and if we need each other's equipment. It's a great system, sort of like family. Whatcha makin'? I smell cinnamon rolls."

"Your smeller is correct. What would you like?"

"Well, you spoil me so."

"I like spoiling you, Mac."

"Bacon and eggs? Then maybe you'd have time to sit and talk to me."

"Can do. You start the urn, coffee in five minutes."

"OK. Over easy, please."

Quicker than quick, Mac's bacon, eggs and hot cinnamon roll was in front of him. He felt a nudge on his knee beneath the tablecloth. Wet lips licked his fingers as he slipped Buddy a piece of bacon while Marybeth stared at him.

Mac looked Marybeth directly in the eye and said, "Don't worry, I won't feed him in here," as he pulled his greasy hand out from under the table.

"HA, HA, HA! Oh, Mac! You are trouble! You and Buddy! Now, while you eat, let me go finish breakfast prep."

Fifteen minutes later, Marybeth brought a pot of coffee, refilled Mac's mug, poured herself a cup in her bone china and sat down. She couldn't help but notice how his hands bore the scars of a hundred battles.

"OK, so what are we talking about this morning, Mac?"

"First, to the future," said Mac.

"Yes, to the future," said Marybeth, clinking her fine cup against his heavy mug.

"So Marybeth, do you think Tim Riley suspects that we think he and his buddy Joey Minetti were both involved in my parents' death?"

"Well, he's been coy with you, but they've gotten away with it for forty years, so other than your library inquiry with Rosie, I don't think you've actually done anything to seriously worry Tim, or the Minettis."

"*High winds do not last all morning; heavy rain does not last all day*[21]," Mac said.

"That sounds like a proverb, Mac."

"That's *Lao Tsu*[21], saying nothing lasts forever; things always return to normal. So, Joey Minetti killed my parents, and he's gotten away with it for forty years. He figured he was safe, even though a little voice is always whispering in his ear that he may not get away with it forever."

"Now, the ten-year-old kid who knocked him out with a rock is all grown up and back here asking questions, poking my nose into his affairs. He knows I wasn't afraid of him forty years ago, and I'm not afraid of him now. He's worried all right."

"Marybeth, if the Minettis were involved in Jim's death, my staying here could also be worrying them. They must be wondering '*what does the Murphy woman suspect about her husband's death? Will she discuss her suspicions with the Morrison guy? And who is this Morrison guy, anyway? Why is he here? What is his game?*'

"Yes, the Minettis must be very worried, Marybeth."

Marybeth said, "But the autopsy said Jim drowned, although they did note a bump on his head."

"M, last time you said the autopsy called it a crease. Which was it?"

"Well, hang on, let me get it."

She went into her office and returned with a sheaf of papers she pulled from a pouch.

"This file is all the stuff from Jim's and Mom and Dad's death. I should organize it, but it makes me numb, so I just dump it in this pouch."

Mac read Jim's autopsy report aloud, pausing to let the meaning sink in.

"*Cause of death: accidental drowning. 4 ounces of water were extracted from the lungs. There is a contusion on the left side of the head, caused by blunt force impact with a flat object. A deep crease in the center of the skull is one inch wide and 1/2 inch deep, which resulted in loss of hair and skin. There are blackened pores of the skin over the skull the length of the crease. There is a black paint-like substance in the skin crease. Laboratory analysis reveals the identical black material found on a gunwale of the victim's boat, suggesting he may have struck his head*

121

on the gunwale when pitched overboard. The impact to the side of the head and top of the skull may have contributed to the loss of consciousness and resultant drowning. Victim was wearing a full wrap-around chest flotation vest when found."

"Marybeth," said Mac, "a Coroner's office is a busy place in a county as big as this. They never looked past the obvious. So, a guy gets fished out of the lake, floating, been in there a while, looks like a drowning. But 4 ounces of water, Marybeth, hold up your little cup."

She held it up.

"If you take a sip, it's half empty. That's 4 ounces. You would choke on that, but you would never drown on that. Hell, I've spit up more water in basic training."

"But..."

"So the two head traumas either killed him or knocked him out. The vest held him up vertically so he wouldn't drown. I tested it last night after you went to bed."

"But, after being knocked out, his head could have tipped over in the water. If he was conscious, his face might have submerged, in which case he ingested a little water, possibly suffocated. But he didn't drown, in my opinion, M."

"So... how does this all fit with..."

"Be right back," said Mac.

Mac walked out to the Chevy as the spy camera followed him. He came back with the shopping bag.

"This is the black material I scraped off the gunwale of Jim's boat. The autopsy report said this material matched that taken from his skull crease. But they did not analyze it because they had already concluded he drowned. That's sloppy work."

"They speculated he could have hit his head on his own boat rail going overboard. That makes no sense. It would be almost impossible to fall overboard and somehow land head first on the gunwale's steel rail *outside* of your own boat, and magically turn a glancing blow into a crease of the skull. And the black substance would have had to already be on there, and I don't buy that. This was a bang-bang play, as they say in baseball. His boat was swamped after being hit by a taller black boat."

"It's either sloppy coroner work, or some nefarious tampering and collusion. I don't know which, but I am not buying the whole drowning conclusion. I am going to take a scraping of black paint off Joey Minetti's boat hull and look for any signs of a two-year-old repair to the gel coat. Gonna have both samples analyzed. If that paint sample in the jar matches the gel coat on the *Deadly Serious*, he wasn't pitched off his boat by any rogue wave. And by the way, lake conditions were calm that day, I checked."

"No, Jim's boat was side-swiped by a heavier, bigger black boat. Possibly the *Deadly Serious,* Joe Minetti's boat. Its hull is taller, so Jim's stainless steel gunwale and the side of his head took the impact of the black boat's hull, which probably knocked him unconscious. He pitched overboard into the water and then was run over by the same black boat, causing the crease in his skull."

Marybeth's hands began to shake uncontrollably. Her coffee cup rattled against its saucer as she spilled it on the white tablecloth, and screamed!

"AAAAAHHHHHH!"

Mac jumped up and wrapped her in his arms, pressing her face to his chest.

"It's OK, Mac," she said, "I'm all right, I'm all right, Mac."

The Labradoodles surrounded her like her little army of protectors.

"Oh, Mac, how horrible!"

A bald man with a fluffy bathrobe wrapped around a large belly poked his head through the dining room doorway to the porch.

"Uh, is everything OK? I heard a scream."

"Oh! Mr. Steinaker! I just got some bad news. Someone I loved very much has passed away, and it was a shock. I'm sorry I woke you."

"You sure you're OK, Mrs. Murphy?" he said, eyeing Mac suspiciously.

"Yes, I'm fine. Mr. Morrison broke the news to me; I don't think I could have handled it from anyone else. Please go back to bed. I'm fine now. Tell your wife I'm sorry I woke her."

"Velma? She wouldn't wake up if a train ran through the bedroom!" he snorted. "Well, I'm up now, guess I'll take some coffee back to the room and watch TV until breakfast. Sorry if I disturbed you."

"Oh, it's okay, yes by all means, take your coffee, and there are freshly baked cinnamon rolls in the kitchen, help yourself."

"Mmm, hot cinnamon rolls," he said as he returned upstairs.

*****

123

"So Mac," Marybeth said, still shaking a bit and wringing her hands, "you think a black boat, maybe the *Deadly Serious,* struck Jim and killed him? So, therefore, you think the killer was Tim Riley or Joe Minetti? Why? Do you think the motive was to stop Jim from investigating modified stolen cars with legal salvage titles?"

"Possibly. It fits, but it's just speculation, M. But, I am going to find out."

"Mac, suppose the paint samples match, what does that prove? There must be a hundred black boats with the same paint."

"Yes, but every impact transfers unique material onto both surfaces. And even if the paint on Jim's rail is common to many other boats, the hard impact of scraping another hull left traces of metal on that hull."

"But wouldn't it have been repaired?"

"Probably, but I do auto and boat restoration, remember? Fiberglass is a tough surface to repair smooth and blend paint. Factory applied gel coat is baked on. Even if a professional body man like Joey Minetti did the repair with exactly the right materials, he probably can't cure it the same as the factory. There might still be a scar, and under that scar, scrapings subjected to spectroscopic analysis might be able to peel back the layers. It's a long shot, but I think I'm on the right trail."

"Sorry I got so emotional, Mac, but all of a sudden…how horrible for Jim."

"I'm sorry too, Marybeth."

"Oh, Mac," she said, tears dropping from her eye.

"But we're not going to let them get away with this," Mac said in a dark tone.

Marybeth shivered.

"Mac, promise me you'll be careful. I just…couldn't bear if it if…"

"Marybeth," he said, changing the subject, "you need to make your guests' breakfast."

"What are you and Buddy doing next?"

"Walking down to the pier, chat with some folks, kick over some stones and see what slithers out."

*****

"Nice boat you got there. What year is it?" Mac said to an old timer in a wrinkled flannel shirt and ratty boat shoes. His boat was pristine and polished.

"1966 Bertram. She's a thirty-one-foot with fly bridge, and a '93 Mer-Cruiser inboard. Built way better than how they make'em today. "

"She looks brand new," said Mac.

"Well, I take care of her, not like some of these yahoos with big money and no respect."

"I see you have the slip next to Tim Riley."

"Huh!" He spat overboard, and it hit the lake with a 'splat.'

"Joe Minetti, you mean. It's his boat. Riley just uses it. His slip used to be mine! But when he got that bigger boat, he wanted to be on the outside, because he couldn't dock it for shit. Harbormaster made me move, but it backfired on Minetti."

"Oh? How so?"

"We had a big storm with wind outta the west. Being on the outside, those waves just crashed against his boat over and over, slammin' it against the dock fenders. His spring line let go 'cause he didn't tie it right. He told the insurance he had storm damage, but I knew that wasn't storm damage."

"No?"

"No, he had a scrape all along his starboard hull facing me. I saw it when Joe came in one day. He hauled it out and repaired it. He did a good job, you can't hardly tell. I live on this boat all summer; I see everyone come and go. Saw you and your gal Marybeth last night. Also saw you go for a swim. Must have been chilly, eh? Hee, hee!"

"I did go for a swim. How could you see from here?"

"It was a nice night, but cool. I was smoking my pipe up by the Santa Maria," he pointed to the picnic table above the beach. "Nice dog you got. He woofed at me, but you was in the water and didn't pay him no never mind. What's your name young fella?"

"Mac Morrison, glad to know you..."

"Call me Pops, everybody does. Real name's don't matter when you're older than dirt, but mine's Roy Rodgers, and don't laugh, that is my real name, spelled with a D."

"Pops, can you describe the damage you saw on Riley's boat?"

"Sure, like I said, it was a scrape, 'bout an inch wide, scratched through the gel coat to raw fiberglass, probably 25 feet along his hull and just about two feet above the water line. So that wasn't storm damage, because when that storm tossed his boat against them fenders, that's an up and down motion for one. And second, them fenders are soft white vinyl, made to give and not leave a mark. There is no way that scrape along his hull was caused by up and down waves rubbing against fenders."

"My boat survived that storm fine because I know how to tie a spring line. I rode'er out below decks, so I adjusted them lines when they got stretched. Proper care, proper respect, that's what it is."

"You don't think much of Tim Riley," Mac said.

"Not him, nor his friend Joe Minetti. Riley's unpredictable, he scares a lotta people."

"Pops, can I give you my cell number and get yours? I'm staying at the Captain Murphy Bed and Breakfast across the street."

"Sure, I know Marybeth, she's good people," Pops said.

"I'd like to invite you to dinner while I'm here, would you like that?"

"Come to dinner? Would I have to get dressed up?"

"Absolutely not, come as you are."

"OK then!"

As they swapped each other's cell numbers, Pops said in a serious tone, "Mac, you wasn't swimming last night."

"I wasn't?"

"Not with that life vest on. You was experimenting. Don't know why, but I got an idea. Has to do with you bein' friends with Mrs. Murphy, don't it?"

"Might, Pops."

"Well, I see things, and I think about them. Never believed her husband drowned. Known him all my life; he swam like a fish. He used to go out with me on this boat. No, I think he was looking into something that got him killed. That was no accidental drowning."

"Pops, I've only been here a week, and I believe that too."

"One more thing, Mac, can you keep a secret?"

"I can."

"That scrape on Minetti's boat...it happened the same day Jim Murphy died. Say, that's a nice dog," he said, pointing at Buddy.

Buddy snapped to attention and wagged his tail.

'wuf!'

"That means he likes you Pops. I'll call about dinner."

"You do that, and tell Marybeth I said hello."

"Will do."

Mac and Buddy returned to the cottage for Buddy's breakfast, made an appearance for the spy camera, and then went into the back porch where guests were eating. Mac walked into the dining room, waved at a busy Marybeth and found the pouch they looked at the previous night.

Pops had just reinforced his theory about Jim Murphy's death: the scrape on Minetti's boat occurred the same day.

There was a jumble of stuff in the pouch. Mac made two piles: one for Jim's death and one for her parents' death.

The Sheriff's report said Jim Murphy died June 6, 2021.

Mac carefully read all the papers on the 'accidental drowning.' He still felt like his theory made sense. He needed to get paint samples off the *Deadly Serious*.

As he was organizing the papers, Mac noticed a yellow carbon of a Sheriff's report on top of the other pile. It described an accident location 'near 5910 Sherman Road.'

Sherman Road. That caught his attention. Had Marybeth's parents died in a car accident on Sherman Road? Mac took this other stack of papers and organized them with the Sheriff's report on top, then the coroner's report, then newspaper articles, obituary, cemetery burial receipts, notes and letters from friends.

The Sheriff's accident report was dated Easter Sunday, April 4, 2021. The deceased were John and Beth Waterman, 314 Elm Street, Westfield, NY. Her parents died two months to the day prior to Jim's death.

Now he understood the depth of Marybeth's grief, and why she threw herself into her work.

Mac used Marybeth's computer to call up *Google Earth* and search for 5910 Sherman Road. It was the seventh of the seven curves from Sherman to Ripley, the last one before descending to the Ripley flats.

Ironically, it was only a mile and a half from where his parents died.

The Sheriff's report noted conditions were clear and dry. The time of the accident was 10:30 a.m. Easter Sunday. Responding Deputy M. Rinker stated their vehicle left the road at the apex of the curve in a straight line and ran down into the ravine striking a large tree. Excessive speed was blamed, possibly a distracted driver.

There was a Sheriff's photo taken from the side of the vehicle jammed against a tree, but no Sheriff's photos taken from the road above.

The vicious impact had blown out the windshield. Her father had been ejected. Her mother's seat belt tore out its anchor in the floor pan and she was hurled forward, striking her head against the A-pillar and crushing her skull. Both were pronounced dead at the scene.

Once again, Mac was looking for newspaper stories and photos in Marybeth's pouch. A fatal car crash is big news in a small town. The local paper usually gives a big spread with multiple photos.

And they had.

Marybeth had saved the clippings, but she said they made her numb, so she had probably read them too hurriedly before shoving them in this pouch. And she did not know what to look for. Her parents had been driving a 2010 Ford Crown Victoria. It was a large old-school rear wheel drive car. There were millions of them still running the roads like trusty tanks. Theirs was a light color.

The Westfield Press article showed a black and white photo of the road at the runoff point and broken branches where their car smashed through, tumbling sixty feet to land on a large tree. No pictures were shown with bodies in the car, but the car was shown as it landed. The photo was taken from above with a zoom lens looking down from the road. Two dark vertical lines scarred the plastic rear bumper cover. Even though the photo was grainy, the lines were noticeable.

Now Mac moved to Marybeth's computer and searched for the Westfield Press. He hoped they had an online version.

And they did.

This time, the photos were sharp, color digital images. He hit 'print-screen,' copied and pasted to a blank document and zoomed in.

He could clearly see two dark vertical lines in the Crown Vic's bumper, approximately 2" wide and two feet apart. There was an obvious indentation shown by a slight shadow line, meaning the foam under the plastic had been crushed.

A second look at the road photo showed two sets of skid marks in a straight line before the car went off the road. So, her father had braked hard. If he had been driving at the 30 mph posted speed, he could have easily stopped before going over the embankment.

If her father had a heart attack, he could have failed to negotiate the curve, but he would not have slammed on his brakes, he would have drifted straight off the road. The Coroner's report made no mention of a heart attack or other medical cause of death.

Failure to negotiate the curve, speed too fast for the geometry, and driver error, the Sheriff's report concluded. Why did it not mention the skid marks on the road? Why did it not mention damage to the rear of their car?

Now Mac's Spidey Sense$_{11}$ was tingling!

If it could be done once, forty years prior, could it have been done again, here?

He printed out the sharper digital photos, shut down the computer, put the papers back in the pouch and laid it on the desk.

"Come, Buddy, we're goin' for a ride."

'Woof!' He raced ahead as the screen door 'whapped' shut behind them.

"Marybeth, be back in an hour!"

Mac cranked over the Bel Air's V-8 and looked to see if the spy camera was following him.

It was.

He snicked into gear and rumbled down the pea stone drive.

He wanted to drive the same road, the same direction Marybeth's parents had driven. It was a clear morning, sunny and dry, with similar conditions. Mac and Andy had driven those curves just two days earlier, but they were driving uphill in the opposite direction. So this time, he drove Route 394 through Westfield, up the incline to Mayville, and turned right on Route 430.

As he passed Andy's house, he saw him outside washing his truck. Mac slowed and turned into his yard. Buddy stuck his head out the window and barked a happy greeting.

'Rowrf! Rowrf! Rowrf!'

"Mornin' Mr. Mac! What brings you up my way?"

"Taking a ride. Day off, Andy?"

"Yep. Weather's so nice I figured I'd golf with my wife."

"What's your tee time?"

"After lunch."

"Ride over to Ripley with us. I'll bring you back in half an hour."

In two minutes, they were rolling past fields of young corn, mature wheat and horse pastures.

"Andy, we're going to drive these seven downhill curves into Ripley."

"There have been a lot of accidents on those curves over the years, Mac, especially in winter. Locals know to slow down, but tourists and kids will drive too fast and either wind up in the guardrails, or off the road at the final curve."

"Do you remember where Marybeth's parents were killed? Last curve before the Ripley flats?"

129

"Of course. That was a huge shock to the community. I knew them well; good people. And it happened right before Jim Murphy died, doubly hard on Marybeth."

"Ever stop her Dad for speeding?"

"Never."

"Accident report said excessive speed, plus poor road geometry. The coroner's report found no evidence of a medical emergency like a heart attack, stroke, or seizure."

Mac pulled over at the apex of curve number seven, a mile above the Ripley Flats.

"This is the spot. They went off the road over there, right Andy?"

"Yes."

"The curve is well marked 30 mph. The Sheriff's report said he went straight off over the embankment and did not try to negotiate the curve, or try to stop. It did not mention tire marks."

Mac held up the prints of the newspaper article and the enlarged color digital photos.

"I see skid marks, Andy. He was braking in a straight line."

He held up the best digital print he had made off the computer image and handed it to Andy. It was the zoom-lens shot from above, showing the rear of the car after it smashed into the tree.

"See the two vertical lines on their plastic bumper cover, Andy?"

"I do."

"See the shadow lines of those creases?"

"Yes."

"So, Andy, the bumper had been hit at some time. Possibly when backing up. What might a driver back into that would crush the bumper in those locations?"

"Probably a shopping cart corral."

"Could be, but those pipes are round, and the spacing would be farther apart, to my builder's eye. I doubt they would leave a knife edge shadow like that. Besides, it would be odd that a driver would back directly into both corral pipes straight on and hit that hard."

"True."

"Looks more like the marks were made by square-shaped flat bars. The impact was direct and forceful."

Andy said nothing.

"Some State Trooper cruisers have flat push bars, right Andy?"

"Mac, are you thinking…"

"They were pushed off that curve. Yes, that's what I'm thinking. And here's what else I am thinking. Do we know someone with a hair-trigger temper who drives a retired State Police cruiser with push bars? Maybe someone who had a beef with Marybeth's parents? Hello? Andy…?"

"I know, I know, I just don't want to say it."

"Andy, I gotta trust somebody."

"And you're willing to trust me? You hardly know me."

"You were a good camper. You got the Bar-B sermons. Buddy likes you, and Marybeth trusts you."

"Mac, you already know that Tim Riley has an old Crown Vic cop car with push bars."

"Is he a possibility?"

"I've known Tim all my life, Mac. I can't believe he would do that."

"But it's possible?"

"Anything is possible, but why, over a fence dispute? No, I can't believe he'd kill over a fence, Mac."

"OK, Andy, we keep this to ourselves, we let it stew. We do NOT tell Marybeth; are you in?

"Yeah, I'm in. But I won't have my mind on golf this afternoon!"

"Andy, there is one tricky thing I need you to do."

"What's that?"

"I took black paint samples off Jim Murphy's boat. I believe it was side-swiped and swamped before he was run over. Maybe I can prove it. I'm gonna get paint samples off Riley's, that is, Joe Minetti's boat, and you need to get your crime lab to see if they match."

"That wouldn't necessarily prove it was Minetti's boat. There are a lot of black boats in the area."

"I know, but modern science is amazing. Maybe a good crime lab might find the metal from Jim's gunwale under a repair patch on a boat: maybe Riley's boat."

"You'd need a search warrant to get those samples, Mac. A state crime lab would have to take the samples, and there's no reason for law enforcement to reopen that case based on speculation."

"Hm. OK, you're right. So I need a good private lab."

"The best is near Buffalo. That's a dangerous game, Mac. You think Tim Riley killed Marybeth's parents and her husband?"

"Either Tim Riley or Joe Minetti."

131

"What's Tim's motive for murdering her parents? Can't be a fence dispute, Mac."

"I don't know. Tim's a loose cannon."

"That doesn't make him a murderer. What's Minetti's motive for murdering Jim?"

"He was investigating a possible criminal enterprise by Joey Minetti, that's all Marybeth knows. I have a theory that takes that further, a theory Marybeth finds plausible, but we're not ready to share it with you yet Andy."

"Jeezuz, Mac. You certainly can stir the pot. Be very careful what you are doing and saying, man."

"Not my first rodeo, Andy."

So, Mac returned Andy home within the hour, but Andy wasn't concentrating on golf.

*****

Before going back to the B & B, Mac stopped at Lake Chautauqua and called Angie on his cell phone.

"Angie!"

"Mac...is everything OK?"

"Maybe not."

"Doing the Lone Ranger[1] again?"

"Yep."

"Mac!"

"Morgan busy?"

"In trial. You need the boys?"

"Might need one."

"I'll send Roger. What level?"

"Level II. It's complicated. Not sure I can trust anyone here except Marybeth at the B & B. I believe her husband was murdered. Coroner said accidental drowning. I don't think so. It could be the same guy also killed her parents. And he could also be the guy who covered up the killing of my parents forty years ago. He's a big dude, with a hair trigger temper. And he's a state cop."

"Oh shit! Mac! Could you, for once, just help a little old lady across the street without unearthing a friggin'murder plot? Don't answer! I'll charter a plane, Morgan will pay for it."

132

"I'll pay for the charter, Angie."

"Doesn't work like that, and you know it! Morgan and I can never pay you back, and since he can't come, at least he can feel like he's contributing. Bring gear?"

"Yep."

"Airport?"

"Looks like Chautauqua County-Jamestown Regional is the closest. I'll pick him up. It's only a half hour from me."

"Anything else?"

"Text me his arrival time. He'll be staying with me. I'll take care of it."

"OK. Mac"

"Thanks, Angie."

"You take care, Mac."

✳✳✳✳✳

Chapter Twenty One

Tuesday, May 23
11:00 a.m.

"Marybeth?" said Mac.

"I'm in the office, Mac."

"Are you feeling better, M?"

"Yes, thanks."

"Do you have guests for lunch today, M?"

"No, not today."

"Pops says hello. I invited him for dinner when it works for you."

"Oh, I love Pops! He's got a galley kitchen, but he can't really cook a good meal. I'll fatten him up!"

"M, I want to test Jim's boat in the harbor. I thought we'd get sandwiches at the gas station, collect Pops and have a picnic by the Santa Maria while we enjoy the many happy returns of the day."

"Are you quoting *Pooh-Bear*$_{22}$, Mackenzie Morrison?"

"Most certainly, I am."

"Full of surprises, you are."

"Yeah, and I have another one. I'm going to fill your downstairs room with my friend Roger. He's flying into Jamestown this afternoon. Too many ghosts in this town, too many relationships I can't sort out."

"OK. Where did you go, Mac?"

"Picked up Andy, drove around. I hope I can trust him. What do you think?"

"Absolutely! Bar B Camper!"

"OK, good, I was hoping you'd say that. I've got a hitch on the back of the Chevy, M. I'll hook up the boat and we can launch at the ramp."

*****

The ramp was not busy at midday. Tim Riley's boat was in its slip, and Pops was on the Bertram's deck as they launched.

134

"Pops!" shouted Marybeth, "we're going for a spin around the harbor. Would you join us for a picnic lunch?"

"Sure, I'll get ready!"

Marybeth released the trailer's cable from the bow cleat, jumped in and started the boat engine. Mac pulled the trailer out and parked the Chevy. Marybeth met him and Buddy at the dock, and they jumped aboard.

"OK, M," he said, "let's motor around the harbor nice and slow. Everything sounds OK, how does she feel?"

"Smooth, as always."

"I'm looking for eyes on us, M. If we make several slow laps, whoever might be watching may get bored. Slow down when we swing by Pops, OK?"

"Aye, Aye, Mac. Engine runs good, Jim would be pleased."

"That proves that there was no mechanical problem the day he died. If he was swamped, it's not because he couldn't maneuver. He could. He was purposefully swamped, and my guess is he knew the boat coming at him, or he would have taken evasive action, but by then it was too late. Here's Pops."

"Pops," Mac said, "is Tim Riley aboard his boat?"

"Nope."

"You said the long scrape on Riley's boat was starboard side about two feet above the water line."

"Yep."

"M, cruise us along the starboard side."

Using his LED flashlight, Mac traced the hull at the level of the Tracker's gunwale. There was no evidence of a scrape, until…

"Hold it, M, back up and idle."

And there it was. Joey Minetti was very good at bodywork. The color was perfect and smooth, but the repair was high in some areas and low in others. At an oblique angle, you could faintly see the striped path.

"The scar is right at Jim's rail height; it's a perfect match. OK, let's turn around and position me against the stern."

Mac pulled out his Leatherman™ multi-tool and flipped out the curved cutting blade. He ripped off a piece of green painter's tape and stuck it to the hull a foot above the water line. Using the razor-sharp curved blade, he carefully sliced under the tape until he had a one inch square of black gel coat. He lifted the painter's tape and pulled the sample from the hull. Next, he took a rattle can of gloss black spray paint and sprayed the small spot on the hull. To the casual observer, it was perfect.

"OK, let's go for a quick blast on the lake."

135

Marybeth expertly turned the Tracker around and idled out to the end of the pier. She opened the throttle, and the boat skimmed along on the smooth water. After a half mile, she did a sweeping arc and headed back for the harbor. Mac jumped out onto the dock, trotted to the Chevy and backed the trailer down the ramp.

Buddy twisted his head in a question mark as Marybeth expertly slipped the boat into its cradle. It was his first boat ride, and he liked it, but he didn't like Poppa Mac jumping off. With Marybeth and Buddy still in the boat, the Chevy pulled her out of the water, across the street and into her barn.

❋❋❋❋❋

"What's good today, Todd?"

"Hey Marybeth! Grilled yellow perch sub."

"I'll take two large, Todd."

"And for you, Mac?"

"Cheesesteak."

"Subs will be out in two shakes."

Mac sipped a cold root beer and rubbed Buddy's ears.

"Marybeth, tomorrow I go to Buffalo to have a private lab compare these samples. If they match, then we know the damage done to Tim Riley's boat matches exactly with the gunwale paint and elevation on Jim's boat, and the crease in his skull. That's probably not enough for the Sheriff to reopen the file on Jim's death, but it's enough for me to run a bluff. I have an idea how it could play out. In case it goes wrong, Roger and Buddy will be with you so you'll be safe."

"Here's your subs, folks!"

"OK, let's go get Pops!"

❋❋❋❋❋

"Pops, Marybeth tells me you live on this boat all summer. I don't see any hookups for power, water or black water dump."

"This is just a dry slip, Mac. But with LED lights and gas cooking, I don't use much power. I run the engine to recharge the batteries, and I take on water and pump out at the marina across from me. I can use the pier restroom, walk the beach, and talk to folks. It's good for an old hermit like me. Boy! This is a great perch sandwich! You got this at Todd's?"

"Uh-huh. So, Pops, where do you live the rest of the year?"

"I got a little log cabin in Tennessee."

"Why Tennessee, Pops?"

"I got my 20 years in the Navy by the fall of '76, so I retired with benefits at 38 years old, still had to figure out what to do with my life. Came home to Westfield for Thanksgiving, but after seeing the world, this town was too sleepy for me. A big snow storm was headed this way, so I got in my Chevy 4 x 4 and headed south. Stopped on the Little Tennessee River for some lunch, and saw a sign that said 'hillside lots for sale.' This old feller was a dealer for log cabins like his. I bought a lot and a small cabin kit and hired his son to lay a block foundation and pour a cement floor. We decked it with thick plank flooring, then laid up the logs and beams, and put on the potlatch pine plank roof, which we shingled in a day. In two weeks, the cabin was up."

"Pops, that is so fast!" said Mac, "and I know 'cause I'm a builder!"

"Well, the cabin is small, only 22' x 24', with three stories, including walkout basement. Only the first floor has log walls, the top floor is under the eaves. Logs are precut, so you just stack'em and nail'em with giant spikes and a sledge hammer. There's no siding, and no drywall. Soon as it's framed, you start interior walls. Simple."

"I lived there 'til '03, when I came back here for a friend's funeral and saw this Bertam for sale. I decided to live on it summers. See, not too far from my cabin is 'The Tail of the Dragon'23, a curvy mountain road that attracts thousands of cars and motorcycles every day. I rent the cabin for $2,000 a week from Memorial Day through October, have a housekeeper who cleans it. I can live easy on that $40,000 rent plus my Navy pension."

"Fall is beautiful in the mountains, but after Christmas, I go down to Daytona Beach. Got an old 30' RV at a campground where I stay until the 500 race. That's a lot of fun; meet a lot of old farts like me. We drink beer and tell lies. Good times.

April 1st, I go back to the cabin for the Tennessee mountain spring, and then I come here late May."

"Pops," said Marybeth, "it seems like you've done what you wanted with your life, and your intuition always paid off. Wasn't there ever a girl in your life? You never married?"

Pops' face collapsed in a sad frown.

"No. Thought I would. Met a real pretty girl in San Diego, it was 1966. We were both young and in love. Sun rose and set on her."

"What happened?"

"Got sent to Nam, did a year, got wounded, so they air-lifted me to Japan to patch me up. By the time I got back to San Diego, she'd married another guy. Never met another I liked as much. Finally realized I just it wasn't gonna happen for me."

"So here I am, an old hermit, but my life is good. I come and go as I like. Still have a few folks in town I know from way back, but most have passed. Folks at the gas station give me my coffee and donut in the morning with a smile and hello to start my day. I read yesterday's paper and smoke my pipe here by the water. At my age, can't ask for more."

"Do you have any living brothers or sisters?"

"Nope, they've all passed."

"Ever have a dog, Pops?"

"Always, but now I'm too old."

"Pops," said Mac, "Marybeth is about to give you the senior dog pitch, so Buddy and I are gonna take a walk." He winked at Marybeth and she winked back.

"Come, Buddy!"

'Rowrf!'

Mac's phone buzzed. He checked the text. 'Roger 4:30, Jamestown.'

His mind snapped back to the chase. It was an idyllic lunch by the harbor, but now he had to plan.

✳✳✳✳✳

138

Chapter Twenty Two

Tuesday, May 23
Jamestown Airport
4:30 p.m.

The King Air 350 floated out of the sky like a giant seagull, touching down with a gentle kiss of wheels on hot tarmac. It taxied to a small terminal where the blue Bel Air was waiting.

Roger Lemonier stepped out in khaki garb with a large gear bag slung over his shoulder.

"Good flight, Rog?"

"One hour and twenty minutes, Mac. Just enough time to wonder what the hell kind of trouble you are into this time. Angie mentioned three murders and other mayhem, so I came equipped."

"Murder tally's up to five."

"Balls!"

"I'll brief you on the way back. How's my job site?"

"Shed footers poured yesterday. Steel's coming in a week."

"Did Angie pay you?"

"Yep, thanks, Mac. Early season, cash is king."

"OK, Rog, my deal is complicated, but yours is simple. You act like a B & B tourist, but protect a very nice widow named Marybeth Murphy. You never leave her; never let her out of your sight, no matter what happens to me. If, for any reason my plan does not work out, you call Morgan to clean up, but you never leave her unprotected."

"So, you're doing this alone against how many bad guys?"

"That's the thing. One, two, three, maybe even four. A lotta faces are all intertwined, hard to know good guys from bad. Here's how it goes..."

It was a 30 mile drive from the airport to the B & B. Mac parked in front.

"Rog, there's a spy camera trained on the back of the house. Guests normally check in at the rear, but you're going in the front so the camera doesn't see you getting out of my car. Grab your bag and ring the bell. She has a doorbell cam and is expecting you."

"Got it."

"Meet you in the dining room in fifteen minutes. Buddy is inside with Marybeth. And, Rog?"

"Yeah, Mac?"

"Thanks for coming."

"Course, Mac!"

*****

"What about this Trooper Andy Gregor, Mac?"

"Pretty sure I can trust him, Rog. Buddy likes Andy, and that counts for a lot."

"Man, you putting your life in the jaws of a dog?"

'Grrrr!'

"Be careful what you say, Rog. Buddy could bite your balls off under the table."

"HA, HA! Man, you crack me up! OK, now, your bluff plan bothers me, Mac. What if you're out on the lake with Riley, and it goes wrong?"

"I'll be expecting that. I won't be wearing a vest if I have to dive overboard. My phone is submersible for thirty minutes so Pops can track me."

"I don't like it. You need me with you."

"Can't do it. I gotta run my bluff, and you gotta protect Marybeth. If I don't come back, he'll be coming for her next. You stay on her."

"What if you lose cell service?"

"Yeah, that's the big if. It's spotty. That's why Pops will be tracking me. If he loses my signal, he still has my last location coordinates."

"How will we know if you need help?"

"You won't if I have no cell service."

"What's the lake temp?"

"55 degrees at the surface near shore, colder farther out."

"Man..."

"Remember, no matter what, you stay with Marybeth. And if you lose that signal, keep an eye out for Riley's boat returning. If he comes back without me, it's up to Pops to find me because someone will be coming for Marybeth. Whoever that person is, that's the bad guy. You take him out."

"What about her guests?"

"They leave tomorrow; she's vacant for six nights, just us."

140

"Mac…"

"How else do I flush this guy, Rog?"

"Dunno. OK, my brain is crushed. What next?"

"A little light bulb job, c'mon."

Marybeth brought cold drinks to the back patio. Meet and greet, she called it. The sun was warm. Guests gathered.

Mac sat down and chatted with a group, including Roger. Buddy sat by his side, getting his head scratched. Marybeth called next door and asked the girls to please turn off their outside cabin lights and unscrew the camera bulb, but not remove it.

"This is so cool! Is someone going to get shot?" they giggled.

"Heavens no, girls!"

"But this is so mysterious!"

"Yes, it is, so you must do *exactly* as I asked. We'll keep the camera focused on the guys at the back patio. You approach the bulb from the far side, turn off the cabin lights, and unscrew it. Got it?"

Marybeth heard them giggling as they put down the phone. She walked out back to be in the picture when the camera went dead. She nodded to Mac. The Shavely girls snuck up on the cabin door, unlocked it, and the lights went off. Waiting a bit for the bulb to cool, they reached up and unscrewed it, but let it hang loose.

Marybeth nodded to them, and they bounced off like kangaroos.

❉❉❉❉❉

Chapter Twenty Three

Mac left Buddy with Marybeth and headed out. He had his paint samples, and his brain was cranking all the possible ways this could go.

The Chem Systems lab was in Hamburg, a Buffalo south side suburb fifty miles east of Westfield, so Mac entered I-90 at the Westfield toll ramp, figuring on a leisurely trip.

Before he had driven very far, a dark colored sedan fell in two cars behind him. Mac noticed it immediately because it held that position, even though he was driving five miles below the 65 mile per hour speed limit. Commuters were passing him in a steady stream, but the dark car kept its position two cars back. It never advanced, and always kept two cars between itself and the Chevy.

Mac slowed to 50 miles per hour. The dark car slowed, and stayed a hundred yards behind him.

He sped up to 55, 60, 65, and then 70 miles per hour. The dark car matched him. It kept its distance as they both threaded their way through light morning traffic.

For fifteen miles, Mac kept an eye on his rear view mirror as they played the cat and mouse game. The dark car would speed up and slow down, matching Mac's blue Bel Air, allowing traffic to filter past, but never approaching him.

All commuter traffic exited at Fredonia, leaving just Mac and the dark car traveling east. Now there was nothing but farms and woods on either side of the divided interstate highway, with no other cars in sight.

Suddenly, the dark car zoomed up behind him. It was an older green Buick LeSabre, one of those '90s squat bodies that looked like a crushed bug. The windows were tinted too dark to see the driver. Mac's déjà vu flashed to his parents, and the Waterman's. This guy's intent was obvious.

Mac floored his 450 horsepower Bel Air, and it rocketed ahead to 90 miles an hour, leaving the Buick far behind. Mac held his speed at 90 and watched as the Buick again approached him. At the last instant, Mac's hot rod Chevy leaped ahead again!

Now the old Buick was struggling to keep up. It took a long time for it to close the gap and get behind Mac, but it couldn't quite catch his Chevy.

Tenth-mile-markers were flashing past every four seconds as they whipped along at 100 miles per hour. As the Buick pulled left into the passing lane, Mac moved left to block it.

The Buick quickly shifted to the right lane, but again, Mac blocked it. As he did so, the Buick dropped its passenger window, darted left, and sling-shotted itself beside the Chevy.

Mac slammed on his brakes as gunfire spit out the Buick's open window! Three shots flew wildly off into farm fields.

Now Mac was behind the green car! It tried to speed away, but Mac's hot rod had too much power. The Bel Air pulled up close behind the Buick as Mac positioned his chrome front bumper so its rubber 'bullet' tips could push the Buick's plastic rear bumper. He didn't want to damage his Bel Air, but he wanted to wreck that car and see who was driving it! He got it tight, and right, and shoved the Buick, then braked hard to back off and let it spin. The Buick swerved wildly, but did not spin!

Now, Mac locked onto the Buick's bumper and began pushing! He shoved the evil green bug along at 110, 115, and 120 miles per hour, and he was still gaining speed! As they flew past a wooded median, a State Trooper flashed his lights, and surged out after them.

Mac opened his window and waved to the Trooper to 'get the Buick'! But instead the Trooper zoomed up behind Mac, with flashing lights and screaming siren.

Mac flicked on his right blinker and slowed as the Buick raced off.

The Chevy drifted onto the shoulder and stopped. Mac waited for the Trooper to run his plate and approach. The Trooper quickly radioed the stop, got out of his cruiser and walked up to Mac's window.

"MAC! WHAT THE HELL WERE YOU DOING? I CLOCKED YOU AT A HUNDRED AND TWENTY MILES AN HOUR PUSHING THAT GUY!"

"Hey, Trooper Andy! I was trying to spin him into the median. Did you see him shoot at me?"

"He shot at you?"

"Three shots! That Buick shadowed me from Westfield, Andy. I sped up and slowed down for 15 miles trying to shake him, but he held back as long as we were in traffic. When all the cars exited at Fredonia, he sped up and tried three times to wreck me, but I easily pulled away. Finally, he got beside me and fired, but I anticipated it when I saw him lower his passenger window, so I slammed on my brakes and the bullets overshot me.

"You think it was road rage?"

"No, Andy, this guy wanted to wreck me. Just like my parents, Andy. Just like the Watermans. So, you know who I think this was."

"Did you get a look at him?"

"No, his windows were tinted too dark."

"Did you get his plate?"

"No, he smeared it with mud, Andy."

"Where are you headed, Mac?"

"To a chemical analysis lab in Hamburg. I got the paint sample off Minetti's boat. We're going to compare it to the paint on Jim's boat."

"Mac, I warned you. Now, this is getting dangerous. You think this guy was out to stop you from poking your nose into those old deaths?"

"I do. And you let this guy get away, Andy!"

"Sorry, Mac, but you were the guilty one, pushing him. And you were driving way too fast for public safety."

"You gonna give me a ticket, Andy?"

"Not since you got shot at. I think that's enough excitement for one day."

"Thanks, Andy. Any chance of grabbing that Buick?"

"I'll radio his description, but he'll probably pull a U-turn at the next median and head back for Ripley so he doesn't have to exit through a toll booth. And I'm the only Trooper on this section this morning, so all I can do is call for a BOLO eastbound, then I'll head back west myself."

"He must have been watching my car somehow when I left the Harbor, Andy. Now I'm more interested than ever to see if these paint samples match."

"OK, well, slow it down. Get there safe, Mac."

"Will do, Andy. And thanks for believing my story."

"Of course, Mac. My Bar B counselor would never lie to me."

*****

Mac rolled into the Chem Systems parking lot at 8 a.m. He clutched five hundred dollars in his right hand and the two paint samples in his left as he pushed open the glass door and approached the counter with authority.

144

"Good morning!" he boomed, "I need two paint samples analyzed!" He dropped the $500 on the counter in front of a startled young woman in a white lab coat.

"We usually ask for an appointment," she said.

"My name is Mackenzie Morrison. I represent Attorney Morgan Hillman, who is in trial this week on a murder case. This is evidence that he vitally needs today. If this deposit is not enough, tell me what the cost is, and I will pay it."

"Well, please wait just a second, Mister..."

"Morrison, Mac Morrison. Would you like to speak with Attorney Hillman's secretary? She can confirm the urgency. Here, I'll call her."

Mac knew that when Morgan was in trial, Angie opened the office early. The phone buzzed once and she picked up. He put her on speaker.

"Attorney Hillman's office, how may I help you?"

"Ms. Morelli, this is Mackenzie Morrison, your investigator in New York. I have the samples and am at the chemical analysis laboratory now. I have implored them to do this urgent work while I wait. I know Attorney Hillman is in trial, and we need to get these results to determine *if* this is a match, and *if* we can determine that this was the boat that killed his client."

"I have told them that money is no object; we will pay whatever it costs, so long as they are competent to do the analysis and could give a deposition regarding this fatal accident. I have not told them that this case is related to four other deaths or that this may not be an accident, but murder. Did I state that correctly, Ms. Morelli?"

Picking up his cue, Angie replied.

"Who am I speaking with at the lab, please?"

"Uh, Brittany Coleman...*Doctor* Brittany Coleman, PhD, Molecular Chemistry and Biology, and half-owner of Chem Systems Lab. We are an ISO 9000 certified chemical and biological analysis laboratory, approved for DOD work. We have provided courtroom testimony in more than a dozen cases, including fatal car accidents."

"All right, well, I guess we will have to trust that you are qualified. Can you do this today?"

"We will have to adjust our schedule to make it a priority."

"What would that cost?"

"Mr. Morrison has given me a $500 deposit to begin. If it is more than that, it will simply be our hourly rate, plus equipment time and materials."

"That is acceptable," said Angie. "I will leave it to Mr. Morrison to describe what we need. Thank you for accommodating us. Mr. Morrison, please phone me the minute you have results, and ask the lab to email me the data sheets and explanation."

"Understood; thank you, Ms. Morelli. Goodbye."

"OK," said Mac, "who will be doing the analysis, Dr. Coleman?"

"I will. Now, what is it you are trying to determine?"

"The pilot of Boat A was fishing on Lake Erie when his boat was struck by another unknown boat, which we'll call Boat B. The scrapings in this jar were taken from the gunwale of Boat A, left by the impact from Boat B. The scrapings in the plastic sandwich bag were taken from a boat that we believe is Boat B."

"The impact of Boat B into Boat A killed Boater A, and the case has gone unsolved. His widow needs closure and the ability to sue for damages in her husband's wrongful death. Meanwhile, time is of the essence because we have every reason to believe this was not an accident, it was murder."

Dr. Coleman gasped.

"And, there is a link between this suspect and four other deaths dating back forty years. It is a very complicated and tragic case."

"So," Dr. Coleman continued the thought, "you want to know if we can determine if Boat B is the boat that, upon impact, left the deposited material in the jar taken from Boat A."

"Exactly."

"Well, let me get started. Have you had breakfast?"

"I have not, thank you for asking. Do you have a suggestion?"

"Yes, drive into old Hamburg to Boulangers Café, the best breakfast spot in town. It's on Main Street."

"Sounds like a recommendation."

"As soon as I have results, I will phone you."

*****

Mac got to the Chevy and called Angie.

"Attorney Morg…"

"Great performance!"

"Mackenzie Morrison! You could give a girl some notice! Did you make that up on the fly, you rascal?"

"I did. When Dr. Coleman balked, I had an inspiration, and it was you!"

"OK, Mac, remember its Gabriella's birthday. Did you call her?"

"Gonna call her right now."

"Did Roger get there OK?"

"He did. Thank you, and thank Morgan. Next couple of days will tell if my bluff pays off."

"Stay in touch. And Mac…"

"Yes?"

"Take care."

"Will do, Angie. Bye."

❋❋❋❋❋

8:30 a.m.

Boulanger's parking lot was almost full. Mac found a spot farthest from the front door and parked half on the grass. The tinkling of forks and knives, rattling of plates, and 'order up' calls meshed with the rush of busy waitresses as Mac pushed open the ancient glass and wood door. A server spotted him and pointed to an empty counter stool.

"Coffee?" she asked.

"Please. Any specials?"

"Bacon-cheese-avocado croissant."

"Sounds good."

"Five minutes, set your watch. Our kitchen is fast."

Mac spotted a 1950s era wood and glass phone booth. He left his coffee and slipped inside.

It was period correct, and could have come from a high school, judging by the carvings on the walls. Calls were 10 cents, and the mechanism was a rotary dial. He lifted the receiver, and, as expected, there was no dial tone. This was a quiet booth for cell calls. Genius!

Mac tapped his cell phone, and Gabby answered.

"Hi, Dad!"

"Happy Birthday, Honey."

"Thanks, Dad, how's the rebuild going?"

"It's going, in my absence. I'm building a new steel barn on the old pad, plus a large steel shed."

"That doesn't sound like a place to live."

"Nope, strictly work. I'm going to rent four bays in the barn and keep two. It will be for small contractors like me."

"What about a house? You still in Jordan's cabin?"

"When I'm there."

"OK, this is getting too deep. Where are you, and what are you up to, Dad?"

"I'm in Barcelona Harbor, New York, on Lake Erie. Came here to revisit my boyhood farm, but it's turned into something much bigger."

"Oh, not another Lone Ranger deal!"

"Afraid so, Honey. But don't worry, Roger's here to protect my backside."

"Dad, you are like Velcro™ to trouble!"

"Can't help it, Honey. So, you're 25, congratulations!"

"Thank you. Guess I'm supposed to feel all grown up, but honestly, life seems more complicated."

"Welcome to the big time, kid. You'll figure it out. How's the café job?"

"Not my cup of tea, but the first 3 days, I made $700 in tips working half-time."

"Well, you get a special birthday present this year, and it keeps on giving for the next eight years."

"Really? What is it?"

"It's a Trust, Gabby. Starting today, you can withdraw up to $25,000 a year for the next eight years. Hopefully, you will use this money to do something for your future, so you can have a better life. If you squander it, that's your privilege, but I hope you won't."

"One more thing, if you have a good reason, and need more than the annual draw, you can request it through Morgan. He has to get override permission from me. Got it?"

"Got it! Wow. I'm overwhelmed, thank you, Dad! This is so unexpected, and so generous, but don't you need the money to rebuild?"

"I'm going to sell some land. Already got one lot sold to Roger."

"You're not selling the back 15 acres on my pond, are you?"

"Nope; that's where I'm going to build us a cabin. Hey, my breakfast just arrived, so I gotta go. Just wanted to say love you, and happy 25th Sweetheart. Angie will call you to answer any questions and take your first year draw from the trust. Talk to you soon, OK?"

"OK! Thank you so much, Dad! Love you, bye!"

*****

After breakfast, Mac walked out to the Chevy, juggling his phone in one hand, and a coffee in the other, while pulling his keys from his pocket. His fingers slipped, and the keys dropped to the pavement with a 'clunk.'

"Well, better the keys than the coffee or my phone," he muttered.

He bent down to grab his keys, and a woman's voice behind him said, "While you're down there, could you see if my bracelet is under your car?"

Mac swiveled his head to see a very stylish woman of a certain age over-dressed for breakfast.

"Your bracelet, under my car?"

"Yes, you see, I put these bangles on this morning, but they're so big they slide off my wrist if I'm not wearing my big watch. I forgot to wear the watch, so when I got out of my car one of them fell off. I think it rolled under your car. I can't get down on my knees dressed like this, so when I went inside, I kept my eye out to see who owned this car."

"Oh! I'll have to lie down to see."

"Good of you, thank you. Its solid gold, otherwise I wouldn't bother."

"Of course," said Mac, smiling as he lay down on the asphalt.

"Yep, it's there, but I'm gonna have to slide under to get it."

"I hope you don't ruin your clothes, I'm sorry."

"It's OK...got it!"

As Mac slid back out, he was facing directly up at the underside of his chassis. He noticed a small black object the size of a matchbox stuck to it, with a bright dot glowing.

"Here's your bangle," he said, reaching out with his right hand while reaching up with his left and pulling at the black box. It was magnetic, but came away with a tug. He slid out from under the car, looking at it. It said GPS on it.

"Thank you so much. What do I owe you?" she said.

Mac looked up from a seating position.

"Owe me? You don't owe me anything, you did me a favor. I just saw something under there that needed attention."

"Oh! Well, that makes me feel better. Thank you again!"

"You're welcome."

Mac sat behind the wheel of the Chevy, staring at the little box. He held it to the steel dashboard and it stuck. He pulled it away and used his phone to Google 'tracking devices.'

This was a GPS tracker. The web site said, *'Magnetic, waterproof, 180 day battery. Follow on your cell phone. Uses satellite service, no cell towers.'*

"I underestimated these guys," Mac said out loud, "so, not only a spy camera, but also a tracking device. Now I know how that Buick followed me! So the question is: do I want to leave this on the car? Can I use that to my advantage, or do I trash it? And if so, where do I trash it?"

"Whoever is tracking this saw that I went to the lab, and they will be wondering, why? I don't want them to see where I am all the time, but it could be handy some of the time. Problem, how do you turn it off?"

He referred to the tracker website.

"Ah, long press on the square button, and the LED light should go off. OK, let's leave it on and go find a full service car wash."

Using his phone, he located the nearest drive-through full service wash.

"Full service with underbody wash," Mac said, handing cash to the attendant.

So the big '57 Chevy got a whirling brush wash, undercarriage cleaning, blow dry, and hand toweled by some busy young attendants. Mac tipped them $5.

"OK, now we press the Tracking device one long press, and, bingo, the light goes off, so it's off."

Just then, his phone buzzed.

"Hello?"

"This is Dr. Coleman at the Lab. I have results for you, Mr. Morrison. Are you nearby?"

"Be there in 20 minutes," Mac said.

He was as excited as a ten year old with a new bicycle. What did she find?

*****

Wednesday, May 24
Chem Systems Lab
10:45 a.m.

"Mr. Morrison, both samples are marine gelcoat."

"Sample B is called S1500 Moon Black Gelcoat. The sample was generous, and we had no problem identifying it."

"Sample A was a bit more difficult. These scrapings from a stainless steel rail were left by abrasive impact by a surface that was coated with a black substance. We rehydrated them using a chemical solution and determined that these scrapings also represent deposits of S1500 Moon Black Gelcoat."

"Can we tell from the two samples if Boat B is the one that left its deposit on Boat A?" Mac asked.

"No," she said, "and here's why. If I bumped into you, evidence of that collision, even if microscopic, is deposited on each other. For example, I could determine that you wore a navy blue pullover."

"But I could not determine that it was you specifically that bumped into me, unless I could sample your clothes to see if there was evidence of my clothing deposited on you."

"So, in this case," she said, "the metal gunwale of Boat A left some metal deposits on Boat B from their impact, but we would need to take samples from suspected Boat B to see if we could find metal particles that matched those from Boat A."

"Got it," said Mac. "And even if we could do that, it would not prove which boat was the striking boat and which was the struck boat."

"Correct. Furthermore, if the damaged boat had been sanded down and repaired with new matching black gelcoat, obtaining metal samples beneath the new gelcoat would be almost impossible."

"So," Mac said, "the gelcoat samples from Boat A and Boat B are identical in their manufacturing makeup. But that does not prove that Boat B is the boat that struck Boat A. Boat B could be any boat that was painted with Moon Black Gelcoat. Correct?"

"Correct."

"Doctor Coleman, what do I owe you?"

"Your $500 will cover it. Here is your receipt and your printed report."

"Will you please email a copy to Attorney Hillman? I've written the address on this card for you."

"Be glad to, and one favor, Mr. Morrison…"

"Yes?"

"This is an intriguing case, so would you let me know the outcome? I'm curious, and interested to have been part of it."

"Sure will. Thank you, Dr. Coleman, thank you very much."

✳✳✳✳✳

As soon as Mac was back in the Chevy, he called Roger.

151

"Anything happening, Rog?"

"Nope, but I had a great breakfast. This lady can cook! How about you, Mac, find out anything?

"The paint samples match, I found a tracking device under my car, had a high speed chase and got shot at. That's all."

"No shit?"

"No shit. Was in pursuit of the guy who shot at me, but I got stopped by Trooper Andy Gregor. The other guy got away."

"You think Trooper Andy let the other guy get away on purpose?"

"No, he saw me trying to wreck him at 120 miles an hour. He thought I was the bad guy."

"You had all the fun, Mac! Someone is really getting nervous about you, dude."

"Yep, but I think I know how to use this tracker to our advantage. Tell you when I get back. Be there in an hour. And Rog, do not tell Marybeth about my morning adventure!"

*****

Wednesday, May 24
Murphy B & B
12:30 p.m.

The smell of chili wafted through the house as Mac walked in the back porch door with its customary 'gronk' and 'whap'!

"You'd think by now I would either have fixed that, or gotten used to catching it before it whaps my ass," Mac said as Roger came to see who entered.

'Rowrf! Rowrf! Rowrf!' Buddy did a whirling welcome dance and pushed Mac backwards with giant paws to his chest.

"Oh, Buddy, you knew I was coming back. I missed you too! How are you all getting along?"

"Fine," said Marybeth. "Roger has told me a few of your escapades with him and Morgan. Sounds like the *Three Musketeers*24."

Mac looked at Roger. He wondered how much he had told her.

"Marybeth" said Roger, "the three of us saw a lot of evil in war, and we also learned special skills to defeat it."

Mac added, "So when we see a problem, sometimes we get involved."

"Oh, it's that simple is it?"

"Rog, how many bodies have we left behind?"

"Women with broken hearts? At least three dozen."

"You guys!" Marybeth quipped.

"I found a magnetic GPS tracker stuck to my car, so someone knows everywhere I've been, including my trip to the lab, and probably the airport," said Mac.

"We didn't want that known, did we?" said Marybeth.

"No, but it's too late now. Never would have found it except for an overdressed lady's bangle that rolled under the Chevy. Found it stuck to the chassis when I slid under to get it. Now the question is: who put it there, and when? I think it was done off-site."

"Really? Where, Mac?" said Marybeth.

"At the Cruise-In, probably by Joey Minetti. We know he was there. Remember, I parked next to Andy, and we walked down a ways so he could introduce me to Tim Riley. Our backs were turned, and we were a hundred feet from the Chevy. It would have been easy for someone to walk between the aisles, drop down, and stick it to the frame in five seconds. People are always looking under classic cars to see how they've been modified. No one would pay any attention."

Roger said, "But you didn't trash it?"

"Nope. It's pretty cool. The signal is bounced off satellites and read by your cell phone. It's sealed, waterproof, and does not need cell service. It can read you anywhere!"

"Amazing," said Roger.

"I turned it off at a drive thru car wash. Whoever is tracking me is going to think it got knocked off in there. If we get the opportunity to run my bluff, we'll reprogram it to Roger's cell phone. Now we have no worries about cell service on the lake."

"Well, this whole thing seems like layers on layers of complexity that only you can unwind, Mac," said Marybeth.

"And that's why it will work."

"Let's hope," said Marybeth. "We were waiting for you, so let's eat: homemade chili with garden herbs."

Mac said, "Roger and I will go see Pops after lunch and get him up to speed. Gotta make sure he stays in port until we need him. He needs full tanks, charged batteries, whatever."

"Meanwhile, Roger,"…Mac turned sideways and held three fingers down towards the ground, meaning Level Three, High Alert.

Roger nodded.

❊❊❊❊❊

Chapter Twenty Four

T he rain began as they ate lunch, gentle drops at first, then a pitter pat-
ter on the back porch roof, then a harder, more determined pelting against
the windows. The first booms of thunder echoed across the lake as lightning lit up darkened skies.

"Looks like a fast moving spring storm coming across the lake," Roger
said as he watched the Weather Channel on Marybeth's living room TV.

"All along, I've been thinking how to make them move," Mac said, "and
they've been playing with me. We have suspicions, but not enough to force
an action, like an inquest. There is nothing I can do officially about my
parent's death, but maybe..."

"Marybeth," said Mac, "where is your car? Not the Merc, your daily driver."

"My Outback? It's in the garage."

"May I use it?"

"Are you going out in this rain?"

"Yes. Would you make me copies of all the documents in this pouch?"

"OK."

When she left, Mac huddled with Roger.

"Roger, is Morgan licensed to practice law in New York?"

"I think so."

"Call Angie and ask her."

Roger walked into the hall to call. Thunder shook the house, tinkling
the Victorian crystal chandelier. Marybeth's Labradoodles huddled around
her feet at the copier.

Roger returned.

"He's licensed."

"Good. Call Angie back and have her email Marybeth the paperwork
to retain Morgan. I'll pay for it. Print them and have Marybeth sign
with witnesses."

"Where are you going?"

"To the Jamestown body shop that received her parents' car after the accident. If we get lucky, it wasn't crushed. Maybe it went to a junkyard for parts. Do *not* tell Marybeth. Let me see if this is a dead end first."

"You got a hook?"

"Maybe, let you know later. Remember, Level Three, Rog."

"No worries, Mac."

*****

2:00 p.m.

Marybeth's Subaru was perfect for three dogs, thunderstorms, and lake effect snows, Mac mused.

After 20 minutes of hard rain, he punched the satellite radio and found Richie Havens singing *Freedom$_{25}$*. Suddenly, the car was filled with that rasping soulful voice and frenzied guitar chords made only by his left thumb.

Freedom, freedom, freedom, freedom....

Sometimes... I feel...

Like a Motherless child

Whoa, ohh looooong... ways... from Home...

Just then the swift moving rain cloud turned north, and Mac drove out of the storm. The roads ahead were dry, bathed in sunshine.

The little voice inside the Outback's navigation system announced he was at his destination, Johnson's auto body shop. Mac turned up the radio and let Richie blare out the windows:

Sometimes I feel,

Like I'm already gone,

Soooo faaaaaaar from my home!

Mac shut off the radio and stepped out of the car.

A large black man with a regally shaved head looked up from an open garage door.

"That's Brother Richie at Woodstock," boomed the man's deep baritone.

Mac froze at the sound of his voice, instantly flashing back to the day in Kuwait when he lost 'Lonzo.

The booming baritone voice echoed again outside the fog of war in Mac's head, but Mac did not hear it. He was already far away, hearing explosions as he dragged 'Lonzo to cover from heavy gunfire, applying pressure to stop his bleeding, urging him to hang on for medics.

156

'Hang on 'Lonzo, hang on dammit!' But 'Lonzo could not hang on, and as his eyes rolled back in his head, he whispered 'Mac', before he slipped away and sent Mac spiraling down into a hellish hole of guilt.

Next, Mac was charging the sniper, screaming with blind rage at the top of his lungs, zig-zagging back and forth as bullets thudded into the sand around him until he lofted the grenade and it sailed through the open window and the concrete walls exploded with a 'BOOM'!

"HEY MAN!" the large man yelled, "YOU OK? You look like you seen a ghost."

Mac snapped back to the moment. He grasped for words.

"Sorry. Flashback. You reminded me of a buddy I lost in Kuwait. Alonzo Thompson, a good buddy. You look and sound a lot like him." Mac's voice broke. He turned away. "Sorry. So many emotions this week," Mac said.

"A death?" the big man asked.

"Five."

"Five deaths? Man, you got a right to be emotional."

"Mac Morrison," Mac said, extending his hand.

"Juan Johnson."

"Juan, I had many Black brothers in the Army. They were proud fighters who wore their emotions on their sleeve. You always knew how they felt. I liked that. White folks hide their emotions. It eats you up inside. Anyway, how did we get so soul-searching?"

"You were playin' Brother Richie Havens at Woodstock, man. My Momma used to play that album. She was the right age to be at Woodstock, but weren't many black folk goin' to Woodstock. Now, what has brought you here on this dark and stormy day, with the clouds just parting and the sun shining down on your arrival at my fine establishment? Sort of a sign from heaven, like Moses parting the Red Sea," he chuckled.

"Juan, two years ago, a wrecked car was towed here from Sherman Road in Ripley. It was a light colored 2010 Crown Victoria from a fatal accident that killed an elderly couple."

"You're describing the Waterman car."

"Yes, the Waterman car."

"I remember it well. I'm a qualified collision shop for Farmer's Mutual. Tow truck brought it here with pretty heavy damage in front of the engine. Grille, radiator, hood, windshield and even the fan were crushed, but the engine, transmission, and drivetrain were OK. Back end of the car was pretty much undamaged."

"Repairable?"

"Not worth it. Car was eleven years old."

"What happened to the car? Was it crushed?"

"Actually, I bought it from the Insurance. Sold some parts off it, but it's still here."

"Can I see it?"

"If you tell me the reason. You don't come out here two years after the accident if you don't have a reason."

"Juan. You have a military bearing. Am I right?"

"Captain, U.S. Army, twenty years."

Mac snapped to attention and saluted. "First Lieutenant Mackenzie Morrison reporting, Sir!"

"At ease, Lieutenant. I thank you for the respect. The Army's a great equalizer. We're all brothers in combat, like your buddy 'Lonzo Thomson. You broke up remembering him. No corporate white bread dude would even *know* a brother named Alonzo Thompson. We're Army, and proud of it."

"You are so right, Juan. Let's see that car, and I'll tell you the reason."

It was behind a large steel building, sitting on an asphalt pad. The crumpled hood was up and folded back on the roof. The engine and transmission were gone.

"Looks like you did sell some parts, Juan."

"Man, this was a good buy. I paid $1,000 for it; scored $3,000 selling the engine, tranny, radio, brake booster and seats. Now, what're you lookin' for, man?"

"I'm looking for this," Mac said, walking around to the rear and pointing to the back bumper.

"You looking for a plastic bumper-cover? This one's damaged, man."

"That's what I came to see. How much do you want for what's left of this car?"

"I'll take $200, if you tell me why. And I got a reason for asking."

"Deal. I'll pay you for storage if you move it inside and keep it locked up. No one's allowed to see it."

"Mac, are you a private investigator?"

"Nothing official. I'm looking into the deaths of five people over forty years. And this is a clue."

Juan paused, turned his head sideways and nodded to the far corner of his fenced lot.

158

"C'mere Mac. I want to show you the last car at the end of the row. Bet I can contribute another clue. Bein' Army, I gotta help you out."

It was an older State Trooper cruiser with the same body as the Waterman car, and Tim Riley's car.

Juan said, "This cruiser got hit in the ass by a distracted driver on the Thruway. Trooper was lucky he was writing a ticket, not in the car. Crushed the rear frame, so the insurer totaled it, and I bought it from them. Figured someday I'd find a Crown Vic hit in the front, take the two and make one ba-dass cop car. You know, cop motor, cop tires, cop suspension, cop shocks..."

"*Blues Brothers*[26]" Mac chuckled.

"Right on."

"So when you saw the Waterman car..." Mac said.

"I said here's the back end. But I had some personal issues at the time, so it just sat. Later, when I got back to work, there was a lot to catch up on, and I don't get paid for my own hobby cars, so I never got around to it. Someday, maybe I will. Now, here's what I want to show you."

Juan walked around to the front of the Patrol car.

"See the push bars?"

Mac nodded.

Juan reached into his overalls and pulled out a roll of masking tape. He peeled off one end and handed it to Mac.

"Put that on the outside of the push bar, left side, stick it down."

Mac did.

"OK, now I'll stretch the tape to the outside of the right push bar, stick it down and tear it off."

"OK, now," he pulled a black marker from a chest pocket in his coveralls, "let's mark the inside of each bar on the tape. OK?"

"Juan, you have been reading my mind."

"I figured. OK, let's match up the dents on the Waterman bumper."

They walked back to the pinkish Crown Vic and placed the tape on the marks.

"Perfect fit," Mac said.

"Yep," said Juan. "Perfect fit; this car was hit hard by a cop car with push bars."

"Like a State Trooper cruiser," Mac said.

"Yep, at some time, it was pushed. Don't know when..."

"Could have been pushed down into a ravine," Mac added.

159

"Could have," Juan said. "Not my affair. Don't pay to mess in cop business, if you get my drift."

"Not good for me to mess in cop business either."

"You stirring the pot, Mac?"

"To a boil."

"Man, be careful. Everybody knows everybody hereabout. Where you from?"

"My parents owned a vineyard in Ripley until they were killed. I was ten."

"That'd be the deaths forty years ago?"

"That'd be them."

"Where do you live now, man?"

"New Hampshire."

"But you're back here, poking your nose in old business. The hornets have left the nest to come after you, am I right?"

"Right as rain."

"Well, not good business for me to judge what cops say. I just fix the cars or scrap them. But I never understood why the Sheriff never made more out of that rear end damage, especially since it was fresh when towed in here. *Fresh damage, Mac*! And it's obvious it's from push bars on a cop car. They called it an accident. Yeah, it was an accident all right, but what caused it? You think it was pushed over the edge?"

"I do," said Mac.

"I know that road," Juan said. "Lotta wrecks. Couple people a year get hurt on those curves."

"Here's $200," said Mac, handing him two bills. "Do you have the title?"

"I do."

"Sign it over, and I'll give you $100 for the first month's storage, is that fair?"

"That's good, Mac."

"When I'm done with the car, I'll give it back to you, Juan. Looks like you still have enough to put together one badass cop car someday."

"Good deal, man. Let's go get that title and exchange cell numbers."

*****

"Funny thing," said Juan, handing the Waterman title to Mac.

"What's that?"

160

"I kept that car for two years. Could have sold it to this one dude several times, now you come in here, a total stranger, and I sell to you."

"Maybe I had the better story."

"You did. This other dude, Joe Minetti, he had a bullshit story. He has a body shop over in Ripley. He wanted that car real bad. Him and his buddy came over and looked at it."

"Is his buddy a big dude, big as you, about 60, military haircut?"

"That's the one. "

*****

Chapter Twenty Five

Wednesday, May 24
Driving the east side of Lake Chautauqua
3:00 p.m.

Mac's phone buzzed. "Still in one piece?" said the voice.

"Morgan! I thought you were in trial."

"Hillman's the name, acquittal's my game. Six-figure payoff, which allows me to help poor schmucks like you and my new widow client. Angie emailed the docs, and Mrs. Murphy signed them. So, what do you need me for?"

"I need you to reopen an official investigation into three deaths from two years ago. They are linked, in my opinion, the killer is still running around, and he could be a former state cop. If so, he just happens to be the same young state trooper who was at the scene of my parents' fatal accident 40 years ago. Which was no accident: it was an execution. It was planned. He may have been covering for his good buddy 40 years ago, who is the guy who pushed my parents into the path of an oncoming truck."

"Mac, next time you decide to take a vacation, just stay home where we can keep an eye on you."

"And what would you do for fun? Look, Morgan, I've got a lot of speculation and a little bit of evidence. If you could demand an inquest, maybe we can get the bad guys out in the open to make another play for me."

"*Another* play, Mac?"

"Someone shot at me today while I was driving. It was no road rage, it was planned. They had a tracker on my car, which I discovered later. Unfortunately, I have no clue who it was, because the cops let him get away."

"OK, Mac, I'm coming down there, and I better bring Angie."

"Great. Morg, I'm pretty sure we have a leak in the law enforcement community. A guy I'm looking at could have friends at every level of the cops, but we should be able to trust the Bureau of Criminal Investigation. Marybeth's husband was a BCI Investigator. He was killed in a boating accident...which, in my opinion, was not an accident, it was another execution. I'm sure BCI would like to avenge their own, but we gotta tread lightly because, as I said, the guy that could be the killer is a retired New York State Trooper, now working for the BMV."

"Mac, I am friends with Colonel Trammel Bradford, head of the New Hampshire State Police. In a delicate situation like this, it would be a great help if I had a letter of introduction from him. Even better, a phone call from him to the Field Superintendent of the New York State Police, outlining the delicate nature of the inquiry, not making any accusation but requesting discreet cooperation by a top trusted investigator in New York BCI to assist us relating to the death of Investigator James Murphy. I'm sure that will get their attention," said Morgan. "We will make whatever evidence you have available to them, and let them determine if they see enough to reopen the file on the death of Investigator Murphy."

"See? I knew I needed you, Morg."

"Well, because my trial ended early, I've got a few free days. We can fly out first thing in the morning. Angie says it's a short flight, so pick us up at Jamestown around 8:30 a.m. Do I need tactical gear?"

"Hope not; just your crafty legal mind."

"I'll pack a piece or two just in case, and check on concealed carry laws on my way down."

"Good idea. Now that I got shot at, we need to gun up legally. Trooper Andy Gregor from State Police Troop A was at the scene when shots were fired. He is a friend and will vouch for me."

"I'll try. And Mac..."

"Yes?"

"Don't do anything stupid until I get there."

*****

Wednesday, May 24
3:45 pm

'Rowrf! Rowrf! Rowrf!' Buddy did his welcome home dance and pranced all around Mac.

"Hey, Buddy, gimme a smooch."

"Rog, all good here?"

"All good, Mac."

163

"Morgan and Angie will be here in the morning. Marybeth, you have a room, right?"

"They'll have my best suite on the second floor."

"Great."

"So, Mac, are you going to tell me why I need an attorney?"

"Yes, M, after dinner. What do I smell?"

"Chicken Tetrazzini, baked French bread and raspberry pie. Let's have a nice candlelight dinner in the dining room. Buddy can stay on the porch. Not because his manners are bad, but because you won't behave with him under the table."

"Got you again, Mac," Roger said.

"Buds, you and I are in the dog house."

"OK, boys, dinner at 6:30 sharp."

"Rog, Buddy can guard Marybeth for a few minutes. Let's walk across the street and talk to Pops."

*****

"How do you know he'll ask you to go out fishing?" Pops said.

"He already asked," Mac said, "so I can call him, and he'll take me."

"Mac, that plan's got a lot of problems," said Roger. "Let's wait and see what Morgan comes up with first. We should give him the complete briefing, show him all the evidence, and let him call the shot. You are too close to this one."

"I agree with you, Rog. We'll give Morgan first chance, but if he can't get these guys, *I will*! It's my parents. I can't let this go unpunished. And now that I figured out what really happened to Marybeth's husband and her parents..."

"Wait a minute; what do you think happened to her parents?"

"Let you know after dinner. It's all speculation, but I know I'm right. OK, thanks Pops. Stay ready and gassed up. I'm paying expenses."

*****

May 24
7:00 p.m.

"Never had tetrazzini before, Marybeth, but now it's one of my favorite meals."

"Thank you, Roger. I like to please with my cooking. Now, Mac, what did you do in Jamestown?" asked Marybeth.

"Let's clear the dishes. I'm gonna tell you quite a story."

✶✶✶✶✶

"Marybeth, was your parent's car ever pushed by a State Trooper's vehicle?"

"That's a strange question. No. Why?"

"Did Tim Riley ever push your parent's car with his old cruiser?"

"No."

"Did your parents have enemies?"

"No. I wouldn't even call Tim Riley an enemy."

"What were their jobs?"

"Mom was an accountant. Dad was an executive search consultant for college presidents."

"OK, focus on your Mom. What kind of accounting did she do?"

"Forensic."

"Do you know what she was working on at the time of her death?"

"No. Accountants can't divulge their audits, Mac."

"But think back, any little comment she might have made in the months prior."

"No. I mean, well...there was one ironic coincidence. Jim and I talked about it."

"What?"

"Mom's firm was hired to do an audit for a trade group of food distributors. They collected dues to pay for advertising and lobbyists."

"How big an organization?"

"All of western New York, some of central New York and northwestern Pennsylvania."

"Hundreds of members?"

"More like thousands."

"What was the ironic part?"

165

"Well, you know how clubs elect officers. The Treasurer of the Western New York Food Distributors Association was…Rosemary Minetti."

"Bingo!" said Mac, snapping his fingers.

"What, Mac?"

"Tomorrow morning, you are going to call your Mom's accounting firm and find out who took over that audit, and what happened."

"Oh, I don't have to wait until tomorrow, Mac. I know what happened."

"What?"

"The WNYFDA members hired an attorney to find a hundred thousand dollars they suspected had been embezzled. That was public information because he filed a lawsuit accusing the three officers."

"The officers, including Rosemary Minetti as Treasurer, countersued claiming libel, etc."

"The WNYFDA attorney hired Mom's firm to do the audit. Mom was preparing to give him her findings, but all of a sudden, the WNYFDA membership dropped the case."

"Wait a minute," said Mac. "Exactly when did that happen: before or after your Mom's death?"

"After. I remember because they came and took her work laptop. I had to let them into her house."

"Oh, man, there is your motive, right there! Your Mom's audit found something hinky. If the lawsuit had entered the discovery phase, they would have had to turn over their financials. Maybe restitution was made by the officers, specifically by Rosemary Minetti, and the missing money got 'found' by the members. They dropped the suit to avoid defending themselves from the officers' libel suit."

"That's it, Marybeth! Rosemary made restitution and cooked the books. They had to get the laptop, but your Mom, she would still be a problem, she would still know. And once she reported her findings to the Attorney… they had to get her too."

"Marybeth, brace yourself."

"What, Mac?"

"I believe your parents' death was no accident. They did not lose control, run off the road and plunge down a ravine by accident. They were pushed. And I believe Tim Riley's old Patrol car pushed them. But now the question is: who was driving that car?"

"WHAT?" she shrieked, "Mac, what are you saying?"

"I have recovered evidence from your parents' car."

166

"WHAT?" she covered her ears with her hands, "wha... what is happening?"

"You want to know the truth, don't you?"

She was trembling, but this time, Mac could see her face turning dark with anger.

"IT'S THE MINETTI CRIMINAL ENTERPRISE!" she shouted.

"THE MINETTI FREAKING CRIMINAL ENTERPRISE! They killed my husband...and my parents, too? Damn right I want to know the truth. I WANT TO MAKE THEM PAY!"

"They ruined my life, my husband's life, and my parents' life? Oh! I'm sorry, Mac! They ruined your life, too. They killed your parents!"

"So, Marybeth, now murder has come to Barcelona Harbor, right into your not-so-safe B & B. And the question becomes, what are you going to do about it? You said you'd help me find Jim's killer. OK, here's your chance. We have one case, one chance for the law to handle it, if we help them."

"Which one?"

"Your parents," said Mac. But we've got to move fast to get Riley's cruiser impounded. That car is the smoking gun in your parents' death. Morgan has to take this over as your attorney and file some kind of motion with BCI to reopen your parent's death. Meanwhile, I need to set a trap."

"You know Marybeth? I might have been wrong about Tim Riley. I was forming this picture of an unstable psycho; I'm talking first impressions. That was sloppy on my part. I was letting myself point at the obvious, but there could be a different side to this. Maybe Tim Riley is actually a pathetic, mentally compromised schmuck, who still needs to work part time to make ends meet, and who can't afford a new car, so he drives his old patrol car."

"Well," said Roger, I think you're right about one thing, Mac. Riley retired and immediately took a job at the BMV. You said he needed money for his wife's medical bills, OK, that fits. But why did he get that specific job? Was it so he could help his 'best bud', Joey Minetti, to modify high-end stolen cars with legit parts from Gino's salvage business, so he, as BMV inspector Tim Riley, could pass them?"

"Rog," said Mac, "I agree. I bet if we checked the BMV log of cars that Inspector Tim Riley has passed, we would find a pattern of expensive cars titled to Gino Minetti. Joey modifies stolen cars using Gino's legit trackable parts, then Riley gives them the green light, and the BMV issues a salvage title. The cars get sold for big bucks, probably online. Riley probably gets a kickback from the Minettis for each car."

"So Tim Riley could just be a pathetic, mentally compromised schmuck, a tool used by the Minetti Criminal Enterprise," Marybeth repeated, half dazed.

"Point is," said Mac, "I've only been looking at Tim Riley in Jim's and the Waterman's deaths."

"Why only Tim?" asked Marybeth.

"If the *Deadly Serious* is the boat that hit Jim, I initially figured Tim was the one piloting it, because he goes fishing so often. I can't prove it's the death boat, but I'm pretty sure of it, and Pops believes it, too. He saw that boat come back with a big scrape on it the day Jim died, but *Joey Minetti* was piloting it. It's been expertly repaired, obviously, because Joe Minetti is an expert in body repair."

"But, we don't know *who* could have been piloting that boat at the time Jim was killed. It could have been Tim Riley, or Joey Minetti, or someone else. And we don't know who was driving Riley's car when it struck your parents' car. But first, we have to prove Riley's car was the murder weapon. Your parents' case is the best case, M."

"How can we do that?" asked Marybeth.

"I bought their car from the Jamestown body shop where it was towed two years ago," Mac said. "It was still there. There are two distinct dents with black paint scrapes in the plastic back bumper-cover. I measured against the push bars on a junk State Trooper car at the body shop. The width between the dents was a perfect match. Now we need to get Riley's car to actually match the push bars against those dents."

"Oh my Gawd!" Marybeth started shaking again.

'Arf arf arf arf arf!'

"Come here, my babies, I need a hug!" She picked up all three of her dogs and held them tight to her chest. The largest growled at Mac as if to say, 'Why are you hurting my Mommy?'

Mac continued, "In my parents' death, there is no physical evidence that can be used to bring Joey Minetti to justice forty years after the fact. And in Jim's death, it's gonna be almost impossible to get physical evidence off Minetti's boat, now that it has been repaired."

"They botched both those cases, Marybeth. Sloppy police work, intentional or unintentional, but my guess is that Tim Riley had something to do with those reports. Even if we could build a mountain of circumstantial evidence, Minetti will never crack. But maybe I can get something from Tim Riley."

"How?" Marybeth asked.

"If there is a sliver of good in Tim, I can try to turn him, make him give up Joe Minetti," Mac said.

"Failing that, Mac and I can 'persuade' him with...*other means,"* said Roger.

"Like the excavation contractor and the beaver dam," Marybeth said. "Oh, my God! I can't believe this is happening! Here I was, running a peaceful B & B, you sweep in here, take over my life...and now this!"

"It's why we're here," said Roger, "it's what we do. But it's a last resort. Look, guys, we got our ace lawyer, Morgan Hillman, coming tomorrow. Let's all calm down and have a quiet evening. Tomorrow, we'll brief him and show him the locations of these so-called accidents."

"Right," said Mac, "My hope is he'll be able to demand an inquest into the Waterman's death. He has to work it through BCI since they are the overseer in cases of police error, or corruption."

"MAC!" shouted Marybeth. "THAT IS ENOUGH FOR ONE NIGHT! NO MORE MINETTI TALK! Please!"

"Agreed," said Mac.

"All right," she said, "geez, Mac, just let a girl catch her breath, OK?"

"OK, Marybeth, sorry, it's a lot, I know."

"OK, guys," she said, "Let's have a quiet, candlelit dessert on the back porch...with a bottle of 30-year-old cognac! Tomorrow we'll look forward to meeting Attorney Hillman, then the Three Musketeers can put their heads together and make a plan."

❖❖❖❖❖

May 24
11:59 p.m.

The rain returned at midnight. Thunder shook the little cottage as lightning flashes pulsed through the curtains. Mac was glad the Bel Air was safely locked up in the barn. Things were beginning to stir, and his juices were beginning to flow. He was on the hunt, and it felt good.

"MOM, DAD," he said out loud, "I'll get'em!"

Then he dropped back to sleep, with Buddy's back tucked against his leg.

169

Chapter Twenty Six

Thursday, May 25
5:30 a.m.

Hard rain fell all night. Near dawn, Mac heard the last drips in the downspout. He pulled back the curtain. The rain gauge held four inches of water, but a bright sky promised good weather.

"Gonna be a nice day, Budso."

'Woof!'

Mac slipped into his all-terrain pants, stretched a tee shirt over his wide shoulders and stepped into running shoes.

Buddy led the way outside, tail held high and eyes scanning for Poppa Mac. The spy camera was still pointing in the wrong direction, and the light was out. Mac wondered what his nemesis was thinking. He'd lost his eyes on the cottage, and he'd lost his tracker on the Chevy. He knew Mac had been to a lab in Hamburg, but what else had he surmised? Had he seen him go to the Waterman death scene? Had to presume he did.

The strawberries were bursting on the vine, so Mac picked a bunch for Marybeth's breakfast group. The Steinakers would be checking out this morning. He went to the Captain Murphy website's calendar. The weekend was free, but the following weekend was Memorial Day, and all rooms were booked.

"So we gotta be outta here by then," Mac said to Buddy. He was thinking about his new barn and shed. He needed to put out the word and get them rented. *He stopped right there*. No. He was close, he could smell it. He needed to stay focused on this situation.

He decided to use the tracker to his advantage, so he and Buddy trotted out to the barn, crunching on soggy pea gravel. He unlocked the door and backed out the Chevy. It was a short distance to Todd's Gas n Go. As Mac stuck the nozzle in the gas tank, Buddy growled.

"Up early, like a fisherman," boomed the voice behind him.

"Tim Riley!" Mac said, spinning around to see 'Officer Tim Riley', in his BMV uniform.

"Going into work today, Tim?"

"Yeah, got inspections in Fredonia. Boy, you keep your Chevy clean."

"Ran it through a car wash, even did the undercarriage. No fishing for you today, Tim?"

"Nope; maybe tonight, but the offer still stands, Mac. If you want to go out, give me call."

"Let's do it, Tim."

"OK, I'll find you, Mac." There was a menacing undertone to Tim's words.

Tim Riley backed his old black Patrol car to pull around the Bel Air. As he did so, Mac got a close look at its push bars. And, unbelievably, there was a pinkish scratch six inches long on the driver's side bar!

*****

Thursday, May 25
Jamestown Airport
8:30 a.m.

The King Air touched down at 8:15 a.m. Morgan Hillman jumped down the steps like leaping into a war zone. Angie Morelli stepped down with athletic grace, carrying a laptop case and small clothes bag.

"Thanks for coming, Morg, Angie!" Mac shouted over the din of the plane's propellers as it twirled around in preparation for takeoff.

"Easy flight, very relaxing," Morgan said once he and Angie settled into the Chevy.

"Morgan, I'm going to tell you the damnedest story. We'll stop for coffee and briefing before you see murder exhibit A. Then we hit the library, where Morgan is going to role-play the heavy."

"Oh boy!" said Morgan, rubbing his hands with glee. "Start at the beginning."

"Well, it all began with my parents' death, and Abe's mysterious envelope."

"Cut to the chase Mac."

An hour later, Mac loaded them in the Chevy.

"OK, guys," Mac said, "now you know what I know."

*****

171

Thursday, May 25
Johnson's Body Shop, Jamestown
9:30 a.m.

"Juan Johnson, meet my attorney and friend Morgan Hillman, and his secretary Angelica Morelli."

"Juan," said Morgan, "thank you for preserving important evidence. Can we take a look?"

"Sure, right this way." Juan led them into the garage, pointed to a bay, and pulled back the car cover.

"So Juan," Morgan said, "this car came to you two years ago. Did you tow it?"

"No, a local company towed it from the accident. It has been secure in my yard ever since. I'm a qualified repair shop for Farmer's Mutual, the owner's insurer. They totaled it. I bought it, and sold all the parts that are gone. I was gonna use the back end to repair an old Crown Vic cop car."

"Mac noticed these dents," Morgan said, pointing to the Waterman bumper. "He said they appear to be damage from push bars typically found on certain State Trooper cars."

"We did a tape comparison to the bars on the wrecked Trooper car I have out back. The width between dents matched."

"Has anyone other than yourself and the insurance rep touched this car?"

"No. Any parts I sold, I removed myself. But there was a dude who owns a body shop in Ripley..."

"Joey Minetti Jr," Mac interjected.

"Yeah, Joey Minetti, he pestered me to sell him the car. Came here a day after the accident. I told him I'd sell the engine and transmission, but he wanted the whole car."

"Juan, we may be stirring up this fatal accident, and this car is material evidence. It's possible someone may come here wanting to see this car. It needs to stay inside and undercover. If anyone asks, simply say it has been disposed of."

"Got it."

*****

172

Thursday, May 25
William A. Banks Memorial Library
10:30 a.m.

Mac pulled the Chevy as close to the front door as he could, and gave the tuned horns a blast that echoed off the stone edifice.

Rosemary Minetti peered out the window, saw the Chevrolet, and dropped the curtain with a shiver.

"OK, here we go," Morgan said. "Let me do the talking. I'm going to sweep in and bowl her over."

He put on his dark suit coat and tie, held his head up, and charged through the front door with a swiftness that even caught Mac and Angie off guard.

"GOOD MORNING!" Morgan boomed as he strode up to the front desk.

Rosemary Minetti looked up over her reading half-glasses, startled.

"My name is Attorney Morgan Hillman. I have been retained to investigate certain events that should have been covered by the local newspapers two years ago. May I have the pleasure of your name Madam?"

He held out his card.

"I, I'm Rosemary Minetti, I'm the Librarian...Chief Librarian!" she said, regaining some poise. She took the card and looked at it.

"New Hampshire?"

"You will note it says licensed in New York as well. Could you kindly assist me to find whatever resources you have regarding two events from two years ago?"

Rosemary pushed her glasses down on her nose and adjusted the sleeves of her baggy gray sweater.

"Do you have the dates?"

"I do. Sunday, April 4, and Sunday June 6, 2021." He drew a folded paper from his vest pocket and laid it on the counter. "The first event is the death of Mr. and Mrs. John Waterman, and the second is the death of BCI Investigator James Murphy. Do you remember those events Ms. Minetti?"

"Uh...yes, I think so...it's a small town."

"Good. Where do we begin?"

"The Westfield Press articles are on-line. The Jamestown Journal and Buffalo News may also have something."

"May we use two computers so my confidential secretary can assist me?"

"Those two over there."

"Can we print out?"

"Send to the printer on the wall, 25 cents per page."

"Thank you."

Mac slipped out the front door and dialed Morgan's cell.

Inside the library, Morgan's phone buzzed.

"Go!" said Mac, as Morgan answered his call.

"GOOD MORNING COLONEL JUSTICE!" Morgan shouted loud enough to be heard throughout the library.

"YES SIR, THANK YOU VERY MUCH. I DID, YES HE CALLED ME AND ASSURED ME OF YOUR AGENCY'S FULL COOPERATION. I HAVE THE POLICE ACCIDENT REPORTS. YES, I'M STARTING HERE IN TOWN, AND THEN I WILL LOOK AT THE OTHER EVIDENCE GATHERED BY MY IN-VESTIGATOR. ONCE I'VE DONE THAT, I WILL MEET WITH YOU BEFORE WE FILE AN INQUEST ON THE WATERMAN CASE. I'LL BE LOOKING AT THE EVIDENCE WE HAVE ON THE MURPHY DEATH ALSO. YES, SIR, YOU WILL BE THE FIRST TO KNOW, AND I WILL COORDINATE WITH BCI AS YOU KINDLY OFFERED. THANK YOU COLONEL JUSTICE."

He hung up and said, "I'm sorry, Ms. Minetti, where was I?"

"Uh, sending to the printer. Is that all you need? If not, I must get ready for other patrons."

"Yes, I can see you are very busy, thank you so much." There were no other patrons; the library was empty.

Rosemary slipped into the side room. This time, she shut the door behind her with a 'thunk.'

Mac reappeared inside the front door and nodded to Morgan. Morgan spoke in a hushed tone.

"Mac, this is going to take a while. I have access to some records courtesy of the real Colonel Justice. After he spoke with Colonel Bradford of the New Hampshire State Police, he called me to give me his personal cooperation. If he has a serial killer in his ranks, even retired, he wants to be first to know.

"Angie is going to be searching for the WNYFDA lawsuit online. If Rosemary Minetti checks our browser history like a nosey Minetti, she'll know how deep we are going after them, and that should elicit a reaction. I suggest you go back to the B & B and wait for my call."

"OK Morgan. Are you carrying?"

"Yes, got temporary permits for me and Roger from Colonel Justice, although I think you're the one who needs one. Colonel Bradford personally vouched for us and confirmed we had valid permits in New Hampshire. Colonel Justice checked with Trooper Gregor. He confirmed you were shot at."

"Morgan, it's better for me naked. With the leaks inside law enforcement, I don't want adversaries to know I'm armed. I want them to come after me. An unarmed target is better bait."

*****

Thursday, May 25
10:40 a.m.

Mac's phone pinged as he walked out to the Chevy: incoming text. *Dr. Coleman. Please call me.*

She answered Mac's return call the first ring.

"Mr. Morrison! Thank you for calling. I am very sorry to inform you that there has been a slip-up in our internal procedure here."

"What, you got the test results wrong?"

"No, no, the results are good. No, I'm afraid that one of our summer interns was handling the front desk early this morning when the Officer came in. She unfortunately divulged some information about your tests to him. He was a very large man in uniform who showed a badge for the New York State Police. She was intimidated. He asked what work you had done, and she retrieved it."

"She didn't give him a copy, but she did tell him the gist of what we tested for, Boat A, Boat B. And I'm afraid I had told her it could be linked to a murder case, and she was so excited she blabbed that too. But she did not give him a copy of the report."

"Tall man, about 60?"

"Yes."

"Was he wearing a New York State Trooper Uniform?"

"That was the funny thing. We have a security camera, so when I found out what she had done I replayed the video. He was very persuasive, and she wilted under the pressure. I am so sorry."

"What was the funny thing?"

"I got stopped by a Trooper last week. He was nice and just gave me a warning. So, I know what a State Trooper uniform looks like. This man

175

was not wearing a Trooper uniform. It looked official, but not the right patches or colors."

"And he showed a State Trooper badge?"

"Yes, it's on the video."

"OK, what's done is done. I appreciate your calling me. Under no circumstance are you to release that report to anyone but me, and you are to retain those samples until I tell you they are no longer needed. Please preserve that video of his visit and email a copy to me and to Attorney Hillman's office."

"Yes, absolutely, Mr. Morrison, and once again, I can't tell you how bad I feel about this. We pride ourselves on our secure data. This has never happened before."

"It's going to be all right, Dr. Coleman. Thank you."

*****

Thursday, May 25
Inside the private conference room at the William Banks library
10:45 a.m.

Rosemary Minetti fumbled her cell phone out of the saggy cardigan and punched the screen.

"Yeah, Rosie?"

"Joey, we got a bigger problem. Morrison just came back with an attorney. He's looking into the accidents that killed Jim Murphy and the Watermans. He's in the library now. And he got a phone call from someone called Colonel Justice, who sounded like BCI. He was talking about an inquest."

"I don't like the sound of that. Let me call Tim."

"Joe...Morrison is driving the Chevy, it's easy to spot."

"OK. The tracker stopped working after he drove through a car wash. Let me call it up on my phone. Oh, hey! It's working! I'll be watching him from my shop. This is good, this is good. Ciao."

*****

Officer Tim Riley's cell phone rang at the BMV station. "Hey, Joey," he said.

176

"We got a problem, Tim." Joe repeated Rosemary's report word for word.

"Colonel Justice? She said Colonel Justice?"

"She did."

"Mmm. That's bad."

"Who is he, Tim?"

"Colonel Samuel Justice is Field Superintendent of the New York State Police, all branches, including BCI. But you might have another problem, Joey."

"What?"

"I followed the tracker coordinates and found the place Morrison went to. It's a chemical analysis lab in Hamburg. He had them run some tests on black paint from two boats, trying to determine if one boat struck another. It was supposed to be related to a murder. The paints were a close match, but they couldn't prove anything. You had a big scrape on the *Deadly Serious* the day Murphy drowned, Joey. Something you want to tell me about that?"

"I told you, I hit a log. State Police, huh? Tim, remember that body shop in Jamestown where the Waterman car was taken two years ago?"

"Course I remember."

"Go see if the car is still there. If it is, we need to get it. Use your old badge."

"Why, Joe?"

"Just do this for your best bud, OK Tim? I'll explain later if the car is still there, and you can get it."

As Joe Minetti clicked off the call, he went back to the GPS tracker and watched the Chevy drive down Route 394 towards Barcelona Harbor.

*****

Thursday, May 25
Captain Murphy B & B
11:00 a.m.

'Gronk!' groaned the wooden screen door. 'Whap!' it went as it slammed behind Mac.

"Hello?" called Marybeth. 'Rowrf!' alerted Buddy.

"It's Mac!"

Roger stepped onto the porch with his hand on his Colt pistol. "Are they here?" he asked Mac.

"Yes, I dropped them at the library. Morgan got a personal call from the Field Superintendent of the New York State Police, and he issued both of you carry permits. Then we faked that call out loud for Rosemary Minetti, leaving out the part about guns. I think he gave her quite a scare, definitely stirred the pot."

"Tell us," Marybeth said.

Mac gave them a full report of the sketch Morgan played out.

"Bet her first call was to Joey," Marybeth said.

"And his next call was to Tim Riley," Mac said. "Now that they know State Police is involved, they will be starting to panic."

"So they'll make a counter move," Roger said, "we gotta be alert."

"Tim Riley already made one stupid move by coercing the Chem Systems lab into telling him about our paint tests," said Mac. "But I think that's gonna be to our advantage. Ratchet up the pressure."

"Unless this gets resolved quickly, I might have to close," said Marybeth. "That would disappoint a lot of people, and be a bad start to my summer."

"Well," said Mac, "let's take it an hour at a time, a day at a time. Roger is right, the pot is simmering; when it boils, stuff will happen fast."

*****

Thursday, May 25
Johnson's Body Shop, Jamestown, New York
11:30 a.m.

"MR. JOHNSON!"

Juan Johnson was hammering out a body panel. He looked up to see the shadow of a large man standing in the open garage door. With glaring sunlight behind him, it was impossible to see his face.

"Yes?"

"I'm Officer Tim Riley, Inspector for the New York State Department of Motor Vehicles, and Special Investigator for State Police." He flashed his former Trooper badge and quickly put it back in his pocket.

"Two years ago, you received a wrecked vehicle from a fatal accident on Sherman Road near Ripley. I am here to inquire if you still have that vehicle."

Juan moved so he could see the man's face. He recognized him as the buddy that came with Joe Minetti two years prior.

"This is an official inquiry," Riley said, keeping his hat brim tilted down to hide his face. "BMV has been tasked with finding and impounding the vehicle for New York BCI."

"What vehicle?"

"A 2010 Ford Crown Victoria, light rose color, VIN ..."

"The Waterman car?" Juan said.

"Uh, yes, the victim's name was Waterman. Do you still have that car?"

"I sold most of the parts and disposed of that car, Officer Riley."

"Well, just to be sure we are talking about the same vehicle, do you mind if I look out back at your wrecks? I will be looking at VINs to properly ID the vehicle."

"Help yourself, Officer."

"Thank you. I'll just be a few minutes while I check your cars."

Officer Riley turned the corner and walked to the rear of the windowless building.

Juan looked at Officer Riley's vehicle. It was an old Crown Victoria Police Interceptor resprayed black, not an official BMV car. He looked closely at its push bars. The side of one bar had a very distinctive pink stripe. Juan whipped out his cell phone and snapped several photos. Then he snapped a photo of the dashboard VIN. Next, he grabbed a roll of masking tape and a razor knife and quickly placed it under the pink stripe while he scraped pink paint onto the sticky tape.

Then, he went back to work on the body panel. In a minute, the shadow of Officer Riley loomed large in the doorway against the backdrop of bright sun.

"OK, Mr. Johnson, I did not see it. Your other vehicles checked out. Thanks for your cooperation."

Tim Riley backed his black Crown Vic and sped off. As soon as he was out of sight, Juan pulled out his cell phone, tapped Mac's number, and sent him an email with three photos attached. Then he called him.

"Mac?" It's Juan Johnson in Jamestown."

"Hey, Juan."

"Just had a visitor. BMV Officer Tim Riley, who said he was a 'Special Investigator' for the New York State Police. Flashed a State Trooper badge, said he was here on an official visit for BCI, looking to impound a specific vehicle involved in a fatal accident 2 years ago."

"The Waterman car," said Mac.

"Yep. I played like I had never seen him before, but this is Joe Minetti's buddy, the one who came here two years ago. A guy that big is easy to re-member. He put on a show about an official investigation being reopened into that wreck. I got the whole thing on my security cam. He said he had to find the Waterman car to impound it. I told him I had disposed of it. He wanted to go out back and check my wrecks to see if the car was gone."

"Did he go out back, Juan?"

"He did. And while he did, I took pictures of his old black patrol car. The one you're interested in."

"He drove that to make an official call to your business?" said Mac, incredulously.

"He did. I got three good close ups, just emailed to you. There is pink paint on one push bar."

"Wow! Great work Juan. Quick thinking."

"Even better, Mac. I pulled a pink paint sample off his push bars. Got it stuck to a piece of tape here in my shop. I figured you might want to come get it."

"Juan, you might have cracked a murder case, man. Be there in half an hour."

✷✷✷✷✷

"They made their countermove," Mac said to Roger and Marybeth. "We need to call Morgan. I'll put it on speaker."

"Morgan?"

"Yeah, Mac."

"Go outside where you can talk."

"OK, gimme a sec... OK, go."

"Juan Johnson just had a surprise alleged 'official' visit from BMV Of-ficer Tim Riley, who claimed to be a 'Special Investigator' of the New York State Police. He said he was there to impound the Waterman car for 'an official BCI investigation.' Sloppy. He showed up in BMV uniform driving his retired patrol car, flashing a State Trooper badge."

"Wow, that didn't take long," Morgan said. "So, Rosemary took the bait and called Joe, Joe called Tim, and Tim immediately went to the body shop."

"Yeah, listen," Mac said, "Tim saw me at the gas station this morning. He told me he was going to Fredonia to do inspections. But, no, he's been a busy boy. First, he went to the lab in Hamburg and conned them into giving him the results of my paint tests. They got him on video impersonating a State Trooper. Check your email for that video. Dr. Coleman should have sent it by now."

"Next, he shows up at the body shop and tries to con Juan Johnson into giving up the Waterman car. Again, he was impersonating an officer of the State BCI."

"Good thing you beat him to it, Mac. He didn't see the car, did he?"

"No, Juan was cool; he told him the car had been disposed of. And he got that visit on video too."

"Good, we can nail him for both of those," Morgan said. They're getting scared. Now we have a hook for BCI: impersonating a State Police officer, making false statements in BMV uniform, and using an expired Trooper badge to intimidate and impound the evidence car."

"Yep, and get this, Morgan. Riley insisted on searching Juan's lot. While he was doing that, Juan took photos of Riley's old black patrol car and got samples of pink paint off his push bars!"

"Excellent!"

"I'm headed back to the body shop to grab that paint sample, and to get a sample from the Waterman bumper, then back to the lab for comparison."

"Mac, if it's the pusher car that killed the Watermans, I can't believe they never got rid of that old cruiser. Even worse, that they left paint traces on the push bars. And Minetti's a body and paint man."

"Criminals always make a mistake, Morg."

"OK. Since they now believe Waterman's car is disposed of, they don't have that evidence to worry about. But if they're smart, they'll still get rid of Riley's cruiser. We've got to get that car, and State Police has to do it for us. Go get those samples and get them to the lab. I'll watch the Chem Systems video of Riley's visit, call Colonel Justice and forward it to him. Based on Riley's visits to the lab and the body shop faking an official inquiry, BCI has enough to pick him up for questioning."

"Pot's starting to boil, Morg. Level Three."

"Hey, one more thing, Mac. Waterman's bumper had very distinct dents. You should be able to take an impression and match it to some small protrusions on Riley's push bars, maybe a bolt head, or something like that. Get some Silly Putty™₂₇ and make an impression of the dents while you're at Johnson's. Make sure Juan videos when you're doing it."

"OK! Call Roger when you are ready to be picked up at the library."

"Will do, now, get going! I've got to get BCI to grab Riley's car!"

*****

Thursday, May 25
Perfect Restoration Shop
1:00 p.m.

Joe Minetti's phone buzzed.

"Yeah, Tim."

"I've been to the body shop. He disposed of the car."

"Good, so we catch a break."

"I got ears inside Troop A, Joey. If anything is said, I'll know."

"Tim, why don't you let me crush your old cruiser? I can pay you and give you a newer, better car."

"I'm guessing why you want that car, Joey. But the Waterman car is gone, so you don't have to worry. I'm keeping my old cruiser."

Thursday, May 25
Minetti Council Room
1:15 P.M.

"Poppa," said Joey Minetti, "this is getting dangerous. State BCI is looking into Jim Murphy's drowning, and the car accident that killed the Watermans. And the Murphy woman hired a lawyer. He's snooping around both of those cases and reporting to the head of BCI."

"Joey, those were accidents. Why are you worried?"

"Uh, Poppa...I might have had some involvement in both of those."

Joseph Senior sighed and sat down. "Joey, what did you do? No! Don't tell me. You already said too much. Why tell me this now, Joey?"

"I gotta make another move on Morrison, Poppa. My guy at the marina saw him slice some paint off my boat. He's been to a chemical lab, and they

182

compared my boat paint to paint on Murphy's boat. I put a tracker on his car, and saw him go to the Waterman accident site. He's getting too close on both of those cases. I gotta take him out to stop this investigation."

"Whattaya mean, 'another move,' Joey?"

"I had him in my sights on the Thruway, but his car was too fast. He must have a hot rod engine in it. I couldn't catch him to wreck him, you know, make it look like an accident. So I got next to him, and took three shots, but he slammed on his brakes and I missed, all three missed. Then he tried to wreck *me,* but a Trooper saw him pushing me and pulled *him* over. I got lucky and got away. Don't worry, it was a stolen car with a blacked-out plate, and I ditched it. No way it can come back on me."

"Stupid, Joey, stupid! I told you to avoid that guy! How can you be so foolish! You could bring this down on the family! Any move you make now on Morrison, his lawyer or the Murphy woman will have the State Police pounding on our door in two minutes! NO! You already did too much. You gotta ride this out, keep Tim's ear inside the cops, and find out what's happening. If it looks bad, then I call our people in Jersey, and we get you outta the country. But stay outta this! I'M TELLIN' YOU JOEY, STAY AWAY FROM MORRISON!"

"...OK, Poppa, ...OK."

*****

Thursday, May 25
Murphy B & B
1:30 p.m.

"Marybeth," said Mac, I'm going back to Johnson's to get Riley's paint sample. Morgan will call Roger when they are ready to be picked up from the library."

"Are you going to scrape a sample off my parents' bumper and go back to the lab in Hamburg?"

"Yep, they owe me a favor."

"Wow, stuff is happening!"

"Roger, Level 3.9," Mac said, pointing to Marybeth.

*****

Thursday, May 25
Johnson's Auto Body, Jamestown
2:00 p.m.

"Mac, I've been to court many times on accident cases. The State Police will not accept my samples as best evidence. They take their own."

"But we want our own samples to find out if Waterman's car was pushed by Riley's car, Juan."

"Right on. So, I took two samples off Waterman's bumper. One I sliced with a razor; one I took using sandpaper. Each one is in a plastic freezer bag and labeled."

"Great."

"Riley's push bar sample is on this tape in the envelope, stuck to a piece of glass."

"Perfect, Juan. I want to take impressions from that bumper. Would you video me?"

They walked inside the body shop. Juan lifted the cotton cover off the Waterman car and shined a flashlight at the rear bumper.

"Mac, look close at the center of those black grooves."

"Looks like a cross with a circle around it."

"It's a mark left by a Phillips-head screw with a buggered slot from being over-torqued. Note the square dent around it. It took a hard hit to make that distinct impression. A normal cop 'pit' maneuver is a shove. I don't normally see such a hard hit from a Trooper doing a pit-push."

"There's one in the right groove and one in the left, said Mac. "And next to the right hand one is another ding, sort of round but irregular, and rough with little tiny dings inside it."

"OK," said Juan, pulling out his cell phone. ''Here are the photos of Riley's push bars, the same ones I sent you. Zoom in. See the two rusty Phillips-head screws?"

"I do".

"See this? Weld spatter where the dent is next to the screw mark on the bumper."

"I do, Juan."

"Push bars are spring steel, Mac. These got damaged. Someone clamped two flat bars to the top and bottom of the crack, drilled them and screwed

184

them together. They used cheap Phillips-head screws that rusted. Later, they welded the crack, ground the weld and touched it up with black paint. Probably rattle can stuff. That paint is probably on Waterman's bumper. After they welded, they hacked off the flat bars, leaving rusty screw heads, which made the distinctive dents. If we had the matching push bars, we could press them against this bumper to see if they match."

"Juan, I'll push some silly putty into these dents while you video using my phone."

❉❉❉❉❉

Thursday, May 25
Chem Systems Lab, Hamburg
3:00 pm

"Dr. Coleman, thank you for doing this."

"It's the least we can do. My staff and I will work on the paint stuck to the tape first and then do the comparison to the bumper samples."

"Think I'll grab a bite to eat," said Mac. "I saw this 1940s roadside hot dog shack on the Net. Charcoal broiled dogs, with outdoor picnic tables, totally primitive."

"You're describing Red Hots," she said, "and we give them 5 stars! I'll call you."

❉❉❉❉❉

Thursday, May 25
3:15 p.m.

Marybeth drove while Roger kept his hand on his Colt. They tooled up SR 394 into sleepy downtown Westfield and parked directly in front of the William Banks Memorial Library. Marybeth gave a honk of the horn, and Morgan and Angie descended the stairs like royalty. Morgan had that effect on juries too.

They squeezed into the back seat with a quick head rub to Buddy.

Roger said, "Well, you bluffed Rosemary, so what else did you guys find?"

185

"Pretty much what Mac already had, plus the Waterman fence feud, and more details on the embezzlement lawsuit. That one is definitely a motive for the Waterman murders. Riley really screwed up making a play for the car at the body shop in BMV uniform. Colonel Justice watched the video I sent him. He called Juan Johnson, got the whole story, and then called the BMV. Tim Riley will be called into his supervisor's office. He will be disciplined, and could be fired."

"Can State Police impound his car?"

"Not yet; we have to make the connection to the Waterman car. Maybe Mac's new lab results will help. Based on our findings, plus the WNYFDA embezzlement lawsuit, we have a possible motive on Waterman, so Colonel Justice has assigned Senior Investigator Jonetta Pope to meet with us and open an investigation into both the Waterman and Murphy deaths. The motive in both cases leads back to protecting the Minetti criminal enterprises, such as may exist."

"Jonetta was so kind after Jim's death," Marybeth said. "BCI staff and Troopers came from all over to Jim's funeral. Even though she did not know Jim, she made a great effort to comfort me."

"What Angie and I need now is to check into our room," said Morgan, "and then we need brain food."

"I'll take care of that!" said Marybeth.

Fifteen minutes later, Morgan and Angie were seated at the dining room table sipping iced tea while Marybeth was cooking and Roger was grilling burgers.

"Angie," said Morgan, "let's make a timeline of events, starting forty years ago with Mac's parents' deaths. We are not trying to reopen that case, but we want to show the link of Joey Minetti and Tim Riley at the accident scene. We will argue there is probable cause to believe Minetti caused the accident, and Riley may have covered it up in his report."

"We are going to need a statement from Trooper Andy Gregor regarding the implausibility of the 1983 Morrison accident reports and the witness statement given by Minetti in contrast to Trooper Gregor's observations of the accident scene, and how it could have actually happened."

"Then we fast forward to the Waterman deaths and the suspicious circumstance about their so-called accident. We add that Mrs. Waterman's audit of WNYFDA had ostensibly turned up embezzlement within their ranks, and before she was able to successfully submit her findings, she was killed, her laptop was confiscated, and the lawsuit was dismissed."

"The link for BCI will be that Rosemary Minetti was the Treasurer of the WNYFDA when $100,000 had been embezzled. We are again going to need a statement from Trooper Gregor regarding the implausibility of the Deputy Sheriff's accident report on Waterman, and how it could have actually happened. And, we need to find out what happened to the Waterman laptop. That was less than two years ago. Does it still exist within her firm? Do her files still exist? Investigator Pope will have to get a court order for it."

"Then we look at Jim Murphy's death, the motive being his investigation into criminal activity by Joe Minetti Jr, possibly including Gino. We question the coroner's report alleging drowning as the cause of death and believe we have sufficient evidence to warrant an inquest."

"Next, we tie in current BMV Inspector and former State Trooper Tim Riley's unauthorized visits to both the Chem Systems Lab and the Johnson body shop, and his attempt to confiscate the Waterman car for an alleged official investigation. We will specifically note that he showed a New York State Police badge and stated that he was acting on behalf of New York BCI."

"And finally, we need to weave in our layman's collection of evidence. First, paint samples from the two boats in the Murphy death. Second, a statement from Pops about the scrape on the *Deadly Serious,* and when he first observed it, and third, the paint lab results from Riley's cruiser push bars and the Waterman bumper as soon as we get them."

"Oh! If Mac gets good impressions from the bumper damage, we need to compare those to Riley's cruiser bars. If we can do it surreptitiously, we will, but it would be better if BCI could impound his car and do the lab work themselves. Make sure to note that we have secured the Waterman car at a third party site and will make it available to BCI whenever they want to see it. OK, Angie, that is our outline for Jonetta Pope. Hopefully, she will find it's sufficient to present to Colonel Justice and that he will order an inquest and impound Riley's car."

"All right guys!" Marybeth shouted, "Lunch is served on the back porch. Grilled burgers, hand cut French fries, fresh fruit, and garden salad."

"Brain food!" Morgan said as he high-fived Angie.

⁕⁕⁕⁕⁕

Thursday, May 25
Buffalo Bills Stadium, Hamburg, NY

4:45 p.m.

As a kid, the Buffalo Bills had been Mac's team, and still were. There is no New Hampshire Lumberjacks NFL team, and never will be. Mac's phone buzzed while he stood in front of the Bills Stadium.

"Mr. Morrison? Dr. Coleman calling. I have some interesting results for you. Are you nearby?"

"At the Bills Stadium. See you soon."

*****

Thursday, May 25
Chem Systems Lab
5:00 p.m.

"Staff, this is Mr. Morrison. Mr. Morrison, this is Elizabeth, Angelo, Damon and Woodley. We all worked on your samples to get quicker results. The staff will give their individual reports."

"Elizabeth?" said Dr. Coleman.

"There were three distinct paints present on the samples you gave us. Pink Sample A was taken from the bumper of the rose colored car that was struck, and Pink Sample B was the tape sample pulled from the black steel bars on the front of the vehicle that allegedly did the striking."

"Angelo?"

"There were two different black paints from Tape Sample B. One was an automotive OEM paint that had been baked on. It was the smaller of the black samples detected. The other paint was an over the counter rattle can variety, not the same black color but similar to the casual observer."

"Damon?"

"Both black paints were found on both surfaces, meaning the black scrapes on the bumper of vehicle A are identical to the black paints found on the steel bars from vehicle B. Because we had two different paints, the possibility of both these exact paints being in combination from random wear and tear is virtually nil."

Mac said, "Does that mean..."

"Please wait, Mr. Morrison."

"There is no question, from the black paints alone, that these two samples were created by a unique impact," said Damon.

188

"But there's more," said Dr. Coleman. "The rose color sample is an automotive paint specifically applied to plastic trim panels like bumper covers because it is flexible. It is covered with a clear coat that is also flexible. Both the rose base coat and the clear coat from the bumper sample A are identical to the deposits from the push bars on vehicle B."

"Although all these paints exist in the general universe, the only way that these four paints could have left their distinct molecular structure on both vehicles A and B was by a violent impact. Our conclusion is that the black push bars from sample B caused the damage to the vehicle's bumper from sample A."

"100%?" Mac asked.

"100%," said Dr. Coleman.

"Wow! Great work, staff! When can I get the written report? And what do I owe you?"

"Well," she continued, "to make up for our mistake the last time, there is no charge. We will write a detailed scientific report with layman's conclusions and email it to you before morning. Is that acceptable?"

"Terrific, really appreciate your hard work." Mac pulled out his wallet and handed her $200. "This should cover a late dinner for the five of you at Boulangers."

Dr. Coleman held the $200 out for all to see.

"Yay! Boulangers!" they yelled.

Mac said, "Please retain the samples. I look forward to getting your report."

❈❈❈❈❈

Thursday, May 25
Captain Murphy B & B
6:30 p.m.

"Well!" said Morgan, "I am fried. My brain has been taking in all day but Mac still keeps heaping more on. I'm concentrating on the Waterman case because it is the only one we have a chance of convicting, but we are going to need a lot of help."

The group of five was in the dining room. Buddy and the Labradoodles watched from the open door to the back porch.

"Mac, you did good finding Waterman's car and securing it; well done. That was critical; we could not proceed without it. And, good job matching the paint samples; they are good circumstantial evidence, but it goes to the res gestae."

"What the fuck is res gestae!" Roger snapped. "Speak friggin' English, Morgan! Pardon my cursing, Marybeth, but this guy does this shit to us all the time."

Morgan grinned at Marybeth.

"It's a little word game we play, Marybeth. The worlds of lawyer, builder and excavator collide too infrequently for a learning experience. Res gestae refers to those acts and declarations which are such an intimate part of the criminal event that their existence must be known to the court. In other words, evidence that would not ordinarily be admitted in court may be allowed because it is deemed vital to the case, and the court must know it. Usually, it is an exception to the exclusionary hearsay rule."

"Well, that certainly cleared that up!" snorted Roger with a smirk. He winked at Mac, who winked back.

"It means, you clods," Morgan sighed, "that it's good, it may be useful, but you better have something more compelling to point the finger at someone."

"Next," he continued, "the Sheriff's police report on the Waterman accident did not make reference to rear end damage or push marks on the plastic bumper-cover. But clearly, there was damage. The news photos showed it, and the actual vehicle, which Mac secured, shows rear end damage that suggests it was pushed. Sloppy police work? Maybe. Or was the report influenced by outside forces? Don't know."

"BCI Investigator Pope should interview the Sheriff's Deputy, who I hope is still alive and available. If she could get the Deputy to say the report was changed under duress, and who provided the duress, *that* would be a criminal conspiracy."

"Now, matching the paints and dents on the bumper to the protrusion on Riley's' push bars, that would be even more compelling. But first, BCI would have to take possession of Riley's car. Do we have enough to allow them to do that? And even if they did, and even if the dents match the protrusions, it still is only evocative because Riley could say he hit their car another time. For example, he could say he rammed it in anger while it was parked in their driveway. He had a record of vandalism against them."

"Now, I'll grant you, there may be a motive. Riley's fence feud with the Watermans? No, the better murder motive is the WNYFDA audit being done by Mrs. Waterman, which may have pointed the finger at Rosemary Minetti for embezzlement. But, we do not have the audit and again are speculating."

"The one great hook we have is Riley's two colossal mistakes."

"First: impersonating a New York State Trooper to intimidate the Chem Systems Lab employee into giving him private lab results that could implicate himself or Joe Minetti in the death of Jim Murphy."

"Second: showing up at Juan Johnson's body shop in BMV uniform, driving his personal car and attempting to impound the Waterman car by stating it was part of an official BCI investigation. That is falsification by a law enforcement officer, threat by deception, improper impersonation of a legal State Police officer, and probably many other crimes. That action alone shows he is involved in something nefarious."

"Now, when we put that together with my bluffing Rosemary Minetti a few hours earlier at the library, she obviously called Joey, who called Riley, who went directly to the Johnson body shop. That *is* evidence of a criminal conspiracy regarding the Waterman accident. They are trying to obtain and destroy possible evidence, cloaked in a supposed official investigation by an imposter State Police officer."

"That most certainly will garner some disciplinary action against Riley by Colonel Justice. But, by itself, it does not put Tim Riley behind the wheel of his black former police car pushing the Watermans over the edge of a cliff. Even if his car did the deed, we do not know who was driving it."

"Res gestae, Morgan?"

"Yes, Mac, but we are building a case in the mind of BCI Pope, which she can hopefully take on and push."

"Which could drag on forever," Roger said. "We gotta be outta here by next weekend, Morgan, Marybeth has guests coming."

"Look, guys, you don't put a timetable on criminal investigations, and you can't predict the outcome in court."

"Which is why Mac and I are here," said Roger.

"And, which is why," said Morgan, "Angie and I are going into the kitchen out of earshot to help Marybeth bring out our dinner."

*****

The rain began again at midnight, pounding Mac's cottage roof and waking him. Buddy looked over at him and groaned. He pressed his big paw against Mac's face, and they both dropped back to sleep.

*****

Chapter Twenty Seven

The rain again fell hard all night, finally ending at five a.m. An hour later, Buddy nudged Mac with his nose, and woofed.

"I'm up, Buddy, I'm up. Let's go outside."

They walked down to the pier in the dawn glow. Pops was smoking his pipe on deck.

"Mornin' Pops!"

"Mornin' Mac. Mornin' Buddy."

'Rowrf!'

"Pops, will it be good fishing today?"

"Maybe. This time of year, we get a lot of bugs that come alive after a rain. We'll see if we get a bug bloom in about an hour. Water temp is 55 degrees near shore at the surface. Air temp's gonna be high-seventies by afternoon. If fish eat early on bugs, they'll go down deep in the heat. In that case, night fishing under moonlight would be better. Water's gonna be muddy near shore from storm runoff, so the best fishing will be offshore."

"But that's gonna be dicey, Mac, because after these last two big rains, there'll be a lotta flotsam in the lake, I mean big stuff. Whole trees will slough off into the lake. The west wind blows all that shit east to this harbor. See all that trash on the beach?"

Mac turned and looked. There were piles of branches and logs that had washed ashore overnight.

"Yes," he said.

"I call it the coffin corner, Mac. On the lake there'll be a lotta that stuff. If a guy goes out today, he better have a good eye and a slow hand on the throttle, and watch out when night fishing. Best to stay in port, but there are two kinds who will go out night fishing after a rain: fools who don't know better, and fools who do. Now, if you go out at night after a big rain, you better have a powerful spotlight."

193

"See that?" said Pops, pointing to his fly bridge. "Those two spotlights have a million watts each. Light up the lake like day, but even then you can't see over waves. Logs can hide in the troughs. Why are you asking, Mac? You goin' fishing tonight?"

"Dunno Pops. Stuff is happening. We put a scare into Tim Riley and Joe Minetti. State Police are now investigating two accidents that I believe were murders, and Minetti and Riley know it. Riley made a bad mistake that might have cost him his BMV job. With his temper, no telling what he might do."

"He'll go fishing," said Pops. "That's what he does when he's troubled."

"If he knows my snooping has cost him his job," Mac said, "he'll be pissed, so he might ask me to go out with him as a trap. That could give me a chance to run a bluff on him, and crack this case. So, Pops, I may need you today. If you go out, you'll be bringing my buddy Roger with you. He's legally armed."

"I'm ready, Mac. When will you know?"

"Spur of the moment. Call me if Riley comes to his boat, OK?"

"OK, Mac. Boy! This is gonna be exciting!"

"Hah! Yes, that would be one word for it. I need a quick course in Walleye fishing and tackle. Do you have a floating tackle box?"

"Yup. Let's get to work," said Pops. "First, this is the pole I'm gonna have you use."

*****

Friday, May 26
7:00 a.m.

"Good morning, Mac," said Marybeth. "Morgan and Angie are working on their outline, and Roger is on 'protective patrol,' as he calls it. Jonetta Pope will be meeting us here at noon. Your Amazon package is on the front porch."

"Rog," said Mac, "let's take a walk."

*****

Mac rolled back the big barn door and flipped on the blazing LED lights.

"Rog, there's a rattle can of Day-Glo orange paint in the cabinet. Would you wipe down this tackle box and spray it while I grab my Amazon package?"

The Amazon box was six inches square and weighed less than a pound. Mac slit the tape and pulled out the battery-operated flare. He trotted back to the barn and installed three AAA batteries. Fifteen LEDs flashed with a brilliance that dazzled.

Roger was spraying the tackle box using an old stump for a paint stand. Mac found a box of quart size freezer bags in the cabinet and grabbed three.

"Looks great, Rog. Now let's get some tackle for you." Jim's fishing cabinet had six poles with reels. Mac picked one that looked like Pop's.

"Let's find a lure like the one Pops gave me, maybe one of these."

"What's the plan, Mac?"

"We're gonna fish on the pier and see if Riley comes to his boat. If he does, and he asks me out, I bring my own tackle box with this LED flare inside. Can be seen a mile."

"Does it float?"

"Dunno. Let's try it."

They put it in the rain barrel and it sank. Mac placed the flare in a triple lock freezer bag, blew some air in it and pinched it shut. It floated.

"I'm going to let Riley believe I've given up on my parents' accident," said Mac.

"That's the distraction," said Roger.

"Right. He knows that I'm pursuing Jim's and the Waterman's accidents with the State Police. So, I'm going to act like the whole investigation is being taken over by Morgan and BCI, and I'll be going home soon."

"That's the bluff," said Roger.

"Once we get offshore with no witnesses, I'm going to hit him with my suspicions on all three "accidents" and tell him about the boat scrapes, the bumper damage, the paint chips, and the 1983 cover-up. Maybe I can get him to confess to something or turn on Joe Minetti. My cell phone will be recording from my pocket."

"That's confronting him, Mac. He can either play dumb and say he has no idea what you are talking about, or kill you and throw you overboard."

"Right, but I'll be prepared. If it's a struggle, I should be able to overpower him. I'll zip tie him and drive the boat in."

"I dunno Mac, he's a big guy, and has cop training in close quarters fighting. You're not carrying a weapon?"

"Can't, because he's a cop and he'd spot it. Nope, I'm gonna have this toolbox, the flare, and the GPS tracker taped to my ankle, which you are going to reprogram to your phone. I'll have my Leatherman™ on my belt, like any fisherman would carry, and my wits. He'd have a hard time explaining a body with a bullet washing ashore after I was seen leaving the pier with him. If he pulls a gun and I have to bail, I'll try to take the toolbox with me. He could try to run me over to make sure I'm dead, but I'm wearing dark colors and no life vest. I can dive and blend in the water. My phone is submersible up to 30 minutes. You follow the GPS tracker, which is waterproof. Pops will be following my phone using an app. So you have two locators, and hopefully, I'm alive when you get there. If I can locate the tool box, I'll turn on the flare."

"Not the best plan, Mac."

"Worst case, Rog, let's say he pulls a gun, takes my phone, frisks me and rips off the GPS, then forces me overboard."

"Then you're miles off shore, no way to find you, it's dark, water's cold, and you are shit out of luck, Mac."

"Rog, if you don't hear from me, and you see that my phone is coming back to you, intercept him, even if you have to shoot him. Try not to kill him. If you see my phone hasn't moved, but you see Riley's boat returning, fix my last location and have Pops go for that spot, call Morgan and tell them to gun up. Minetti or Riley will be coming for him and Marybeth. She's got guns, and she's a dead shot on a stationary target, but she's never had to kill. They gotta be ready."

"Mac, Pops and I will be just out of sight on the water following you. We shouldn't be too far behind."

"That's the plan, Rog, any flaws?"

"Too many, Mac, but hell, we always wing it. I'm starting to feel the juices. This is why I'm here!"

*****

Friday, May 26
Barcelona Pier
8:00 a.m.

"Pops, give us a few pointers," Roger said.

"Toss your lure out there. Give it a second to slow dive, then reel in steady, not fast. If they're biting, you may catch one first cast, or you may not catch one in a hundred casts. But that's fishing."

"Oh! I think I got one," Roger said.

"Keep tension," Pops said, "Keep reeling, lemme get my long handle net! That's a nice one, Roger. Do you want to keep him?"

"No, put him back," Roger said. "Say, don't look now, but an old black Trooper patrol car just parked by that big black boat."

"Um hm," said Mac. "That will be Officer Tim Riley."

But Tim Riley did not even look over at them. Instead, he unlocked the *Deadly Serious*, cranked the twin engines, and in a minute was idling away from the dock.

"OK, Rog, I got an idea; let's go!"

They ran back to the B & B. Mac opened the Chevy's trunk.

"I bought lots of Silly Putty to take the impressions on Waterman's bumper. Let's take impressions off those push bars!"

They walked casually down to the pier parking lot. Riley's boat was gone. They sauntered over to his Patrol car and looked at it.

"Rog, take a video of the impression with me in it and the pier behind. Then take a pic of the VIN tag on the dash and zoom out to me standing here with the Silly Putty."

"Is this an illegal search?"

"It's in plain sight, Rog, and we did not force entry. Do you give a shit if we catch a murderer?"

"Hell no, murderers don't get rights. Anyway, that's Morgan's bag, not ours."

Mac quickly pressed the pink glop onto the screw heads on the left push bar. Next, he did the same to the right push bar, and last, he made a separate impression of the weld spatter. It only took 30 seconds.

He marked the left bar sample L, the right one R, and the weld spatter, R-Weld.

"OK, Rog, back to the barn!"

There was a bag of plaster of Paris in Marybeth's garden locker. Roger whipped up a stiff mix and poured it into the Silly Putty impressions like a mold.

"Rog, this should be nice and hard by the time BCI Jonetta Pope gets here. It's time to reprogram that GPS tracker to your phone. Then we can kick back, walk the Buddy-boy, and do chores for Marybeth until Jonetta arrives. This has been a very good morning!"

❈❈❈❈❈

Chapter Twenty Eight

Friday, May 26
Captain Murphy B & B
12:00 p.m.

A charcoal Ford Explorer with six roof antennas glided to a stop in front of the Captain Murphy B & B. The driver pulled off onto the shoulder of Route 5 with two wheels on the lawn. The Shavely twins were doing somersaults in their front yard next door. They stopped, stared, and bounced over like kangaroos.

"Hi!" the two girls said as a woman stepped out of her State Police SUV. She was in plain clothes: a charcoal vest and pants with a cream long sleeve starched cotton shirt. Her sidearm was hung on her belt. The girls looked up at her in awe. She was a very fit, tall black woman with handsome features that commanded respect, even from teenagers.

"Wow, you're tall," they said in unison.

"All Troopers are tall, didn't you know that?" said BCI Investigator Jonetta Pope, giving them a wink. "That's a fib; we have normal size folks too. How old are you, girls?"

"13!" they said in unison.

"I'm Investigator Jonetta Pope with the New York State Bureau of Criminal Investigation. Who are you?"

"I'm Linda! I'm Belinda! We live next door!"

"Would you like to be a State Trooper when you grow up?"

"Wow! Could we?" they said like two parrots.

"If you get good grades and stay in shape, you could."

"Watch this!" they said, bounding off doing hand springs and flips, tucking and rolling up from a somersault, and assuming a judo stance.

"Hey!" clapped BCI Pope.

"We know why you're here, but we won't tell," Belinda said.

"You do?"

"Yep, spy cameras and spooky things happening. It all goes back to the death of Mr. Jim and Marybeth's parents, that's what we think. Even though we were eleven, something didn't seem right. Weird stuff has been happening here, too, right in our back yard!"

"Really?"

"Yep, but we can't tell. Mac can tell you if he wants. Bet that's why you're here."

"Bet it is girls, so let's just keep this to ourselves, OK?"

"OK, nice meeting you, Secret Agent Pope!" They turned and bounded off like kangaroos.

"Hello, Jonetta!" Marybeth called from the front door. "Won't you come in?"

"Thank you, Mrs. Murphy. How are you doing?"

"I'm fine. Please call me Marybeth. I'll introduce you, and then we'll all gather for lunch."

"Thank you. That is very kind of you."

"Investigator Jonetta Pope, this is Mac Morrison, Attorney Morgan Hillman, his confidential secretary Angelica Morelli, and their friend Roger Lemonier."

"Pleased to meet you all," said Investigator Pope. "Please call me Jonetta."

"All right, guys," said Marybeth, "give Jonetta ten minutes to freshen up. Lunch will be served as soon as she joins us. No business talk until after lunch, house rules! C'mon guys, yes, she's tall, we know."

*****

Friday, May 26
Captain Murphy B & B
12:45 p.m.

"Jonetta," Morgan began, "I prepared an outline of the events that led Colonel Justice to appoint you to investigate three deaths that were originally classified as accidents. The one with the most available physical evidence is the Waterman automobile accident that killed Marybeth's parents two years ago on State Route 76, also known as Sherman Road. It occurred just outside the Village of Ripley."

200

"We believe this was not an accident, but rather, they were shoved off the road intentionally by a person, as yet unknown, driving a car belonging to a former New York State Trooper named Tim Riley, who is currently employed as a State BMV salvage vehicle inspector. We can absolutely prove, by physical evidence, that Riley's personal car, which is a retired State Police cruiser with push bars, did strike the Waterman's car. What we cannot prove is when. This proof of impact comes from paint samples taken from both cars and tested by an ISO 9000 chemical analysis laboratory in Hamburg, New York, that is certified to do State and DOD work. Therefore, we believe Riley's former Trooper cruiser pushed the Waterman's car off the road to their death."

"BMV Officer Riley was the Waterman's next door neighbor and had been involved in a feud with them over a fence he constructed on their property, and which he refused to remove. Watermans obtained a court order allowing them to remove the fence, after which Riley became unhinged. Police were called."

"To be clear, we do not imply that the fence feud was a motive for vehicular murder, because we do not know that Riley was driving his car, and because there is a stronger alternative motive that may implicate his lifelong friend Joey Minetti, owner of an automobile collision and restoration shop in Ripley. Minetti has served time in prison for dealing in the sale and transport of stolen cars."

"At the time of her death, Mrs. Waterman had been doing a forensic audit that allegedly implicated Rosemary Minetti, Joey's wife, of embezzling $100,000 from a business organization for which she was Treasurer. Jonetta, we believe the real motive for the Waterman's alleged 'accident' was to kill Mrs. Waterman and thereby suppress her audit before it could be released in the discovery phase of a lawsuit involving the missing money. Her laptop computer was retrieved from her house, and the contents of her audit were never made known. The lawsuit was dismissed, and Mrs. Minetti was never charged with theft."

"Now, Jonetta, you will want to know what our physical evidence is."

"First, the paint samples, analyzed by a New York State approved lab, which conclusively, 100% indicates that the Riley car did indeed strike the Waterman car. But, we cannot say when, or who was driving."

"Second, we secured the Waterman's car and made impression molds of the damage to their rear bumper. We also made impression molds from Riley's former Trooper cruiser's push bars. We did this on our own, but the

Riley car was parked in a public place, namely the pier parking lot across the street, and we did not hide our actions."

"Whether or not these impressions would be allowed by a court is a matter for a court to decide. But for your purposes, they are strong material evidence to be considered. The molds are in the barn out back, locked securely. We took videos of Mac making them."

"Lastly, regarding the Waterman accident, we purposely let Rosemary Minetti know that, as attorney for Marybeth Murphy, I was looking into her husband's and her parents' deaths, whereupon BMV Officer Tim Riley immediately showed up at the body shop where the Waterman car was being stored, and stated that he was there acting as a New York State Police special investigator seeking to impound the Waterman's vehicle."

"He had obviously been tipped off by either Rosemary or Joe Minetti, and was attempting to use his New York State BMV uniform, his former State Police badge, and intimidation tactics to obtain the Waterman car by deception. The reason is obvious: he and the Minettis want that car destroyed so it cannot be used as evidence in an inquest, which I intend to request through your boss, Colonel Samuel Justice."

"We have actual video of this visit with Riley in his BMV uniform trying to intimidate the owner of the body shop, falsely claiming to be there on behalf of the BCI, and using his former Trooper badge as credentials."

"We also have actual video of Riley, in his BMV uniform, impersonating a New York State Trooper by showing his former State Police badge to intimidate an employee of the chemical lab that did the paint sample analyses. He was successful in his tactics. They told him the results of the tests, but did not give him the written report."

"Our second case is the death of Mr. Morrison's parents 40 years ago, May 14, 1983."

"Their 1970 Ford F-100 pickup truck was struck in the driver's door by a heavy tractor truck at the intersection of U.S. 20 and State Route 76, also known as Sherman Road. The police report concluded that the Morrison vehicle ran a red light, and they were at fault."

"We have no physical evidence to prove that this was also a murder, but we have facts that are in the written outline that may link suspects in that case to the Waterman case, and which show a pattern of criminal behavior."

"Lastly, Riley and/or Minetti are also implicated in the alleged drowning death of BCI Investigator James Murphy two years ago. We have some preliminary evidence in that case and a statement from a local boater who witnessed certain occurrences the day of BCI Investigator Murphy's death, but I will leave that story to the outline."

"OK, I am going to stop there. All of this is covered in your written copy."

"Thank you," said Jonetta Pope. "I appreciate your being direct and offering possible evidence, which I will have to evaluate. Now, you say you have actual video of this Officer Riley at the body shop and the Chem lab stating he was acting officially on behalf of BCI, and using his former State Police badge to deceive and intimidate those employees?"

"We do," said Morgan.

"And you have taken molds from Riley's former Trooper patrol car's push bars, which you say will match the rear bumper of the Waterman car?"

"We have."

"Well, this *is* an interesting story," Jonetta said. "OK, let me read the outline, and then I'd like to see these impression molds and visit the accident scenes. Marybeth, may I have some coffee?"

"The urn is hot, and mugs are on the buffet, Jonetta. Please help yourself. Guys, let's all go outside and take the dogs for a walk."

*****

With the sun now high in the sky, the garden thermometer read 78 degrees. There was no breeze.

"Walleye will be going down to cooler waters this afternoon," Marybeth said, "no sense fishing at the pier."

"On the contrary, M," said Mac. "We're hoping to catch a murderer, not a walleye." He winked at her.

"Roger, I want to do a sound check, so let's leave these guys and go in the barn." Once inside, Mac turned on his cell phone, slipped it into the leg phone pocket of his all-terrain pants, and faced the microphone outward before zipping it.

"OK, Rog, let's start the car and let it idle down. That should be about the same as a boat engine."

Roger got into the Mercury Cyclone and started the V-8.

"I'll stand by the Merc and you talk," Mac said. "I'm recording."

Roger spoke for 30 seconds and they did a playback. There was some droning, but the thin pocket fabric did not muffle the voices; they were clear.

"Now, if there's wind, maybe it's worse. OK. Any last thoughts, Rog?"

"Yeah, let's hope he asks you to go fishing."

"All right, I think we're good. Ready, Buddy?"

'Wuf!' Buddy did the whirling dervish, and out the door he ran.

*****

Friday, May 26
Murphy B & B
2:30 p.m.

Jonetta Pope put down the multi-page outline.

"OK, I have the sequence of events and your reasons for an inquest. I must say, you've been inventive in your inquiries. Not sure if your samples would be admissible in court, but if BCI pursues this, we will retake our own samples and determine the chain of evidence."

"Let's go see these impression molds and then take a drive. I'd also like to visit the Jamestown body shop to see the Waterman car, speak to Mr. Johnson and watch his video of Officer Riley's visit. Morgan, can you accompany Mac and me? Angie, would you come as a witness and possibly take notes?"

Mac said to Roger, "If Pops calls me, I'll let you know."

The four of them walked out to the barn. Mac unlocked the door and began by showing her the black gelcoat on the gunwale of Jim's boat. Mac pointed out the vest Jim was wearing when his body was found floating. He also noted that the boat's engine started up and ran, so there was not a problem with a breakdown on rough water. He noted the waters were calm that day.

Next, he showed her the "male" plaster cast made from the putty impressions of Riley's patrol car push bars, and the video of him taking the impressions at the pier in plain sight. He also showed her the 'female' plaster casts made from putty impressions off the Waterman bumper.

They mated perfectly.

He placed the molds in a cardboard box, and they all walked out to Jonetta Pope's Explorer. She made a short radio call before they drove to the pier and parked next to Tim Riley's Crown Vic.

"Looks like an old State Trooper cruiser," said Jonetta.

204

"It was," Mac said. "Tim Riley bought it when Troop A retired it. This car could be the murder weapon in the Waterman's death."

"OK, we start with that," said Jonetta.

Mac brought the cardboard box with him. They stood looking at the front push bars as Mac reached into the box and withdrew the first of three molds made from the putty impressions.

"Jonetta, I made these putty impressions from these bars with Roger Lemonier as my witness. We then used the impressions to make these plaster of Paris molds. You notice the putty impressions perfectly fit the four screws and weld spatter we see on the push bars. The plaster of Paris molds we made also fit perfectly to those taken from the Waterman bumper."

Morgan added: "They were taken in plain view with the car parked in a public parking area without entry into the vehicle and the objects in question were also in plain view."

"But Mr. Morrison is not a sworn officer of the law or the court," BCI Pope said.

"No, but he has the ability to make a citizen's arrest, and, as such, to gather obviously available evidence in plain view, not on private property," Morgan said.

"OK, let's leave it at that. Let's see them match. Hm...OK, OK, OK, yes they do seem to match up. What else did you want to show me about this car?"

"When we get to the body shop, I will attempt to match these castings with the damage on the Waterman car's rear bumper."

"By the way, Mac, that was very shrewd of you to go to the body shop two years after the accident and actually find the Waterman's car. Why did you think it would still be here?"

"It was the only lead I could dream up. We needed some physical evidence. Did you see my Blue '57 Chevy parked behind the B & B?"

"I did. She's a beauty."

"I restore old cars, Jonetta. So I know that a good Crown Vic like the Waterman's car is a valuable parts car. Since it was front end damage, it stood to reason that there might be a lot of good salvage parts on that car, and that a body shop might be able to sell those parts."

"Like I said, Mac, very shrewd."

"OK," said Mac, "now the last empty slip at the end of the pier, that's Riley's, actually Minetti's, boat slip. He owns a 34' Pursuit off-shore fishing boat. It's big, heavy, fast, and black."

"And you matched the gelcoat samples from his boat to the Murphy boat."

"Correct."

"But that only means the Murphy boat was hit by a black boat with that gelcoat, not specifically the Riley boat."

"Correct. But we also have the statement from 'Pops' Rodgers, who owns the boat next to Minetti's slip, that Joe Minetti took his boat out early the day that Jim Murphy was killed, and that Minetti's boat had a long scrape on its starboard hull when it came back in. There is still a trace where that scrape was repaired, and it matches the gunwale of Jim Murphy's boat when it is in the water."

"OK, are we ready for our tour?" asked Jonetta.

They drove the Police Explorer south on State Route 5 and crossed over to U.S. 20 to the former Morrison farm, now Minetti Wines and Enterprises.

Jonetta Pope parked in front of the Wine Store while Mac gave her a quick recollection of growing up in the old house. Next, they parked outside the fence protecting Perfect Restoration, Joe Minetti's shop, and Mac again explained how the businesses of Gino and Joe meshed to acquire and restore wrecked high end cars.

Driving east on U.S. Route 20 toward Ripley Center, they stopped and parked the car just short of the Sherman Road intersection as a large pickup truck swerved around them, turned left and parked in the elementary school.

Jonetta Pope, Mac, Angie and Morgan got out of the BCI Explorer.

"Have there been any physical changes to this intersection in the past forty years?" Jonetta asked.

"Not according to Trooper Andy Gregor, who lives locally, and who examined this scene with me," said Mac. "Perhaps that pocket park on the corner wasn't there. But that would not have affected sight distance to the west, which is the direction the tractor truck was coming from. The truck that struck my parents' pickup was eastbound on U.S. 20 and rammed them here, in the intersection, pushing them 75 feet past the intersection."

Mac paced off 75 feet and stopped in the center of the road.

"This is where their pickup came to rest and burned with them inside."

"Hm!" said BCI Pope as she did a pirouette and assessed the scene with the expert eyes of a State Trooper trained in accident reconstruction.

"OK, so your parents were coming..." said Jonetta.

"They were traveling north on Sherman Road, approaching the intersection," Mac said. "And they would have been turning left to go to our farm. The police reports assumed they were speeding straight through the intersection, having run a red light. That could not have been the case. I was staying at a friend's house next door to our farm. They had to turn left at the intersection to pick me up and then return home."

"The police report said they were struck in the intersection by a heavy tractor truck running bobtail, no trailer…" said Jonetta.

"Correct," said Mac.

Jonetta continued her thought out loud. "This is an intersection of two, two lane roads, with a 25 mile per hour speed limit in a rural village. Now, if I am your parents' vehicle approaching the intersection northbound on Sherman, this old commercial building on the corner sits right on the sidewalk and it completely blocks my vision to the west if I am making a left turn, as you say they would have done."

"Correct," said Mac. "Since a northbound vehicle's sight distance to the left is blocked by those buildings until you are right in the intersection, it makes no sense that my parents would run a red light, not knowing what might be coming. This is a truck route into the vineyards and to the grape processing plant in Westfield. My father knew that. He was a safe driver. Under no circumstance would he run a red light if there were no emergency and he could not see in both directions."

Jonetta added, "The tractor had to be traveling at a fairly high speed to push them 75 feet and explode their truck's gas tank."

"Correct. The gas tank in my Dad's truck had its filler cap behind the driver's door at shoulder height. It was an unsafe design where the steel tank actually was behind the front seat inside the cab, making it vulnerable to a hard side impact."

Jonetta thought for a moment.

"So, how did it happen? Did your parents blindly run a red light while making a slow left turn and crash into a speeding truck coming at them? They were only a few miles from home, and there was no emergency…"

"Doesn't make sense, does it, Jonetta?"

"No. OK, what were the other alternatives? Let's say they had the green light, and the truck ran the red, so it was moving already. But would a truck tractor with no trailer doing 25 mph have enough momentum to push their pickup 75 feet? And the eastbound tractor truck could not see around the corner either, so why would it run the red light?"

"And that also does not jibe with the witness statements, Jonetta. Witnesses Joe Minetti and the truck driver said my parents' pickup ran the red light. If my father had run the light on yellow, then the tractor truck should have been stopped for the red eastbound and only just begun moving when it turned green. It certainly would not have had the momentum to push them 75 feet."

Morgan's phone pinged, and he looked at an incoming text.

"Oh, this is interesting," he said. "My private investigator has been running down the registration on the truck that struck your parents' vehicle forty years ago. New Jersey registration, owned by an LLC leasing company; it's the same LLC that bought Mac's parent's farm."

"And Minettis bought your farm from that New Jersey LLC," said BCI Pope. "Mac, your theory is that Joseph Minetti Junior, who was driving behind your parents at the time, colluded with the tractor truck driver by some means of radio communication and pushed them into the path of the speeding truck, killing them. And you judged this by the damage to the back of their truck, caused by something striking it. That damage was noted by the Ripley officer, and is clearly visible in the newspaper photos, but was dismissed as old damage by 22 year old Trooper Tim Riley, who also happens to be best friends with Joey Minetti."

"Correct."

"Hmm. So, Mac, do you think Trooper Riley covered up for his friend?"

"Possibly. To be fair, he arrived at this scene after the vehicles had burned, so, giving him the benefit of the doubt, he did not carefully reconstruct the accident because he was immediately called away for a major wreck on the Thruway. He could have taken his buddy Joe Minetti's word for what happened, and that was why he dismissed the rear end damage to my Dad's truck when he wrote his accident report hours later."

"Or, Jonetta, he may have been involved in a cover-up by dismissing the damage to the rear of my Dad's truck. There is no way to know. And, being charitable, I now know that Trooper Riley was brain damaged in a wreck on active duty twenty years ago, so his memory of events preceding that accident may be poor. It's possible he was not being evasive when I questioned him. He just may not remember what happened here 40 years ago. But either way, I still believe Joey Minetti pushed my parents into that speeding tractor and killed them. And that was murder."

"Well, these are serious allegations," Jonetta said. "But, I am beginning to see how the physical facts, namely the accident scene, do not jibe with the police report or a common sense interpretation of how this could have occurred. OK, are we done here?"

"Yes, now on to the location of the Waterman's accident."

As BCI Jonetta Pope pulled away from her parking spot, a large pickup truck with dual rear driving wheels slowly left the elementary school. It drove through the intersection and let her get almost out of sight before following over the double railroad track and creeping up Sherman Road.

"There will be no good place to pull off in this direction, Jonetta," Mac said. "Even though it's very rural and there is no traffic, I don't want you to get hit on this narrow road with these blind curves and heavily wooded shoulders."

"OK, Mac, show me where the Waterman's car left the road."

Mac said, "It's here on your left. They went off at the apex of this curve, then down a ravine that drops sixty feet, slamming against a large tree. Why don't we drive ahead until you can turn around and then approach it as they did, going downhill."

"Good idea." Jonetta proceeded slowly up the curvy road, noting the guardrail on both sides as they crossed over a creek far below. She continued until they had cleared the last of the seven curves, found a cross road and stopped to make a U-turn. As she waited for a clear view, a large pickup truck rumbled past, its driver hidden behind tinted glass. It was a Ford 350 Platinum with dual rear wheels, she noted to herself.

She turned around and proceeded back downhill. She drove through the first six curves at the posted 30 miles per hour. As she approached the Waterman accident site, Mac said, "Just ahead on the right, where there's no guardrail. If someone were going to push them off the road, this is the spot."

"That would require local knowledge," said Jonetta as she pulled onto the shoulder and stopped.

Just then, the large pickup truck with the dark windows rolled around the blind curve, saw the police SUV, slammed on its brakes, paused, and then sped up to drive by.

Jonetta Pope hit her squawker 'Wip! Wop!' as she pulled out behind the truck, closing fast and hitting it with her flashing lights. It kept going, and she kept following until they arrived at the Ripley flats. She reached out her window and signaled for the driver to pull off. The pickup, a Ford F350 Platinum dually with the license plate *DedlySrs,* stopped on a grassy lawn.

Jonetta called in the stop, ran the plate, got out and walked up to the driver's window, which was too dark to see through. She rapped on the glass and held her badge up to display. The window buzzed down two inches.

"Put it down all the way, driver. And keep your other hand on the wheel where I can see it." She looked into the cab and saw a mop-headed young man in his mid-twenties.

"License and registration, driver."

He fumbled in his wallet and handed them over.

"Gino Minetti, is that you?"

"Yes sir, uh, ma'am."

"Why are you following me, Gino?"

"I wasn't following you. Hey, can you make a traffic stop in a plain clothes cop car? Doesn't seem fair."

"Yes, I can, and don't lie to me, Gino; I've been watching you in my mirror ever since we left Minetti's Wine Store. You pulled into the school in Ripley, you followed me up this road and then passed me when I turned around, so you turned around and followed. But you didn't expect to see me at this curve, so you tried to stop, but it was too late, so you tried to be cool and drive by. And by the way, I could cite you for tinted glass; it's way too dark. So, why are you following me, Gino?"

"I was just...uh...going to the auto parts store in Sherman, officer."

"Then why did you turn around and come back before you got there?"

"I...uh, forgot my cash, I had to go back to get my cash."

She handed him his license. He opened his wallet to slip it in. She could see a wad of bills inside with credit cards.

"Looks like you have cash, Gino. And credit cards too. Step out of the truck, please. Registration says this truck belongs to Minetti Enterprises LLC, is that you?"

"No, my father."

"Does he know you're following a state police vehicle in his truck?" She gave a quick look inside the cab and saw nothing suspicious.

Gino looked at the ground. "I saw you checking out our business and decided to see what you were doing, so I followed."

"OK, I'm going to let you go, Gino, but get the tint off these windows, and stop following people unless you have a better story to tell. Now go on."

BCI Pope got back in her cruiser.

"Gino Minetti, she said, "in his father's truck."

210

"I recognized it from a couple of days ago," said Mac. "I followed him make a delivery in Ohio."

"So all of this cloak and dagger between the Minettis, Tim Riley, Mac Morrison, and now the Waterman's was all unearthed by a simple inquiry into old newspaper stories forty years ago?" asked Jonetta.

"Welcome to my world, Investigator Pope!" said Mac.

*****

Chapter Twenty Nine

Friday, May 26
Johnson's Auto Body Shop, Jamestown
3:45 p.m.

"Juan Johnson," said Mac, "this is Investigator Jonetta Pope, New York State Police, Bureau of Criminal Investigation."

"Call me Juan," he said, extending his hand to her.

"Mr. Johnson, I am making inquiries into a fatal accident in 2021 regarding Mr. and Mrs. John Waterman and their 2010 Ford Crown Victoria. I understand you have their vehicle here, and have had it here for the past two years continuously. Is that correct?"

"The Waterman car? Yes, Ma'am."

"And is it true that you had a visit from Officer Tim Riley of the New York BMV, who attempted to impound that car, saying he was acting on behalf of the State Police and BCI?"

"Yes, Ma'am. Would you like to see the video?"

"I would."

"Come into my office." Juan placed a thumb drive into his laptop and started the file.

"Here is Officer Riley arriving," Juan said. "You see that old black Crown Vic with the push bars? State Police hasn't used those in 10 years. Not an official car. I recognized this dude from two years ago. Right after the Waterman car was towed in, he showed up with his buddy, a guy who runs a restoration shop in Ripley."

"That would be Joey Minetti," Mac interjected.

"That's the one. Minetti wanted to buy the Waterman car," said Juan.

They watched the video in silence as Tim Riley made up one lie after another.

When the tape finished, Juan popped the jump drive and handed it to Jonetta Pope. "Figured you might want this," he said.

"Yes, thank you, Mr. Johnson."

"Juan, please."

"Thank you, Juan. May we see the Waterman car?"

"Right this way."

Mac went to the Police Explorer and got his cardboard box. They walked into the long garage, where the car was draped with a blue cotton cover.

"You can see the damage on the plastic rear bumper cover Investigator Pope."

"Please Juan, call me Jonetta."

"Jonetta. The impact was hard enough that it punctured the plastic and dented the crushable foam behind it."

Mac took his left bar plaster casting and handed it to Jonetta Pope.

"Try this on the left side," he said.

It fit the dents perfectly.

"Now try the one on the right."

It fit the dents perfectly.

"Now try the weld spatter."

It fit perfectly.

"It would seem," said BCI Pope, "that Juan and Mac have introduced new evidence into the Waterman accident case. Not sure if the way these castings were taken would be legally admissible, but standing here, there is no question. Riley's push bars on his cruiser, which I observed today, hit this car pretty hard at some time. Did it hit it and shove it over into the ravine? I don't know."

"But I do know that this video of Officer Riley impersonating an agent of the State Police and attempting to confiscate the Waterman car under false pretenses is serious enough for me to question him. I want to take possession of this car and have it sent to our crime lab, Juan."

"It's OK with me," he said, "the car actually belongs to Mac. I sold it to him."

"I give you permission to take it," Mac said, "with the understanding that whenever you are done with it, you will return it back to Juan. That was my agreement with him."

"That's fair," said Jonetta. "I will get a tag from my car and call for a tow truck. Juan, it will probably be a state truck, but if they are busy, it could be a private one. Just make sure he gives you authorization from the State Police Troop A to pick it up. Do not release it if the driver does not have that authorization."

"I won't."

"Your sign says you're also open on Saturday, Juan. That's a long week for such hard work."

"Just until noon. It's a good day for customers to come see their car. Lotta people are curious how repairs are going. Most of my work is paint and body, not heavy collision. Those customers like to come, see it, and chat. You know."

"Your wife doesn't mind you working Saturday?"

"She did mind, but I lost her two years ago. Cancer."

"I'm very sorry for your loss, Juan. I didn't mean to...."

"It's OK, Jonetta...I'll help Mac any way I can. I don't like Minetti or Riley. Figure they're up to no good."

"Well, guys, said Jonetta Pope, I guess we are done here. Let's take you home. Attorney Hillman and I have some talking to do."

*****

Friday, May 26
Captain Murphy B & B
4:30 p.m.

"Well, Jonetta, what do you think?" asked Morgan.

"As far as the Waterman accident, I need to interview Sheriff's Deputy Rinker. He wrote the report."

"I also need to question Officer Riley. We'll see if he has a valid alibi for the time of the Watermans' death. He could make up some reason why the marks on his push bars match the damage on the Waterman's car, such as he drove into their driveway to confront them about the fence, didn't stop in time, banged into it."

"I will start an internal investigation into Riley's misuse of his uniform and misrepresenting his authority to procure the Waterman car at Johnson's body shop. And as soon as I can see the video at Chem Systems Lab, I can nail him for that too."

"Jonetta," Mac said, "Angie will send you the Chem Systems video right now. Hasn't Colonel Justice already called Riley on the carpet?"

"I asked him to hold off until I had a chance to speak with you and see your evidence. Juan Johnson's video speaks for itself. He could be fired for that and could face charges from the State Police also."

Mac said, "Maybe we want to hold off questioning Riley until you talk to the Sheriff's deputy. It might spook him if he gets called in before we can make a case for an inquest. He could destroy his cruiser and we would lose that evidence."

"OK," said Jonetta, "I can wait."

Morgan said, "So, as of right now, how do you see this situation, Jonetta?"

"Right now, these cases certainly seem related and are suspicious. But with what we've got, I don't know if it's enough for an inquest on Watermans or Murphy. The Assistant Attorney General assigned to work with me will have to determine that."

"Meanwhile," said Mac, "the Minetti criminal enterprise gets away with murder."

"I'm sorry," Jonetta said, "it seems unfair, but there needs to be more substance and less speculation to build a case for prosecution. The Attorney may feel different; she may think there's enough to initiate an inquest not only on Waterman but also on Murphy. But look, guys, my next step is to interview Deputy Sheriff Rinker, and then talk to Tim Riley. We know the Riley patrol car's push bars match the damage to the Waterman bumper, but your unofficially obtained evidence might not hold in court, and that could definitely spook him to trash the push bars or the whole car before BCI has the opportunity to impound that car and do our own tests."

"I see," said Morgan. "Well, please keep me posted. Thank you for coming down and looking into this. When will you speak with Officer Riley?"

"After I interview Deputy Rinker, which should be tomorrow morning."

"Please let me know the outcome of those conversations," said Morgan.

"I will, and thank you for your cooperation," said Jonetta. "Thank you for your hospitality, Marybeth. I'm staying in Jamestown tonight. Here's my cell number if you need to call me."

*****

Friday, May 26
Barcelona pier
4:45 p.m.

"Well," said Pops to Mac, "you tried."

"No," said Mac, "Morgan tried, through legal channels, but Minetti and Riley have been clever. Looks like they could get away with five murders unless..."

"Shhh," said Pops, "here he comes now."

Tim Riley walked up the dock with his tackle box in hand.

"Lousy day," he muttered, "water's too warm, fish are down deep, nothing's biting. Muddy near shore."

"Be good tonight, though," Pops said. "Gonna be clear with a half moon over the lake. With no clouds, it'll get chilly fast, and fish will be up top looking for bugs. Shad may come up top too, and then there will be a feeding frenzy. Fishing a few miles offshore should be good."

"Hmm," said Riley. "Well, if you think so, Pops, maybe I should get some different tackle and go back out. Say, Mac, would you like to go out with me? Ever been night fishing on Lake Erie? It's really beautiful with the stars, moon, and maybe some swells."

"Yep, there'll be 2'-3' swells" Pops said, "count on that. You can see them rolling in now, and the breeze is picking up. Too rough for small craft, Tim, but your boat can handle them."

Mac said, "Well, I had planned to pack up tonight and leave for New Hampshire in the morning, but this is a once in a lifetime offer. What time do we go out, Tim?"

"Let's say seven p.m. That gets us out there before dusk, sound right, Pops?"

"Dusk is always good fishing on a clear night, yep."

*****

Friday, May 26
Murphy B & B
5:00 p.m.

"Hey, I'm going fishing with Riley tonight," said Mac.

"No shit?" said Roger. "How did that happen?"

"He didn't catch anything today. Pops told him night fishing will be good."

"Mac, did you know we painted a very expensive carbon fiber tackle box orange?"

216

"Well, if Pops is pissed, I'll buy him a new one."

"...If you're around to buy one."

"C'mon, Rog, we got this!"

*****

Friday, May 26
Joe Minetti's Perfect Restoration Shop
5:15 p.m.

Joe's cell phone buzzed as he laid body filler on a Porsche 911.

"OK, Joey, we're goin' out at seven p.m." Tim said.

"Good. So, they were messin' with your Crown Vic, eh Tim?"

"Yeah Joe, my guy across in the marina saw them do something while I was out on the lake. They put some pink stuff on my push bars. And later, when they came back with the lady cop, they did it again."

"Pink stuff?"

"My guy has good binoculars. He said it looked like modeling clay or Silly Putty, you know."

"Silly putty? Not good. This could come back on us. We shoulda crushed your car."

"Joey, you know I love my old patrol car!"

"Tim, I'm gonna come get it right now. Leave the title in the car with the keys. I'll call Banks scrap yard. Old man Weinstein closes at 5 p.m., but he lives there, so he'll open up for me and take the car. Once it's crushed, we got no worries."

"What am I gonna drive, Joe?"

"I'll give you a new Explorer that I repaired. It's only a year old, Tim. I'll drop it at your house and take yours. You take Morrison fishing and find out what he knows. And Tim: if he knows too much, leave him out there in deep water, way offshore."

*****

Chapter Thirty

Like most war plans, it went wrong from the beginning.

Instead of driving his old patrol car to the pier, Tim Riley stepped out of an older Toyota 4 Runner. He had a pole rigged for night surface lures and a different tackle box.

"Anna," he said, "I'll call you no later than 10:30."

"OK darling, be careful. Love you."

"Love you too, Anna."

As they boarded the *Deadly Serious* Mac asked, "Got a tackle box for every type of fishing, Tim?"

"Yeah, I learned a lot about fishing, but I'll never know as much as Pops. Where'd you get your rig?"

"Borrowed it from Pops," said Mac.

"All right, Mac, cast us off."

As the twilight glowed purple, Tim Riley steered the 34' *Deadly Serious* out into the huge expanse of Lake Erie.

"How far are we goin', Tim?"

"Three miles to start. We'll use the fish finder and make a few casts to see if we get any action. Some big swells are building, gonna be real rough ten miles out. You'll see hills on the horizon. Those are big waves, but we won't go that far offshore."

Mac started his distraction. "Man, its 72 degrees at sunset in Barcelona Harbor, New York. In New Hampshire, we might still be wearing flannel shirts and kicking on the wood stove tonight."

Once they were clear of the no-wake zone, Tim pushed his throttles to half-way and timed the rise and fall of the rolling swells to avoid crashing the hull against them. It was slow going, and the ride was pitching the boat up and down like a roller coaster, over and over and over.

218

Once they were three miles off shore, Tim cut the throttles to idle as darkness settled over the lake like a blanket. A half-moon was slowly rising. The swells were bigger, rhythmically lifting and dropping the boat three feet every ten seconds. It was like riding a bucking Bronco, only smoother. It was difficult for Mac to stand in one place without bracing against a seat. Tim had hold of the ship's wheel; he looked comfortable in his element.

The drone of the engines was low, so Mac pressed the record button on his phone and zipped it in his pants pocket.

"What's the biggest walleye you ever caught, Tim?"

"Eight pounds."

"Keeper?

"Took a picture and released him. Maybe I'll catch him again someday. Be even bigger."

"Fishing is good times, isn't it, Tim."

"The best. Relieves my stress."

"You got a lot of stress now, Tim? I mean, you're semi-retired."

"Yeah, bad stress headaches."

Mac said, "For me, stress makes blood clots that block my brain. Snaps like an electric shock, with a wicked headache, like yours. Probably doesn't help that I've had concussions, probably brain damage."

"Jeezuz," said Tim, "what's your stress from, Mac?"

"Building custom homes for rich people, Tim. They're a pain in the ass, always changing their mind. Move this wall, raise the roof, make the kitchen bigger, on and on. They give me foolish change-orders that I know won't work out. I usually wind up undoing it and going back to the original plan. What's your stress from, Tim?"

"Bad decisions, doing things I never wanted to do, things I knew I shouldn't. Eats me up, so I go fishing, but the headaches are bad. Sometimes I lose control. Anna always knows what to do. Anna keeps telling me I shouldn't...." Riley stopped, looked at Mac and kept quiet.

"Tim, you gotta get rid of the people that make your life bad. Know what I mean?"

Tim turned around from the wheel and looked at Mac like he had struck a chord in his heart.

"I know, Mac."

"Seriously, Tim?"

Mac was looking for a reaction to Tim's favorite high school phrase, and he got it.

Tim snapped around with a grin on his face.

"Yeah, seriously, I know."

"When did your headaches start, Tim?"

"High school football."

"Big dude like you probably hit hard as hell."

"Hit'em hard, Tim! That's what they used to yell. Hit'em hard!"

"You play Tackle, Tim?"

"And Center. Our team was so small some guys had to play both ways. Sometimes my head would be spinning after a game. 'Member how the TV shows would laugh and say 'that guy got jacked up'!"

"I remember," said Mac.

"They thought it was funny. But gettin' jacked up ain't funny."

"I had a CAT scan of my last concussion, Tim. You ever get a CAT scan?"

"Once, after the crash that retired me."

"What happened?"

"I was on Thruway traffic duty. It was early December, with a lake effect storm dumping wet snow faster than the plows could salt. It was snow over freezing rain, real slick. Snow on the grass median was like grease. If your tires ran off the road, grass would suck you in and you spin."

"So I was sittin' in the median, flashing my blues to slow folks down. Guy passes a big truck, loses control, and slides into the grass straight at me...BOOM! Right into my cruiser!"

"Wow! How bad, Tim?"

"They had to cut me out with the Jaws of Life™. Broke my left arm and leg, fractured my skull. They put a metal plate in my head. Still got a scar under my hair."

"Your arm and leg healed, but your brain wasn't the same, right Tim?" said Mac.

"Right; ever since then, I've had the bad headaches. One time I lost my temper on duty and roughed up a guy, so they pulled me off the street. I loved being a Trooper. It was my life."

"Why didn't they give you medical disability?"

"Docs said I was OK. What the fuck do they know? Are they inside my head?"

"Keep it simple, Tim. Hang with good people who do right by you. Go fishing and do cruise nights with Anna in your old patrol car. Good times with good people. Keep it simple."

"My patrol car, the last one I had. No one ever drove that car but me. I loved that car…"

"Left your patrol car home tonight, huh, Tim? Anna dropped you off."

Riley looked at him, started to speak, and thought better of it.

"You keep that car clean. I'll say that, Tim. Good memories. Hey, speaking of memories, I gotta take some photos. Look at that moon rising over the water."

Mac whipped out his cell phone and did a panorama, starting with Tim at the wheel. He made sure it was still recording before slipping it back into his zippered leg pocket.

"Looks like a good spot," Tim said, checking his fish finder screen. "Go ahead and make a few casts, Mac."

Mac grabbed his pole, opened his tackle box, and set it on the transom bait locker. He selected a lure, clipped it to his line, and made his first cast.

He closed the tackle box, and made his second mistake. He had turned his back on Tim Riley.

"Reel in slower, Mac," said Tim behind him. "Sorta sneak it past them, give'em a tease. Say, what was you guys doin' to my patrol car today?"

Mac turned around. Tim was holding a lead fish billy the size of a bowling pin down by his side, tapping his leg.

"Is that for the fish, or for me, Tim? Gonna club me and toss me over? How do you explain that when you come back without me, eh? Everyone saw me go out with you. Marybeth, Pops, and Roger, they were all watching, Tim."

"Look Mac, I got a guy watches my boat, he's moored across in the marina. He's got good binoculars. He saw you guys put pink putty on my push bars, so don't bullshit me, Mac!"

"Tim, I gotta be honest with you. We took impressions for the BCI Investigator. She's looking into the Waterman deaths two years ago. You're in a lotta trouble, Tim. We matched those impressions from your push bars to the Waterman's rear bumper, they were a perfect match."

"Don't bullshit me, Mac, that car is gone, crushed."

"No, it's not Tim. I bought it. And the BCI Inspector took possession today after we made the impressions. It was inside Johnson's shop while you were looking for it."

Tim's eyeballs clicked left and right, trying to figure: wait, what's happening?

"Yeah, Tim, we know you were at Johnson's body shop. That was a big mistake going down there, pretending to be on official State Police business to impound the Waterman car. We got you on video lying to Mr. Johnson in your BMV uniform. You wanted that car to destroy it, but I beat you to it, Tim. Big mistake. Colonel Justice has that video right now."

Tim was clearly agitated, thumping the lead billy against his leg.

"Yeah, Colonel Justice will be calling you in for questioning, Tim. BCI knows your car pushed the Waterman's car off the curve at Sherman Road and killed them. No question about it. Lab results 100% match your car to Waterman's, Tim."

"I never did no such thing, never pushed them off the road. Not me."

"Can you prove that, Tim? Where were you that Easter morning two years ago? Can you even remember? 'Cause your bars match their bumper. BCI is opening an inquest into their death now that they have those impressions. They are going to put you in the driver's seat, and that's going to be first degree murder, Tim. Seriously, no bullshit. You just said no one ever drove that car but you. You're gonna hang yourself with your own words."

Tim cocked his head like a dog hearing a far off whistle.

"Just remember something, Tim? Remember where you were that morning? Sunday, April 4, 2021? Easter Sunday. Were you behind the wheel of your old patrol car following the Watermans as they left the D Line ranch after their trail ride? Were you matching their speed when they arrived at the last curve above the Ripley flats, the one without an outside guard rail? Did you speed up and shove them off the road down the ravine and kill them? Was that you, Tim?"

Tim cocked his head left and right, like a dog hearing something weird and he couldn't place it.

"I remember. Easter Sunday," said Tim, "Anna was at the D Line. She was on the trail ride with Watermans. I remember. They were our neighbors, our friends, for 30 years."

"But you were mad at them, weren't you, Tim? They took down your fence. The cops had to come, you went nuts."

"Somethin' in my brain snapped with the fence. Terrible headache. It happens. Lost control. Didn't mean to hurt them. No, no, I wasn't driving my car that day. I had Joey's truck to tow Anna's horse over to D Line. While she was riding, Joey asked me to drive down to Erie and pick up some parts for him, but when I got there, it was closed. Easter Sunday, it was closed."

"So where was your patrol car, Tim?"

"Joey's shop, where I picked up his truck. I left the keys so he could move it."

"So, your best bud Joey Minetti set you up, Tim. Can't you see it? He used your car to kill the Watermans by pushing them off the road. If there was a snag, it was gonna be your car that was the murder weapon, and everybody knows you never let anyone drive your car. He set you up Tim!"

"Why, why would he want to kill the Watermans?"

"Because Rosemary Minetti embezzled $100,000 from her trade group, and Mrs. Waterman was auditing the books. Rosie was gonna go to prison, Tim, so Joe had to kill the Watermans to protect Rosie! Don't you get it? He set you up, Tim!"

Tim Riley just stood there, dazed, taking it all in, shaking his head. Suddenly, he seemed to grasp what had happened that Easter Sunday.

"HE DID SET ME UP! JUST LIKE THE DAY JIM MURPHY DIED! HE SET ME UP THEN TOO, I CAN SEE IT NOW! I KNOW HE DID!"

"Jim Murphy, Tim. What did Joe do?"

"He took the boat out early, told me I couldn't use it that day. It was good fishing, walleye were biting like crazy. I had to pier fish. He came back early with no fish, and a big scrape on the side of the boat. He said he hit a log. Told me to go ahead and take the boat out. So, I did. I stayed out 'til I caught my limit. When I came in, I heard Jim Murphy drowned. They found him floating two miles out and towed his boat in."

"Tim, Joe hit Murphy's boat and swamped it, knocked him overboard, then ran over him and split his skull. Tim, BCI is looking at that, too. We matched the paint on this boat with the paint on Jim's boat and his skull. We know this boat is the one that hit him. Murphy didn't drown; the *Deadly Serious* killed him. BCI is going to dig up his body and do a new autopsy. He didn't drown, Tim, Joe killed him with this boat, Tim!"

"You see what Joe did, Tim? He wanted people to see you going out before Jim's boat was found. He wanted you driving this boat with the big scrape on it. He set you up again, Tim! Seriously, your best bud, Tim? Joe was your best bud?"

Tim's eyebrows flew up. Joe Minetti's words rang out in his head (*"If he knows too much Tim, leave him out there, far offshore"*). Like a wet dog, Tim shook his head to clear his brain, but the anger clouded his judgement.

"AAARRGH!" Tim shouted, "FUCKIN JOE MINETTI!"

He charged at Mac, swinging the lead fish billy just as a big swell lifted the boat three feet and dropped it! The heavy club missed its mark, knocking him off balance and he crashed awkwardly into Mac, knocking him backwards over the stern seat. Mac's leg scraped something sharp as it kicked the tackle box and he fell overboard, splashing into the lake!

Three miles off shore, the deep water temperature was in the 40s and it took Mac's breath away! He dove to get below the propellers until he heard the sound of the engines throttling up and moving away from him. He surfaced for air, but Tim Riley wasn't looking for him. The *Deadly Serious* was headed for port, leaving Mac treading water in the frigid lake, miles offshore with darkness hiding him and three foot waves crashing over him.

"SHIT!" shouted Mac, "how the Hell!" *But*, he thought, *I got him on my phone!*

But no, he didn't have him. Tim didn't admit to anything, but he did put Joe Minetti behind the wheel of his car the day the Watermans were killed, and at the wheel of the *Deadly Serious* the day Jim was killed.

"FREAKIN' RES GESTAE!" Mac shouted, spinning around, trying to get his bearings. He kicked off his sneakers so he could swim better and realized how really cold the water was.

Sunset's last gasp of pink light washed the wave crests as Mac floated up on a large swell. He caught a glimpse of the *Deadly Serious* running fast for the harbor. A glint of light across the lake hit something orange floating in the distance.

The tackle box!

With a surge of adrenaline, Mac swam towards the box, keeping his head above water and his eyes on it. He had to get that box! The two minutes it took him to reach it felt like ten in the cold water. It was bobbing up and down like a cork as he carefully unlatched the lid to pull out the flare. He switched it on. Its blinding yellow LEDs lit up like a Christmas tree as it floated away.

With the tackle box latched back tight, he held onto it like a life preserver. Bobbing up and down on the swells, he reached down and unzipped his flank pocket. He pulled out his phone and held it up over his head. It was working. He tapped the screen, and dialed Roger.

"ROGER! LEVEL FOUR! REPEAT! LEVEL FOUR! I'M IN THE WATER!"

"COPY MAC! WE'RE COMING!!"

"LOOK FOR THE FLARE, ROGER! LOOK FOR THE FLARE!"

"WHAT ABOUT TIM, MAC?"

"HE'S HEADED FOR SHORE! TIM IS NOT THE MURDERER! JOE KILLED WATERMANS! JOE KILLED MURPHY! HURRY UP, ROG, WE GOTTA STOP TIM!"

"WE'RE COMING! WERE COMING! KEEP TALKING!"

"I'LL TRY, ROG!"

Mac held his phone out of the water with one hand, hanging onto the tackle box with the other while his feet were treading water.

Something heavy thumped him in the back!

He spun around as a large log with no bark slowly floated past, forty feet long and two feet thick. It had obviously been the water a long time and was slimy, riding up and down on the swells. Mac let go of the tackle box and tried to grab on, but his hand just slid off. The log was too slippery!

He shoved his phone back in his pocket and zipped it tight, then unsnapped his Leatherman pouch, pulled out the tool and unfolded the knife as the tackle box floated away.

Reaching up as high as he could, he stabbed the sturdy pointed blade into the log. Using it as a handhold, he scrambled out of the cold water, sitting astride the log with his legs dangling in the lake.

"YOU STILL THERE?" Roger shouted from his pocket.

"YEAH, I'M ON A LOG, ROG, I'M OUT OF THE WATER!"

The warm air felt wonderful! Mac laid down flat on his chest. Using his hands to paddle the log, he maneuvered it until he could grab the tackle box and set it up on top with him. He opened the box, cut off a length of fishing line, closed the box and tied its handle around the knife.

Mac scanned the black lake and saw the bobbing LED flare floating 50 feet away. He dove back into the cold water, swam to it, grabbed it and swam back.

Using the knife as his handhold, he again climbed back onto the slimy log. Now he opened the tackle box, cut off more fishing line and tied the flare to the tackle box handle. It sat high and proud, two feet above the swells. Mac yelled:

"ROGER, CAN YOU HEAR ME?"

"I HEAR YOU! WE'RE COMING, MAC! WE'RE COMING!"

"I'M ON A LOG, ROG, LOOK FOR THE FLARE! DON'T HIT THIS FRIGGIN LOG!"

"I SEE IT!" Pops shouted in the background.

Now Mac could see two spotlights coming at him. He could hear Pops' engine roaring.

He smiled.

"Been a good day, but it isn't over yet," he said to the log.

"C'MON POPS!"

✻✻✻✻✻

Friday, May 26
On Lake Erie, 3 miles off shore
8:00 p.m.

Had he been in a normal, calmer state of mind, Tim Riley would not have been running wide open in rough water on a dark night with so much flotsam, all of which was headed for the coffin corner at Barcelona Harbor.

But Tim was enraged! All he could think about was getting his hands on Joe Minetti and beating him senseless! He pulled out his cell phone and called Anna.

"ANNA!" he shouted over the roar of the engines.

"MEET ME AT THE PIER! TEN MINUTES! TEN MINUTES, ANNA!"

"TIM! ARE YOU ALL RIGHT, TIM? WHAT'S HAPPENED?"

"THAT FUCKIN' JOEY SET ME UP ANNA! HE SET ME UP! HE KILLED THREE PEOPLE, AND HE MADE IT LOOK LIKE I DID IT, AND NOW THE COPS ARE AFTER ME, AND I'M GONNA GET FIRED FROM MY JOB, AND EVERYTHING IS TURNING TO SHIT, AND IT'S ALL BECAUSE OF THAT FUCKIN' JOE MINETTI! TEN MINUTES, ANNA!"

He hung up and stared through the windshield, trying to make out obstacles that were coming at him too fast, but it was too dark, and he had no lights. He knew running fast was dangerous, but he wasn't going to slow down.

He was blasting through the swells. The boat was crashing down on every other one when, suddenly, a log appeared, directly ahead! He heeled the boat over onto its starboard gunwale...

"*WHUMP!*"

The starboard engine's propeller whacked the log, snapping off all three blades! The engine spun up like a turbine: 'wheeeeee'!

As the speeding boat skidded over the top of the log, one blade on the port propeller clipped it and bent! The engine kept running, but a strong vibration shook the boat.

226

'WA-wa-WA-wa-WA!'

"SHIT SHIT SHIT!" screamed Riley.

He yanked back both throttles, shut down the starboard engine and ran the port engine at quarter speed. It still vibrated, but he could limp home. But he wouldn't be there in 10 minutes; it might take him half an hour.

"DAMN, DAMN, DAMN! Nothing to do but ride it in," Tim said to the waves slapping the stern. His head hurt too much to think. He would talk to Anna. Anna would know what to do.

*****

"FLARE!" Roger yelled at Pops, pointing at the dark horizon!

Flashing yellow lights were bobbing up and down above the swells.

Pops heeled the Bertram over to starboard and made course adjustments.

"BE THERE IN 30 SECONDS," he said, throttling back. "TRAIN THEM SPOTS ON THAT LOG!"

Roger held one spotlight in his left hand and one in his right. There was Mac, sitting on the log with his legs in the water, as happy as *Tom Sawyer*[28] floating down the Mississippi.

"AHOY, THE LOG!" Pops shouted.

"PERMISSION TO COME ABOARD, CAPTAIN?" Mac shouted back.

"PERMISSION GRANTED, MAC!"

Pops expertly swung the stern around so his port side kissed the log.

"Get yer ass up here, you piece of crap!" Roger said. "You know I was worried about you?"

"Love you too, buddy!" said Mac as he untied the tackle box and handed it to Roger. Mac yanked his knife out of the log, shoved it in its pouch, grabbed Roger's outstretched hand, and stepped up and onto the Bertram.

"Now that's what I call a rescue!" Mac said, "Great job Pops!"

"Haven't had this much fun since shore leave!" Pops cackled.

"Pops, how fast can we get back to the harbor?" Mac asked.

"We got a following sea. If I time the swells right, we can run 15 knots, so long as Roger lights the way with the spotlights. Fifteen minutes if we're lucky."

"Roger!" shouted Mac, "Call Morgan. Level Four! Tell him to gun up and take Riley when he docks. I think he's mad enough to kill Joe Minetti and I need him alive!"

227

"Will do. Lucky it's a clear night, Mac. We tracked a strong cell signal, and you weren't too far out."

"Hey, Pops," Mac said, "got any towels?"

"In the port side locker. Say, Roger, point that top spot over there to port 15 degrees. Mile ahead."

Roger shined the top spotlight off to the left. There was a boat in the distance headed for port.

"OK, Roger, put your other spot on the transom. Mac, use the binoculars in the cubby. You see gold against black?

"I do. Is that the *Deadly Serious?* How'd we catch up to her so fast, Pops?"

"Dunno, she's runnin' slow. Let's see if we can overtake her."

When they were within 100 yards, they could clearly read the name on the stern, and it *was* the *Deadly Serious*. Tim Riley heard their engine coming behind him, turned his pilot's chair and was blinded by their spotlights.

"AHOY, *DEADLY SERIOUS*!" shouted Pops into his microphone. The sound blasted out from a cabin-mounted loudspeaker. "HEAVE TO! YOU ARE UNDER CITIZEN'S ARREST! PREPARE TO BE BOARDED!" They were now 50 feet off its stern and closing fast.

Tim Riley reached into his cabin and came out spitting fire! The crack of a pistol split the air. "Pow! Pow! Pow!" but the pitching of both boats made his shots go astray.

In a flash, Roger had his heavy Colt 1911 out of its shoulder holster. He fired five quick shots.

"BAM! BAM! BAM! BAM! BAM!"

Tim's windshield exploded and showered him with glass!

Riley held his hands up over his head, dropped his gun, and pulled his throttle to idle as the *Miss Bertie* came alongside the *Deadly Serious*.

"TIM!" Mac shouted, "YOU'RE NO KILLER! YOU'VE DONE SOME BAD THINGS, BUT YOU CAN MAKE A DEAL AND TESTIFY AGAINST MINETTIS!"

Tim looked exhausted. He held his hands up in surrender.

"MR. RILEY!" Roger shouted, "I AM MAKING A CITIZEN'S ARREST FOR THE ATTEMPTED MURDER OF MAC MORRISON. DO YOU UNDERSTAND?"

Tim nodded and lowered his head. Roger leaped aboard the *Deadly Serious* as the two boats kissed gunwales.

"Turn around Tim, hands behind your back!" said Roger. He whipped a long zip tie from his belt loop, cuffed Tim's hands, and sat him on a stern bench seat. He then zip-tied Tim's belt to a cleat.

"It's all over now, Tim. You're gonna be OK. Just glad we caught you before you did something stupid."

"My head hurts so bad," Tim said. "I just wanna see Anna. Gotta talk to Anna, please let me talk to Anna."

"You'll see her soon. Now I'm gonna bring this boat in, so just rest easy. It's gonna be all right Tim. MAC, YOU GOT YOUR PILLS?" Roger shouted.

Mac nodded and pulled his aspirin from his pocket. It looked like they were still dry inside the watertight box, so he tossed the pillbox to the other boat. Roger tipped Tim's head back and shook four pills into his mouth.

"Chew those Tim."

Pops shouted, "LOTS OF SHALLOW WATER AND ROCKS ROGER! FOLLOW ME AND WE'LL GO IN SLOW!"

✻✻✻✻✻

Chapter Thirty One

Friday, May 26
Barcelona Harbor Pier
8:30 p.m.

As Pops berthed *Miss Bertie,* a soggy Mac jumped off into the waiting arms of Marybeth Murphy. She gave him a bear hug and a kiss and then pushed him away, stabbing his chest three times with her trigger finger.

"MAC MORRISON!" she scolded, "You had us scared to death! Roger called and said you were Level Four in the lake, what the hell?"

"All part of the plan, M. Hey, Buddy, miss me big boy?"

"Rowrf!' Buddy did the Buddy-dervish, twirling around him.

"Hey," said Mac, "Who've we got here? Investigator Jonetta Pope!"

Roger said, "Jonetta, I am turning over my prisoner to you. I placed him under citizen's arrest for the attempted murder of Mac Morrison. He tried to club him with a lead fish billy, shoved him overboard and left him in rough seas three miles off shore. He also fired three shots at us when we tried to overtake and arrest him."

"However," interjected Mac, "if Tim will cooperate with prosecutors to bring down the Minetti criminal empire, then I will ask the prosecutor to drop my charges."

"Wait," said Jonetta, "I have to read him his rights."

She read him his rights, and he waived them.

"Mr. Riley, do you wish to cooperate with BCI to investigate possible criminal activity by certain members of the Minetti family?" Jonetta Pope asked.

A woman's voice called out, "DO IT TIM; DO IT!"

"ANNA! Anna, I'm so sorry, Honey! I've been wrong a long time!"

"You were hanging out with the wrong guy for a long time, Tim!"

She came over, hugged Tim and held him by the arm. "May I ride with him in your car, Officer Pope?"

Jonetta informed Tim Riley that he was being held on the charge of attempted murder, and that his wife, Anna, was being taken into custody for questioning. She placed both of them in her Police SUV.

"Jonetta," Mac said, "I have a recording of Tim Riley saying that he was not the driver of his old patrol car the day the Watermans were killed. Tim had borrowed Joe Minetti's truck to run an errand for him and left his car at his shop during the time Watermans were killed."

"Can he prove that? And...where is Riley's old patrol car?"

"I don't know," Mac said, "his wife dropped him off at the pier at seven p.m."

Jonetta opened the back door to her SUV and faced the Rileys.

"Mr. Riley, where is your old State Trooper car?"

"Joe told me to leave it at home. He took it to Erie to crush it."

"Where in Erie did he take it?"

"Bank's Breakers and Scrap, it's down by the docks."

Jonetta said, "We need to get that car. If Joe Minetti was the driver, the motive was obviously to kill Mrs. Waterman before she could submit her audit findings. If Riley has an alibi, I think I could charge Joe Minetti with suspicion of the Waterman's murder, but we need that car. Marybeth, may I use your house? I need to call for a Trooper to take the Rileys to Fredonia while we go to Erie. I want them secure off this public pier."

"Of course you may, Jonetta. I'll meet you all inside the back porch."

"And I need a dry shirt and sneakers!" Mac said.

✵✵✵✵✵

Friday, May 26
Murphy B & B office
8:45 p.m.

"Can I hear the recording, Mac?" Jonetta asked.

Mac pulled out his phone and put it on speaker. There was background engine noise, but all the words could be understood. It was a damning shift of blame from Tim Riley to Joe Minetti for the Waterman deaths.

Trooper Andy Gregor was watching the late innings of the baseball game when his phone buzzed.

"Hello?" he said.

"Trooper Gregor, this is BCI Investigator Jonetta Pope. Sorry to disturb you, but I need you to report to me ASAP at the Murphy B & B. How soon can you be here in uniform?"

"Fifteen minutes."

"Make it ten, Trooper, lights and siren."

"Jonetta," said Angie, pointing at her computer, "I got Banks Breakers and Scrap in Erie on *Google Earth* view. Here is the address."

"OK," said Jonetta, "I'm putting it into my phone. Mr. Riley, you don't have to answer…"

"He'll answer, Officer, we want to help," said Anna.

"Is that an accurate recording? Did you say those things?"

"Yes."

"And did you leave your car at Minetti's shop the day the Watermans were killed, Easter Sunday two years ago?"

"Yes."

"I know he did, Officer," Anna Riley said, "He towed my horse trailer to the ranch, dropped me off and then went to Minettis."

"How do you know he left his car there?"

"Because it was a beautiful morning, so he took a picture of his car with Minetti's shop in the background with the message, 'Happy Easter, Love Tim.' I could never forget that. And he was sitting in Joe's F-350 when he took the picture. You can see the garage door opener clipped to the passenger visor. I always said he should have gotten out of the truck to take the picture, but now I guess it was meant to be that he didn't."

"Do you still have that picture, Mrs. Riley?"

"Of course, it's in my phone! Give me a minute, and I'll find it."

"Tim, do you have an alibi when the Watermans were killed? 10:30 a.m. April 4, 2021."

"Joe sent me to a parts store in Erie, but when I got there, they were closed for Easter."

Mac said, "He might show up on security video, if it still exists."

"Mr. Riley, do you remember the name of that store you drove to on Easter Sunday, 2021?"

"Um, it's a national chain, same one as in Sherman. It has a red, white and blue logo.

"American Auto?" Mac said.

"That's it!"

"Angie," said Morgan, "let's find that store!"

232

"Hello!" shouted Trooper Andy Gregor, "OK to come in?"

"Come in, Andy!" Marybeth called out. "We're in the office!"

"It would help if Tim Riley had an alibi for that two hour gap," said Jonetta.

"Found it!" Anna Riley shouted. "Here's the picture of Tim's car at Minettis, Easter Sunday 2021. Its date and time are on the bottom!" She brought her phone and turned it so they all could see.

"Hey guys!" shouted Angie, "I have the manager of the American Auto store on the phone. Good thing they stay open late! They save security video to the Cloud, and it is not purged. He's got someone looking back for that date now, said it should only take a few minutes."

Investigator Jonetta Pope got on her car radio and called for two State Troopers to go to the Minetti compound to arrest Joseph Junior and Rosemary Minetti on charges of suspicion of murder and conspiracy.

When she came back into the house, Mac was anxious to get going after the Riley car. And he needed Jonetta's authority to do it.

"Trooper Gregor," Jonetta said, "take Mr. Riley and transport him to Fredonia Troop A for booking. The charge is the attempted murder of Mackenzie Morrison. We are also going to take Mrs. Riley in custody so she cannot speak with anyone until we have the Minettis. She is being brought in for questioning, but is not being charged at the moment. I've got to go to Erie to recover the Riley car before it gets crushed, and Mac is coming with…"

"THEY GOT IT!" Angie shouted. "American Auto security cam, Sunday April 4, 2021, 10:30 a.m. Big dude, their description, looking in the glass front door and shaking the handle, turning around, getting in a light colored Ford F-350 dually pickup, vanity license plate reads *DedlySrs*. I'm having them email the video to me, and I'll forward it to your phone, Jonetta."

"Wow. Sometimes all the tech stuff actually works," Jonetta said.

"Well, Mr. Riley," said Jonetta, "sounds like you have your alibi in the Waterman case. Congratulations, one less thing to stress about. And that could put Joe Minetti in the driver's seat of Tim's cruiser for Waterman's murder. OK, I have enough. Let's see if we can pick up the Minettis."

"Thanks, God," Tim said with his eyes looking up and his hands clasped together like a little boy.

Anna gave him a hug. "Tim, we're going to get through this together! If they put Minettis in prison, our lives will be better than ever!"

"Attorney Hillman, while we are gone, would you, Roger and Angie write up the events of this evening?" Jonetta said.

"Glad to. Now get going, you two! Get that car and catch a murderer!"

"Stay, Buddy," said Mac, "I'll be back soon!"

'Rowrf!' Buddy pushed his giant paw into Mac's hand for a last touch goodbye.

*****

Friday, May 26
I-90, En Route to Banks' Breakers and Scrap, Erie, Pennsylvania
10:00 p.m.

"Take the Bayfront Connector to East Avenue, Jonetta," said Mac, as he watched the navigation system.

"Got it," said Jonetta. She was driving 95 mph. Roads were dry, the night was clear, quarter moon, good visibility and traffic was light.

"Here's the Bayfront Connector, hope we're in time, Mac."

"Jonetta, Tim really loves his old cruiser. He would never let it be crushed, but Joe Minetti has some kind of weird hold over him. I think Tim has a traumatic brain injury that was misdiagnosed 20 years ago after a car crash on Trooper duty."

"Feeling sorry for him now, Mac?"

"Kinda. I think he's a pathetic brain-damaged schmuck who came under the power of an evil, manipulative Rasputin$_{29}$, namely Joe Minetti. But I think his life can still be salvaged. I think he has a good heart, and a good wife to help him."

"Who knew a softie humanitarian lurked in the heart of the New Hampshire Avenger!" smirked Jonetta.

"Hey! Here we are, take this ramp for East Street!" Mac pointed as he spoke.

The tall chain link fence had a spool of razor wire on top, like a prison. They pulled up to the front gate. Jonetta reached out her window and pressed a call button. A moment later, a scratchy voice responded.

"Vee closed! Come back Monday!"

"NEW YORK STATE POLICE, SIR!" Jonetta shouted, "WE NEED TO TALK TO YOU. ARE YOU HERE, ON SITE?"

"State Police? Vats da problem?"

"No problem with you, sir. Are you here? Can you come out and speak with us? I'm going to turn on my lights. I am Inspector Jonetta Pope of the Bureau of Criminal Investigation, New York State Police."

Jonetta turned on her blue flasher and hit her squawker 'wip! wop!'

The scrap yard office was located in an old house behind the fence. A light blinked in a second floor window. A man appeared and looked out. He cranked the window open and yelled.

"OK, OK, I BE RIGHT DOWN."

"Huh! Is that Mr. Banks?" asked Mac. "He lives at his scrap yard?"

In a minute, the front door rattled open. A short fireplug of a man with broad shoulders and thick legs like a small sumo wrestler shuffled out. He had to be 80 years old, Mac thought. He carried a large ring of keys jangling at his side, which he used to unlock a stout padlock and slide back the front gate.

"Come in, come in, I lock behind you."

Jonetta pulled her Explorer inside the gate.

"OK, vassa deal?"

"Are you Mr. Banks?" she asked.

"I'm Sol Weinstein." He pronounced the W like a V, 'Veinstein.' "Dis iss my scadap yard, for fifty years. Banks vas before, I bought from him. Vat is da trouble?"

"Mr. Weinstein, did you accept a black Ford Crown Victoria tonight for crushing? I want you to know, you are not in any trouble, but that car is part of a murder investigation. We are here to recover that car if you have it."

"Yah, I have da car. I got a call, guy I know, he says he wants to bring me a car tonight, can I take it at seven o'clock. My yard closes at five, but I say, OK, I can take it, but it's Shabbat, so I don't take any money."

"Did you crush it?"

"No, because of Shabbat, my Jewish holy day begins at sunset, tonight, Friday night. So vonce I close, no more business until sunset Saturday. Also, som-ting seems suspicious; I'm tinking, 'vatsa hurry?' So, Monday, I vass gonna call New York and see, is it stolen?"

"Can we see the car?" said Jonetta.

"Sure, sure, I alvays cooperate vit da law. Come, come."

He walked with sturdy strides like a man who knows every inch of his domain and can find his way in the dark. They turned a corner behind the scrap yard office and there sat Tim Riley's Crown Vic, undamaged.

Mac used the flashlight on his cellphone to check the dashboard VIN plate.

"It's the Riley car. I took a photo of the VIN plate when we made the impressions, this is it."

"So, vat's da deal, officer?"

"Mr. Weinstein," Jonetta asked, "who brought this car here?"

"It vass Joe Minetti from New York. He brings cars from his body shop, usually just da scadaps after he pick it over for parts."

"Mr. Weinstein, this car is material evidence in a murder investigation. It belongs to a person who was arrested this evening. Mr. Minetti obtained this car under false pretenses and should not have brought it to you. I am going to ask you to release the car to me. I will give you a receipt."

"It's OK, I'm glad you take it. Title and keys are in it."

Jonetta Pope began writing out a receipt.

"Mr. Weinstein," Mac asked, "what is your accent, Polish?"

Sol Weinstein blinked back a thousand years of Polish history at the mention of his motherland.

"Yah, Poland. You know Poland?"

Mac said, "My uncle Abe Solomon was of Lithuanian ancestry. He fought in World War II. We had many relatives who came to the U.S. after the war and they stayed with us in New Hampshire. Their accent was like yours."

"Ahhh, Lithuanian! Kissink cousins! Did you know Lithuania and Poland ver one country, tvelve million people, da richest country on earth in da 1600s?"

"I did not."

"Dey had a kink, a proud kink, grand palaces, and da second democratic constitution in da vorld, after USA."

"When did you come here, Mr. Weinstein?"

"After da vor. My parents vass killed at Auschvitz. I vas a baby. Nazi doctors experimented on babies. Made me look like I do. Short, but strong, like bull. After da vor, I vass sent to camp vit other Polish Jews who survived, and brought to America, my home, very proud to be American."

"Mr. Weinstein, I'm sorry for the loss of your parents. In a way, I am here because of the death of my parents forty years ago. I believe Joe Minetti is the man who killed them, so I will not rest until we have him in prison."

"Vaa?"

Sol Weinstein lunged forward and gripped Mac in a bear hug!

"Ve haff to go on, ve haff to, it's all ve can do. Vat iss your name, son?"

"Mackenzie Morrison, Mr. Weinstein. I'm so glad to know you."

"You haff respect, Mackenzie Morrison, you know Lithuania and Poland, you haff the heart of this old Polack. You come back and see me sometime, ve sit and talk. Even on Shabbat, ve can sit and talk. OK?"

"It's a deal, Mr. Weinstein, I'll come back."

"OK, you go now in peace, my new friend."

"Jonetta, OK if I drive the Crown Vic?"

"Yes, follow me to Troop A in Fredonia. I'm impounding that car. We'll start the crime analysis tonight by comparing it to the Waterman car."

"I'll be right behind you. This is going to make Tim Riley very happy."

"Oh?"

"We saved his beloved patrol car. Something to look forward to: driving it again someday."

*****

Friday, May 26
In A Truck Stop on I-90, City of North East, Pennsylvania
11:00 p.m.,

"Thanks for stopping, Jonetta. The car needed gas, and I needed coffee. I still feel clammy! Brrr!"

Jonetta Pope looked at the huge waffle Mac was devouring and said, "Well, I'm glad we stopped, too. I need to call Trooper Gregor. I'll put him on speaker."

"Trooper Gregor? This is Investigator Jonetta Pope. Give me a full report."

"I booked the Rileys. They are in a holding cell waiting for you to finish the paperwork. Regarding the Minettis, responding Troopers did not find Joe Junior and Rosemary at home. Gina Minetti said they left. Troopers searched the house and confirmed they were not there."

"Did she say where they went?"

"No. They got a phone call about 8:30, after which Joe went out to his shop, put some stuff in his truck, and they left in a hurry."

"8:30," said Mac. "That's about the time you arrested the Rileys on the pier."

"Huh!" Jonetta nodded. "OK, Trooper Gregor, where are you now?"

"I'm at Troop A, figured you might still need me tonight. Did you get the car?

"We did. We are on our way back to Troop A now. Can you wait for us and give Mac Morrison a ride back to Barcelona Harbor?"

"Sure can."

*****

Chapter Thirty Two

Saturday, May 27
New York State Police Troop A Quarters, Fredonia, New York
12:30 a.m.

Jonetta Pope climbed out of her Explorer. "I'm bushed," she said. "It's been a long day, but we made remarkable progress in twelve hours."

"I agree, but we let the real killer get away," said Mac.

"With Riley's in custody," she said, "I'm going to wait 'til morning and have a state's attorney meet me here. We'll go over all the casework you prepared for me, show her the two cars, and let her hear the recording you made of Riley on the boat. Let's see what she says. I'm also going to interview the Sheriff's deputy who responded to the Waterman accident scene and submitted the report."

She continued, "It's possible that, by then, the Minettis will have returned home, and we can pick them up. They don't know how close we are to cracking the Waterman case, and with the Rileys in custody, they can't warn them, even though I don't think they would."

"So, I think we have a little time, Mac. Let's get a few hours rest, take a deep breath, and let the lawyers catch up with us. We preserved the evidence, and we have a lot of other circumstantial to back it up."

"Jonetta, can I ask you one favor before I head back to the Murphy B & B?"

"Sure."

"Can you bring Tim Riley out into the bullpen? I want to show him his car. He thinks Joe crushed it, and as bad a day as Tim has had, and as much trouble as he is in, let's give him something good to sleep on."

"Mac Morrison, you are a softie."

"I never kick a man when he's down. Unless he's a murderer, then I never let him up."

"OK, wait here, Mac. I'll go get the Rileys."

They both looked defeated as they walked out holding hands. They were kind of a sweet sight to Mac, down, but not out. He was going to help the Rileys, the same people he wanted to put behind bars just a few hours earlier.

"Tim, Anna, how are you doing?"

"We're OK," Anna said. "They gave Tim some more aspirin for his headache, and its better. We're both still in shock, but I told Tim, it's going to be good in the end. We are going to cooperate, ask for leniency and get through this together."

"Tim," said Mac, "I told you, and I meant it, if you and Anna cooperate fully with BCI, I will drop my charges against you. You tried to brain me with the fish billy, and you left me in the lake three miles out in damn cold water. Then you fired three shots at us. That's three times attempted murder, Tim. But nobody died, nobody even got hurt, and no hard feelings on my part *if* we can nail Joe Minetti for murder. I won't stop until we do."

"We understand," Anna said.

"Anyway, it's been a hard day for all of us, so I thought a little good news might cheer you up before you go to sleep. Come with me."

They walked down a long hall. Mac opened the door, and there, parked in the middle of the bullpen lot, under a brilliant spotlight, sat Tim Riley's black Crown Vic Trooper car.

"MY PATROL!" Tim shouted. "How did…?"

"You have to thank Mac Morrison, Mr. Riley," Jonetta said. "He pushed me hard for twelve hours on this case. We raced down to Erie, got Mr. Weinstein to open the scrap yard, and by the good luck of his holy day, the car had not been touched. I took possession, and the car is now impounded for criminal analysis. We strongly believe that your car was the murder weapon that killed the Watermans."

"Tim," said Mac, "someday, when this is all over, I'm going to give your car keys back. You and Anna are going to have a good life again, maybe the best ever, in your old patrol car."

Big fat tears splashed down Tim and Anna Riley's cheeks.

"Good night," Mac said. "I'll help you."

He turned and walked away as they were led back to their cells.

*****

Andy Gregor was waiting in the lobby.

"Hey, Andy, glad to see you. Man, it's been a whirlwind day, but I think we are on the right track. I am ready to get outta these stinky clothes, take a scalding hot shower, and hit the sack."

"Well, I'm back on duty at seven, Mac, so I'll probably just stay in uniform after I drop you off."

"Tell you what, Andy, how about you and Sandy come over for dinner tonight. I don't think much is going to happen today, it sounds like all lawyer time. I might just go pier fishing with Buddy, sit in a lawn chair and snooze."

"Boy, that sounds good. Let me talk to Sandy, and I'll let you know."

"OK, back to Barcelona Harbor!"

*****

Saturday, May 27
Murphy B & B
1:30 a.m.

Trooper Andy Gregor's tires crunched on the pea gravel as he pulled up to the back door of the Captain Murphy B & B. The house was ablaze with lights like a Christmas homecoming.

"Looks like they waited up for you, Mac."

"Oh, all I want is a hot shower and a big soft bed!"

"Hey, Mac, maybe I'll talk to you in the morning. I'm gonna go get a few hours sleep."

"Sounds good, Andy. Thanks again."

'ROWR! ROWR! ROWRF! ROWRF!'

Buddy came charging out the porch door with the old wooden screen going 'gronk' and 'whap' behind him!

"Hey, Buddy-boy, did you miss me?"

'ROW! ROW! ROWRF!' He did the Buddy-dance for Mac, round and round and round him.

"I know. That's the longest we've ever been apart. I am gonna sleep good tonight, Buddy-boy!"

"NOT BEFORE YOU GET IN HERE AND TELL US EVERYTHING!" shouted Angelica Morelli.

"Ohh, do I have to?"

241

"Yes, you do! We have been worried sick about you! We figured Jonetta Pope had to shoot it out with Joe Minetti in an Erie scrap yard."

"Nothing so dramatic."

"Did you get the car?"

"We did. I drove it back to Troop A in Fredonia."

"Didn't get crushed?"

"What? On Shabbat? With the scrap yard owner being an 80-year-old Polish guy named Sol Weinstein?"

"Wow!" said Marybeth. "Talk about luck. What about Minettis?"

"Gone."

"Any idea where?"

"No. And it's odd because we had Rileys under wraps. Minettis didn't know we could be closing in on them."

"Someone tipped them," said Roger. "You think it was Trooper Andy?"

"No, I do not. Gina said they got a call about 8:30, loaded up their truck and left. That was before Andy even got called by Jonetta to come and assist. He couldn't have known."

"So Morgan, tomorrow Jonetta Pope is going to interview the Sheriff's deputy who was at the scene of the Waterman accident. Maybe we'll get some answers from him, or maybe we'll get lies, but maybe we can catch him in a lie, too. Next, with both cars at Troop A, she will have her criminologist go over them before she meets with a state attorney."

"Lotta strong circumstantial evidence," said Morgan.

"You think it's enough?" asked Mac.

"I do. BCI can do their own impression analysis of the two cars and reopen the file, see the photos taken at the scene, and see the rear damage that is still present on the Waterman car. We know the chain of possession was secure at Johnson's. Plus, Tim Riley's attempt to confiscate the Waterman car indicates a conspiracy to destroy material evidence. And we have a motive: Mrs. Waterman's audit of Rosemary Minetti's books. Yes, that's enough."

"So now all we have to do is find them," said Mac.

"Well," said Morgan, "once the state attorney agrees to prosecute, my job will be done, so Angie and I can go home."

"WAIT A SECOND, MORGAN!" shouted Mac. "You are going to sue the Minetti estate for punitive damages and wrongful death on behalf of Marybeth for her parents' murder! And that is just for her parents. Maybe you can get the Murphy case reopened, too!"

242

"Yes. And I can do that from my New Hampshire office and come back here as needed."

"Well, if the cops can't find the Minettis, *I will*!" said Mac.

"Mac…" said Angie, shaking her head.

"And I'm staying," said Roger, "haven't had this much fun in a long time!"

"Well, let's all sleep on it," said Marybeth. "Due to this late hour, breakfast will be served at nine a.m. And Mac…"

"Yes, M."

"You stink. Strip those clothes off and toss them outside your door. I'll wash them overnight."

"Yes, Ma'am."

"And one more thing…"

"Yes?"

"Gimme a smooch, but don't touch me. Just wanna say thank you, and good job!"

"Yes, MA'AM!"

*****

Mac desperately wanted a hot shower before he turned in. As he stripped off his pants, he saw that the GPS Tracker he had taped to his ankle was gone! And he had a long scrape on his legs.

'Must have bled some, better wash that out,' he thought, 'can't imagine how filthy the lake is.'

He had to think. He taped it to his ankle. Where could it have fallen off?

Did he scrape it off on the log?

He was too tired to think, or care. Buddy groaned and rolled over when Mac finally laid down to sleep.

*****

Chapter Thirty Three

Saturday, May 27
Port Stanley, Ontario, Canada
Aboard the former *Deadly Serious,* (now badged *Rosie's Revenge*)
8:00 a.m.

"Sleep OK, Rosie?"

"Little stiff, Joe. How far did we come?"

"90 miles."

"Any food aboard?"

"Instant coffee, pop and some of those freeze dried emergency meals in the fridge."

"How long are we gonna stay gone, Joe?"

"Long as it takes. It's time for us to retire, Rosie. We're 62, got no debt, the kids can run their businesses and Gina can take over the vineyard from Pops. They don't need us."

"How much do we have?"

"I took $3,000 shop cash, all I had. Gino gave me another two."

"That won't last long. It costs $2,000 to fill these fuel tanks. And we can't use credit cards if they're looking for us. You disabled our phones right, Joey?"

"Yep."

"What'll we do for money?"

"I'll sell the boat. Already got a buyer. I texted him last night before we left."

"Where?"

"Conneaut. The guy runs a scrap yard in Ashtabula. He's a friend of Sol Weinstein. All those scrappers know each other. He deals in a lotta cash."

"Can we get a good price?"

"Rosie, it's like this, he knows I'm jacked up, or I wouldn't be calling him wanting cash today. He's wanted this boat for a while. I told him I'd call him first."

"So, he lowballed you? "

"Not bad, 300 grand. He knows it's worth 350. Plus, he's tossing in an old cop car. We got no good options and this really works for us. I planned for this, Rosie."

"We'll be in Conneaut by noon. I got the title on the boat, clean, no liens. From Conneaut, we'll drive to Jersey. Poppa arranged for our friends there to sneak us on a freighter that's shipping our Minetti juice to Sardinia. We disappear. 300 grand lasts us a long time in Sardinia. And Gino can send us cash with the grape juice shipments. You know they give you an old house in Sardinia if you promise to settle there? You're gonna love that Mediterranean climate, Rosie."

"What about passports?"

"In the cabin locker."

"OK, good, Joe. You always plan ahead."

*****

In a crack between the bulkhead and the fold down seat on the after-deck of the hastily renamed *Rosie's Revenge*, a square black box, no bigger than a matchbox, was jammed in tight. The folding scissors hinge that held the seat in deployed position jutted out just enough that it had caught Mac Morrison's leg as he pitched overboard. The metal strap had scraped the tape loose from his ankle and jammed the Tracker Box in a dark crevice out of sight. The box was still activated, and its little electronic heart was cheerily beating out its signal, beaming its position to a satellite in the heavens.

*****

Saturday, May 27
Captain Murphy B & B
8:00 a.m.

"Morgan," said Mac, "you've got to push hard, demand an inquest into Jim Murphy's death, and keep the pressure on the state to indict Minettis on Waterman's death. With the cooperation of the Rileys and Jonetta Pope's investigation, aren't they ready?"

245

"They probably will be as soon as they interview the Sheriff's Deputy. No matter what, I'll file Monday."

"I hate wasting time. Minettis could be 1,000 miles away by now."

"Could be, Mac, nothing we can do about it. What are you doing this morning?"

"Guess I'll check on the progress at my barn site. Maybe call the surveyor and make sure he filed the subdivision. Let me check my phone, see if I got messages overnight. Oh! Hey!"

Mac suddenly got up and called to Buddy.

"C'mon, Buds, walkies."

'Rowrf!' Buddy scrambled to his feet and danced to the door.

Once outside, they walked down to the pier with Buddy running ahead and scouting. Mac wanted to see if the GPS Tracker was still on the boat.

The *Deadly Serious* was gone.

Pops was mopping bird poop off his deck. He waved to Mac and Buddy.

"Pops!"

"Morning Mac. Mornin' Buddy."

'Rowrf!'

"Pops, where is the *Deadly Serious*?"

"Don't know. They left last night."

"Who's they?"

"Joe Minetti and that wife of his."

"They left in their boat? But, it was busted!"

"About nine o'clock last night, they came down in that fancy pickup. Someone dropped them off and left. They tossed some gear in the boat, chugged over to the marina, and took it in the boat house. I couldn't see after that. Maybe an hour later, the boat backed out, engines smooth as silk. Joe must have fit new propellers."

"Huh!" said Mac.

"One more thing," said Pops, cackling.

"What's that, Pops?"

"I was watching when they backed her out. Didn't say *Deadly Serious* on the stern no more."

"No?"

"Nope, painted her stern over in black; now she's *Rosie's Revenge*."

"Could he do all that in an hour, Pops?"

"Easy. Haul the boat, wipe the stern and spray with fast-dry rattle can paint. Pull cotter pins, take an impact driver and pop the props off and on. New name is just stick-on vinyl letters."

"And Joe would know how to do that," Mac said. "He's planned ahead. But boats are slow, why flee on a boat?"

"To sell it, Mac. He's on the run. How much cash would he have laying around on a Friday night? How much could he get from an ATM? This time of year, he can sell that boat and get cash on the spot. It's probably worth $350,000. He paid cash, so he's got the title. Plenty of buyers."

"Huh! Hey, that GPS tracker worked great, didn't it, Pops?"

"No; not so great, Mac."

"But you found me right away!"

"Yeah, but not using the tracker."

"No?"

"No, it was working good going out, but then it turned around and came back in. When you called and said you was in the water, it didn't make sense. So we used the app and tracked your phone, that's how we saw the flare."

"Wait! The GPS Tracker went out and came back?"

"Yup."

"Somehow, it got scraped off my leg, Pops. I thought I lost in in the lake. But maybe it got scraped off and fell in the boat! Let me check Roger's phone and see if it's still broadcasting. I'll call him."

"Rog? Hey, check to see if the Tracker is still broadcasting. What? It is? Where? Holy shit! OK, come down to Pops boat."

"It's still active, Pops. It's in...Port Stanley...Ontario!"

"Port Stanley?" said Pops. "Why, that's only 90 miles or so. I've done day trips there. Nice tourist town. Canadians are friendly, sidewalks are clean."

"Why would he go there?"

"Safe harbor, Mac. He could sneak back across between here and Detroit, or just motor all the way up to Lake Superior. But if he wants a quick sale this time of year, it's a harbor town between here and Detroit. That's where the money is."

"We might have to go to Port Stanley to catch him, Pops. Can't wait for the cops, they gotta get permission from their lawyers to take a shit."

"I could take us to Port Stanley in four hours. You got passports?"

"Roger does. Would we get boarded?"

"Possibly, but not likely. I can top off tanks and be ready."

"Look, Rog." Mac pointed to the empty dock next to Pop's Bertram.

"Boat's gone? How? It ran like shit, Mac."

"They fixed it. Joe Minetti came down here last night while we were chasing our tail to Erie, put two new props on it, painted out the name and stuck on new vinyl letters, '*Rosie's Revenge,*' and off they went. The Tracker must've scraped off my leg when I got shoved overboard."

"Huh! Pops figured the tracker came off in the boat 'cause we watched it go out and come back at us. It's not moving Mac."

"Rog, someone must have tipped them that Rileys were arrested, and they panicked."

"Leak inside BCI? Or Troop A? Remember, Mac, Jonetta called for back-up to get Riley's and take them there for booking. "

"Dunno, Rog, but somehow, they knew Rileys got arrested."

"Could be one of his marina watchers saw us bring in the Rileys and put them in the cop car."

"Hell, yes! That's gotta be it!"

"BCI needs to track Minetti's phone, Mac."

"You can bet he trashed it. He'll buy a burner."

"They'll have some kind of ship-to-shore radio on that boat. If they're smart, and they are, they won't contact their kids. Not until they know it's safe. But they could call a friend."

"Rog, we need to set up an extraction, you, me and Pops. Jonetta Pope's bogged down with lawyers, and Morgan's getting itchy to go home."

"Yep," said Roger, "these guys could get away."

"While killers get away, lawyers take coffee breaks. They worry about successful prosecution and future promotion," said Mac bitterly.

"Lawyers are assholes!"

"Ha!"

"I got my Passport, do you Mac?"

"I have an expired passport in the Chevy. Is that any good?"

"Dunno, let's Google it...hey! Canada will accept a USA driver's license and an expired U.S.A. passport."

"I say we go now, Rog. If they find the tracker and destroy it, they'll be on their way to who knows where."

"But if we land on Canadian soil, there could be a scuffle, they might not be on the boat, lotta things can go wrong."

"Best thing would be to take them on the lake."

"I'm on Google Earth, Mac. Port Stanley is opposite Ashtabula. The lake is 65 miles wide. We'd have to get them 30 miles out to be in American waters."

"Hm, dunno how we're gonna do that, Rog."

"Well, if you can't lure the bear out of his cave..."

"We go in after him. OK, let's gear up and go. And we don't tell anyone what we're doing, except you, Buddy, but you won't tell, will you?"

'Rowrf!' Buddy stuffed his big paw in Mac's hand and shook it.

*****

By mid-morning, the sky was blue with high puffy clouds painted in place. The lake was flat with no breeze. The big MerCruiser engine was churning the waters behind the stern, and Roger was working on his tan for the 'three hour tour.'

"You remember what happened to Gilligan and the Skipper$_{30}$ on their three hour tour," said Mac.

"I'll take MaryAnn," said Roger behind dark glasses, "you can have Ginger."

"No way! Ginger is too muckety-muck for me, buddy boy."

Pops said, "I always liked Ginger, fine lookin' woman."

"What're you talkin' about, Pops? You're the Skipper! He didn't have a love interest!" said Mac.

"Always allowed to dream!"

"Hey, the tracker is moving!" said Roger.

*****

Chapter Thirty Four

Saturday, May 27
New York State Police Troop A Substation
Fredonia, New York
10:00 a.m.

"For the record, I am Investigator Jonetta Pope of the New York State Bureau of Criminal Investigation. With me are Chautauqua County Sheriff Lowell Buckman and Deputy Sheriff Marvin Rinker. This interview is being video recorded."

"Deputy Marvin Rinker," Jonetta began, "you have been advised of your rights before we begin this interview, and you have agreed to speak with us. Is that correct?"

"Uh, yes. I don't even know why I'm here, except the Sheriff said to be ready at ten a.m. and drove us."

Jonetta continued: "This is an investigation into two deaths on April 4, 2021, which you reported as a one vehicle accident caused by driver error. We are reopening that case with new evidence that suggests these deaths were not accidental, but were murders conducted as a vehicular homicide."

"Specifically, this investigation concerns the deaths of John and Beth Waterman on State Route 76 outside of Ripley."

"Your accident report has been called into question and will be the subject of an official inquest by the New York Bureau of Criminal Investigation. Whatever you say can be used against you. Your Sheriff is here as a witness because of the seriousness of this investigation."

"Let's take a walk, Deputy. I think you'll understand once we get outside."

Jonetta Pope opened the steel door to the vehicle storage lot behind the Troop A substation. The pinkish Waterman car had its ass end facing them. It was pressed up against the front of Riley's former Trooper car. The space between the two was mere inches.

"I ask you to recall Easter Sunday, April 4, 2021, Deputy Rinker. You were on patrol in the Ripley area and were first to respond to the scene of a one car accident on a downhill stretch of Sherman Road, which is State Route 76. The accident occurred at approximately 10:30 a.m., according to your report. The driver and passenger in the car were John and Beth Waterman."

"The car went off the road at the apex of the curve where there was no guardrail, and continued sixty feet down a ravine until it smashed into a large tree. Mr. Waterman was ejected through the windshield and died at the scene. Mrs. Waterman's seat belt was torn from its floor anchors. She was violently thrown against the door pillar and sustained fatal injuries."

"Do you recall this accident, Deputy Rinker?"

The Deputy looked shaken.

"DEPUTY!" Sheriff Lowell Buckman bellowed. "Answer the question."

"Uh, yessss...I recall the accident."

"I have here a copy of your accident report, Deputy. It states that, in your opinion, the accident was caused by excessive speed and driver error. Would you like to read your own words and refresh your memory?"

"Uh, yes."

"Now, Deputy, would you like to explain how you came to that conclusion?"

"Well, the car just went straight off the road."

"As if it made no attempt to round the curve?" she said.

"Yes."

"Did you find that odd?"

"Odd?" Deputy Rinker said, defensively.

"Yes. This was an elderly couple who were known to be cautious drivers. They lived locally, which you saw from their registration. They were familiar with this road and these curves. They had just left the D Line Ranch and had successfully completed six tighter curves, all marked for 30 miles per hour in this downhill section. If they could negotiate those six curves at slow speed, all of which had guardrails, how did you come to the conclusion that excessive speed caused them to simply drive straight off the side of the road, making no attempt whatsoever to turn their wheels?"

"Uhhhh...there were no tire marks showing they had tried to make the curve?" he said without conviction.

"Is that your answer, or is that a question, Deputy?" Jonetta said.

"Uh..."

"Deputy Rinker, I show you now digital photographs taken by the reporter for the Westfield Press at the accident scene. You will notice that there are indeed tire skid marks that indicate all four wheels' brakes were locked up, yet the car continued in a straight line off the road down into the ravine. If the driver, being elderly and cautious, as his daughter has told us he was, had successfully negotiated six low speed curves, what could have caused him to accelerate so hard in a straight line yet brake at the last second?"

Deputy Rinker did not respond; he stared straight ahead.

"Deputy?" Jonetta inquired. He still did not respond.

"And why, Deputy Rinker, did you make no mention of these brake skid marks in your report, nor did you mention obvious rear end damage to the Waterman vehicle? I note once again the photos taken at the scene by the Westfield Press reporter with the Waterman car lodged against a tree. You can clearly see two vertical dark lines on the damaged back bumper of the Waterman car. Yet you did not mention this in your report. Why? Did you not notice them, just like you did not notice the brake marks in the road?"

"Uh… guess I missed it," he said.

"YOU MISSED IT!" roared Sheriff Buckman, "HOW THE HELL COULD YOU MISS IT?"

"Deputy Rinker, I ask you now to closely examine this car, the pink colored Crown Victoria before you. I can verify that this is the Waterman car. Some parts have been sold off, it but the rear end is untouched since the accident, and the chain of possession has been secure at the body shop in Jamestown, where it was towed. It has been under 24 hour video surveillance behind a locked fence for the past two years until it was brought to our station yesterday. Do you recognize this as the Waterman car?"

"I'd have to check the VIN."

"Please do, here is your report with the VIN listed."

"…OK, it's their car."

"All right. Now, do you see the vertical dents in the bumper?"

"Yes."

"Do you see how they match perfectly with the push bars on this old patrol car?"

"Uhhh, y-yessss?"

"Now, drawing your attention to the specific punctures made into the plastic bumper and the foam beneath: do you see these punctures, Deputy Rinker?"

"Uh, ok, yes."

"Now, looking at the push bars, do you see these four screw heads and this glob of weld spatter on the push bars?"

"Uh, yes."

"Now, does it appear that these push bars could in fact have been the ones that made these dents?"

"I don't know, maybe."

"All right," said Jonetta. She turned around, snapped her fingers, and two State Troopers pushed the Riley cruiser until it touched the bumper of the Waterman car.

"Do the screw heads and weld spatter on the patrol car's push bars perfectly match the dents on the Waterman bumper Deputy Rinker?"

"Uh, seems so, yes."

"OK, I will now tell you that two sets of tests, one by a BCI criminologist and one by a state certified lab, both found evidence of paints on both these two cars indicating that this paint exchange occurred by violent impact and, together with the matching impressions from the push bars to the bumper, that this car, this black patrol car, did in fact impact the rear bumper of the Waterman Car at some time."

"What the labs cannot tell us is when that impact occurred."

"We now believe, based on many other facts that have come to light in our preliminary investigation, that this black patrol car was the murder weapon, that it pushed the Waterman car over the brink, causing it to plunge 60 feet down a ravine, crashing and killing its two occupants."

"What we cannot understand, Deputy Rinker, is why your observations neglected to note these physical facts at the scene, and why you quickly, and we believe wrongly, concluded that this was a single car accident caused by driver error and excessive speed."

"Your report defies logic, common sense, facts in evidence, photographs taken at the scene and physical matching of these cars."

"What is your explanation, Deputy?" Sheriff Buckman snarled.

"Uh, I refuse to answer any more questions without legal representation," he replied.

"OK," said Jonetta, "that is your right, Deputy, but just so you know, Monday morning, when your bank opens, we will serve them with a search warrant to see if there was any deposit of a large amount of cash into your account in the weeks following this accident: cash that cannot otherwise be accounted for. We will also be looking at any major purchase you made, or lifestyle changes like lavish vacations."

"We are going to turn your life history inside out for the weeks and months after this accident to see if you were influenced monetarily to turn a blind eye to these obvious facts, facts which should have led you to conclude this was a suspicious accident needing further investigation. That's all you would have had to do to clear your name and involvement in this obvious cover-up."

"So you have every right to refuse to speak. We will make sure your union provides you with an attorney. But this is not over. In fact, it is just beginning."

"Uh," stammered Deputy Rinker, "may I have a moment to speak privately with Sheriff Buckman?"

"Sheriff Buckman, are you agreeable to speak privately with Deputy Rinker?" said Jonetta.

"Yes, so long as the nature of the conversation is not confidential and can be reported subsequently to you, Investigator Pope."

"Deputy Rinker? Is that agreeable?"

"Yes."

"OK, I am going inside. Come in when you are ready."

Ten minutes later, Sheriff Buckman and Deputy Rinker reentered the building. Deputy Rinker stared down at the floor.

Sheriff Buckman said, "Deputy Rinker would like to amend his report of the Waterman accident, noting the rear end damage to their car, noting the tire marks, and admitting he did, in fact, see them that day, Easter Sunday, 2021, and that he did not include them in his report for two reasons. He is willing to make this admission, and understands that there will be legal consequences, and that he may lose his job as a result. He only wants to know one thing first."

"Ok, that's fair. What do you want to know?"

"Who owns that old black patrol car?" asked Deputy Rinker.

"There are actually two questions you should have asked Deputy Rinker," Jonetta said. "The answer to the first is Timothy Riley, a retired New York State Trooper, formerly of Troop A. The second question that you should have asked is: who was driving that car on Easter Sunday morning, April 4, 2021?"

"We believe the answer to the second question is Joseph Minetti Junior, of Ripley. Mr. Riley has an absolute air tight alibi. He left the car at the

Ripley body shop of his friend Joe Minetti that morning. No one else had access to that car, and the keys were left with it. We believe Joe Minetti drove this car and shoved the Waterman's car down the ravine to kill Mrs. Waterman for reasons which I will not disclose to you at this time."

"Deputy?" said Sheriff Buckman.

Deputy Rinker shook his head and looked at the floor. "I should have known this would all come out." He sighed, paused to collect his thoughts, and then continued.

"Tim Riley was friends with a lot of the guys, my fellow deputies. He'd go out and have beers with us now and then. He always bought. Good guy. One night, I had too much to drink, never should have driven home, it was late."

"I fell asleep at the wheel and crashed my car into a tree. It was in the middle of nowhere, no witnesses. I just wanted to make it go away. It was an old car I didn't care about. I called Tim. He was still at the bar. I told him what happened, asked him could he help me."

"He said sure. Next thing I know here comes Tim with Joe Minetti in his flat-deck ramp truck. They winch the car onto the flat-deck and haul it away. Tim drove me home. Minetti had the car crushed; I didn't report it to the insurance. No harm, no foul."

"Until..." said Jonetta.

"Until next time I see Tim Riley, he says, 'Just remember, you owe me and Joe a favor. Whenever we call it in, remember.' And he told me Minetti took pictures of the car at the scene. Tim said he wouldn't report me driving drunk, just return the favor."

"OK, so what happened with the Waterman accident?" asked Jonetta Pope.

"While I was at the accident scene, I got a call on my personal cell from Joe Minetti. He said he heard it on the scanner. He asked me, did I need a flat deck for the wreck? I told him no, there was one already on the way. He asked me what I was putting in my report. I told him it looked suspicious, tire marks, rear end damage, made me wonder."

"He said, 'Remember the favor you owe me?' Just call it driver error, write it up and I'll show my gratitude."

"Payoff?" asked Jonetta.

"A week later, Joe Minetti came to my house with his son in that red Ferrari. He shook my hand. When I looked down, there was a fat envelope. It had $10,000 in it. It took it. I knew it was wrong, but I knew if I didn't play along, somehow that picture of my wrecked car would be sent to the

Sheriff, and someone would tell him how drunk I was when I left the bar. It could have been the end of my life as a Deputy."

"Well, I think it's the end of your life as a Deputy now," Sheriff Buckman said. "Consider yourself on paid leave pending an official hearing, but you did the right thing, finally, by making a clean breast of it. Investigator Pope?"

"Yes, Sheriff?"

"I'll have Deputy Rinker dictate a statement and sign it. Will you be charging him?"

"I think maybe you would like to do that to clean this up in your own house. So, I'll release him to you, Sheriff, on one condition. I presume you will charge him with filing a false report, and then he will face charges and disciplinary action, potential dismissal."

"Agreed, what's the condition?"

"Under no circumstance are you, Deputy Rinker, to communicate with Joseph Minetti Junior, his wife, his father or his children. If I cannot get that assurance, I will lock you up now on obstruction of justice charges, and hold you incommunicado until we arrest the Minettis."

"Agreed."

"OK, I think we are done here. Sheriff Buckman, thank you very much, sir."

***

Chapter Thirty Five

Saturday, May 27
Aboard the *Miss Bertie*, heading northwest across Lake Erie from
Barcelona harbor
11:00 a.m.

"Pops, how're we doin?"

"Engine's running good; speed 23 knots, less than one hour to intercept, Mac."

"We got a problem, Pops," said Roger.

"What?"

"They changed course and increased speed, now heading for Conneaut, Ohio. Their boat is faster than ours. They are going to get there before we intercept."

"How close to shore are they?"

"Less than five miles. And we're still forty miles away. Even if we push it, they still will beat us to shore by an hour unless they change course or break down."

Mac's cell phone buzzed. Angie was calling.

"Yeah, Ang, what's up?"

"Mac, we're all pissed at you and Roger for not telling anyone where you were going! You're off on your own again, aren't you?"

"Couldn't say, Angie; any news?"

"Jonetta Pope got a confession from the Deputy. He left out facts from the accident report on Waterman: coercion and a payoff from Joe Minetti. BCI criminologists confirmed Riley's car was the one that struck Waterman's, and with the rest of our evidence, BCI has enough to place Minetti behind the wheel of Riley's car. They issued an arrest warrant for Joe Minetti, suspicion of first degree murder, vehicular homicide and obstruction of justice. The warrant for Rosemary is accessory after the fact, a little thin, but they want to grab her to avoid flight. They need to do more work on the audit trail and find out how much she knew of Joe's killings."

"OK, good. Put Morgan on, Angie."

"I'm on speaker, Mac. What possessed you and Roger to go off like that?"

"We're trying to catch Minettis while you guys sit on your asses! And I couldn't tell you because I couldn't tell you. I figured you would tell BCI Pope."

"Oh, shit! What have you done?"

"Nothing, and it looks like we're not going to be able to grab them. Somehow, my GPS tracker is still broadcasting from Minetti's boat, so Roger is tracking them. They fixed their boat and fled last night to Port Stanley, Ontario."

"We were headed there to intercept, but they left and are back in U.S. waters approaching Conneaut, Ohio. We are an hour offshore from Conneaut. They're gonna get away again."

"What is their ETA Conneaut?"

"They are there now. The GPS tracker just stopped. They beat us."

"I need to notify Jonetta Pope," Morgan said, "and get her guys going. She can contact Ohio State Highway Patrol and local law enforcement. Can you get an address or GPS coordinates?"

"Yeah, coordinates. I'll text Angie the location. But they gotta hurry. They could have a car waiting and be gone forever, Morg!"

"OK, well, while we're here sitting on our asses, I'll try to get some real cops to grab them."

"Good."

"And don't do anything stupid without calling me first!"

Mac hung up.

"Shit, can't tell that guy anything!" said Roger.

"Lawyers are assholes, even Morgan when he's playing one."

*****

Saturday, May 27
Conneaut Public docks
11:15 a.m.

"You made good time, Joe, how fast were you running?"

"Thirty knots steady; crossed from Port Stanley in one hour forty five minutes."

"Jeez, that was quick, Joe."

"Yeah, hey look Mace, I appreciate you meeting us here, but we're in a hurry, so let's just do the title, gimme the cash, and you own her. Sorry about the one busted glass in the windshield, but to make up for it, I'm giving you two hundred eighty gallons of gas, and that's worth $1,500. Everything else is perfect on her."

"Hey, that's great! I'm going to take her out right now. Say! You changed the name!"

"Yeah, it's vinyl letters. If you don't like it, just peel them off."

"OK, I will."

"Here are the keys. An extra set is on a hook in the cabin. I've signed the title, there are no liens. You got cash?"

"Three hundred grand, Joe."

"Count it Rosie. What about this car we get?"

"Right over here. Runs great."

"The Impala Interceptor?"

"Yep, 2016, only 99,000 miles, fully serviced. I like these old cop cars. This was an undercover car, so it didn't get abused. With a 302 horsepower V-6, she flies. Got a full tank of gas. Did you bring a plate?"

"Yeah, I got a plate. OK, this car is good. Hey, listen, thanks Mace, enjoy the boat. Rosie?"

"It's all here, Joe."

"All right, we're good. Rosie, did you get my sweatshirt off the boat?"

"No, couldn't find it."

"Hm. Oh! I bet I closed it up into the gunwale bench seat."

"I'll get it," she said.

"OK. I'll put the plate on the car."

Rosemary stepped back on the renamed *Rosie's Revenge*, pulled the fold-down gunwale bench seat and there was Joe's black sweatshirt. She grabbed it, but the sleeve was stuck in the crack. She tugged, and it came loose. She closed the seat back up, wadded the sweatshirt in a ball and ran to the waiting Impala.

Joe Minetti waved to Mace Wilkins as the Impala spun its tires in a quick burnout.

"We're off, Rosie! To Sardinia and the good life! Wine, woman and song!"

On the floor behind the front seat, wadded up inside a black sweatshirt, a little black box no bigger than a matchbox was clinging to a sleeve by a piece of sticky black tape that still had a few hairs from Mac Morrison's leg stuck to it. Its little electronic heart was cheerfully beating out its signal to a satellite in the heavens above!

*****

Mace Wilkins proudly jumped onto the deck of his new toy, the *Rosie's Revenge*. First order of business: peel off that horrible name!

Leaning over the stern, he used his pocket knife to slip under the new vinyl and peel off the strip of letters. He would rename her *Mace's Mistress*. The engines growled like a lion. He backed away, turned and headed out into the lake, ready for a quiet afternoon cruise. His course heading was Erie, where he would have lobster salad at the Yacht club and show off his new boat.

*****

No more than five minutes after he left the pier, a Conneaut Police cruiser and an Ohio State Highway Patrol car both arrived at the dock. They found no sign of a black 34 foot Pursuit named *Rosie's Revenge*.

*****

Two miles offshore from Conneaut, the *Miss Bertie* was cranking her heart out.

Mac said, "Pops, you can slow down, no need to hurry now."

"Why?"

"Roger's phone shows the GPS tracker is moving again, and this time it's headed east on surface roads. We lost them."

260

"There's a nice boat going out of the harbor, Mac, and it looks a lot like the *Deadly Serious*," said Pops. "Roger, put your glass on that boat!"

Roger dug out his binoculars.

"She's turning northeast, running a mile off shore," he said.

"Can you read the name?"

"No name on the stern. And there's an old fat guy at the wheel. Don't see any other passengers. We gonna follow?"

Pops said, "We can follow, but we can't catch him. He's got 800 horsepower. I got 330 and more weight. What do you want me to do?"

"Let me call Morgan. "

"Morg? We lost him. I think he may still have my GPS Tracker cause it's moving east on surface roads, dunno how. No clue what kind of vehicle it could be in, and I don't' even know if it's still with Minetti. We might have just spotted Minetti's boat with no name on the stern. Minetti was not seen, an old fat guy was the pilot. What do you suggest?"

"Ohio State Highway Patrol should be waiting at the pier, can you confirm?"

"Yes, we're just a mile off and we can see a couple of cop cars."

"OK. I think you should stop, talk to them and thank them. I'll get Jonetta Pope and let her know. It was a good try, Mac. Will you be returning with Pops?"

"Yeah, probably get some lunch on the way. Be back late afternoon."

"OK. See you then. I've got some work to do here, and then I'll wrap up with Jonetta Pope. Angie and I will probably fly back in the morning if I can get my charter plane to pick us up."

"All right, thanks Morgan."

*****

Saturday, May 27
Truck Stop, Conneaut Interchange of Route 7 and I -90
11:45 a.m.

"Joe, let me call Gino from a pay phone. Make sure they're OK."

"OK, but don't tell them nothing."

Rosie walked to a pay phone booth, put in the money and dialed Gino's cell.

261

"Gino?"

"Ma! Where are you! Are you OK? The cops were here!"

"What cops, Gino?"

"State Police. Trooper Gregor. They got a warrant for you and Dad."

"A warrant?"

"For your arrest, Ma!"

"What for?"

"For Dad, murder, vehicular homicide and something like obstruction, I don't remember. For you, they said accessory after the fact. What does that mean, Ma?"

"Means we got trouble, Gino. Did they leave?"

"Yeah, but I think they're watching the place, just not all the time. Trooper cars pass the house, but they don't stop. Ma, I'm worried. Do you think they'll arrest me? What about Gina, Ma?"

"It's gonna be OK, Gino. I won't let them hurt you or Gina. She's not involved in any way, and you just run errands for Joey. You're gonna be OK, I promise."

"But Ma, what are we gonna do without you? I need you, Ma."

"Yes, yes you do, Gino, you still need me. Gina's good, she can take care of herself, she's not like you. She doesn't have Minetti blood. But you, Gino, you are a genius with cars like Joey, but you always need direction. And you are still so young. Only 25, you're still my baby."

"So Ma...."

"Listen, Gino. Here's what I want you to do. And don't tell nobody, not even Gina, you understand?"

"I understand."

"I want you to wait ten minutes after I hang up. You tell Gina you need her to run an errand for you. Make something up; say you need something from the store. Tell her it's important and have her drive Joey's big truck. Then you wait five minutes, you watch to see if the cops are there. Make sure they're not hiding in the vacant lot, right?"

"OK."

"You drive one of your old junker cars with a dark color, real plain looking, and you come and pick me up. Make sure you're not followed. I'm at a truck stop In Conneaut, the one at I-90 on the west side of Route 7. I'll be in the coffee shop watching out the window. You pull up. I'll wave if it's safe. If I don't wave, you just drive home, OK?"

"What about Dad?"

"I'm coming home, Gino. Just me, I'm coming home. You come pick me up, OK?"

"OK Ma, see you in an hour."

✻✻✻✻✻

"That was a long call, Rosie. What did you tell him?"

"Joe, listen, the State Police were at the house. They got arrest warrants for both of us. For you, murder. For me, accessory. Listen, Joey, I'm going home. You go to Sardinia, maybe I'll meet you later. Gino's scared. He needs me, I gotta go. They won't go hard on me, I didn't kill anyone, I didn't know you were gonna do that. I can't be made to testify against you. I say nothing if they arrest me. What case have they got against me?"

"What about the audit, Rosie?"

"They dropped that case, Joey. The members dropped it."

"What about the money?"

"I made restitution and changed the books two years ago. I can say the auditor made an error, the books balanced. I'm not Treasurer any more. It's done. I'm good. So I'm goin' back. Gino's gonna pick me up. You go on. Go on now, Joe! I love you. I don't want you to go to prison. Go on. You got a good plan, you can make it. Maybe I can join you later. Now go!"

"Rosie..."

"GO!"

✻✻✻✻✻

Saturday, May 27
Still at the Truck Stop, Conneaut
12:00 noon

"Frank, it's Rosemary Minetti. I'm sorry to call you on a Saturday, but it's very important. You've been our business lawyer for 30 years, I didn't know who else to call."

"It's no problem, Rosie. What is it?"

"Frank, the police have been to my house, they spoke to Gino. They have a warrant for Joe, for murder Frank, for murder. They have one for me too, accessory, Gino said."

263

"Murder! I'm not a criminal lawyer, Rosie…"

"I know Frank, but please, I need advice. I never killed anyone, I never was an accessory. I wanna turn myself in, post bail, get out and take care of my family, see how this works out."

"What about Joe?"

"Joe is gone…somewhere. I don't know where he is. He's running."

"What cops came?"

"Trooper Gregor, Andy Gregor. We know him, he's with Troop A. I want to surrender to him."

"OK, look, Rosie, where are you now?"

"I'm safe, not at home. I want to arrange this so I don't get arrested. I want to surrender with my lawyer. Can you help me?"

"Of course, Rosie. I'm gonna call Joe Delmonico, the best criminal lawyer in Western New York. He's got offices in every county, got one in Jamestown. I'll call him right now, and we'll get his best hotshot lawyer. We'll take care of this. Can I call you back, Rosie?"

"No, I'll call you back."

"OK, give me 20 minutes and call me back, OK?"

"OK, Frank, thank you Frank."

❈❈❈❈❈

Chapter Thirty Six

Pops brought *Miss Bertie* into an empty berth just as sweet as chocolate icing on angel food cake. Mac jumped off the bow, and Roger jumped off the stern. They tied her to dock cleats and dropped fenders over the sides.

"Man, I am starved!" Roger said.

"Bein' on a manhunt, eat when you can," said Mac. "Pops, are you coming?"

"In a sec, gotta lock up the cabin."

The dining room had glass walls facing all directions, the better to admire the view and the expensive toys floating at their member docks. It was an atmosphere of modest money. There were no gazillionaires in Erie, but there was wealth in that city, and wealth still liked their toys.

Mac and Roger had already ordered when Pops came in, grinning like a fiend.

"You look like the cat that got the canary Pops!"

"Maybe I got the tail feathers! Hee, hee."

"What?"

"Now, look way down at the end of the dock leeward of the dining room. See the black offshore boat?"

"Hmm. Yes."

"Look like the *Deadly Serious*?"

"It does."

"I spotted it and walked out to have a look. Guess what? It's the same boat we saw leave Conneaut harbor. No name on her stern, and another thing...she's got the same pair of red fuzzy dice as Joe Minetti had."

"You think it's the *Deadly Serious*?"

"I do. Let's see who goes out to her while we eat lunch."

Just then, a fat man with a silly looking Captain's hat walked out towards the boat with a gaggle of fat old men in tow.

"Looky here Roger, is that the guy you saw through your glasses?" said Pops.

"Hard to be sure, but it could be."

Pops said, "I think I'll go play detective for a change and let you landlubbers have some lunch. Order me what yer having."

Pops got up with new energy and almost trotted out to the dock. Soon, he was at the tail end of a group of admirers to the 34 foot black Pursuit off-shore fishing boat moored at the member's docks.

"She's a beauty," a man said to the fat man in the captain's cap. "How fast?"

"Did thirty knots all the way from Conneaut. Smooth as silk. Nice quarters for a fishing boat, too."

"How many hours on the engines, Mace?"

"Only 300, can you believe it?"

"Wow, looks like she's been well cared for. Where'd you find her?"

"Friend of mine owns a body shop in Ripley, moored her at the Barcelona pier. Kind of a distress sale. I got a helluva deal."

"Congratulations Mace. Well, enjoy!"

The gaggle turned and dispersed back to their bar stools, leaving only Pops standing there.

"Sure is a nice boat, really looks like the one been moored next to my Bertram the past couple years," Pops said.

"Are you in Barcelona Harbor?"

"Have been for 20 years."

"Well, this could be the boat."

"Joe Minetti's boat?"

"That's the one."

"My, my, she was called the *Deadly Serious*."

"I'm going to rename her *Mace's Mistress*."

"Well, congratulations, Mr. Mace."

"Oh! Wilkins is the name, Mace Wilkins. What do people call you?"

"Pops. Just Pops. Mind if I'm nosey and ask what you paid for her?"

"Well, let's just say I got a great deal. Some cash and an old car I had layin' around the yard."

"Old car?"

266

"Yep, an old Impala Police interceptor. Nice car, detective car. Man, helluva deal."

"Well, congratulations, Mr. Wilkins, maybe I'll see you again some time, buy you lunch."

"Hope you do. See you, Pops!"

*****

"Well, boys," said Pops, "Minettis sold their boat, just like I figured. And guess what? Part of the deal was they got an old police car, an Impala Interceptor. Detective's car, the man said."

"No shit," said Mac. "So, Joe picked up a set of wheels in Conneaut. Where is he, Rog?"

Roger pulled out his phone. "He's approaching Olean on I-86. How the hell is that GPS tracker still with him?"

"Must be the sticky black tape that I used got stuck to something that was transferred to the car. Maybe we can still catch him! Only a matter of time before he finds it or it falls off somewhere. So...he's got a lot of cash, and he's heading east. Pops, did that guy give you his name?"

"Mace Wilkins. Funny name, Mace."

"Enjoy your meal," said Mac, "I gotta see a man about a car."

"Here we go again!" said Roger.

*****

Mac casually strolled out on the dock like he was browsing a flea market. When he stopped at the former *Deadly Serious*, Mace Wilkins said, "Hello there! Come out to see my new boat?"

"As a matter of fact, I did," said Mac. "I'm a friend of Pops; we're on our way back to Barcelona Harbor. I think we saw you leaving Conneaut a while ago, was that you?"

"Sure was. Isn't she a beauty?"

"Gorgeous. This was Joe Minetti's boat."

"You know Joe?"

"In a way. His father bought my parents' farm many years ago. I was hoping to catch him this morning on his way back from Port Stanley, but we missed him."

267

"Yeah, he called me from Port Stanley. Nice place, I'm gonna take a cruise over in *Mace's Mistress*, that's what I'm gonna rename her."

"Good name, catchy ring."

"Thanks."

"You know, I had something to give to Joe, something of a surprise, really sorry I missed him. Something to pay him back for all he has done for my family over the years. Understand you sold him an Impala Interceptor. I had one of those, they're great cars. What year was yours?"

"2016, with the 3.6 liter V 6, 302 horsepower. Man, that car could scoot."

"Mine was a dark green detective's car. Sorry I sold it. What color was yours?"

"All white, kinda plain."

"Joe was in the car business, so I'm sure he had a New York plate."

"Yep, he put it on while I was playing with the boat."

"Well, I hope I get to see him sometime. Just wanted to say nice boat, Mr. Wilkins."

"Thanks, thanks, man."

*****

"Can't outrun Motorola!" snapped Mac as he sat back down. Pops was smacking his lips with the excellent potato soup.

"What's up?"

"I got a good description of the car, but no plate. He's still in New York, so maybe Jonetta can put out a BOLO and get him picked up before he loses the tracker. It's worth a try." Mac hit rapid dial for BCI Officer Pope. She answered first ring.

"Yes, Mac?"

"Jonetta, I've got a GPS tracker on Joe Minetti, I'll explain how later, but somehow, it's still in his car. He sold the boat in Ohio and took an old police car in partial payment. Now he's eastbound, just past Olean, New York on I-86. Repeat: he's *eastbound* on I-86 just past Olean. He's driving a white 2016 Chevy Impala Police Interceptor. No plate number is known, but it will be a New York plate, and it will not match the car. It's probably a dealer plate from Minetti's shop. I can give you constant updates. Can you put out a BOLO and grab him?"

"I can try. Hang on one second. I'm going to radio this in. 2016 Impala Interceptor, all white, on I-86."

"Eastbound just past Olean."

"OK, let me call this in. Let me know ASAP if he stops or changes course."

"Will do, thanks, Jonetta."

"Thank YOU, Mac!"

*****

"Nothing to do now but cruise back to the B & B, have a cold beer and contemplate the future, boys," Roger said.

"Right on, Rog. We've done all we can. He's got a two hour head start and it will be four hours by the time we get back, so I'm out of the chase. I just hope a State Trooper hears the BOLO and sees the car. If they can grab him, man, then all we have to worry about is the state's attorney making a successful prosecution on the Waterman case. If they can put him away for that, we can't kill him two more times for Murphy and my parents."

"All set Pops?" Roger asked.

"Do I get dessert?"

"Oh, by all means," Mac said, "but don't fall asleep on the way back, because Roger would have to pilot *Miss Bertie,* and I thought you didn't let anyone pilot her!"

"Huh! Let's go, boys! You're payin' for lunch!"

"Gladly, my dear friend, gladly!"

*****

Saturday, May 27
Eastbound on I-86 near Corning, New York
In the 2016 Impala Interceptor
2:30 p.m.

Joe Minetti was driving east. He was so happy with this car! Ran great, comfortable, quick, and it even had a police scanner! He had it tuned to the State Police band to locate speed traps.

269

This was going so good. Except for Rosie, he was mad about Rosie. He still could not believe she chose the kids over him. But he was going. She said go. He was going.

The radio chirped, and a scratchy voice blurted:

"BOLO. All law enforcement, be on the lookout for a 2016 Chevy Impala Police Interceptor model, white, New York license plate number unknown but possibly titled to Minetti Perfect Restoration shop. Plate will not match the car's VIN or description. Currently headed eastbound on I-86 in the vicinity of Olean. Driver believed to be Joseph Minetti Junior, wanted for murder. Approach with caution: stop and arrest. Contact BCI Investigator Jonetta Pope at New York State Police Troop A. Repeat: BOLO for 2016 Chevy Impala Police Interceptor model, white, New York license plate, eastbound on I-86 near Olean. Contact BCI Investigator Jonetta Pope at New York State Police Troop A."

"SHIT, SHIT, SHIT!" Joe Minetti yelled. "How the fuck do they know? That goddamn Wilkins? Jeezuz! I gotta get off the highway and figure this out! I gotta ditch this car! But how the hell do they know where I am?"

An exit was coming up. He pulled into the right lane and quickly left the Thruway near the center of old Corning. Once past the toll booth, it was highway commercial to the right and the old city to the left. He turned left. Now, he had to hope.

He pulled into a fast food restaurant and got out of the car. Sliding underneath, he looked everywhere for a tracker but saw none. Next, he looked under the hood: nothing. He opened all four doors and pulled up the back seat. There was nothing underneath, but his black sweatshirt fell on the ground. He picked it up, shook it, and heard a 'clack' as something hit the pavement. He looked under the sweatshirt, and, there it was!

A little black box, no bigger than a matchbox!

Just like the one he had stuck on Morrison's Chevy! He pressed the button, and the red LED dot glowed. It was active, but, how the fuck? He turned it over in his hand. Black tape stuck to it. And, on the tape were hairs!

"Son of a bitch!" he blurted. "That fuckin' Riley shoulda searched that fuckin' Morrison! So, Morrison had a tracker on him. Somehow, it got ripped off on the boat, and stuck in the gunwale seat, and then it pulled off onto my sweatshirt!"

"SHIT! THAT FUCKIN' MORRISON! THAT GUY HAS FUCKIN' RUINED MY LIFE!"

270

Taking a second look at the GPS Tracker, he noted a small chip on one corner, just like the one he had stuck to Morrison's car.

"HOLY SHIT! THIS IS MY OWN FUCKIN' TRACKER! ARRRRRRGH! I'LL KILL THAT GUY!"

He walked over to a truck parked by the door, casually stuck the GPS Tracker under a rear fender, and felt the magnet stick. He walked inside and ordered a cheeseburger and chocolate shake to go.

Now, what to do about the car, he thought. Get some rattle cans, and spray it at a car wash stall?

Could do that, he thought, but let's take a minute, cruise around, look for a park, and eat my burger. He found a small park in the historic district, sat at a bench and drank his shake.

A homemade sign across the street said, 'Garage sale: Sat-Sun 9-5.' A kid sat at a folding table playing with his phone in front of an open garage. Joe tossed his shake in the trash and walked across the street.

"Hey, whatcha sellin'?"

"Lotsa stuff."

"Mind if I look around?"

"Nope. Got an old pickup, too, but a guy is driving it. He'll be back soon."

"Really? What make? "

"2010 Chevy Silverado."

"How many miles?"

"106,000."

"Run good?"

"Runs great. I did all the work in my high school shop class, and it was checked out by my teacher."

"Why are you selling?"

"You know, get something cooler, something faster."

"What motor?"

"Just a V-6, but it runs good, fresh fluids, ready to work. You lookin' for a truck?"

"Always."

"That your ride across the street, the Chevy Interceptor?"

"It is."

"Cool, got the 302 horsepower V-6?"

"Yep. You know your cars, what's your name?"

"Jimbo."

"Jimbo, I just bought that car today, but I already got two warnings for speeding. If I keep it, I'm gonna lose my license. Probably should just get a good work truck."

"Really? Cool."

"Let me look around while we wait for your guy to return it."

Joe meandered to the back of the garage. There were tables with stuff piled all over them. On the corner of one table was a box that looked almost new, with grimy smudges. The label read 'Cowboy Revolver, .22, six-round.'

Joe opened the box, expecting to find a marble collection or baseball cards. Instead, it was a .22 caliber revolver, old west style. Price tag attached to the gun read $125.00. Joe picked up the revolver, spun the barrel, broke it open to check it, pulled the hammer and dry fired on an empty chamber.

"Give you a good deal on that," Jimbo shouted. "I'll take $100. Cost $200 new. Good target pistol."

"That is a good deal. Got any cartridges?"

"Half a box, I'll throw those in."

"I'll take it. Say, here comes your guy."

An old man parked the Chevy in the driveway and shuffled into the garage.

"Runs good," he said. "How much you say you wanted?"

"$11,000, cash."

"Would you take ten on Monday? I gotta go to the bank."

"I couldn't do ten."

"Can I take it for a test drive?" Joe interrupted.

"Sure," said Jimbo, "it's not sold yet."

Joe took the keys from the old man, slid into the truck and started the engine. It fired up and ran well. He revved it; no miss from the engine.

"I'll just spin around the block. Back in 2 minutes."

"OK," said Jimbo.

Two minutes later, the gray Silverado was back in the driveway. Joe Minetti slid out and clicked the door shut like a bank vault.

"Nice truck. Would you take $9,000 cash right now plus my Impala Interceptor in trade?"

"Really? $9,000 cash today, plus your car?"

"Today, in your pocket, Jimbo, and I'll sign the title to the Impala over to you. Want to drive it?"

"Sure! Mom! Come watch the sale for a minute!"

Joe tossed him the keys. "Careful, she's a screamer."

"All right!"

Jimbo ran across the street, jumped in the Impala, adjusted the seat and mirrors and peeled rubber all the way down to the corner.

"Boy's gonna go through some tires," the old man said. "Good luck with the truck."

"Thanks," said Joe, "didn't mean to buy it out from under you."

"I was just gonna flip it. I got ten trucks at home. I buy and sell; it keeps me busy in retirement."

The Impala came roaring down the street. Jimbo jumped out and said, "Mister, you got yourself a deal!"

Joe took the title from his pocket, signed it over and handed it to Jimbo with ninety 100 dollar bills.

"Going on a trip," he said to Jimbo, "just got the cash."

"Thanks, Mister!" Jimbo signed over the title to the Silverado, they shook hands, and Joe handed him another hundred for the revolver.

"Oh, almost forgot. Thanks again!"

"See ya, Jimbo."

"See ya! Yahoooooooooo!"

Joe Minetti unscrewed the plate off the Impala and screwed it onto the Silverado. He hopped in, drove back to I-86 and onto the entrance ramp headed *westbound!*

*****

May 27
Aboard the *Miss Bertie*
3:30 p.m.

"Hm," Roger said. "The GPS tracker stopped in Corning. Now it's moving again. Headed south on I-99."

Mac said, "I gotta call Jonetta." He dialed her cell.

"Yes, Mac?"

"The GPS Tracker just left Corning moving south on I-99."

"OK, thanks. Keep me updated."

"Will do."

"This is not good, Rog."

"What's up, Mac?"

273

"Minetti's headed south. He's only twelve miles to the Penn line. Jonetta is going to lose jurisdiction."

"Can't she get the Penn State Police to help?"

"Probably, but how long will that take? Meanwhile, maybe he finds the tracker and ditches it."

"Maybe he already found it, and stuck it on another vehicle while he was stopped."

"Oh shit! Yeah, could be, Rog! Well, if he did, then we are out of luck!"

"Hey! We did all we could. He's in the wind, not our worry now."

"Yeah, he won't be coming back here, and he's covered his tracks real well."

✱✱✱✱✱

May 27
Murphy B & B
4:30 p.m.

If it had been snowing, Mac could not have gotten a colder reception walking into the Murphy B & B back porch. Except for Buddy.

'Rowrf! Rowrf! Rowrf!' Buddy did the welcome-home-Poppa dance.

"Oh, Buddy boy! Yes, I missed you, you big galoot! Did Marybeth take good care of you?"

"Better care than you guys took!" yelled Marybeth Murphy, shaking a skillet at him from the kitchen, nostrils flared and eyes wide and angry. "Why would you go off like that and not tell us? I was worried about you! Last night on a log, today leaving early, and never coming back! You're like an 8-year-old boy, Mackenzie Morrison!"

"Mmm, maybe 9," said Angie.

"I'll go high as 10," chirped Morgan.

"Love you too, Morgan," said Mac, "you know…"

"When you are on a mission, I cannot know, so no one can know."

"Correct."

"Well, I don't like it, Mac!" shouted Marybeth. "Just for that, you are not getting dessert tonight!"

"Oh no! How about a hug and a beer?"

"Me too!" said Roger."

"Roger gets a hug. No hug for you, Mr. MacInconsiderate!"

"How about the beer?"

"Get it yourself! I'm gonna stay mad for another 20 minutes!"

"Like an old married couple," said Angie.

"Heh heh heh," chuckled Morgan. "Well, Angie and I are heading back in the morning. Charter plane will pick us up at 9 a.m. at Jamestown."

"I might as well go, too," said Roger.

"OK, I'll drop you off," said Mac. "You gave everything to Jonetta Pope?"

"Yep. She'll send a unit to pick up Jim's boat. She wants to test it to see if it can match the *Deadly Serious*."

"Well, she might want to hold off until she can get access to the *Deadly Serious*, since it's now docked at the Erie Yacht Club. It now belongs to a guy named Mace Wilkins. No name on the boat's stern. He's gonna rename it *Mace's Mistress.*"

"Oh, lord, another egotistical chauvinist!" snapped Angie. "Mac, how the hell do you always manage to stir things up so doggoned fast?" Angie said.

"Skill and luck, my dear."

"AND A LOTTA NERVE!" shouted Marybeth from the kitchen. "MAN'S GOT A LOTTA NERVE! NOT SO MANY BRAINS, BUT NERVE, HE'S GOT! STEPS IN HORSESHIT, TRACKS IT IN THE HOUSE AND WAITS TO SEE WHAT FLIES COME TO IT!"

"Great metaphor," Morgan chuckled, "I'll have to remember that."

Mac's phone buzzed: Jonetta Pope.

"Mac, where is your tracker?"

"Hang on. Rog, where is the Tracker? Jonetta, it's stopped in a town called Lindley."

"We're there, Mac. It's a tiny little settlement, and no sign of a white Impala Police Interceptor."

"I wonder if he found it and switched it to another vehicle in Corning, Jonetta."

"Can you give me exact coordinates, Mac?"

"Yeah, let me get them from Roger." He gave her the coordinates.

"Let me relay that," she said, "hang on Mac. OK, they are there now, let's see what they can find."

"Get them to look all around and underneath every vehicle, Jonetta. It's a magnetic, 2" square black box, and it might have a red LED light lit."

"OK, let me relay that info. They're looking. OH! They found it under a pickup truck!"

275

"So, maybe Minetti switched it in Corning, Jonetta. See if you can find the truck owner and ask him where he stopped around 2:30 p.m. today. Let me know if you find anything."

"OK, Mac, sorry he gave us the slip. Maybe there's a surveillance camera wherever he swapped it. I'll call you back when I know anything. Bye."

"Goodbye, Jonetta, and thanks again. Well, Rog, Minetti's vanished, so let's get that beer."

*****

May 27
Murphy's B & B back porch
6:15 p.m.

"Dinner will be served in 20 minutes!" Marybeth shouted through the pass through window. "Mac, I am now speaking to you, so put the kebobs on the grill."

"Oh good, no more detention!"

"You deserved it," she said.

"You do make me laugh, Marybeth Waterman Murphy!"

"Well, you can make me cry, you big knucklehead! Don't you run off on me like that again!"

"If I promise, I'll have to cross my fingers behind my back."

He ducked as a green pepper flew across the porch at his head.

"The menu tonight," she continued, "is fresh garden salad with tomatoes, radishes, grated smoked gouda cheese, and raspberry vinaigrette dressing. Garlic bread, a very nice Bordeaux wine, walleye kebabs with red and green peppers, new potatoes and onions, double chocolate quadruple layer cake with hand cranked ice cream. The guys will do the cranking."

Angie said, "Morgan, can we open an office in this house just to get on the meal plan?"

"Great Idea," said Morgan. "After this week, I should get lots of referrals."

"I always bake when I'm mad," said Marybeth, "so it will be lots and lots of calories, and it will be delicious!"

Mac's phone buzzed: Jonetta Pope. He answered and put it on speaker.

"Mac," said Jonetta, "I've got major updates. Rosemary Minetti surrendered to Trooper Andy Gregor this afternoon at the Jamestown office of

276

the Joseph Delmonico law firm. He's the best criminal lawyer in Western New York. She is going to plead innocent to the charge of accessory after the fact in the Waterman case. At her arraignment tomorrow, I have no doubt the judge will let her bond out and go home. But for tonight, she is being held in the county jail."

"Did she say anything about Joe Junior's whereabouts?" Mac asked.

"Nope, she's not talking."

"OK," Mac said, "well, that's one down. At least you have the warrant out for Joe. She surrendered, he'll keep running."

"Yes. As far as the tracker goes," Jonetta continued, "it was stuck to a pickup truck belonging to a local farmer. He thinks it could have happened at the Big Burger in Corning, just off I-86. He was having lunch there at about 2:30 and then drove to Lindley to leave the truck at a repair garage. His wife picked him up there. It checks out."

"Surveillance video in the Big Burger showed a man who could be Minetti at that time. His hat was pulled down over his face. He ordered takeout, paid cash and left. No parking lot camera, so no idea if the Impala Interceptor was in the lot."

"Dead end."

"Yep."

"OK, Jonetta, do you want to speak with Morgan? He's planning on returning to New Hampshire with Angie and Roger tomorrow morning."

"Yes. Morgan, I'll call you later, OK? I'm working with the attorney getting Rosemary Minetti's paperwork ready for tomorrow's arraignment."

"OK," said Morgan. "I'm going to call Colonel Justice and give you great marks, Jonetta. Mac and Roger's style is disruption and confusion, so when I get called to clean up, my job is to cover their ass. It's rare the police are willing to get in gear and go with us."

"Well, I won't say it's been fun, but I certainly will never forget you all."

"All right, call me anytime tonight."

*****

Chapter Thirty Seven

*"When fighting monsters, beware that you yourself
do not become a monster…for when you gaze long into the abyss,
the abyss gazes also into you."*[31]

-Friedrich Nietzsche

Sunday, May 28
Jamestown Airport
9:00 a.m.

"Morgan, Angie and Roger, I could not have hoped to accomplish, alone, what we've done together in just a few days."

"And this time you didn't get tossed in jail!" Morgan laughed.

"That, too," Mac said.

"Marybeth's a keeper, Mac. You never met a woman like her in the north woods."

"You're right, Rog, but she's got a lot of ghosts now. Maybe there could be a time for us later."

"She gets my stamp of approval, Mac," said Angie.

"That means a lot, Angie. OK, well, thanks again, to all of you. See you back in Sunapee."

The King Air dropped from the sky like an eagle gliding down gracefully, snatching its passengers into its belly and lifting off in a matter of two minutes.

And once again, Mac was alone with his own ghosts.

"Mom, Dad," he said out loud in the privacy of the blue Bel Air with Buddy by his side, "I know who killed you, but I can't prove it. Now he's in the wind, and may never get caught. I just wanted to get my hands on him and wring his dirty neck!"

"But I gotta let it go. It's been forty years, and now it's time. I hope you don't think I let you down. Uncle Abe, I hope you also don't think I let you down. Love you guys."

Mac felt a big tongue on his cheek.

"Buddy! Thank God I have you!"

'Rowrf!'!

"Let's go see what loose ends we have to tie up before we drive back to New Hampshire."

'Rowrf!'

*****

Sunday, May 28
Murphy B & B
9:45 a.m.

Mac parked his baby blue Bel Air in the courtyard behind the porch, close to his cottage, so he could pack up and hit the road after lunch. He was uneasy about saying goodbye to Marybeth. She needed time to get over the events of the past week. With guests arriving soon, she would be busy. That would take her mind off the chaos he'd caused.

The morning had started sunny, but now a dark mass of thunderheads bellowed over the lake, barreling in like a fast moving coal train. Mac and Buddy bolted for the porch door and yanked it open with a 'gronk.' The rusty old stiff spring snapped it shut behind him and the door smacked his ass with a 'whap!'

"GULLYWASHER!" Marybeth shouted from the kitchen, as torrents of fat raindrops pounded the flat porch roof like machine guns.

Mac walked towards the kitchen and shouted over the din, "CAN I USE YOUR COMPUTER, MARYBETH?"

She walked up close to be heard over the noise.

"You have to ask, Mac? You know my password."

"Thanks, I…"

She locked her arms around his neck, hugging him tight.

"Thank you, for all you've done for me, Mac. It's been hard, but it's been good. I think we'll get some justice at last, and maybe I'll get some closure in the weeks ahead."

"I hope so, Marybeth. It's been great being here with you. I never met a woman like you. I must say, you are extraordinary."

"That sounds like goodbye, Mac."

"Sorta is. I was planning on leaving after lunch."

279

"NO, YOU'RE NOT! We are taking target practice with Sandy and Andy at their house! I've already got my Ruger in my hip holster. You and Andy are shooting his rifles. After that, we have a lot of talking to do, you and me...about us!"

"I wasn't sure you were ready to talk about...us."

"Well, you can't crash into my life, stir up forty years of ghosts, sweep me off my feet, and leave me in the midst of a thunderstorm! No sir! There is an 'us,' and we need to let it happen!"

"So..."

"So, Mac, remember I told you that I'm part of an animal rescue network?"

"Yes."

"And remember how we promised to find senior dogs for Hubcap Harry and Pops?"

"Yes."

"Well, come in the office, I want to show you something. Sit at the computer. There! Isn't she adorable?"

"Is that a Labradoodle?"

"Yes, Mac, she's one year old. See her left eye? It's half shut because she got mauled at a dog park. Bad places, dog parks! See her ear? It's half chewed off. God love her! We have to go rescue her Mac! Her nasty owners don't want her now!"

"She's scared and alone at a shelter in Ohio, just three hours from here. So we are going to get to know each other better while we drive down there and get her! And while we are there, we are going to pick up a senior dog for Hubcap Harry and another for Pops! They are all at the same shelter. Don't these old girls look sad? Don't you just love them, Mac?"

"Yes. That sounds like a lot of dogs in the Chevy."

"We'll take the Outback. Buddy can have the back seat, and I'll hold the little Labradoodle in my lap. The two seniors can go behind the back seat in carriers. They're both females in a shelter because their owners passed away. It's just providence that my network got a hit on this sweet girl, and now we've got three new dogs in our life!"

'Rowrf!' Buddy was excitedly watching the computer screen, whapping Mac's leg with his long tail.

"Oh, joy," Mac said, "So, when..."

"Tomorrow. We'll leave early and get there when the shelter opens. We can go over and be back before supper. I'm going to call Harry and send

280

him a picture; I know he'll love her. Her name is Bella. And you'll tell Pops to prepare for Miss Ginger. She's coming to her forever home with him on the *Miss Bertie*."

"He'll love that name," said Mac. He's got a Gilligan's Island fantasy about her."

"HA, HA! See there? Providence."

"So where is it we're going tomorrow, M?"

"Cute little town called Huron, Ohio. Actually, it's not so little, and it's on Lake Erie. We take I-90 to Route 2, drive fifty miles west of Cleveland and bingo! Three hours, easy peasy."

"Hm. Maybe I can do some truck shopping, Marybeth. I need a used work truck to build my house and restart my business. I'll do a search for Huron and the surrounding area. Ohio trucks should be less rusty, and there will be a lot more to choose from."

"You do that while I season my cast iron skillet, Mac. It needs a good salt and oil rub. We're having bacon cheeseburgers for lunch, and since we can't grill out, I'll fry them in the skillet. I made fresh squeezed lemonade and chocolate chip cookies. Comfort food after your last 48 hours."

"Great," said Mac. "I'll bring your laptop to the dining room table, so I can watch you cook while I search for trucks."

*****

Outside, a gray Silverado pickup truck parked at the Barcelona Harbor pier. Its driver was a shadowy figure in a black hooded sweatshirt. He slipped out into the cold, slashing rain, pulled the hood over his head, and was instantly soaked to the skin. Undeterred, he trotted around the stone lighthouse, angled across the road, and cut behind the Shavely house. The storm drowned out the sound of his approach on the crunchy gravel driveway. He snuck up to the corner of the Captain Murphy back porch, staying under the windows until he was crouched by the screen door.

He only saw one car parked outside, a blue '57 Chevy Bel Air.

'Excellent,' he thought, 'that son of a bitch Morrison is still here.' He saw no other evidence of guests.

So, it would just be the two of them. Perfect. Six shots in the revolver, but it was only a .22. He needed two kill shots each, to make sure. That left just two misses. But he did not plan to miss at point blank range. And he had the boat's fish knife in his boot.

Joe Minetti raised his head just enough to get a peek over the window sill. Marybeth was scrubbing a skillet in the kitchen, standing by an open window to the porch. He glanced to his left and saw Mac sitting at the dining room table, twenty feet inside. He'd shoot Morrison first, two shots, then sweep the gun to the right, and take out Murphy.

Still crouched under the window, he reached up and silently turned the handle of the old wooden screen door, slowly pulling it open. The rusty old spring groaned.

'Grooooonk!' went the stiff old spring. The sound blended with thunder grumbling overhead.

Inside, Buddy was lying on the porch floor by the back door. He pricked his ears, lifted his head and growled. 'Grrrrrrrr!'

"It's OK, Buddy!" Mac yelled from the dining room. "It's just thunder!"

'GRRRRRRRRRRRRR!' Now Buddy was standing up and scratching frantically at the porch door. 'Alert, alert!' he was telling Mac, but Mac was looking at the computer screen.

Joey Minetti leaped up, yanked the screen door outward with his right hand, reached for the inner doorknob with his left hand, and pushed! As he lunged inside, the stiff spring pinned the wooden screen door against his back leg, gripping him while he tugged the revolver from his belt.

'ROWRF!' Buddy launched through the air, clamping his powerful jaws onto Minetti's left arm, and yanking it down with all of his hundred pounds! Minetti staggered, freed his trapped leg from the screen door, and raised his right hand to shoot at Mac while Buddy dragged him sideways!

"BAM! BAM!" Minetti's first two shots flew wildly into the wall!

With Buddy still tearing at his left arm, Minetti awkwardly turned and fired at Marybeth!

"BAM-*Clang*! BAM-*Clang*!" His second two shots zinged through the kitchen window, ricocheting off the iron skillet!

Now Mac was on him in a flying leap, grabbing the gun and wrenching it down, while Buddy's jaws ripped at Minetti's left hand!

Minetti screamed in pain, but fought like a madman, kicking and bucking and refusing to drop the gun!

"BAM! BAM!" Minetti's last two shots lodged into the wooden floor! The revolver was now empty, so he dropped it. As Mac let go of him to grab the gun, Joey Minetti whipped the fish knife from his boot and raised it high overhead to stab Mac in the back!

"POW! POW!" Two shots came from the kitchen window!

"YEOW!" yelled Joey Minetti! Mac felt a sting on his shoulder.

Buddy lunged at the knife, clamping down and tearing it from Minetti's grasp!

With both hands free, Minetti turned and punched Mac in the gut, then slung him around, slamming him into the door! Buddy lunged, knocking Minetti backwards into Mac, who grabbed him from behind with his left forearm tight around his neck, and his right palm pressed against his temple!

"GIVE IT UP MINETTI!" Mac shouted over the rain pounding the roof.

"I'LL KILL YOU, YOU SON OF A BITCH!" Minetti screamed, struggling to get free, "I'LL FUCKIN' KILL YOU!"

Marybeth aimed again from the window.

"MARYBETH!" Mac shouted, "DON'T SHOOT!"

"POW!" She fired a third shot as Mac spun away. It zinged harmlessly into the door behind him!

"This is for my parents," Mac whispered in Minetti's ear. Then he jerked his neck with a violent 'CRUNCH!' Joey Minetti stopped struggling and became dead weight in Mac's arms.

"AUS!" Mac commanded Buddy.

Buddy backed away. Mac let the lifeless body sink to the floor. He knelt over it and felt for a pulse. There was none.

Marybeth ran out of the kitchen.

"Oh-my-god, OHMYGOD!" she exclaimed, "I KILLED HIM!"

"NO, Marybeth," said Mac..."you didn't kill him." He held her tight as she stared at the crumpled body.

"But he's dead, isn't he? I shot him three times!"

Mac led her and Buddy into the dining room. He snatched the large table cloth and brought it to the back porch. Joe Minetti's head was lolled over like a broken doll, and he had a spot of blood on his right arm oozing through the sweatshirt. Mac draped the table cloth over the body, and walked back into the dining room. Marybeth sat in a chair hugging Buddy as he stood on his hind legs with his paws in her lap.

"Good dog, Buddy!" she said. "You're my hero! Good dog, Buddy-boy!"

'Woof!'

"You hit him once in his arm, M," Mac said. You didn't kill him."

"I didn't? Did you?"

"He's dead. The monster is dead. That's all you need to know. He can't hurt anyone again. Now, you call Andy Gregor, and I'll call Jonetta Pope."

"MAC!" she shouted. "YOU'RE BLEEDING!" She pointed at his right shoulder. A little stream of blood was soaking his shirt.

"Well, like I told you M, it's a lot harder hitting a moving target."

"WHAT? *I SHOT YOU*? OH, NO!"

"It's a flesh wound, nothing serious, M."

"Oh, Mac, I'm sorry!"

Mac chuckled. "Well, I tried to tell you, don't shoot."

"But I had to help you!"

"You took a big chance with Minetti, me, and Buddy all in the same space. But you took the shot and that took guts. Now, call Andy, Marybeth. Tell him to get here, ASAP."

She sat at the table, dazed.

"MARYBETH!" Mac snapped. "You've got to get it together! Soon, we are going to have a lot of cops in your house. They're going to ask questions. You just say what you saw. Minetti charged in shooting. Buddy grabbed his arm, and his six shots all missed us. You returned fire while I struggled to get his knife."

"We are going to be all right, M. It will just be a lot of questions, and then it will all be over. You tell them you had your pistol in your hip holster because we were going target shooting at Andy's. He'll vouch for that. You fired three shots. One hit him in the arm, one hit the door and one grazed me. Self- defense; that's all there was too it."

"MARYBETH!"

"Y-Yes?"

"SNAP OUT OF IT! We're all right! I'm going to call Jonetta. Are you OK?"

"Yes. I'm OK now, Mac."

"OK. Call Andy! Buddy, you go with Marybeth."

'Woof!'

"Good boy, Buddy."

*****

Trooper Andy Gregor was the first to arrive, then a Westfield cop, and then a Deputy Sheriff. Soon the living room, dining room and back porch were swarming with men and women in uniform, all talking over one another.

284

Mac clapped his hands together like a gunshot. That got their attention!

"Thank you all for coming! Marybeth and I will give our statements one time, as soon as BCI Investigator Jonetta Pope arrives. I think I hear her siren now. Let's all gather on the back porch and take seats."

"Marybeth, please let Jonetta in the front. The body is blocking the back door."

Jonetta stepped inside, took one look down the front hall, through the dining room, and into the back porch. She saw the tablecloth covering a lump by the back door.

"Joey Minetti?" she asked Marybeth.

Marybeth nodded. "He tried to kill us, Jonetta. He fired six shots. If it hadn't been for Buddy we'd be dead. Buddy-dog and Mac saved me."

Jonetta reached out and gave her a big hug.

"It's all right, girl, it's all right now. You've had a shock, but it's OK, now. The monster is dead."

"That's what Mac said, Jonetta. The monster is dead."

*****

Chapter Thirty Eight

Sunday, May 28
Murphy B & B
1:00 p.m.

When most of the law enforcement crowd cleared out, the coroner carried the body away. Mac and Marybeth repeated their statements and signed them.

A search of Minetti's body turned up $5,000 cash. Jonetta took car keys from his pocket and found his truck at the pier across the road. Inside, she found the envelope with $290,000 more in cash.

The coroner noted the preliminary cause of death was a broken neck. Mac said there had been a violent struggle for the gun and the knife. He may have had Minetti around the neck, he could not recall. It happened so fast, and then Minetti fell to the floor and stopped breathing.

Marybeth's shot that hit Minetti was an arm wound. A .22 caliber target pistol did not have much stopping power for a big man like Joe Minetti, but it had stopped him long enough to allow Buddy to grab the knife intended to stab Mac in the back.

Jonetta Pope was the last to leave. She assured them there would be no issues. It was self-defense, pure and simple. Four bullets Minetti fired had been found in the back porch: two were embedded in the porch wall, and two in the wood floor. Two additional mashed lead slugs were in the kitchen where they landed after hitting the cast iron skillet, which now had two dents, and was taken into evidence by the State Police. The gun and knife had been retrieved exactly where they fell.

"Buddy Boy," Mac said, "we are not having pan-seared burgers. We are taking Marybeth uptown to lunch, and I have to buy her a new iron skillet. Then we are going to the market and buy their biggest steak with the biggest bone. Tonight we are going to grill that and eat by candlelight, with good wine surrounded by our dogs. And you can chew that bone and suck all the marrow and make a big mess."

"As long as you eat it outside, Buddy," Marybeth said sweetly, rubbing his head. "You are my protector, aren't you, baby, you and Mac."

'Rowrf!' 'Rowrf!'

*****

And so they did. It was a lovely evening after the storm passed. The air smelled fresh, like lilacs and apple blossoms, as if all the dirt of the world had been washed away. A purplish twilight glanced off the lake, turning the side of the house pink in its glow.

And when the table was cleared and the wine was gone, Mac yawned, barely able to stay awake as darkness fell.

"Well, M, it's been quite a day. Buddy and I are turning in. See you in the morning for Ohio dog day." He gave her a quick peck on the cheek, got up and snapped his fingers for Buddy to follow.

*****

After a scalding shower to wash away all the traces of Joe Minetti, Mac padded over to the king size bed to find Buddy sprawled sideways across it.

"Gotta move, Budso. Make room for me."

Buddy groaned, turned a circle and lay down with a 'thump' against Mac's leg, growling his displeasure at having been awakened. Mac chuckled, and ten seconds later was fast asleep.

*****

It could have been ten minutes or two hours later; Mac was so sound asleep he never heard the tap- tap-tap at his cabin door.

'Wuf!' Buddy snuffled excitedly. 'wuf!' 'wuf!' 'Wuf!' 'WUF!' 'WUF!'

"OK, OK, I hear you," groaned Mac, "and I know what you said. She's outside, you said, I'm getting up."

He padded groggily over to the door and opened it. Marybeth pushed him aside, waltzed in with her gaggle of Labradoodles, closed the door and locked it.

"I want some company tonight," she said, "so Buddy is sleeping on the floor with my babies. Now, turn out the light and kiss me."

*****

Chapter Thirty Nine

Monday, May 29
Mac's cottage
7:00 a.m.

"It's a good thing this is a king size bed," Marybeth said with her head on Mac's chest. They lay locked together, dreamily awake.

"My leg is asleep," Mac said.

"Might have something to do with the 100-pound dog laying on it."

"There's that. I was wondering if your hair grew overnight, but I just realized there are three dogs surrounding your head, M."

"Our babies are protecting us. Did you get any sleep?"

"I seem to remember a few times you left me alone when I might have drifted off. You?"

"I slept the sleep of the reborn. I feel so...out of body spiritual almost, like lying in a meadow of French wildflowers, or seeing the sunrise over the Grand Canyon, or...sleeping with my man for the first time."

"Drama before coffee. Heavy, M."

"You knucklehead!" She punched him in the ribs. "Can't I be romantic the morning after?"

"You certainly can, in the shower, with me. We'll let the dogs have the whole bed to themselves."

*****

Passing through Erie, Pennsylvania
High above Lake Erie, En route to Huron, Ohio
8:30 a.m.

"OK, I-90 through Cleveland, then 50 miles west, and exit at Berlin Road for Huron."

"Aye-aye, madam navigator. How's it feel to ride shotgun with Buddy in the back seat?"

"I like it, but I think he's miffed. You miffed Buddy?"

'WUF!'

"Well, we'll see how he likes having three more dogs riding with him, M. Gotta say, I'm excited to see these dogs, but I'm also interested to make a pit stop in Huron."

"Oh?"

"Yep. There's a Ford dealer there. They have a 15-year-old work truck for sale: Ford F-450 dually, stake bed, diesel, 113 k miles, and they're only asking $8,000. Would be perfect if it were four wheel drive, but a dually with the correct tires will go in the mud and snow. New one would cost ten times that much. Gotta save money to buy equipment, build my house and restart my business."

"See, Mac? Providence. You were meant to come on Dog Day with me."

"Well, let's go meet these dogs!"

*****

"Bella, Ginger, and Emma, come to Momma!" squealed Marybeth, clearly in her element. The three newly adopted dogs all rushed to her open arms, and she hugged and kissed them as Buddy and Mac stood by.

'WUF!'

"Well, you let her, now you gotta be patient and share her, Budso!"

'WUF!'

"Buddy's a bit jealous."

"Come here, Buddy, my wonderful protector. I love you too, sweetie. Come say hi to your new pals!"

Little Emma the Labradoodle was shaking in fear. "Look at this poor girl, Mac! She needs you to pick her up and hold her."

Mac gently knelt, let Emma get his smell and lick his hand before he scooped her up and held her. Her little heart was racing against his chest. "Yes, Emma, you're safe now. We are going to take care of you, baby."

"C'mere Buddy, come say hi to Emma."

*****

They were at the Huron Boat Basin under a picnic pavilion splashed with mid-day sun. The shimmering Huron River swept lazily past the former ore freighter docks. The old lime plant was being leveled and prepped for a riverfront park.

"This place is so pretty, Mac, don't you think?"

"I do."

"And that pier! It's three quarters of a mile out into the lake! Makes Barcelona's pier look puny."

"They both have their charm, M. Same Great Lake, but this town has a different vibe. It's not frozen in time like Westfield. It's moving at a steady pace. I like it."

"You just liked that donut shop. Admit it."

"I did. I liked the donut, the coffee, the sisters and the vibe. Not the same as Eleanor's, but it was homey, although I don't think I could sit on a stool without some serious local seniority. Are you done with lunch?"

"Yes, and that was a great perch sandwich. I'm comin' back here just for Menardi's!"

"That, Marybeth Murphy, is a date," Mac said and smiled at her.

"OK, I have the dogs, now it's your turn, Mac."

"Well, that Ford dealer is located on the river, only three blocks from here. How about you take the dogs for a walk out the pier while I trot over and check out this truck?"

"OK! Come on guys!"

'Rowrf!' Arf! Woof, wuf!'

Forty minutes later, the low rattle of a diesel engine made Marybeth look up from her park bench. Four dogs sat at her feet, waiting for treats. Mac jumped out of an F-450 stake bed truck and waved.

"So...what do you think, M?"

"Did you buy it, Mac?"

"I did, put it on my Visa card. Runs great, has good rubber, stake bed has all new oak planks. Front seat needs redone, but I'll do it next winter. You ready to roll?"

"Ready!"

"Buddy, you ride in the truck with me. Emma can ride in my lap. Marybeth, Bella and Ginger seem to like each other, so let's leave them out of the carriers. We'll fold your back seat down to make a long, flat floor for them. And I'll lay down that carpet scrap you brought."

"Wonderful idea. I'll call ahead and tell Pops and Harry to get ready."

"I'll follow you, M. First stop, Hubcap Harry, Bella's new home. Then we'll introduce Pops to Ginger."

"And I'll be thinking about who should adopt Emma," Marybeth said.

"Buddy already told me who, M."

"He did? Who?"

"Me and Buddy."

"You two? You want another dog?"

"Can't ever have too many dogs, M, and Buddy needs a buddy for days when he can't go to job sites with me. It will be better for him at home with a little buddy to look after and protect."

"Well, he *is* the protector. He already pushed a couple nosy dogs away from Emma out on the pier. One look, one growl, and they moved off."

"That's my Buddy. OK, Hubcap Harry! Let's go!"

*****

"Harry, meet Bella. Bella is 8 years old. Her owner passed away, so she's been at the shelter for three months and is a bit confused. She needs stability and love. She's a sweet girl, and she's perfect for you."

"What breed is she?" Harry said, stroking her ears and patting her.

"They think she's Lab-Pit mix, just as sweet as can be. No trouble at all in the car, loves to have her ears rubbed just like you're doing."

"Bella," said Harry, a tear rolling down his cheek, "I'm gonna spoil you rotten, just wait and see."

Bella jumped up and slobbered Harrys' face. He hugged her to his chest.

"Marybeth, Mac, you made an old man so happy. Thank you so much."

"Harry, you and Bella are coming to dinner soon. I'll call you," Marybeth said.

"Bye Mac, bye Marybeth, bye Buddy! C'mon Bella. Let's go see your new home!"

'Rarf!'

*****

"Pops, meet Ginger, your new sweetheart. Did you get her a bed and food and water bowls?"

"Do I look like a guy who wouldn't prepare a home for his new girl? Course I did! Landlubbers! Ginger, you are so beautiful, come say hi to Pops."

291

Mac lifted her over the side of *Miss Bertie* and placed her in Pops' arms. "Not too heavy, Pops?"

"No, she's fine; let me see if she's seaworthy."

He set Ginger on the deck and let her sniff around. She went directly to the water bowl and drank, then came back to sit at Pops' feet and look up at him.

"She's a small poodle, Pops, about 9 years old. She has a sensitive stomach, so we brought you some starter food from the shelter. Don't give her rich table scraps."

"OK, Mac, I'll get the right food."

"Pops," said Mac, "I'm a little concerned about you getting on and off the boat. I don't want you to lose your balance and fall, or drop her in the lake."

"Got you covered, Mac. Looky hereI"

Pops went into the cabin and came out holding a thick cedar gang plank with wooden cleats every six inches, and an underneath cleat to lock onto his gunwale. He extended it to the dock.

"She'll rise and fall with the lake, strong enough I can walk on it too. I'll be careful."

"Perfect," said Mac.

"OK, Pops," said Marybeth, "you come across the road and visit me often, you hear? Bring Ginger. You're welcome to breakfast any day. You just show up on the back porch, and I'll feed you. Understand?"

"Are you adopting me like I'm adopting Ginger?" Pops cackled.

"I guess so. You'll never know how much you helped me, by helping Mac. I can never repay you."

"It was fun! We'll come over, Marybeth. Ginger would like some female company I'm sure, right Ginger?"

'Woof!'

*****

292

Chapter Forty

Tuesday, May 30
Murphy B & B
10:00 a.m.

"So Mac," said Marybeth, "I'd hoped you'd stay longer..."

"Marybeth, you have a full house coming tomorrow, and your house-keeper will be working all day with you to get ready. I have a shed, a barn and a house to build, not to mention land to sell to pay for it all."

"I just got used to sleeping with you, Mac. I'm not going to wash your pillow until you come back to me. You are coming back to me..."

"I am. Marybeth, do you remember the song *Gentle on My Mind*$_{32}$?"

"I don't think so."

"It was before our time, but it's a country classic. Goes like this..."

He picked up her father's six-string guitar and deftly plucked the notes, singing with a clear voice in the pure morning air...

It's knowing that your door is always open
And your path is free to walk That tends to make me leave my sleep-
ing bag rolled up
And stashed behind your couch
And it's knowing I'm not shackled
By forgotten words and bonds
And the ink stains that are dried upon some line
That keeps you in the back roads by the rivers of my memory
That keeps you ever gentle on my mind

"Mac, are you saying you're a free spirit, and I can never have you?"

"No, no, you have me M. You've had me since our dance at the root beer stand, remember? Marybeth, it's knowing I can go and do my work, and you'll be waiting for me, that makes me want to come back before I've even left."

"Mac..."

"Yes, M?"

"That is the most romantic thing anyone ever said to me. I love you for it, Mac."

"M, instead of leaving my sleeping bag behind your couch, I'm leaving my beloved '57 Chevrolet Bel Air in your barn, so you know I will come back to you. Think of me and Buddy and Emma when you drive her. I will be back just as soon as I get my own house in order. Now give me a big kiss, and turn away. I don't want you to see me get teary eyed."

"You big dope, I want to see you get teary eyed. Dance with me, Mac. I'll sing just for you."

And so, Marybeth's angelic voice belted out a sweet acapella rendition of Etta James' classic, *At Last*$_{33}$. She sang it so loud and clear that it carried over into the harbor as they danced in her courtyard, with Buddy and Emma smiling from the truck's open windows.

At laaaaast...
My love has come along
My lonely days are over
And my life is like a song...
...You smiled, you smiled
And then the spell was cast
And here we are in heaven
For you are mine...at laaaast!

Pops and Ginger were taking their morning walk at the pier. He cocked his ear to the sound of Marybeth's sultry voice and said, "Ginger, this is gonna be a good day, sweetheart."

❊❊❊❊❊

Tuesday, May 30
Morrison Cemetery, on the Eastern shore of Chautauqua Lake
Dewittville, New York
10:45 a.m.

It had become a quiet, sunny morning. A gentle breeze lapped the crystal clear waters against the shoreline. Mac and Buddy walked the few short aisles of headstones, pausing at the oldest, *Mackenzie Clark Morrison, died 1888, age 61.*

Mac strode a few steps closer to the water and sat down cross legged. He touched the headstones for his parents, *Shaun Morrison* and *Claudia Morrison, died May 14, 1983.* Buddy laid his head in his lap.

"Mom, Dad," he said, "I did the best I could. I'm sorry I never got to grow old with you, but you gave me a good start, and I hope you are satisfied with what I've done here. Peace be with you, always. I will return."

*****

Tuesday, May 30
Former Bar B Ranch
Dewittville, New York
11:00 a.m.

"Mrs. Wilson, I insist on paying you for the piano."

"I won't hear of it, Mr. Morrison. I'm just glad it is going to be played again, and by a Bar B camper! It's been so forlorn sitting in that old chapel for years and years. Henry and I do not play, so it will just molder away unless someone gives it some love and brings it back to life."

"Well, I have just the man for that. He's an irascible old German piano guru who emigrated here after World War II as a boy and was taught by his father. He will make this old Chickering sing like new. As for the finish, I wouldn't dare restore it. It has the scratches of a thousand Bar B campers on it. All I will do is clean and polish it to preserve the wood."

"You didn't have any trouble loading it on your truck?"

"Nope. I found two furniture dollies in the shed, rolled it up a makeshift ramp and into the stake bed. There was a tarp and ratchet straps in the truck so it's secure and waterproof. The forecast is for dry weather, so it should be fine. I'll be home tonight."

"Well, it makes an old woman happy to see a piece of Bar B history being revived."

"Tell you what, Mrs. Wilson, once it's done and in its new home, I'll send you pictures. Even better, I'll record her playing one of the Bar B camp songs I found on sheet music in the piano bench."

"Wonderful! Can't wait! Will you come back and visit us?"

"I'll be back for that trail ride. I've been waiting 34 years."

295

"We'll have a horse ready for you."

"Better have two."

"Wonderful! Goodbye, Mr. Morrison."

"Bye, Mrs. Wilson, and thank you again. Ready Buddy, ready Emma?"

'Wuf! Arf!'

*****

Chapter Forty One

"Well, guys, are you ready for a walk and lunch? I know a good spot in this next town."

'Rowrf! Arf!'

Mac exited the Thruway and meandered into tiny, quaint Le Roy, following the familiar streets until he found an old gas station. The faded orange letters over one of the bays still read 'Oil and Lube.'

As he filled his diesel tanks, he spotted a green fender with a chrome bumper peeking out behind the 1950s era garage.

"Whatcha got back there?" Mac asked the attendant. His shirt said Nate, but his face looked like sixty years of hard work underneath old cars.

"1971 Impala. It's been sitting there for two months. Wish someone would haul it outta here 'cause I need the space for customer cars."

"What's the story?"

"It belonged to a local lady. She bought it new. It was her only car for fifty years. For the last forty, I took care of it for her. She was a spinster school teacher who walked two blocks to school, only drove it on weekends. Passed away a couple of months ago, and left it to me. I towed it over here and parked it. Don't know why. I got too many cars already."

"Does it run?"

"Did when she last drove it in here for gas and oil change, that was six months ago. Always garaged, you can tell. Needs a battery, and tires, and probably ten other things by now. But the fuel never spoiled. I always dumped stabilizer in her tank when she filled it 'cause she drove it so little. Only has 50,000 miles on it! Original 350 V8 engine."

"Would you take $1,000 cash, right now, today?"

"Mister, you haven't even looked under the hood."

"I think I can trust you, Nate. I could go to that place down the street, rent a car trailer and tow it outta here after lunch. Do you have the title?"

"I do, but what would you do with it? I'd hate to see it all cut up."

"I restore old cars, Nate. I'd make it look and run like new. I lost three vehicles in a barn fire two weeks ago. One of them was a gorgeous '57 Pontiac Star Chief. This Impala looks like a nice car, with chrome and an all-steel body. It's never going to be as collectible as the '57 Star Chief, but I like the story of the little old lady school teacher, so I'd keep it, Nate, and someday, not too far in the future, I'd drive it back here to show it to you, fully restored. Would you like that?"

"Mister, make it $1500 and you got yourself a deal."

✱✱✱✱✱

Le Roy Diner
1:45 p.m.

Mac drove the F-450 to a gravel lot behind the diner and parked it under a grove of maple trees. Buddy jumped out and Mac set Emma down gently. He snapped a leash on both of them, then poured bottled water into a bowl and fed them dry kibble. Emma ate right next to Buddy, with no fear or aggression. It was clear that these two had already bonded.

Looping a long piece of rope through the end of both leashes, he tied it to the Ford's front bumper and walked inside to order. While he was waiting for his food, his eyes were scanning the horizon. He noticed something odd at the motel across the street, something to check out later.

The new family of Mac, Buddy and Emma ate at a picnic table. There were four hamburgers to share. Mac shredded two buns and tossed them to a flock of sparrows who had long ago figured out that the picnic grove meant tasty crumbs.

After he finished his coffee, Mac pulled out his cell phone and called Roger Lemonier.

"Mac! Where you at, man? I thought you'd be back here by now."

"Had some unfinished business Rog. I finished it."

"Oh?"

"Joe Minetti is dead, Rog."

"Really! How?"

"You remember how we lost his Tracker signal? He turned around, came back and tried to kill me and Marybeth. He put two bullets into the porch wall, two in the floor and two in Marybeth's cast iron skillet. Buddy stopped him long enough for me to break his neck."

"Wow! You clear with the cops, Mac?"

"All good. Jonetta said self-defense in her report."

"Glad you're OK, Mac. That was my job, taking out Minetti."

"Well, you left too soon, Dude. After that excitement, we took a day trip to pick up three dogs at a shelter in Ohio, where I also found a good F-450 work truck. So I'll be ready to get going on my cabin and your house just as soon as I get back, which will be tonight."

"Terrific! Good news, Mac! Your steel shed is up! And I already have four bays full of my equipment. I've got a lotta summer jobs lined up. Gonna have to hire some good help. Know anyone?"

"Let me think about it, Rog. See you at Eleanor's in the morning."

"You got it, Mac. Oh! If you were thinking Manny Charbonneau's crew could frame my house with you, they are all booked up for the summer. After they get your steel barn up, they have other jobs scheduled first."

"I'll figure something out. We can talk about it tomorrow. See ya, Rog!"

*****

After Mac put fresh gas in the Impala and bought a new battery from Nate, the Chevy fired right up and drove onto the car trailer. Mac secured it, thanked Nate, and promised to send him pictures after its restoration.

With the Impala in tow, he stopped at a self-serve car wash with an outdoor booth and gave the old Chevy a proper bath. The paint was faded, but Mac knew he could buff it out to a nice shine. Other than a few nicks and scratches, it looked really good for a fifty-two-year old car.

Time to check out what he saw at the motel.

He drove down the block to the old motel he had stayed at, made the loop around the motor court, and came to a stop in front of a group of well-worn Chevy pickup trucks. Three young men were kicking a soccer ball on the grass infield. They stopped playing when they saw the Impala. When Mac hopped out of the truck, one of them called his name.

"Mr. Mac! It's me, Paco! Where is your blue '57 Chevy? Did you buy a '71 Chevy?"

"The '57 Bel Air is at a friend's house, Paco. Want to see this '71?"

"You bet!"

As Mac raised the hood, Paco was amazed at how clean and original everything looked.

"This is nice, man," said Paco. "There are a lot of these in Mexico. My uncle has one just like this, but no way as nice. Where did you find it?"

"Just down the street, behind a gas station. Paco, how come you're not working today?"

"Our job ended, Mr. Mac. We go to our next job tomorrow."

"Where?"

"Ascutney, Vermont, the orchards are there. We were there last year, and the year before. We trim trees, plant new ones and clear underbrush. The pay is not as good as here, but the farmer gives us housing. It's small, but it's clean, and we can cook outside and laugh and not disturb anyone. We stay there three weeks."

"Do you have work permits?"

"Yes, we are legal, Mr. Mac. We have Social Security numbers, too.

"What do you do in winter, Paco?"

"We go home to Mexico. We find whatever work is available. We frame houses, drive bulldozers and backhoes, jobs like that. We can all drive farm tractors and combines and I have an American CDL license to drive a tractor trailer. So, we go where the work is."

"Do you have work after Vermont?"

"No. We have a jobber we pay. Hopefully, he will find something for us by then, and not too far away. Sometimes there is a job, but it is not worth it to drive a long way to get there."

"I have work for you, Paco."

"Really? Where?"

"Twenty miles from Ascutney, in New Hampshire. I need to build my log cabin, and then build a house for a friend of mine. He runs an excavation business and he is also looking for more help. If you guys really are carpenters, and really can operate heavy equipment, this could become a long term deal for you. Would you like to give it a try?"

"Yes! But what would you pay? And where would we live, Mr. Mac?"

"Paco, for good carpenters, I'll pay $25 per hour, and I'll get you good housing. My friend will pay as much for good equipment operators. But this is serious work; I have not seen what you can do, but I'll take a chance and give you a try for two weeks. We'll see how it goes, is that fair?"

"Mr. Mac, I would like to work for you. And so would Ramon and Thomas. My mother can cook for all of us!"

"That would be great. OK, Paco, give me your cell number. Here is my business card and address in Sunapee. It really is only twenty miles from your apple orchard."

"Mr. Mac, I don't know how to say thank you."

"Just show up in three weeks ready to work, Paco. That will be a good enough thank you."

❈❈❈❈❈

Chapter Forty Two

As the sun dropped in the western sky, flickering candles provided the only light on the back porch, which was exquisitely set for a celebration of life dinner, invited guests only.

'Ting-ting-ting!'

Marybeth Murphy tinkled her fork on a fine crystal water goblet, one of twelve set at a long formal table made up of four square tables pulled together in a line and covered with starched white linen tablecloths. Each place setting had her best china, a crystal wine glass and water goblet with baby blue linen napkins, to celebrate the return of the owner of the baby blue '57 Chevy in the barn.

She raised her wine glass to make a toast.

"I want to welcome you all to the Captain Murphy B & B, and thank you for coming to join us in a celebration of life after death, of life lived forward, and life lived well because of all of your help in our 'adventure' a few months ago."

"Not all of you know each other, so let me make introductions. Please be seated."

The scraping of wooden chairs on the hardwood floor was testimony to the age of the Victorian home. No one noticed the bullet holes. It felt like a real homecoming.

"Starting on my left are my new friend and Attorney Morgan Hillman and his confidential secretary, Angelica Morelli, who I notice seems to be wearing an engagement ring. Is there an announcement either of you would like to make?"

"Only that life is too short," Angie said. "Morgan and I realized after our time with you that we should stop fooling around and tie the knot. You will be invited to a fall wedding. Hope you can come."

Marybeth led the applause. "Well, congratulations and let's have a toast to the prospective bride and groom: many happy returns of the day, and many happy years together to both of you."

"Here, here!" said Mac. 'Woof!' added Buddy.

'Ting-ting-ting!'

"OK, next, Roger Lemonier and his wife Ursula. Roger was the strong, silent type brought to protect me during our May adventure. He and Mac masterminded the capture of Tim Riley, who turned state's evidence, which has allowed Attorney Hillman to press forward on several lawsuits regarding the death of my parents. Without Roger's help, Mac would still be sitting on a log in the middle of Lake Erie."

"Next is Pops, who shall just go by Pops, who provided eyes, ears, and technical knowledge of the lake. He piloted his beautiful boat, the *Miss Bertie,* that dangerous dark night to pick up Mac floating on a log on cold, rough seas. Pops' date for tonight is Miss Ginger, who is lying on the floor beside him. She is his forever sweetheart and canine companion."

"Next to Pops is our new friend Hubcap Harry, who set us on the right path at the right time when we did not know friend from foe, and from whom Mac finally got a pristine set of original 1957 Chevrolet wheel covers. We found a dog for Harry, too. Her name is Bella, and she is lying behind his chair."

"To Harry's left is Juan Johnson, the man who actually cracked the case of my parents' deaths. Juan owns Johnson's Body Shop and Collison in Jamestown."

"Had Juan not bought my parents' wrecked car and saved it for two years, we would never have had the physical evidence to get BCI involved, leading to an investigation and the dragnet for my parents' killer."

"Juan's date for tonight, and I must say you two make a handsome couple, is BCI Investigator Jonetta Pope. Jonetta came to us by assignment of Colonel Samuel Justice of the New York State Police. Her belief in our cause and her tireless marathon to track down my parents' killer deserves a big round of applause from all of us. We so appreciate your effort and professionalism, Jonetta."

Mac stood and led the applause.

"Thank you Marybeth," said Jonetta.

"Next, going round the end and returning back this side of the table, we have Gabriella Morrison, Mac's daughter, who is here with us from her home in Colorado. Gabriella is going to be returning to New Hampshire with her Dad to help him plan their new cabin in the woods overlooking Gabby's beaver pond."

"And next to Gabriella is Gina Minetti. We asked Gina to join us tonight. It was a difficult decision for her to accept, for as you all know, it was her adoptive father who was responsible for my parents' deaths, and he died in this very room in a struggle with Mac Morrison. We invited Gina to be part of this celebration of life to show her that we bear her no ill will. I taught her in school, so I knew she could have no knowledge of her adopted father's crimes. She is always welcome in this house."

"Next to Gina are Andy Gregor and his lovely wife, my lifelong friend Sandy. Andy, Mac and I were all campers at the Bar B Ranch camp a million years ago. Mac was Andy's tent counselor. And it was Andy who steered Mac to my B & B after stopping him on the Thruway for a loose trunk lid, but actually just to get a look at his gorgeous '57 Chevy."

"It was that chance encounter that kick-started the bull-in-a-china-shop rampage that Mackenzie "Mac" Morrison inflicted upon this community. He was looking for the real reason his parents died forty years ago, and in so doing he caused a week of upheaval in all corners of this quiet wine country until he got some much needed justice and closure."

"And last, seated next to me is my protector, my savior, and my man, Mac Morrison, who absolutely exploded into my life, took it over in a matter of days, swept me off my feet, endangered me, protected me, and eventually brought me out of the gloom that had cast over me these past two years."

"Mac, you are an avenging blunt instrument, crashing about and stirring things up, making people come out of the woodwork, some of whom had been unsuspected for forty years. Somehow, in the end, you tied it all up in a bow and made it come out right. I love you for it, Mac, but I never want to go through that again!"

"And to his wonder dog Buddy..."

'Rowrf!'

"Yes, I am talking about you Buddy. You saved my life. You were my protector, my hero, and I love you, and your new buddy Emma at your side."

'ROWRF! Woof!'

"Here, here!" Morgan shouted!

'Ting-ting-ting!'

"All right," said Marybeth, "dinner is served buffet style at the side table."

It was a dinner fit for royalty. Fresh cut fruit, tossed salad, standing rib roast, grilled Walleye, garden peas, and homemade cornbread, served with fine Sardinian wines brought as a peace offering by Gina Minetti.

And when all the guests had left or retired to their rooms upstairs, Mac took Marybeth aside, with Buddy and Emma following along.

"Best meal of my life, M. And you were the perfect hostess. Even your seating arrangements were clever. Pops and Harry look like new best friends, sparks were flying between Juan and Jonetta, and I even saw Gina and Gabriella talking quietly between them."

"Marybeth, I want you to close the B & B for a couple of weeks and come back to New Hampshire with me and Gabby."

"Mac, I'd love to, but I have guests booked."

"Cancel them. Give them double the stay at a future time, make up any excuse. Just come back with us. I want to show you the cabin I have built."

"Is it done? It's only been nine weeks, Mac."

"I bought a precut log kit, like Pops did. Already had the foundation in when it was delivered. Hired three nice young men to help, and we assembled it in a week. There's still a lot of interior finish to do, so it's sort of like indoor camping right now. Needs furniture, but there are two finished baths, a couch, table, folding chairs and a king size bed."

"And for you, my lovely lady, there is a fine old Chickering upright piano pulled from the Bar B chapel, courtesy of Mrs. Wilson! All freshly refurbished by an itinerant old German piano restorer who lives just down the road."

"We'll be temporarily cooking on an outdoor grill with a makeshift kitchen sink, plywood counter and fridge. I need you to help Gabby pick out furnishings and interior colors, design the kitchen, and make it our home."

"So...what do you say, Marybeth? Will you come home with me? Will you build with me, sing with me, accompany me and my new 12 string guitar on your favorite piano and accept me for the 'avenging blunt instrument' I am? I'm asking you: will you dance this dance with me, Marybeth?"

"Yes, Mac; yes, I will. You can have all my dances for the rest of my life, Mackenzie Morrison. Now, kiss me."

"Rowrf! Woof!"

*****

Appendix I
Cast of Characters

Principal characters in bold

Mackenzie "Mac" Morrison: builder, car restorer, trouble shooter, and unpredictably capable investigator of lost causes

Buddy: Mac Morrison's newly rescued dog

Marybeth Murphy: widow owner of the Captain Murphy B & B, Barcelona Harbor, New York

Abe Solomon (deceased): WWII Bomber pilot, Mac's uncle and mentor

Madelaine Solomon (deceased): Abe's wife

Shaun Morrison and his wife Claudia (deceased): Mac Morrison's parents

Doc: Sunapee, NH Fireman #1

John: Sunapee, NH Fireman #2

Frank Notting: Fire Chief, Sunapee, New Hampshire

Jordan Solomon: Abe and Madelaine Solomon's son

Roger Lemonier: Mac Morrison's best friend, comrade in arms and excavation contractor

Flavius Miller: Mac Morrison's Insurance agent

Morgan Hillman: renowned criminal attorney, friend of Mac Morrison

Angelica Milana Morelli: confidential secretary and paramour to Attorney Morgan Hillman

Gabriella Morrison: Mac Morrison's daughter

Doc Halliday: Veterinarian

Melanie Taylor: Doc Halliday's assistant

Eleanor: German-American Café owner

Roland Malouin: police dog breeder

Mrs. Gerrard: Mac's cottage neighbor at Jordan's Pond

Paco, Ramon and Thomas: three Mexican laborers

Andy Gregor: New York State Trooper

Betty Wilson: owner of the former Bar B Ranch Camp

Rosemary Minetti: Librarian, wife of Joey Minetti.

Joseph "Joey" Minetti: automotive genius, cruel son of Joseph Minetti Senior.

Joseph Minetti Senior: patriarch, owner of the Minetti Vineyard

Gino Minetti: Joe and Rosemary's son, automotive genius like his Dad

Gina Minetti: Joe and Rosemary's adopted daughter

Jim Murphy (deceased): Marybeth Murphy's former husband

John and Beth Waterman (deceased): Marybeth Murphy's parents

Tim and Anna Riley: retired New York State Trooper and wife

Sandy Gregor: wife of Andy, and best friends with Marybeth Murphy

Jane Gregor: Andy and Sandy Gregor's daughter

Kurt: owner, Kurt's Kustoms, car builder

Linda and Belinda Shavely: identical twin teens, Marybeth's next door neighbors

Hubcap Harry: owner of Vintage GM Parts and Hubcaps

Mr. Steinaker: B & B guest

Pops: aka Roy Rodgers, owner of the *Miss Bertie*, and friend of Mac and Marybeth

Todd: owner of the Gas n Go station

Dr. Brittany Coleman: PhD, Owner, Chem Systems Lab

Bangle lady: overdressed woman at Boulangers Café

Juan Johnson: owner of Johnson's Auto Body and Collision

Colonel Trammel Bradford: Field Superintendent, New Hampshire State Police

Colonel Samuel Justice: Field Superintendent, New York State Police

Chem Systems Staff: Elizabeth, Angelo, Damon

Jonetta Pope: New York BCI Investigator

Sol Weinstein: owner of Bank's Breakers and Scrap

Deputy Marvin Rinker: Chautauqua County Deputy Sheriff

Sheriff Lowell Buckman: Chautauqua County Sheriff

Mace Wilkins: scrap yard owner, Conneaut, Ohio

Frank D'Angelo: Minetti's longtime attorney

Jimbo: a teen running a garage sale

Appendix II

Footnote References and Credits

1. The Lone Ranger: TV western drama series that ran from 1949-1957 on ABC network, starring Clayton Moore. The Lone Ranger was a masked former Texas Ranger (believed to be dead), who roams the west administering his own brand of justice for people victimized by outlaws. His sidekick Tonto was played by actor Jay Silver Heels.

2. Ella Raines (1920-1988): Film noir actress of the 1940's and 50's.

3. Impact: Film noir released in 1949 by United Artists starring Ella Raines and Brian Donlevy.

4. "You can't go back home to your family, back home to your childhood:"
   Quote attributed to author Thomas Wolfe from the book You Can't Go Home Again, Book VI, Chapter 44, 'The Way of No Return', published by Harper and Row, 1940.

5. Dusty Springfield (1939-1999): Stage name of British singer, songwriter and producer. Born Mary Isobel Catherine Bernadette O'Brien in London England. She had a wide range of song genres including blue-eyed soul, pop, jazz, and country. Her voice was a smoky mezzo-soprano that could be loud and brash or soft and sexy from one note to the next.

6. Son of a Preacher Man: Popular rock and country crossover hit song written in 1968 by John and Hurley and Ronnie Wilkins and recorded on the album Dusty in Memphis, released by Atlantic Records, and sung by Dusty Springfield.

7. Nessun Dorma: Aria with melody and lyrics by Giacomo Puccini, from his Opera Turandot. Referenced herein is the recording of Luciano Pavarotti and the New York Philharmonic Orchestra, January 14, 1980.

8. True Grit: Western film starring John Wayne as Marshall Rooster Cogburn, 1969. Directed by Henry Hathaway, based upon the 1968 novel True Grit by Charles Portis. Film distributed by Paramount Pictures.

9. Wishin' and Hopin': Song recorded by Dusty Springfield, music and lyrics by Hal David and Burt Bacharach, 1964 by Phillips Records (cover of the original recording by Dionne Warwick, 1963).

10. The Spider and the Fly: Poem published by British poet and writer Mary Howitt in 1829.

11. Spidey sense: The tingling sense of imminent danger felt by Spider-Man, aka Peter Parker in the comic book series of the same name. Spider-Man Comics published by Marvel Comics, written by Stan Lee and illustrated by Steve Ditko.

12. Shake Rattle and Roll: Song recorded by Bill Haley and His Comets, 1954 by Decca Records (cover of the original song by Big Joe Turner, 1954).

13. Rock Around the Clock: Song recorded by Bill Haley and His Comets, 1954 by Decca Records.

14. Can't Help Falling In Love With You: Song recorded by Elvis Presley, 1961, RCA Victor Records. Written by Hugo Peretti, Luigi Creatore, and George David Weiss and published by Gladys Music.

15. Perry Mason: TV series starring Raymond Burr as criminal defense attorney Perry Mason of Los Angeles. The series ran from 1957-1966 on CBS network TV, produced by Paisano Productions. Based upon the original Perry Mason novels written by attorney and author Earle Stanley Gardner.

16. Gunsmoke: TV western series that ran from 1955-1975 on the CBS network. Starring James Arness as Matt Dillon, U.S Marshal of lawless Dodge City Kansas in the 1870's.

17. People Are Strange: Music and lyrics by The Doors, from the album Strange Days, 1967, Elektra Records.

18. All Along the Watchtower: Music and lyrics by Bob Dylan from the album John Wesley Harding, 1967, Columbia Records.

19. Wanted: Dead or Alive: TV western show starring Steve McQueen as bounty hunter Josh Randall. The show aired on CBS network from 1958-61. Produced by Vincent Fennelly for Four Star Productions and CBS Productions.

20. Twilight Time: Original song by Buck Ram and the Three Suns (1944) and covered as a hit single release in 1958 by The Platters on Mercury Records.

21. Tao Te Ching: Chinese proverbs believed to be written in the 6th century B.C. by the Chinese philosopher Lao Tsu. This passage is from proverb number Twenty Three from Tao Te Ching, A NewTranslation by Gia–Fu Feng with photography by Jane English, published by Random house, 1972.

22. Pooh Bear: speaking to Eeyore, the depressed donkey in Chapter VI-Eeyore Gets a Birthday Present from the fictional children's book Winnie the Pooh, written by British author and poet A.A. Milne and illustrated by E. H. Shepard. Published in 1926 by Methuen Press, London and Dutton Press, USA. Young boy Christopher Robin fantasizes about a life with his friends Winnie the Pooh (Pooh-bear), Eeyore the donkey, Piglet, Kanga, Roo, Owl and Rabbit in the hundred acre woods behind his home.

23. Tail of the Dragon: A stretch of U.S. Route 129 through the Great Smokey Mountains that has 311 curves in 11 miles. Popular with motorists of all types. Located near Deals Gap, North Carolina in the Cherohala National Forest. Begins at the intersection of NC Route 28 and U.S. 129 and ends at the Tabcat Bridge in Tennessee.

24. Three Musketeers: A French historical adventure novel written in 1844 by Alexander Dumas. Its four main heroes (D'Artagnan, and the three Guardsman Athos, Aramis, and Porthos) are swashbuckling swordsmen who fight for justice.

25. (Freedom) Sometimes I Feel Like a Motherless Child: Song as sung by Richie Havens at Woodstock folk festival, 1969. The song is a traditional black spiritual of pain and suffering that dates back to the era of slavery in the United States. First recorded by Paul Robeson in 1926 and many others. Richie Havens (1941-2013) was an American singer-songwriter of Native American (Blackfoot) descent on his father's side and British West Indies on his mother's side. He had a unique rapid strumming guitar style where he performed most chords with only his left thumb. His voice resonated with a soulful mix of pain and humanity and his outstanding fifty-minute opening performance at Woodstock launched him into the main stream of popular music.

26. The Blues Brothers: A 1980 action comedy film starring John Belushi and Dan Akroyd as Blues singers Jake Blues and his brother Elwood who are on a "mission from God" to raise $5,000 to prevent the foreclosure of the orphanage they were raised in. They drive the Bluesmobile, a retired 1974 Dodge Monaco cop car which Elwood famously describes: "It's got a cop motor, cop tires, cop suspension, cop shocks." Produced and distributed by Universal Pictures.

27. Silly Putty: A moldable rubber-like compound that can be made into any shape and which bounces when made into a ball. Originally developed as a rubber alternative during WWII. Made by Crayola LLC and marketed since 1950 as a child's toy packaged in red plastic eggs.

28. Tom Sawyer: Fictional mischievous boy in the 1876 great American novel The Adventures of Tom Sawyer by renowned author, orator and comedian Mark Twain aka Samuel Clemens. In the book Tom Sawyer and his friends Joe Harper and Huckleberry Finn pretend to be pirates on the Mississippi River circa 1840. Published by the American Publishing Company.

29. Grigori Yefimovich Rasputin (1869-1916): A historical symbol of Evil and manipulation. Rasputin was a Russian monk who alleged he had healing powers, including the power to read minds. Photos of Rasputin show him with long hair, dark flowing beard and wild looking eyes. He became a controversial religious and political fig-

ure in the waning years of the Russian empire by his manipulative control over Tsar Nicholas II and his empress consort, Alexandra Feodorovna. His controlling influence over the Tsar and allegations of rape and other crimes turned many Russians against him. He was stabbed repeatedly in a 1914 failed assassination attempt. The legend of his death by a second assassination in 1916 added to the myth of his alleged superhuman powers. He was allegedly poisoned twice to no ill effect, and shot in the chest, after which he leaped up and attacked his assailant and followed him outside into a court-yard where he was shot in the forehead, and his body was thrown in the Malaya Nevka River.

30. Gilligan's Island: Sitcom TV series that ran from 1964-1967 on CBS. The story line was a 'three hour tour' on the ship SS Minnow which ended by crashing on an island in a storm. The five passengers (millionaire Thurston Howell III, his wife 'Lovey,' actress Ginger Grant, Professor Roy Hinkley and farm girl Mary Ann Summers) and the ship's crew (the Skipper and Gilligan) were stranded on the island, where they inexplicably had an endless supply of tools, clothes and exotic food that they used in their many zany adventures.

31. "When fighting monsters, beware that you yourself do not become a monster...for when you gaze long into the abyss, the abyss gazes also into you:" Quote attributed to German philosopher Friedrich Nietzsche (1844 – 1900).

32. Gentle On My Mind: Pop and country western song covered by Glenn Campbell in 1968 on Capitol Records. Originally written and sung by John Hartford in 1967 and recorded by RCA records.

33. At Last: Song recorded by Etta James, from the album At Last! 1960, RCA Records. Original song written by Mack Gordon and Harry Warren for the musical film Sun Valley Serenade (1941).

Author Profile

PHILIP LAURIEN

Philip Laurien was born in Buffalo, New York, and spent his childhood there.

Although schooled as a community planner, he has also been a lifeguard, lumberjack, Luxembourg tour guide, lecturer, town manager, acting police chief, consultant, car restorer, builder, developer, and Innkeeper. The interesting people he has known in twelve countries and half the United States now inform the characters in his stories.

In 2007, while passing through Barcelona Harbor, New York he was reminded of his summers at a nearby riding camp on the shores of Chautauqua Lake, and the seed for a murder mystery was planted.

Barcelona Harbor Murders is the first novel he has published.

He currently resides in Ohio with his dog Buddy.

Made in the USA
Columbia, SC
18 May 2025

58097770R00176